Second Edition

Also by Rob Walden-Woods

Give yourself a head start.

Give yourself Permission to wi

Give yourself an Edge.

Violent Horizons.

Synopsis

Mid 1960s

Murder Comes to Mojácar is a sequel to Violent Horizons first published 30th June 2022.

Eddie Coleman becomes the most wanted man in England since the James Hanratty incident. A daring raid close to Oxford Assizes liberates Eddie from a potentially long-term incarceration. Police searched far and wide for the escapee not realizing he'd already skipped the country.

The big plan for Eddie is for him to make his way by fair means or foul, to the tiny village of Mojácar in Southern Spain. It is here he intends to meet up with the love of his life, Esme Wren. Together they mean to hide out in a secluded villa until the U.K. manhunt is called off. Old habits die hard as unfortunately did a number of individuals who unluckily got in Eddie's way on his journey South.

Killing came easy, being in a foreign country and holding a forged passport made it all that much easier for a hardened East End criminal cum psychopath to murder and move on undetected, such as Eddie Coleman.

Acknowledgements.

I am wholly indebted to Cheryl Blackmore and her partner Graham who both spent hours, weeks and months tirelessly working with me on this book. Cheryl for proof reading and much, much more and Graham for research.

Writing *'Murder comes to Mojácar'* has been quite a journey.

Dovetailing it into the first of the trilogy *'Violent Horizons'* turned out to be quite a challenge. However, with the help and dedication afforded to me by the above, it became possible and I thank them for their selfless dedication.

I would also like to thank my friend Jason Caulfield-Ware the big boss at Gorilla Consulting who engineered not only the website www.robwaldenwoods-author.com but the launch of this book.

My thanks also go to my friend John McCourtney for choosing the book title and indeed the front cover. Splendid stuff John, that's a few Cappuccinos coming your way.

Finally, may I say a big thank you to my wife Jan especially for your support and encouragement.

The third part of Eddies story is underway. Working title, **Committed to Crime.**Murder Comes to Mojácar

CHAPTER 1

"Almost there now Ted mate, I wish these bloody windscreen wipers would do a better job, it's pissing down so hard I can't see a sodding thing." The driver swung the wheel, pushing the meat wagon hard left. The journey from Oxford prison to the Assizes courts being almost next door is a little over five minutes, it was however deemed inappropriate to walk prisoners. Better to transfer them from cell to court in a suitable prison van. Normally, due to one of the occupants today being in the high-risk category, a police escort would have been employed. On this particular occasion however, for one reason or another, there was not. "Crappin ell Ted what's this?" A coach drove fast and straight out from their left, stopping smack across the middle of the road, blocking the prison van's journey forward. The driver hit the brakes hard catapulting Ted towards the dashboard almost breaking his nose on impact. Bloody hell mate, that didn't half hurt." "Sorry mate, I was trying to avoid colliding with that bleedin coach, where'd it come from anyway." A collision was the last thing they needed to worry about. Before the pair of luckless prison guards could gather their thoughts, five men leapt from the coach, three armed with shot-guns the other two carrying heavy looking lump hammers, all dressed in black with faces covered by scarves and balaclavas. A voice rang out from one "Ten minutes. Go." The driver of the coach remained in the driver's seat, levelled a sawn-off shotgun toward the prison van then loosened off both barrels. The windscreen of the meat wagon shattered into a million shards of glass, showering the two prison officers plus every corner inside of their once warm and dry cab. The five balaclava clad men positioned themselves, three at the front and two at the rear. Those at the front screamed at the prison officers, "Get your fucking heads down, get down now, or you get both barrels again." Driver and Ted froze. The coach driver reloaded and took aim.

Driver and Ted didn't need telling a second time. They dived downwards into their respective foot-wells. Ted started praying, the driver joined in.

Meanwhile two men at the rear of the prison van started laying into the locked and bolted rear doors with persuaders, ten-pound hammers. Such was the onslaught; the rear doors quickly gave up the fight revealing the vans contents. Eddie Coleman sat in his single locked cubicle within the prison van smiling, humming a tune. All the goings on outside had been planned therefore, of no surprise to him. Eddie's fellow passengers, also on their way to the Assizes for sentencing were caught completely by surprise, they both had the right hump. They had no windows to view exactly what type of hell was being unleashed. The noise from the hammering, metal on metal was horrendous, sparks flying everywhere, nerve jangling and scary. The rear doors collapsed inward. Eddie's co-passengers were grabbed roughly and yanked out of the van. Timing was essential. There wasn't enough of it to politely request if they might feel good enough to disembark. One of the hold-up men screamed, "Scarper, go on fuck off, disappear or get shot, your call." They ran for their lives and for their freedom. The five-minute mark passed, leaving five minutes more to release Eddie then get themselves away before the cops descended. Next job was to break into the internal cubicle housing their target for today; Eddie Coleman. A signal to the coach driver saw him drive off towards Carfax in the centre of Oxford, then an onward trip to a scrap yard based at Station Road, Didcot some sixteen miles away. It was to be dismantled, crushed and melted down. Lump hammers cast aside, both men unhitched crowbars from their belts. They had the flimsy metal cubicle door off in seconds. Eddie let himself be unceremoniously grabbed, then bundled out of the van and onto the road.

Crowds of onlookers gathered on street corners, many of them from the country's finest academia, suddenly turning to ghoulish behaviour known as rubber-neckers. Totally fascinated by what was occurring in front of their eyes, some were actually cheering. Eddie was pushed, half running, half dragged to a waiting Ford Cortina Savage, engine racing awaiting its precious cargo. The Savage had been stolen to order earlier that day from nearby Witney. Plates changed to give the car a new identity.

The registration cloned from a random car to piss off the old Bill. If any of the onlookers took note of it then handed it to the police, the law would be on a wild goose chase. It would be a false lead; the correct and lawful owner of the cloned registration might well be in for a dodgy night. Eddie was thrown into the rear seat then covered with a blanket. Once in, the wheel man rammed the Savage into first gear, floored the accelerator causing excessive wheel spin and away they went, the smell of burnt rubber accosted the noses of those nearest. The Cortina Savage had been especially chosen. The Savage version being well known for its ferocious speed, should a police chase happen here in Oxford or elsewhere for that matter, the coppers would lose the chase. By the time police finally arrived on the scene, the five balaclava donned men were long gone, easily melting into the back streets of nearby Jericho. As they walked away balaclavas were ripped off and dumped into five different street bins. The tools of their trade thrown into Castle Mill stream nearby. The job had been satisfactorily completed in eight minutes, two ahead of schedule. The getaway car was now well on its way to its desired destination – Weymouth, on the South Coast. Located in the rear foot-well next to Eddie he would find, courtesy of his mum Ma Val, an overnight bag containing a change of clothes, a bottle of hair dye, a pair of horny-rimmed glasses, a thick wad of reddies in low denomination bank notes together with a one-way ferry ticket to Jersey via Weymouth. There was also a contact number of Forgotten Frenchie the forger, who currently hung out in St. Aubin. Originally a fishing village back in the day, now the hub of the parish of St. Brelade, a few miles West of St. Helier. Back in Oxford, all hell was let loose. Coppers raced to the scene, having received several phone calls from the general public babbling on about shotguns, machine guns, cannons, knives and hammers, all kinds. They began by surrounding the prison van from a safe distance. Fearing that one or two of the hold-up gang might still be hanging around tooled up to hamper and delay things; their collective hands were stayed.

Firearms officers needed to be summoned prior to any attempts made to rescue the two prison officers and whoever else might be left cowering inside the prison van. Uninjured, but in a state of shock, Ted and his driver slowly raised their glass covered heads up to windscreen level and peered out squinting as spatters of rain hit them through the now windscreen-less windscreen. Neither registered the coach that originally blocked their way had disappeared. Gingerly Ted gently opened the passenger door a couple of inches. This action encouraged worried shouts from the police which came thick and fast. "Hands Up" shouted one. "Get out of the van; very slowly" from another. "Hit the Deck" shouted yet another. At a snail's pace, both driver and his mate Ted made their way out of the prison van via the passenger door slithering onto their knees, heads down as low as possible kissing and hugging the tarmac. The surrounding officers continued to hold back, unsure if they should rush forward or stay put, when two unmarked police vehicles screeched to a halt. Three more officers joined the fray, these guys were authorised to carry firearms. Their movements were calculated, measured and cautious. They rather smartly took up their firing positions at three different angles to the prison van, making sure that if and when they fired their weapons, *none* of their colleagues would be in the line of fire. Once in place and happy the situation was becoming under control, a nod from one of them indicated for the unarmed officers to approach the stricken van. The pair of prison officers now presently on their hands and knees shuffled towards some kind of safety. When they reached what they considered to be far enough away from danger, they both stood, slowly. Their bad moment however was far from over. As a precaution, they were immediately cuffed and pushed into a waiting police car. A big burly Sergeant nearby stated in a strong Welsh accent, "Can't take any chances with you two boyos, as far as we know you might have been in on the job." "Bloody hell" replied Ted. "Aint we been through enough?" The police car bearing the two luckless prison officers shot off before anyone else could speak.

Eddie's mum, watched the action from a vantage point, amongst the throng of onlookers, thrill seekers, and general nosey bods gathered on various street corners to gawp, unaware of the danger they were in. Satisfied that her son was safely on his way, she too melted into the myriad of Oxford City's side streets. Raincoat collar pulled up around her face, scarf pulled tightly over her long blonde hair. Smiling to herself, she decided to do what ladies do, when the opportunity arrives, she went shopping. Oxford City Centre is well endowed with a myriad of excellent shops, so why not? As she wandered in and out of the many department stores a thought came to mind. A coach? It was supposed be a bloody coal lorry. After all, the target was indeed Eddie Coleman! Perhaps though the irony would have been wasted on the plod. Thing to do now she thought, was for Eddie to evade the manhunt that will no doubt spark up, and spark up it did sharpish like. She hoped the plan she had devised would see Eddie off and running, literally. News of springing Eddie Coleman from the prison van travelled rapidly through both police force and underworld alike, much akin to a snake in a pot of grease.

CHAPTER 2

It was the month of June, flaming June, they called it. This meant a small percentage of the police force would be on their hols. Police watches however sprang up rapidly at all the likely areas South of the Wash, in order to keep a lookout for such a person as Eddie, who might attempt to escape from England, if indeed that was his plan. Over at Limehouse Police Station in The East End of London, any free 'on duty' officers, and for that matter any of those that were off duty who could be called in, quickly found their way to various known haunts of the escaped villain, just in case he decided to find his way back to home turf. Two officers stationed themselves out front of Eddie's home, 119 Plenva Street on the Isle of Dogs with two more at the back. Other officers roped into the man-hunt went on to cover the infamous Oasis Corner Café and Bar, the centre of Eddie's criminal empire, close to Limehouse. Limehouse pronounced locally 'Lime'ouse', is so called due to the many limekilns that were sited there, converting Kentish chalk into quicklime for London's building industry. Old Bill didn't like the idea of Eddie going on the run.

It had taken an avalanche of police resources plus man hours to get him arrested and up for charging, only to see him slip through their fingers, even before being convicted.

Top Brass at Scotland Yard were severely pissed, as was the arresting officer a certain D.I. Jackson.

The Cortina roared on towards its destination, stopping only to let Eddie out, grab the bag containing a change of clothes and walk casually into the toilet block provided by the roadside truck stop without a care in the world. Taking a look at himself in the only mirror provided, 'Jesus' he thought, as his image stared back. Short and curly bright ginger hair, with a thin wan freckled face. 'Prison life doesn't suit me at all.' Due to his restricted height he needed to stand on his toes to see a passport style image of himself. Eddie got busy. Out came the hair dye, it took a couple of applications to get bright ginger over to mid brown, slipped the horny-rimmed glasses on and viewed the result. He spoke to the mirror. "Even me mum wouldn't recognise me now." He looked more like thirty-five than his actual age of twenty-five. Off came the prison garb, to be replaced by a casual Oxford blue, button-down shirt, v neck jumper and slacks together with a pair of his favourite style of shoes. Ox blood-coloured slip-ons complete with leather tassels. 'That's more like it' he thought. He trousered the bank roll, then put the ferry ticket plus the telephone number of Forgotten Frenchie in his back pocket. Following a long satisfying piss which he had been holding on since his prison breakfast, the idea being, following sentencing, if things got that far, he was going to piss openly in court out of sheer defiance. Oh well he thought, prison escapees can't be choosers. Eddie sauntered back outside and breathed in some free, fresh non-prison air. Meanwhile, a car swop had been arranged, all part of the plan of course.

The Cortina with its hot head driver had disappeared. In its place was a smart looking silver Jag, complete with suited, booted and peak capped chauffeur. It was none other than Little Allen. Eddie threw the day bag into the Jag's open boot, then climbed into the luxurious, opulent rear seat. No need for a blanket over his bonce now. His driver was itching to get underway, but held back until he received a nod from his passenger, his eyes fixed firmly on the rear-view mirror. Eddie rolled his eyes and grinned. The nod came but only after two minutes had passed. Eddie reflected, *'onward ever, backwards never.'* Off they set in a rather more sedate fashion. Little Allen, signalled left joining the main road towards Weymouth. He looked at the back of Little Allen's head and asked. "Who was the mad driver in the Cortina Allen, he was goin a bit hell for leather, didn't recognise him?"

"One of Errol's blokes Eddie, goes by the name of Yapper Yates on account he can't stop yapping on just about everything." "Oh right, bit tasty he was with the driving like, where's he disappeared too then?"

"His order from Mrs. Coleman was to drive to Essex on the 'urry up, then on to Harwich. Something about creating a diversion for the cozzers. With a bit of luck, they will be chasing him, instead of us." "Like it" remarked Eddie. "Like it. What time we due in Weymouth?" "About an hour or so, I've timed it so we get to the ferry shortly before it leaves for Jersey. After that I've to get this Jag back to Errol's scrap yard back at Creekmouth, for crushing." On the journey across the Channel to Jersey, Eddie reflected on the time he recruited Little Allen as his driver when things were a little different. His real name was Allen Little but for one reason or another it got turned around, much like John Little became Little John, in the tale of Robin Hood. Little Allen was a petrol head, car mad. He idolised Eddie Coleman, would kill for him if necessary. In fact, one time he did. A couple of years ago Eddie was about to be arrested on the streets of East London, for visibly carrying a gun in a shoulder type holster. He warned this copper not to come any closer. He let the policeman know how much he meant serious business, pulled out his gun and aimed it directly at his heart. Little Allen who was shadowing his boss in the company Jag, drove at the policeman mowing him down before Eddie could pull the trigger, thereby cementing a life-long bond between himself and his career gangster boss.

CHAPTER 3

In the crisp air at the break of dawn, Eddie Coleman made his way off the Ferry from Weymouth. He stepped on to Jersey soil for the first time in his life. Prison garb ditched, a new look, he felt confident, like a new man. Not like someone screaming around on the run from the filth, but someone who blended in with the other ferry foot-passengers. Looking somewhat like a respectful businessman on the Island coming over from the mainland in search of a contract or two. A glint of sunshine cast early morning shadows across St Helier harbour. 'First things first' he thought. A bit of breakfast somewhere, then on to Frenchie's drum. He made his way up the steps to street level and began searching for an early door's café. Sauntering along the wide Esplanade within minutes he found just the place. He was about to enter this charming looking café when two uniformed police officers came out. One of them had arms and legs like pipe cleaners, the other quite the opposite.

He looked like he was wearing a uniform that was two sizes too small for the poor chap. Eddie stifled a laugh.

He thought, 'now, a villain's weapon is pain and there's no doubt I could deal it out to these two muppets, tooled up or not.' He could hardly believe what happened next. The fat one stood aside, out of Eddie's way and held the door open for him, offering him a cheerful "Morning Sir." Eddie nodded casually, without looking back as he entered the café. He thought of asking directions to Frenchie the Forger at St. Aubin, but didn't think it would go down too well. Mug of tea, bacon sarnie, followed by a cream bun was much more important. Inside the café and behind the counter, the entire wall had been mirrored from waist height up to the ceiling, ostensibly to make the interior seem larger than it actually was. Eddie caught his reflection as he sauntered over to the service area. Hair dye and horny-rimmed specs had worked their magic. Thanks Ma, you're a diamond of a Mum. Breakfast done, and a ton of money burning a hole in his sky rocket, Eddie decided a bus ride to his next destination was in order. The sun was up now, a warm day beckoned for the Jerseyites and Island visitors alike. Sod it he thought, no rush, let's see a bit of the Island. Whilst he was sightseeing, Val Coleman had already made her way back to the Isle-of-Dogs in the East End of London. Her long blond hair now free from the scarf so tightly held down in Oxford, blowing free in a gentle breeze. Breeze, she thought, that just about sums up Eddie's escape, went like a bleeding breeze. It was now, however, up to Eddie to sort himself out and get to his final destination; Spain. Busy in her thoughts, she rounded the corner from Launch Street and made her way down towards her home in Plenva Street. Val became aware of two police officers smoking roll ups and having a conversation right on her doorstep. This of course was to be expected, she was well ready with alibi's as far as her whereabouts were concerned especially at the time her son was lifted from the prison van earlier this morning. Both officers spotted her before she'd clocked them. Val being a bit of a looker, tall, trim, blond and well dressed, officer one on the doorstep said to officer two, almost in a whisper, "Yea, she'd have it. I'd give it one, wouldn't you?" Officer two replied. "And I suppose like all the other nice-looking birds you ogle; you want to drink her bathwater 'an all. You bleeding potty or something. Where's your brain, in your pants?

You do realize who she is don't you?" "Course, I bloody do, I can fantasize, can't I?" Just look at those legs, I bet they go all the way up to her" ...... "Good morning, Mrs Coleman" officer two said, interrupting his colleague's disgusting meanderings. "We have been ordered to station ourselves here for the time being see. You see your son, Mr Edward Coleman has er, um gone missing. Don't suppose you know anything about it do you?" Val shook her head sideways. "There was a breakout you see, from the prison van he was travelling in, over in Oxford and as a result, he escaped from custody see. Before you ask, Mrs. Coleman that is all I am allowed to tell you, you see. We have to report back to the station regarding any comings and goings at this address, including that of your good-self Mrs. Coleman.

So, would it be possible to use your telephone please?" Val looked across the road to see curtains twitching. "What happens if my son turns up here then?" Val asked. "Well, er I guess we'd have to arrest him see. He is of course on the run and now, a wanted man you know." "Do you think you two would be capable of that?" Val asked, sneering sarcastically. At this point, the officers stiffened, held their backs up straight, instantly dropping the politeness. Officer one was about to draw his truncheon nestling in a side pocket of his trousers. His colleague saw the move and decided to calm things down. "From what we understand Mrs. Coleman, your son is not a violent man and we are sure he will want to come with us to the station for a discussion you see." Val decided the conversation had run its course, turned the key in her front door and entered her home. She spun smartly round and spat "Well come on then, whichever one of you wants to bell your station. While you're doing that, I'll put the kettle on." Officer one was about to say it'll not fit, but then dropped the idea.

CHAPTER 4

"Good day Sarge." Officer two was using Val's phone now connected to Limehouse Police Station, a couple of miles from 119 Plenva Street. Officer two began reporting in regarding the appearance of Mrs. Coleman. "Caution her. Don't let her out of your sight. We'll send a car round to pick her up." "Righto Sarge I see, will do."

Officer two relayed on to his colleague what was occurring. Val didn't take too much to being cautioned as an accessory to her son's escape.

"As for that cuppa, you can go and boil your heads, cos I'm damned if I am gonna boil the kettle for you now. What's more both of you get out of my face and out She roared her displeasure, at the top of her voice and shouted,

of my house, now" she ordered. "Ok Mrs. Coleman" officer one replied. "However, I shall have to ask you to remain indoors for a while. A car has been dispatched to pick you up and take you to Limehouse station for questioning. If you try to escape, we will be forced to arrest you." Val was seething. This was happening in her own front room. No doubt neighbours' tongues were wagging at the speed of a dog's tail about to be handed a bone by a butcher. Taking a few deep breaths to calm herself down, she sat back in one of the easy chairs nearest the fireplace and smiled sweetly. Her mind, however, was racing. Carefully she went over her cover story as to where she had been at the moment of the prison van breakout. Val would be more than ready for any smart Alec questioning. Besides, she had already decided she was going to become self-appointed chief of what was left of Eddie's empire. Therefore, careful handling of the coppers was needed, nothing good will come from aggro with them at the moment.

CHAPTER 5

As the bus meandered its way on the coast road from St. Helier to St. Aubin, Eddie looked out on Jersey's picture postcard vista of waterfront properties all possessing magnificent views out to sea. 'If Jersey weren't so small and therefore too easy for the filth to find me, he thought, I could settle here. Put roots down like. Christ I've only been here five minutes and I'm starting to think like a sodding holiday maker.' The bus conductor tapped him on the shoulder, pointing out that he, asked to let him know when the bus was going to stop at St. Aubin. Eddie pulled himself out of his seat and made his way to the rear exit. As the bus moved slowly away from his stop, he had a strange feeling. He was, for the first time in ages feeling completely lost. Lost like a Bedouin's camel in a desert storm. It was time to fish out the bit of paper with Forgotten Frenchie's number on it and give him a bell. It was answered within three rings. "Ello" spoke a low gravelly voice. "That Forgotten Frenchie?" asked Eddie. "Oo wants to know?" "The Queen of fucking Sheba." Spat Eddie "Now, now caller, no need to get shirty" muttered the forger. "Look pal, I aint got time to fuck about, just give me the address of your drum and I'll be round directly."

Eddie identified himself. Forgotten Frenchie suddenly remembered his recent conversation with a certain Mrs. Coleman and the large amount of Nelson Eddy's (reddies) transferred to his bank account for services yet to be rendered. "S-s-sorry" Frenchie stammered. Eddie heard a loud clearing of the throat coming down the phone followed by a much less gravelly voice. The voice climbed up several octaves. "Yes of course m..m... Mr. Coleman, tell me where you are and I will gladly come and get you."

He gave Frenchie his location. He read out the address of the public telephone box via the plastic disc in the centre of the phone's dial. "Oh, so you're already here in St. Aubin. I will be with you in two minutes." Forgotten Frenchie assumed he would need to be on the lookout for a shiny Jag or some such vehicle that befits a notorious and violent gangster with connections. He enquired. "What car do I need to be looking out for?" "You don't, I got here by bus, and very pleasant it was too, just you get your bleedin arse over here."

Forgotten Frenchie was a big heavy man in his late fifties. Getting a move on was not uppermost of his usual daily routine. A quiet thoughtful chap, gentle and caring. Most times a bit dishevelled. Longish greying hair parted in the middle; a droopy moustache covered his top lip. If you were to pass him in the street, you would think perhaps he was a retired professor or mad scientist. Frenchie's home was something of an upside-down house. Bedrooms and kitchen on the ground floor. Reception room, toilets and lounge on the first floor. According to Frenchie, his workshop and darkroom were up in the attic, accessed only by a tiny metal spiral staircase. It was up here they settled down to the business of Eddie's new identity and forged passport. While Frenchie moved over to his work bench to start the process of forging the required passport, Eddie noticed a number of framed photographs all lined up on a shelf. It was like a gallery of criminals. All looking more than capable of knocking your block off if given any aggro. Frenchie was posing with each one of them. There was one however that looked out of place. A single shot of someone's head and shoulders, no Frenchie in this one. "What's that last one all about then Frenchie?" enquired Eddie. Frenchie looked up from what he was doing, and towards the photo Eddie was pointing to. "That's my lover Mike, he will be home later if you want to meet him."

"Lover!" Eddie was shocked. He'd heard of such goings on. He looked at Frenchie like a snake looks at a rabbit before he eats it. "So that means you're a bleeding queer, a faggot?" "If those are the labels you must use, then yes." "That sort of things against the law aint it?" "Yes, so is maiming and murdering people. They may be scum to you, the people that you maim and murder, but they *are* people." Frenchie replied rather softly. Eddie was a bit stumped by this even so, it irked him to be in the same room as someone who takes another man for a lover. "So, what did all these other hard nuts in these photos think?" "Same as you Eddie, same as you." "Well, I'll tell you what Frenchie, you aint fucking posing with me. I don't want anybody that follows me up your windy staircase to get the wrong message about me." "As you wish Eddie, as you wish. Now will you please come and sit in this chair over here, I need to take a number of passport type photos of you. As soon as I have developed them, I can complete the task. "Ready? and don't say cheese." Frenchie quickly snapped off half a dozen shots. Eddie's gaze wandered back to the photo of Frenchie's lover. "He's a damn sight younger than you." "Yes Eddie, he really is only a boy. He can't afford the rent, so he pays me in other ways." This was new territory for Eddie. 'Bloody stroll on, the quicker I get out of here the better.' was said under his breath.

Despite his earlier thoughts of settling down in Jersey, he was now beginning to miss his beloved East End of London. The Isle-of-Dogs had been the centre of his universe for many a year. He was born and dragged up there amid the rough and tough times afforded to most on the Island. His old fella Micky Coleman fled the family home, chasing fanny whilst Eddie was still quite young. Therefore, much to his dismay, he had the title 'man of the house' thrust upon him.

CHAPTER 6

Frenchie broke into Eddie's day dream. "What's your plans then, where you headed to from here?" he asked gently. Eddie smelt a rat, or thought he did. Was Frenchie gonna grass him up to the filth for a few lousy nicker. Was his queer rent boy a plant from the old Bill, should he kill Frenchie here and now to shut him up. No, perhaps best to tell him some porkies', lay a false trail. "Flying back to the mainland Frenchie, then on to Ireland.

I fancy my chances in Dublin's fair city." "Oh, right, seems like a good idea. I just thought, as with all my other customers." He waved a podgy fingered hand out towards gangster's gallery. "You would be off to Sunnier climes. Most of this lot ended up in Spain on the Costa Del crime!" That did it. Eddie blew a fuse. "You stupid, silly old fucker. You've just let on to their whereabouts. Would you be so loose tongued to the filth if they raided this place? And anyhow, why do you keep em? You're not fit to lick their boots you bloody lily livered woofter. If I get wind of you……. or your sodding boyfriend so much as whispering my name, one of my most trusted blokes, Johnny the Turk will be over here to slice your face to fucking ribbons with a cut throat razor. It'll be swift and unflinching. Your lover boy won't be so ready to snog you with half your fucking face missing. Grass me up and you can kiss this gravy train goodbye you bloody ingrate. Frenchie turned white with fear. He was acquainted with some of the goings on that Eddie had been involved in and had no desire for a facial, cut throat razor or otherwise. The thing that was *as* frightening as the threat, which, no doubt was very real, was the look in Eddie's eyes. They seemed to glaze over and peer far into the distance somewhere. It was as if Eddie was actually seeing the skin fall off of Frenchie's face, seeing the blood flowing from the open wounds down the front of his shirt.

Worse still, he seemed to be enjoying the pain Frenchie would be feeling. He couldn't be too sure, but he thought he heard Eddie gently singing a nursery rhyme, *"Half a pound of tuppeny rice, half a pound of treacle. That's the way the money goes, pop goes the weasel."* It would become known to Frenchie, that Eddie had a habit of humming his favourite nursery rhyme whilst slicing up or murdering his victims. Unsure of what to do next, Frenchie gathered up all the gangster mug shots, including the one of Mike and threw them into a waste paper basket located at his tormentor's feet, thinking, hoping this action might calm Eddie down. His entire body shuddered and shook with pure fear.

Eddie certainly had put the wind up him. He felt an urgent need to visit the toilet, however, Eddie held his gaze for a good two minutes. He felt unable to move, he soiled himself on the spot. Eddie smiled, "You'd better go and clean yourself up mate. I'm going to fuck off now, but just remember what I've said. You've been warned." This last sentence was snarled menacingly.

Eddie purposely put his face right into Frenchie's so that his spittle covered the lower part of Frenchie's now ghostly white face. Forged passport in his hand, Eddie said his goodbyes to Forgotten Frenchie shouting it through the closed toilet door. There was a distinct sound of Frenchie throwing up whatever he had had for breakfast. He wasn't going to shake Frenchie's hand for fear of catching the pox or something. He'd even declined using Frenchie's outside toilet, in case something untoward lay in wait for him under the seat. What was that ditty he'd heard a while back? 'It's no-good standing on the seat, the bugs in here can jump ten feet!'

Glad to be out in the fresh coastal air once again, he made his way down to the sea-front area, hoping to find a pub frequented by straight customers where he could have a piss in peace and not worry about anyone standing behind him. Maybe shove a pie and a pint down his neck. After all, threatening Frenchy with a facial made him thirsty and hungry.

CHAPTER 7

"Ok, that's all for now Mrs. Coleman." D.I. Jackson had questioned Val strenuously within the Limehouse nick. He could tell she was lying through her teeth. If her signed statement had the tiniest of tiny holes in it, he would come down on her like a ton of bricks. Nothing would please him more than to be able to put at least one of the Colemans in a cell. "You gonna drive me back home then?" asked Val. No answer was the stern reply. D.I. Jackson made his weary way back to East Ham station for a meeting with his boss Chief Inspector Ellis. Jackson grabbed a couple of teas from the station cafeteria on his way. "Come in" Ellis barked. Chief Inspector Ellis was not a happy man, far from it, an official from the Home Office had been exerting heavy pressure regarding the springing of Edward Coleman onto the Chief Constable, who in turn was bringing pressure to bear on Ellis. Everybody who was anybody wanted Mr. Edward Coleman back behind bars.

Ellis pushed his glasses from the tip of his nose back up to his brow, sat back in his chair and clasped his hands at the back of his neck. As usual, his shirt was stretched to the limit around his vast waist. The bits of his shirt front between each button gaping apart, exposing his belly button. 'Oh god, not that grim sight again' thought Jacko as Ellis occasionally called him. "Well?" barked Ellis before D.I. Jackson had fully entered his office.

Jackson in his usual ram rod upright stance, a legacy from his time as a Colour Sergeant in the royal marines, sat down without being asked. Back straight, carefully placing the teas on place mats situated on the huge and highly polished desk, being careful to avoid cup ring marks from the luke warm teas. He tried with all his might to ignore the beastly belly button complete with fluff which was staring straight at him. It reminded him of the Eye of Horus. However, it was far from bringing to mind the meaning of the symbol; protection, royal power and good health. Egyptology was something that D.I. Jackson had gotten into recently. In fact, he was positively fascinated by the entire spectrum of Egypt's ancient civilisation. The more he delved into it, the more he wished he had been there to appreciate it first-hand. Before Ellis could speak D.I. Jackson outlined the situation that several hours of questioning Mrs. Coleman basically had drawn a blank.

Her statement contained at least seven witnesses in and around the East End, who swore blind that black was blue she was with them at certain times of the day. "Honestly Sir, you couldn't make it up. This person at 10. o'clock, that person at 11 o'clock and so on and so on." "Better get some uniform on it. Have them all checked out, squeeze and squeeze until the pips start to appear." Jackson was about to ask, what if Gladys Knight appeared. He relented on the basis that just now, was not a time for jokes.

CHAPTER 8

The grab crane at Errol's yard swung noisily in a sideways arc dropping yet another unwanted and unloved car into the crusher. That would be car number fifty-two on this fine sunny East-End afternoon. The screaming of the metal in its death throes sounded almost blood curdling to the uninitiated.

Car fifty-two became yet another to be crushed into a metal cube ready to join the others all stacked neatly by the side of the huge hydraulic crushing machine, awaiting collection to their final destination; the smelter.

Creekmouth Yard in East London sat between Beckton sewage treatment works to the West and Dagenham Sunday market to the East. It was owned and run by Errol and his dad, Lee-Roy the Second. Errol was something of an entrepreneur. Most days he wore a blue pin striped suit, tailor made of course, together with a crisp blue shirt sporting double cuffs and a rather nifty tie. Errol was of African descent. His great grandparents came over to England from Nigeria looking for a better life. His grandfather Lee-Roy the First founded the business which then was passed on to Errol's dad. Errol looked after day-to-day activities at the yard, while his dad bombed around Europe gathering orders for quality knocked off cars or at a push, those that had been welded together, more commonly called cut and shut. Amongst other things, Errol's dad owned a number of car-lots in and around the East End. A fair amount of the cut and shut motors along with a few ringers ended up at the car-lots, to be sold as the genuine article but much cheaper. Errol's dad always chuckled at the thought of unsuspecting punters gagging to buy one of the ringers, along with its fake documentation. 'God love East Enders,' he would say, sod the state of the car, if it was half the price of anything else on the car-lot, no amount of steering them to more expensive cars would temp them away from the ringer. Protection from potential gangs muscling in on this lucrative arm of his business empire was supplied by members of Eddie Coleman's crew, notably a pair of right fucking hard nuts, known as the Stratford Two, under Eddie's control of course. Since Eddie's arrest, protection of the car-lots continued without any reduction in intensity or strength. The weekly stipend or protection money had been mounting up due to not being collected from Errol in the usual way. Sitting in the safe at the Creekmouth Yard, owed to Eddie, was the best part of three grand. The main entrance to the yard was by way of two high and wide, heavy electrically controlled wooden gates. They were installed to keep out prying eyes and thieving hands.

An 8-foot-high breeze block wall topped with barbed wire, completed the defence of Creekmouth Yard bringing about a margin of safety and security from unwanted night time visitors. Several break ins, in the not-too-distant past had occurred.

Mostly by geezers who legitimately visited the yard during the day, clocked the bits they wanted to graft onto their old bangers then returned at night, in order to thieve the parts. As a result, when Eddie's crew began providing protection for the Yard all the thieving stopped. The gates suggested by Eddie, together with the barbed wire topped walls did their job. In addition, Eddie's reputation for violence and retribution was known far and wide, therefore unwelcome night visits became a thing of the past.

CHAPTER 9

It wasn't that long ago when the 'Stratford Two' Billy and Mel, visited Creekmouth with an order from Eddie to quell an up-and-coming gang of hoodlums known as the Cherry Boys. The thought was, as the Cherries operated in and around the Creekmouth area, they might be a threat to Errol's yard. As Eddie had put it, "When I offer it and get paid for protection, it's all in, so fuck this new gang up, hospitalise them." The Stratford Two walked into a pub locally known as the Cherry Boys meeting place. They politely asked three of the so-called gang leaders to accompany them to the rear and out into the pub garden, then proceeded to beat the fuck out of them. Billy using an iron bar and Mel, his motor cycle chain. Hearing the commotion, the rest of the gang rushed out to assist their guvnors. Sadly, they were no match for Billy and Mel. These two were hardened street fighters, as well as blood brothers. They were sworn to die for one another. The fighting was furious with no quarter given. After the beatings, they straightened their ties, popped their double-breasted suit jackets back on and strolled back into the pub. Billy suggested politely to the landlord, that he might want to ring for an ambulance or two, as there were a few chaps out the back that might need some medical assistance. Mel leaned over the bar, shoved a ten quid note in the barman's waistcoat pocket and said "We were not here pal got it? If we hear otherwise, you will be next. This is now part of Eddie Coleman's manor." Knees knocking loudly, the landlord readily agreed. Local would-be car-part thieves didn't relish the idea of punishment inflicted on them with an iron bar or a motorbike chain. Henceforth, they took their business elsewhere.

With their guvnors in hospital, the Cherry Boys decided to disband and go their different ways. As far as Billy and Mel were concerned, that was job done. A car horn was heard from outside the gates by the yard personnel. Someone called up to Errol's office "Little Allen's back." Errol pressed the button marked 'Gate'. They opened inward with a gravelly grating noise. The Jag slid quietly into the yard. Little Allen jumped out, slung the ignition key to one of his ex-work mates then climbed the outside staircase up to Errol's office. The office was basically one static caravan bolted on top of another. It gave Errol a panoramic view of the yard and beyond. He pressed the button again, the gates slowly grated and creaked to a close. "All right then Allen, how'd it all go then?" "Smooth as you like Errol, smooth as you like." Together they moved over to the window overlooking the crusher to watch the Jag getting cubed up. They both felt uncomfortable, a bit like two frogs sharing a small pond. "Nice motor that, shame it's got to be all crumpled up and melted down." Yea well," Errol replied, "plenty more of them waiting to be lifted. West-End's teeming with 'em, sometimes the registered owners don't even know their wheels are missing. They don't tell the old Bill until it's too late to do anything about it, stupid noncers. All they get is a crime number, half the time they shoot straight out and buy another one. Errol sniggered. "We should get a rake-off from the dealers for keeping their profit margins up." "I'll leave the negotiations for that one with you Errol, that's right up your Strasse." "How was Eddie then?" enquired Errol. "Well, he didn't say too much, just asked what time we would get to the ferry and that. No small talk. He's changed how he looks though." "In what way?" "Well, his ginge, um, red hair was dark brown and he was wearing thick framed glasses." "That'll be his disguise then won't it dummy." "Yea well, I suppose. I just didn't get informed about it, so it came as a bit of a surprise, that's all." "If I were you, I wouldn't go complaining to Mrs. Coleman." "Anyway Errol, now the Jag's gone, how do I get home?" enquired Little Allen. "Shanks's bloody pony for all I care pal. Can't you get one of the other lads to give you a lift?" Errol turned, walked over to his desk and proceeded to make a phone call. "What's up with you Errol, you still pissed off about me taking that job as a driver for Eddie?" "No not at all."

"I'm pissed off as you call it, about the time Eddie came over here last year, tied me to a chair and roughed me up. What did you do to stop him? You prevented my lads from downstairs coming up to help me. I even wet myself. It was *you* who decided to become his driver and leave my employ" Errol screamed. "Now get out pronto, before I turn the tables on you and get my men to tie you up, slap *you* about a bit." he knew Errol was not capable of carrying out his threat. He also knew Errol's 'men' as he called them wouldn't go near him, due to his association with Eddie Coleman. So, just to keep the peace, plus the need to bum a lift home he kept his cool, and left. After all, now that his boss Eddie was on the run, he was out of a job, unless Mrs Coleman stepped in with an offer. If not, he might need to get his old job back here with Errol sometime in the future. Still suited and booted, Allen asked each and everyone in the yard for a lift home. Each bloke when asked, looked up to see Errol at the window shaking his head. So that was that. Little Allen had to bus it home. His chauffeur's uniform turned a few heads upstairs on the number 16 to Stoke Newington. Little Allen grinned; he couldn't have cared less. He was a free man and he knew, although he had caused a fair old pen and ink at Errol's, Errol would take him back when he calmed down like a shot.

What Little Allen didn't know about motors, wasn't worth knowing. The other thing in his favour, he is all too aware of the seamier side, the unlawful goings on at Creekmouth Yard. Errol would be best set to keep his enemies as close to hand as possible.

CHAPTER 10

Police efforts resulted in the recovery of the lump hammers and crowbars used in order to demolish the police van's coachwork so comprehensively, plus the broken-down pieces of three sawn off, double-barrelled shot guns. Two weeks had passed since the prison van breakout, happening as it did, within sight of Oxford's dreaming spires. What the spires thought of it would be anyone's guess and probably remain a secret for at least a millennium or two.

The Oxford Mail bashed out story after story in an attempt to boost its flagging sales. However, a fortnight on, it was far from being the lead story now. 'The audacious daylight Prison Van raid' as they called it began to wear thin with even the most ardent of crime hungry readers. All five of the discarded balaclavas were recovered from where they had been dumped. Based on information from the public, police divers dragged part of Castle Mill stream. Police officers based at the St. Aldates station in Oxford were tasked with visiting all known retailers of such items within a thirty-mile radius, but to no avail. The conclusion was, all of the items recovered were most likely purchased some time ago, outside the county of Oxfordshire.

At 119 Plenva Street on the Isle-of-Dogs, the officers on rota duty were stood down. Others were to be stood down too at known haunts of Eddie Coleman the following week or so. It was unlikely that he would show his face now. Besides, as always, police man-power was at a premium. Various watches at airports and seaports were thinned out to a minimum. The man hunt would now be cast wider to include Europe. Hence Eddie Coleman's details were passed on to the international Criminal Police Organisation known as INTERPOL. Locating fugitives being the core activity of this organisation, huge records of criminal data is held at Interpol's H.Q. The hope being, if Eddie Coleman was picked up for some minor offence somewhere, police at Scotland Yard would be informed and his likely whereabouts would be revealed. Local police activity had been centred in both Oxford and the East End of London. Shortly after the prison van raid, the Chief Constable at Oxford police station at the behest of the detectives currently working on apprehending Eddie Coleman, posted an appeal in the Oxford Mail. The appeal requested any witnesses to come forward with information about what they had seen or heard. Exemption from prosecution or penalty would be granted by government authority. In other words, 'full immunity' such was the gravity of the situation.

In the East End, Eddie's ancestral home and manor, detectives were hitting on various snouts and grasses for *anything* heard or seen. They might as well be pissing in the wind. East Enders generally keep shtum about any of their own. However, this was Eddie Coleman the filth was asking about. Most snouts suddenly went deaf *and* blind as well as dumb. One actually said, 'I'd rather commit Hari Kari than grass up Mr Coleman!"

For the detectives, it was like to hitting a wall. Three or four of Eddie's known associates were rounded up for questioning. This too proved useless. Each one was put on 24-hour watch, as a precaution. But these guys were Eddie's most trusted and they knew only too well how to play the game. They were all well aware of their individual police tails, and as a matter of course, began to live perfectly normal, even sedate lives. No contact with each other, no contact with Val, early to bed, some even helped elderly ladies' cross busy roads, all the time smirking in the face of the coppers following them around.

It was a sight to behold, big brawny East Enders, some with flat noses gained in the boxing ring, others with cauliflower earholes from the same source, dressed immaculately in double breasted suits, cufflinked shirts, plain ties, finished off with highly polished shoes, now acting the perfect gentlemen. Each one had the mark of a rough-house criminal. They stood out from the crowd in the East End's busy shopping areas like turds in a punch bowl; and for all the right reasons. Hard, tough and sometimes evil looking blokes, the ones you stepped off the pavement into the gutter for if they were coming toward you two abreast. Yet here they were, offering to carry shopping for half bent-over old timers. Kissing babies in their pushchairs, buying cups of tea for some of the down and outs. The locals were not quite sure how to take it. Nobody questioned it though, best not to. Eddie Coleman was something of a legend around here and although no one could put their finger on the correct spot as to why, most of them knew he had been sprung and that he was probably behind this welcome display of conviviality from these gentlemen thugs. For sure no one was complaining.

CHAPTER 11

"Get up off your arse mate, I didn't hit you that hard." Johnny the Turk was towering over his opponent's prone body lying face up on the canvas smack in the middle of the boxing ring. Johnny stepped over the downed fighter, walked casually over to his corner, rested his back against the printed corner padding and hung his arms over the middle ropes either side of him. As usual, Johnny completely ignored the text printed on the four corner paddings which read: 'Sparring Only'.

As far as he was concerned a fight was a fight. Especially when an opponent tried to bite off his ear, as did the guy on the deck. "Johnny, I've told you time and time again, this gym is just for sparring." The gym manager had come out of his tiny office to see what the rumpus was all about. Seeing a body on the canvas, and other guys, usually shadow boxing, rope skipping or bench pressing, crowding round the ring, he jumped to conclusions without first consulting Johnny. "What the bloody ell is going on here then?" he asked. Johnny shrugged his vast shoulders, touched his bloodied ear with a sparring gloved hand mimicking biting. The Turk turned away, climbed out of the ring between the top and middle rope then sauntered off to the changing rooms for a hot shower. The guy on the canvas stirred. Pushing himself up to a sitting position, he slipped off a glove so as to nurse his sore chin with a bandaged hand, then cautiously made his wobbly way to the changing rooms, holding on to the walls, as he went. Sensing a scene, the gym manager cautioned the young ear biter not to clash with Johnny behind closed doors, telling him, Johnny is an accomplished street fighter as well as hell on wheels in the ring. "If you pick on him outside the ring a knockout like todays will seem like heaven. Anyway, if you're into biting, I suggest you take your gloves and your business elsewhere." Johnny had been a member of the gym for many a year. His professional fighting days were almost over. Considering the amount of ring battles he'd fought, his face mostly still intact unlike most of his contemporaries, didn't mark him down as a boxer. Not a broken nose or cauliflower ear to his name!

He was no more Turkish than Andy Pandy. He'd earned the nick name due to having some excess skin collect on his throat. Plus, he would fly around the ring like a turkey trying to avoid the chop at Christmas. Being a southpaw, meant he was awkward to fight too. His natural stance is right hand and right foot forward, leading with right-handed jabs, followed with some left cross hook shots and the occasional uppercut. He didn't brag about it, so most of his associates at the gym, his second home, were not aware of his connections with Eddie Coleman, before and hopefully after Eddie's arrest. The Turk was one of Eddie's most trusted. He would stand in for him, as and when he went absent without leave as he called it. Eddie was apt to disappear every now and then. Nobody knew where, only Johnny was trusted with Eddie's whereabouts.

It was Johnny who would run the crew in his absence. Now that he was on the run proper; and the basement of the Oasis Pub, Eddie's headquarters at Limehouse temporarily closed, courtesy of the old Bill, Johnny simply defaulted back to the ring. His plan being, to keep sharp, keep fit then to plunge himself back into the fight circuit. All that was needed now, was for him to find a boxing promoter who might be able to get him some bouts. An hour or so later, Johnny found himself in the Penny Farthing Café in Vincent Street, just around the corner from the Gym. In front of him perched on the table for two, sat a frothy coffee in a glass cup complete with an accompanying glass saucer.

His face obscured to almost all other seated customers, due to the Racing Post being held close up to his face. He held it up, not to hide himself but in order actually to read it. His one and only pair of specs complete with scratched and cracked lenses sat silently waiting for him, back in the gym, inside his locker.

CHAPTER 12

Betting on the gee-gees was now his main source of income, at least until some paying ring work came up. Whilst he studied the racing form, searching for some likely nags to bet on, a shadow fell over him. He waited; it didn't disappear, or move on. Sensing some kind of retribution from the guy in the ring, Johnny clenched his fists, leapt to a standing position with his two enormous fists out at arms-length boxing style, ready for the fight. The chair he was sat on flew behind him as he readied himself for a bundle. Whoever was standing over him would be on the rough end of a right old hiding. "Whoa! fucking hell Johnny, take it easy." Johnny recognised the voice seconds before recognising the face. "Christ Bomber." Johnny turned to pick up his chair, at the same time as offering profuse apologies to the young couple at the table directly behind him; such was the gentleman in the Turk. The couple looked from Johnny to Bomber and back again, instantly realizing that these two were definitely East End heavies. "That's ok" replied the male of the two. Bomber at six-foot-tall and about as wide, face cut to ribbons courtesy of years in the ring, offered to buy the young couple some coffees, to compensate for those that were spilled. "No that's fine sir." replied the male again. "As it happens, we are just on our way out." Bomber smiled, nodded in their direction. "Just been over to the gym mate, they told me you might be sat in here." "Ok Bomber, now you've found me what is it you want?"

Bomber frowned inwardly. Johnny and he were members of Eddie's crew. It was not like Johnny the Turk to be sharp or uptight with him. Bomber noisily scraped a chair out, sat opposite and pressed on. "Val Coleman wants a meet." "Oh, she does, does she, what's on the agenda then, has Eddie surfaced?" Bomber frowned openly this time. "Not that I know of mate, have you heard something then?" "No Bomber, just idle speculation. So, I will ask you again what does *she* want?" venomously spitting out the word *she*. Bomber looked aghast. This was Mrs Coleman they were talking about. Although being the boss man's mum, the Turk never had much time for Val, preferring male company at all times. "Don't know Johnny. All I know is the meet is at Plenva Street and apparently, Dave Conti is gonna be there along with Billy and Mel." Johnny looked astonished; Bomber was describing all the top guys who were actively involved with Eddie and his murderous and villainous ways. Trusted members, all of them, recruited into Eddie's crew by the man himself. "Ok Bomber, when and what time?" "Tomorrow mate at ten." "Er would that be morning or night time?" "Fuck me mate, I never thought to ask," laughed Bomber. Johnny grinned, suggesting "let's go for the morning shift, Ok? oh, and what about that Errol from Creekmouth Yard? is he coming to the party?" "Not sure mate, never asked did I." Bomber caught the eye of a young blonde girl over by the new Gaggio Expresso coffee making machine. He held up two fingers swirling them around above his head, indicating two expressos' over here darlin. The newly installed Gaggio spluttered into life gurgling, hissing then spewing out the money-making liquid that everyone was into just now. The expresso's arrived and placed carefully on Johnny's table. Bomber thanked the young blonde, bunged her a fiver and said easily "Ta love, keep the change." She nearly fainted, the change due from Bomber's fiver, would have amounted to more than her daily wage. She gave Bomber a quizzical look, wrongly assuming there was something sinister behind the very generous tip. Perhaps he wanted some sort of favour?

However, didn't even look up at the blonde, totally oblivious of her quizzical look. He was far more interested in his conversation with the Turk. So, she turned on her heel, shot over to the till, quietly tucking the enormous tip in the pocket of her apron. This one she thought, was definitely not going into the jar with a label marked up 'tips.' She happily tripped her way back to her work space with wings on her feet, thinking quietly 'what she could blow this windfall on.' Bomber, message delivered, coffee cup drained, stood to go. Johnny looked up. "You still got the flat above the Oasis Bar?" "I do, why do you ask?" "Curious, just curious, and what about the bar?" the Turk asked. "Well, the filth has buggered off at last. Stood guard for weeks they did in case Eddie showed his boat race. Stupid, I thought, as if he's daft enough to. Couple of good blokes they were though, for the filth that is. Got a bit of decorating to do to get the smell of the old Bill out of the place. Should have it ready to open up again in a couple of weeks." "Ok so you've got the flat above and the bar about to go live again, what about the basement." "You're asking a lot of questions Johnny, what's your angle then?" "I just thought I'd be one jump ahead of Val tomorrow at the meet that's all.

Did she question you about Oasis Corner?" "No mate, she didn't." Johnny smiled and sank back into his copy of The Racing Post. No attempt was made to look up as Bomber bade him farewell then disappeared out onto the street. Hmmm Johnny thought, if she thinks she's gonna become the matriarch of Eddie's crew, she will come a right cropper. That is my destiny and mine alone. And as for that bleedin Errol, he can keep his snivelling nose out of it too. Snivelling bloody git, he is. All fucking pinstripe suits with bum freezer and fart flaps. What sort of tailor does he use anyway? Johnny reckoned the 'Stratford Two' Billy and Mel, would be more than willing to toe the line if he was in charge. They were not management material by a long chalk. Those two maniacs were much more interested in inflicting pain to whoever stood in their way. As for Dave, bit of a loose cannon that one. Bit of a dark horse. Brilliant at nicking up-market jam jars and shagging anything with a pulse. Given the circs, he might just be harbouring thoughts of running the show himself.

Johnny knew he would need to deal with Dave in no uncertain terms, to keep him toeing the line. Might be best to get hold of him tonight, before tomorrow's big pow wow for a little word in his shell like. He knew bees and honey was Dave's God. Turned him on big time it did. Especially when it's fat wedges of money. Johnny held the one and only key to the safe down in the Oasis basement and was hoping he could grab some of the cash held in it, if only to line Dave's pockets as a massive bribe. He needed to reassure himself that old Bill had not taken the safe away as evidence following the raid and shutting the Oasis club down. Probably not, the bloody thing weighed a ton. Several streets later, he caught up with Bomber. Both were fast walkers, the Turk however just a little faster. "You were a bit handy with the cash back there in the café, weren't you pal?" Bomber stopped abruptly. "What's that got to do with you mate, if I fancy flinging a bit of cash now and then that's up to me 'init?" "Yea well your right on that one. It's no skin off my nose. Question, can I get into the basement today?" "I suppose so, what's the 'urry?" "No reason, just want to see what mess the old Bill has left it in." Johnny smiled a toothy grin. "Well, I told you mate; I need to do some painting and that." "Ok, ok I get that, I just want to see how bad it looks. Perhaps if it's just a lick of paint that's needed, we could get ourselves back down there and get things moving again. Bomber narrowed his eyes. "Fine see you there in an hour or so."

CHAPTER 13

Eddie cursed himself for rearing up at the Forger back at his bloody upside-down house. Blowing a fuse though is business as usual for Eddie. Rage, rant, scream then stab first, ask questions after. For all that was bad about him, Freddy did actually live on the Island and probably would've been a good source of local information. Too late, not going back there he thought, I'm on me Jack Jones now, best get myself back to St Helier and find some digs. Being midday, the sun was up, together with a piercing blue cloudless sky above the entire Island. He felt blessed. That cheered him up somewhat plus, as a bonus, it was lovely and warm. As he sauntered along the sea front Esplanade, Eddie's thoughts went back to his childhood days on the Isle-of-Dogs. We never got weather like this, he thought, too much of that smog-shit and smoke about. It's no wonder blokes were queuing up to get into the London Chest Clinic, coughing and spluttering on their way over there.

He remembered; it was always a good thing to avoid the open ground floor windows of the Clinic early on in the mornings. The noise of blokes heaving up the phlegm then gobbin it out the window, was enough to make even the hardiest of smokers to at least, *think* about packing up the fags! At the Westerly End of St Aubin's Esplanade, a solitary taxi sat in a single bay for it to park undisturbed. It was a big old Humber Super Snipe. Red paintwork with a white roof and stripe along each side. Polished to within an inch. The sun danced off it almost blinding Eddie. In it sat an oldish gentleman, perhaps in his early seventies, greying at the temples who looked like he had earned his life stripes. He wore a white, half sleeved shirt coupled with a smart blue and black regimental type tie. Dead smart it looked too, pure silk, probably from Saville Row. As Eddie approached the car, the distinguished looking gentleman stood out of the Snipe and threw a warm smile at Eddie. "May I take you somewhere Sir?" he asked. Eddie stood quite still for a moment. People displaying good manners was foreign to him. His life to date had been a collection of beatings, rough housing, stabbings and finally a murder or two. Good manners or niceties didn't come into it. Here was this bloke smiling at him, a complete stranger. For all he knew, I could be an escaped murderer on the run. And he wants to let me into his car and into his little world. "How's tricks mate?" Eddie said by way of a greeting. He smiled back at this bloke. "What makes you ask?" "No reason Sir, it's just that I have been sat here most of the morning and yet to have a fare, so I thought I would be a little pro-active." Eddie had no idea what he was talking about and was the verge to question him as to what the hell pro-active meant. However, to Eddie, he looked harmless enough so he slid into the red leathery passenger seat whilst the gentleman driver fired up the Snipe. As they drew gently away, he asked, "Where to Sir?" "As it happens pal, I'd like to see a bit of the Island, I guess you'd know your way round a bit." "Oh, indeed I do Sir, indeed I do. You see, before I retired, I was a senior officer in the States of Jersey Police."

CHAPTER 14

"Hello, sorry Hola, my nombre is Esme Wren." "It's ok, it's ok, I speak your language." Esme smiled and relaxed a little. She'd stepped into the offices heralded by the sign above the door Agentes de la Propiedad. The rather good-looking young Spaniard continued. "I spent my learning years in London at the Imperial College studying vernacular architecture for my sins, came back home to Moxakar, or as you would say, Mojácar and here I am. So, how is it we can help you?" On instructions from Eddie, before he was arrested then sent to the Assizes court in Oxford, he told Esme to find somewhere in Southern Spain, well out of the way and buy a Villa. He wanted them to live out there until heat from the jewellery raid in Hatton Garden and Lennie the Scrotes murder died down. Esme, paying for the journey from her savings, arrived at her desired destination by way of a coach from Alicante airport to Mojácar. It being in the South East within the Province of Almeria, it is a good two hours' drive, longer, if the coach made any stops on the way. Having booked in to a hotel conveniently situated across the road from the coach terminal, Esme asked the porter on duty where she might find the Spanish equivalent of an English estate agent. She was directed to a particular street in Mojácar Pueblo. The Pueblo or town as such was tiny compared to what she'd been accustomed to back in London. It was situated at the top of a winding two-way road that led down to a couple more hotels, that sat on the beach area. Esme soon found what she was searching for, amongst the souvenir shops, Tapas bars, El Dorado type Cantinas and Restaurante's, all cobbled together. A number of dusty alleyways stretched outward and down-hill between each one leading to clusters of Haciendas, most with little grills outside to fire up the evening meals with. These would-be homes were for the locals and perhaps Cantina workers. A few dogs roamed free, skinny looking things, no doubt acquiring the odd meal from round the back of the many cafe's and eating places. Cars parked haphazardly here and there, which didn't seem to worry the locals.

Time stood still in Mojácar. She remembered hearing a while back, something about Spanish siestas. During the summer months, shops would close around midday then reopen in the evening when it was cooler, some staying open well into the night. As it was approaching midday, she was glad to be in the office of the local agents for villas and haciendas. A bonus being they had several fans on the go. One was sweeping from side to side meaning that every ten seconds or so, she got a refreshing breezy blast. She wanted to raise her arms when the sweep came her way to cool her sweaty arm-pits, but thought better of it. "I'm hoping to rent, lease or buy a villa in this neck of the woods." Puzzled by the idiom *'neck of the woods'* the young Spanish chap moved on then introduced himself. "Ok, firstly, my name is Javier and you have arrived at just the right place. Please do take a seat. He waved a hand toward a plush white leather recliner with a second one adjacent to it. May I offer you some refreshments, tea, coffee or perhaps a glass of chilled sangria?" Esme opted for coffee, insisting on a weak affair with two sugars. Javier asked "how weak?" "About the colour of khaki" she replied. Javier nodded solemnly as if to know exactly what she meant. Whilst he disappeared into the tiny kitchen, hidden by a door fully mirrored from top to bottom, Esme sneaked a quick look at the paperwork neatly piled on Javier's desk. 'Old habits' she thought, it was all down to the training she underwent, as an officer in the London Met. By the time the khaki-coloured coffee arrived, Esme was sitting where she was told. At the age of 27, she was not tall.

In fact, sat on the plush recliner as requested, her feet failed to reach the white marbled floor. Her green eyes, darted this way and that and especially darted towards Javier's cute little backside as he leant down to place her coffee mug on his desk within easy reach. Esme had long since ditched her gold wire rimmed circular specs, opting for something a little more business-like. Esme fished out a hankie from her handbag, took off her heavy framed glasses and began absently polishing the lenses. Instead of sitting behind his desk, Javier sat in the recliner next to Esme. She felt a little uncomfortable with him so close by, but thought 'hey I'm a grown up', and let it pass.

Javier turned to her blurting out "Wow, you have the most beautiful green eyes and I love your jet-black hair." Esme had heard it all before, admittedly not from a Spanish stud though. Being a copper in the Met for all those years she was well hardened to male come-ons. Besides, she was head over heels in love with Eddie. Since Eddie, she had had many offers. Mostly from blokes she served beer to when working at the Oasis Bar. Funny she thought, Eddie, big time crime boss and murderer, sitting in the Oasis basement or the dungeon as he called it. Lording it up over his gang members, cooking up new money-making illegal doings. He would have gone ballistic if he knew. Most likely killing one of her would be suiters, thereby bringing his murder tally up to three or was it four, as a message to all others. 'Keep your bloody hands off'. He needn't have worried though. All offers were politely declined. Eddie was the one. There would be no other. Glasses back on, she grabbed her coffee and hid a little behind the mug smiling sweetly. Javier got the vibes and retreated to his professional work space on the opposite side of his desk. "Ok, let's get some details from you." He grabbed a new client form and pen. "Shall we start with your name?" "It's Esme Wren." Javier wrote, at the same time as asking, "May I address you as Esme please?" "You may." "And what Esme, are you looking for and where?" "Well, as mentioned earlier, **we** are looking to rent or buy a villa for two. Can you underline *for two* please?" "Javier looking at Esme, physically aching to kiss her lips got the message then proceeded to finish the form. Perhaps another time he thought. What was his lothario Father's words to him? Never give up at the first hurdle!

CHAPTER 15

As the Super Snipe powered away in the direction of St. Brelards Bay, Eddie had second thoughts. Here was he, on the bloody run from the plod, now sitting next to an ex-copper, in *his* taxi with *him* at the wheel. This is not good; I've got to do something fast, otherwise I might strangle this old boy right now and dump him and his car in the briny, just to shut him up. Eddie quickly worked out, the forger and this driver bloke both lived in St Aubin. Might even drink in the same pub, swap stories and all that. It was common in the East End for plod to mix with gangsters.

Made them feel excited, gave them an adrenalin rush. Some of them for a few quid would turn their backs when things got a bit naughty. Eddie was beginning to regret having a pop at the Frenchie. He might just give this bloke a bell, just to turn me in, then be the local bloody hero. "Is there a high spot on the Island where we can look down on the water below?" Eddie asked. "Yes, yes, in fact there is. I used to work at just the place you are describing when I was a boy. It's called Sorel Point, North of the Island it is. It is the highest point of the Island too." "If you worked there as a kid then what job did you do?" asked Eddie. "Well, Sorel is a growing area, arable farming stuff and the like, you know. Daffodils up there are grown in their thousands, early on each year. Acres and acres of them. They're cut, boxed and sent over to the mainland. My job since you ask was to box up all the bunches and ready them for the van that would take them to St. Helier, put on the ferry and that was that. Of course, they fly them over now, ferry was always too slow for living things like cut flowers." "Well, let's go there then" instructed Eddie. "How long will it take?

only I've got to find some digs for a week or so. I was thinking of finding a drum in or near St. Helier." "Drum Sir, are you in a band?" Eddie explained, back in London, a drum was local parlance for somewhere to live, as in drum and base, my place. "No need to worry about that old chap, in addition to the taxi business, my wife and I run a bed and breakfast establishment, not far from where I picked you up a little earlier. We have some beautiful rooms, mostly sea facing. Quite reasonable prices too at a couple of pounds sterling per night. That includes a full Jersey breakfast of course!"

"Look mate" Eddie was getting a bit twitchy and paranoid. "Forget about the thingy point, whatever it's called, and for that matter the Island tour, just get me to St. Helier. Thanks for the B&B offer pal, but I would prefer to stay in the main town." "Yes of course Sir, on to St. Helier it is then. Anywhere in particular?" Thirty minutes later, Eddie jumped out of the Snipe as it cruised to a halt near the Pom D'or Hotel close by Liberation Square in St. Helier. He bunged the old boy a deep-sea diver, waving away the change. With an imposing frontage the Pom D'or sat squarely on the Esplanade, it overlooked St. Helier's harbour area, which at this time of year, was bristling with private yachts of all shapes and sizes. With the weather still on the warm side, Eddie decided to take a stroll around the harbour, getting amongst all the shining white hulled yachts gently bobbing about at their moorings. 'These are the bee's knees, thought Eddie. 'Stinks of money down 'ere it does.' "Ahoy there" came a voice behind him. Eddie spun round to see where the voice emanated from. Two berths back a chap, middle aged-ish, wearing a captain's hat, dressed in white roll neck jumper blue jeans finished off with a pair of deck shoes was walking towards him. Eddie thought, 'Christ, what is it with this bleedin Island nobody wants to leave me be.' "Hi there" said the voice, "I'm Lee, Lee Dean, I've just moored up after crossing over from Brittany." Eddie's geography outside London being close to nil replied. "Don't you mean Britain?"

Lee chuckled. "No, Brittany France. Anyway, I was looking to get some provisions, you know food and stuff. Would you be local by any chance?"

Eddie started to chuckle too. "No mate, I got here myself only this morning. Look pal, it's been a long day, so if you don't mind, I'd rather just leave it out and say cheers for now." "Oh ok. Sorry to jump on you like that. Look if you need a sit down, and maybe a cuppa and a slice of cake, why don't you come aboard and put your feet up then I can make us both a brew." Eddie looked carefully into his eyes. He held sailor boy's gaze for a good twenty seconds. Seeing no immediate threat, Eddie nodded whilst taking a few cautious steps towards the yacht Lee was generally waving towards.

Under his breath he said, 'I hope this bloke doesn't turn out to be the filth an' all. I've had it up to here with coppers today.' He lifted up his hand as if in mock salute. Ok sailor boy, lead on I could do with a cuppa as it 'appens.

CHAPTER 16

Johnny the Turk was the last to arrive. It was ten minutes after ten in the morning. The front door of 119 Plenva Street on the Isle-of-Dogs stood ajar. Still, he thought, show a bit of respect and courtesy, best to knock first. Grabbing hold of the little brass knocker, before he could rap it on the door, Val appeared. Opening the door to its widest point, she beckoning Johnny to step inside. As he made his way along the hall through to the tiny living room, muffled voices talking and laughing could be heard. Johnny stiffened, almost turning to leave, he didn't want to be a part of this especially in *her* house. His hand surreptitiously slid to a pocket inside of his jacket and felt the comfort of a claw hammer. The claw-end ground down and sharpened to a vicious looking point of some four inches long. More than enough to do serious damage to someone's skull. Johnny was tooled up and ready for agro. Billy was the first to greet him, followed by Mel then Dave Conti. Both Billy and Mel, known as the 'Stratford Two.' were dressed in smart double-breasted suits, cuff-linked shirts together with plain ties. Billy nodded at Johnny; Mel smiled that smile that always melted young lady's knicker elastic at twenty-five yards. Billy's swarthiness had him marked down from Romany decent. Mel by contrast had more of a baby-faced pretty boy look. These two, whilst working within Eddie's crew, had carved out a fearsome reputation for malicious wounding, violence, torture and mayhem. They were pain givers. None dared cross them, their violent wrong doings preceded them. They would eat pain like candy then dole it out multiplied by ten in return. Their main task within the crew was to look after Errol's ten or so car-lots, providing protection against anyone attempting to muscle in on the lucrative business.

It was Eddie who tasked them with carrying out their job unfettered, as in - do what you think fit, in return for a weekly wedge from Errol. Dave Conti sat on one of the two fireside chairs grinning like a Cheshire cat as Johnny entered the room. He had slipped off his black leather jacket draping it over the back of his chair. At six foot plus, Dave had just about the longest legs going.

Nobody understood how he was so smart at nicking motors, how on earth did he managed to fit in some of the smaller sporty two-seater types? Johnny the Turk previously had sparred with Dave down at the gym a few times. Dave was a bit of a handful in the ring. A longish spell in prison had seen to that, hardened by the bare-knuckle fights with inmates whilst enjoying time spent at her Majesties' pleasure. However, due to his recent slacking off from the fight circuit, Dave was not hitting his opponents so hard. Especially because, just lately, he was more interested in hitting on the birds. Never seemed to be without one on his arm. Always blond, tall and slim, mostly with long black shiny high heeled boots. Must be down to Dave's height and his Elvis style hair-do. Plenty of Brylcreem with a neat looking duck's arse at the back and a kiss curl to the front. The style seemed to turn a few blond heads in his direction. As it happens, Johnny had not been able to get hold of Dave and whisper in his shell like, that would have to wait for now. "For openers, I'm assuming you all know about Eddie being lifted?" asked Val. All nodded. And I'm assuming you all know where he's aiming to get to?" All shook their heads. Good, that's how it's gonna have to be for now. The less anyone knows, the more chance he will have of keeping out of old Bill's way. The filth parked themselves outside here for a fortnight. They've buggered off now but no doubt will be keeping an eye out for him." Johnny interrupted Val's flow. "Where's Bomber then?" "On his way" Val Coleman scowled at Johnny. Being interrupted was not on her agenda. Her agenda had her rebuilding Eddie's empire. Her agenda was to put her firmly in control. Eddie is her son, therefore whilst he is absent, she felt it was her duty to take control. Not too bad a leap from bus clippie to gangland boss, she thought. Her old job as clippie was history now and why the hell not? "Bomber has instructions, from me, to get the basement at The Oasis back up to scratch, is that good enough for you Johnny? The filth turned it over several times and didn't have the grace to clear it up. He'll be here any moment."

Val, having answered Johnny's query pressed on. "As and when we get the basement back, we can start to meet there again." She ordered Billy and Mel to continue with the protection of Errol's car-lots and for Dave Conti to resume stealing top end motors from up West.

"I've spoken to Errol. He is more than happy to continue taking delivery from you Dave, same deal as before. Soon as you nick them, drive straight to Creekmouth Yard and drop them off. Errol will see to it that the motors get new registration plates and false paperwork and fresh paintwork, before they are shipped out to Europe." Bomber Brown breezed in and stood in the doorway. He nodded to all individually. Val continued. "According to Errol, his dad Lee Roy has lined up a number of contacts ready and willing to part with cash for as many motors as we can supply. That's if for now, when we can get into the Oasis we'll talk again." So began the revival of Eddie's crew, albeit with a different Coleman at the helm. The men filed out of number 119 on to Plenva Street, leaving Val in a state of intense excitement and happiness. During one of her many visits to Eddie while he was on remand, not only had they discussed the plan to lift him, Eddie was adamant that she would take control. She was the only person in the world apart from Esme he could trust now. Bomber was last to leave, as he got up to go Val held him back and used the magic word, *Eddie*. "Eddie wants you to act as my number one, my right arm as it were. If I am to run this show properly, I need you to keep me in the loop with what's going on with the rest of the blokes. It's not grassing, Eddie's ordered you to do it." She lied. "From now on, I want you to meet me here once a week. Eddie said it's most important. Got it?"

CHAPTER 17

Javier stopped the car, shut down the engine, got out and walked to the other side of the road. "Come look as this Esme." She did the same, feeling the heat as soon as she stepped out of the car onto the dusty by-road. "Look." Javier was pointing down to an area across and below them that looked like part of an old Western cowboy town. At first all Esme could focus on was a large herd of goats mooching around clearing brush and anything else remotely edible. Javier continued "Some filming took place here a little while ago. Big American film company came to stay in Moxakar. They built what you can see here, then left it. Now tourist travel on a pilgrimage just to visit what you see down there and to soak up the atmosphere. El Paso they named it. I think the film was called 'For a Few Dollars More.' Some call it a Spaghetti Western."

Esme turned to Javier. "Ok, so why are we here, I thought we were going to view, what was it you said? a spectacular villa, with a spectacular view." "Yes, yes and we will. This is such a beautiful place though. Look over there." Javier pointed above and beyond the abandoned film set of El Paso to the slopes of the Sierra Nevada Mountains way off in the distance. See, here we are in the heat of the day. There they are, snow-capped. Don't you think it is lovely?" He turned to her, not waiting for an answer. "So, on to the villa then. By the way, it is called Villa Hermosa Vista, which in English, translates to 'beautiful view'. And when we get there, you will see why. It is no more than twenty minutes away, on the road back to Mojácar. The Villa turned out to be a stunner, fully furnished, nothing was left wanting. Esme went for it without question, she would take out the minimum three-year rental period with an option to purchase thereafter. Standing by the pool Esme admired the far-reaching, uninterrupted view out to the sparkling azure blue Mediterranean Sea. Over to the right, she could just make out somewhere the locals called Goats Head Bay. From here it looked like it offered a quiet sandy stretch of deserted beach. Real 'Robinson Crusoe' stuff, she purred, "It's perfect Javier." High up on the hillside it was, with not too many neighbours and just a short drive to Mojácar. You were right about the beautiful view. I could look out on the sea all day." "You will be pleased to know the owner had it specially built to be Westerly facing." "This means you will be able to watch the sun setting on the water's horizon, sitting here by the pool. Just think how romantic that would feel, some classical music on the record player, a glass or two of wine, contemplating the beauty of the golden sun as it disappears over the horizon." Privately he wished 'if only it could be just you and me'. Esme seemed to read his mind. So, to take the steam out of his steamy thoughts, she switched the conversation to more mundane subjects. "What about maintenance, servicing the villa, cleaners and the like?"

Javier began to feel the rising sap, once again drain back down. Esme smiled thinking, *now to get the ice dagger in deeper.* "Bit of an old romantic at heart 'aint you mate, bubbling on about sunsets and that." "Show me a young Spaniard that is lacking romance and I will call him bereft of life itself" smiled Javier. "Well, I reckon it's all this heat and Sangria. Come on, drive me back to your office and let's get the initial paper work done." Esme turned to walk around the side of the Villa back towards Javier's car. Javier eyed her slim figure, shapely legs, pert little bottom and let his imagination and sap run riot.

CHAPTER 18

To Eddie's relief, the offer of a cuppa and slice on sailor boy's boat held no threats. All seemed calm, all seemed well. He had no intention however of going below. As it turned out, the yacht sported a small seating area at the back end in a semi-circle from one side to the other. Scatter cushions had been scattered for comfort. The craft bobbed gently and rhythmically at anchor, causing the now seated Eddie to yawn and close his eyes momentarily. Lee called from below, "One sugar or two? Sorry I don't yet know your name, what would you like me to call you?" Eddie grinned. "Anything you like but definitely not early in the morning mate." No laughing at his attempt at a joke emanated from the cabin. So, Eddie offered up "Mr Rolex will do." Lee arrived with two steaming mugs of tea. "Hope two sugars is ok for you? Because, Mr *Rolex* that's what you've got." Lee eyed the Rolex Submariner strapped to Eddie's left wrist the value of which was somewhere close to that of his yacht. Eddie caught his admiring gaze. "Champion mate two sugars are just fine." He slurped the nectar and bit heartily into a massive slice of cake. "Do you ever sail to Spain mate?" "Well, yes, I have done a couple of times, it's a bit of a longish passage, why do you ask?" "Thing is Lee, I could do with getting to Spain sooner or later." "Anywhere in particular?" "Not too sure pal, not good on foreign soil geography wise." Lee disappeared below again, returning almost immediately with some charts. "Ok let's have a look." Clearing some of the clutter on a nearby flat surface Lee rolled out a complete map of Spain. Some of the clutter was used to hold down each of the maps four corners. Sounding like a primary school teacher, he asked "Point to where you might want to go then."

Eddie was still confused. Not wishing to look totally ignorant he shrugged his shoulders and said, "Somewhere South". "Hmmm. Well ok, but that would mean passing through the Strait of Gibraltar, that's quite an undertaking what with crossing the Bay of Biscay thrown in. The very best I could offer you is here, up in the North." His fore-finger rested on Bilbao.

"We can sail down the Estuary of Bilbao and land you more or less in the centre of Bilboa. From there I would presume you will be able to find links to the South, you know, trains, coaches that sort of stuff." "How long?" asked Eddie. "Well, this time of year, with a fair wind and so on, at least two days maybe three."

Eddie hadn't planned for things to happen this fast. He knew Esme was going to make a trip to Southern Spain in order to find somewhere. Somewhere he could keep his head down well off of old Bill's radar. How long that would take or if it were even possible, he had no idea. Ok, he knew now, prior to meeting Esme that she was a copper. A copper clever enough to become part of his crew. Clever enough to work her way in so far, as to be around when meetings at the Oasis were convened. Meetings when raids were discussed, robberies were planned, methods of murders arranged, who and when. Worst still, everything she witnessed or heard he now assumed relayed back to the police! She was a plant. An undercover cop planted very carefully right at the heart of his operations. So, finding her way to Spain and renting somewhere shouldn't be too much of a problem, perhaps. Her downfall from her unique position at Eddie's top table, came from a most unexpected source. She fell headlong, cartwheels, head over heels, base over apex in love with Eddie. Shortly before the outrageous (*as Eddie called it*) and infamous police midnight raid at the Oasis Bar, Esme shoved her notice to quit the Met under her bosses' nose. If they needed her to attend a trial in order to give evidence, now being a civilian, she would be obliged to attend and if not be subpoenaed. Being on the force for some years, she was well aware of all the angles, which is why, when talking through Eddie's planned escape with Val, she was more than willing to run with the idea of scarpering off to Spain, perfect! Get across to Spain, go into hiding with Eddie. As far as she was concerned, a blissful new life beckoned, sunsets, Sangria and siestas in bed with her beloved Eddie.

CHAPTER 19

"So, what do you think then Mr Rolex, will that suit you?" Before Eddie could reply, Lee continued. "If it's yes, I will need to stock up on provisions and suitable sailing togs, unless you have some in your luggage perhaps?" Eddie cut in "No mate what you see is what you get, my luggage didn't make it to Jersey" he lied. "In that case Mr Rolex, if we are going to sail all the way to Bilbao, we will need to kit you out with some suitable sailing gear. Come on, let's drink and eat up then go find an outlet for your needs. Do you have money with you?" Eddie stiffened. Was this bloke out to do him or what? "What sort of question is that pal?" Eddie growled. Lee sat down again. "Ok if you're short of a bob or three, I've got just about two of everything that you should need for the trip, might be a bit on the large side though." Eddie pulled out his bank roll. Not too far, just enough to let Lee see he was nowhere near being potless. Lee got the message, "okay, understood. Let's go shopping." "One thing, I shall need to log our trip with the authorities." "What the bloody 'ell for?" "Well, apart from being maritime law, I have to give a destination, a planned sailing route and an ETA, so that if we dock at our intended destination as stated, people don't need to go looking for us." "ATA, what the fuck is that when it's at home?" Eddie was getting twitchy again. Self-preservation was kicking in. Lee smiled at Eddie's mistake. "ETA, simply means estimated time of arrival." Eddie stood and thought it through as best as he could. "Look pal I know you fancy my watch. I've seen you gawping at it. If you can get me across to Billyboy Bay or whatever you call it, without letting anyone know, when we get there, you can 'ave it." Back in the East End, Eddie's home turf, this bloke would be on the end of a right hiding about now, he held back. Just for the moment, he needed sailor boy. Lee grinning a big grin said, "deal, let's shake on it." They shook. "Now let's go shopping." Lee momentarily envisaged a more luxurious and sea worthy yacht coming his way. The money from the sale of his yacht and of that Rolex, would see to that.

CHAPTER 20

The explosion was so loud, it could be heard as far as Hoxton, the best part of four miles away. The blast being so immense shattered windows, shopfronts, eardrums, car windscreens and anything else shatterable within two hundred yards. Amazingly not one person was injured or killed. Perhaps being four o'clock in the morning had something to do with it. A police officer some streets away walking his beat, was knocked to the ground. Jumping up he screamed "Fuck me" at nobody in particular, followed by "everybody run for the shelters, Germany's bombing London again the bastards." Once the ringing in his ears ceased ringing like Big Ben on speed, fumbling for his police whistle, he gave it three blasts in an effort to attract any other beat bobbies within earshot. Just in case they might have temporarily lost their hearing too, he gave it a further three blasts. What he couldn't have known at that moment, the blast and subsequent flames shooting up in the air from a fractured gas main, had grabbed the attention of Limehouse and Clerkenwell fire stations. As the beat bobby was busy dusting himself down, the night crews at both stations would be busy donning their fire tackling kit such as it was in the mid-sixties whilst the fire engines were being started up ready to race to the scene. The lone beat copper was soon joined by a colleague, equally stunned and equally dizzy from the blast. He spoke in shouting mode in an effort to hear his own voice. "What the hell was that all about then?" "Dunno mate" shouted the other "But I couldn't half go for a gasper, got any fags on you?" As they lit up and took deep drags of nicotine infested smoke way down into their lungs, the bells they could hear ringing, were not inside their heads this time, but the clanging bells of the fire brigade charging towards the scene.

Fags stubbed out, they decided it was time to get their arses in gear and practice the four-minute mile in the general direction of the fifty-foot flames which were now lighting up the location of the explosion like a giant fiery beacon, as in *over 'ere pal*. By the time they arrived at least one fire crew and engine were on site. The crew busied themselves unfurling hoses whilst the fire chief began assessing the situation and cobbling together a hasty plan. The beat bobbies were told in no uncertain terms the best thing for them to do was to get the gas main turned off.

One of them raced to a nearby police phone box and relayed the request to the Sergeant on night duty at the station. The other was told to keep the small number of gathering onlookers well back. The onlookers, mostly attired in pyjamas and nighties, were beginning to organise themselves in the best of London's East End tradition, brewing cups of tea and handing out biscuits and fags plus blankets for those that had dashed out following the blast in just pants and singlets. Several guesses as to the reason for the explosion passed from onlooker to onlooker as they gawped at the flames. "Gas main I bet" ventured one. "Nahh it's a bleedin V2 Bomber in it."

This from an elderly lady who had managed to live through the bombing blitz laid on by the thoughtful Luftwaffe during World War Two. "Seen it all before I 'as" she grinned. "It was a plane crash" from yet another. "I saw it plummet down from the sky, I even 'eard all the passengers screaming, 'orrible it was." Amazingly, not one of the collection of onlookers guessed the blast might have been a deliberate act, which of course it was. The entire building known locally up until one minute to four o'clock as the Oasis was completely demolished, simply a pile of smoking rubble. By now, the second fire engine arrived to ably assist in dousing the flames.

A couple of ambulances turned up, seeing there were no casualties obvious or otherwise, the crews mingled with the onlookers, whose numbers had now risen up to thirty or so. They mingled, snaffling mugs of teas and as many biscuits, cakes and fags as they could snaffle. A bit of an East-End party atmosphere was beginning to develop. The heat from the flames was warming the growing crowd, someone introduced a bottle of two of mother's ruin for others to swig which warmed them up even more.

One or two people actually began to sing. The old dear who swore blind it was a V2 bomb that landed, laughed a toothless laugh "just like the old days" she shouted. "Bloody Gerry won't break our spirit, 'ere you, giss another swig o that gin," she cackled, like an old witch. As more constables arrived a collective "oh noooo" rang out. The gas main which serviced the entire street had been shut down and with it the nice warm flames. The extra officers on site began to politely shuffle the onlookers back to a safe distance, then with the aid of some rope and posts, set up a cordon around the smouldering rubble. The fire crews would stay on until well into the day in order to assess any damage that may have occurred to the neighbouring buildings. Luckily the adjoining buildings were uninhabited, unless of course any dossers had broken in to doss down for the night.

Although, they wouldn't perhaps have heard the blast, being too hammered on Meth's let alone be harmed. Therefore, it appeared not to be a requirement for both ambulances to remain at the scene. Reluctantly, following a final swig of gin, the driver of ambulance one disappeared into the night, shooting off erratically to the crew's next exciting destination. In the rear of ambulance two, a young crewman chanced his arm with a tasty looking bird and was having it off with her on one of the stretcher beds. Thank God he thought for the blacked-out windows.

CHAPTER 21

The Oasis, *(current owner Eddie Coleman),* comprised of a two-storey corner building situated on the junction of Mill Place E14 and Basin Approach. The ground floor, with double doors that opened out and onto the pavement, housed a bar-cum-gambling den by night and café by day. Below the ground floor a dingy dungeon type basement existed. The disused basement a while ago had been hollowed out then fashioned into a smart meeting place for Eddie and his most trusted villainous crew members for get togethers. Ironically, Eddie christened it the Dungeon.

Above the bar sat a two bedroomed flat decked out as living accommodation. It was occupied by Bomber, an ex-heavyweight boxer, a true and trusted friend of Eddie Coleman. Bomber's pro boxing days were over, his main task now being gatekeeper of Oasis Corner, old Bill look out and official bouncer for the basement office, when Eddie was in residence. Oasis Corner was well known in the gangland underworld. Before Eddie's arrest it became a place to avoid so far as other gangs or firms were concerned, when he and his crew of henchmen were most active. Indeed, on one occasion, a bunch of Scooter type mods from Tottenham decided to plague the place and knock it about a bit. Ten of them tried turning the place over one night, scaring most of the customers away. Big mistake. Eddie, Johnny and Bomber made sure the mods left a few pints of their blood and many teeth behind before scarpering for their lives, never to return. None of tonight's gas explosion onlookers felt inclined to mention to the police about Bomber Brown living above the bar. They were all too aware of Eddie's reputation for anyone with loose tongues especially where the police were concerned.

He'd cut them out and feed them to the dogs. If Bomber died in the blast, it was not for any of them to speak up about it, as ever; the usual East End wall of silence descended.

When dawn came, most of the onlookers had retired back to wherever they came from. The police closed off Basin Approach which pissed off anyone needing that particular route to get to their place of work. Men from the gas board arrived but were frustrated by the amount of building rubble heaped up on the areas they needed to work on. The boss gasman told all the workers to bugger off until the site was cleared enough to work on. Heavy earth moving equipment would be needed to do the clearing up. How long that would take was anyone's guess.

In essence, the nerve centre of Eddie Coleman's activities, Oasis Corner in Limehouse which included protection rackets, jewellery heists, thieving, violence of one kind or another, torture, terrorism and general thuggery was snuffed out. The Oasis was no more, and with it the crew of villains, thieves, safe breakers and henchmen. Val Coleman's plan to take up the reins from her son had been well and truly thwarted. Johnny and Bomber sat in Eddie's steak bar and restaurant up West discussing the ins and outs and ups and downs of starting up again. Almost certainly Mel and Billy, the Stratford two would want to be roped in, which put the crew up to four quick as you like. Next on the list would be Little Allen followed by Dave Conti, then it was over to Creekmouth to pay a visit to black Errol and check out his breakers yard. "Why blow the bloody the place then up Johnny?" "It's business Bomber mate pure and simple. I read somewhere something that went like this, 'To the victor go the spoils.' If Eddie's mum keeps to her word, we could well be pushed aside and I'm not 'avin that. I always was his right-hand man therefore it should be me being the bloody victor, not 'er." "So, if you're coming in with me, we'll get some of the men together and form up a fresh crew of blokes with you and me in charge." Bomber posed a question, "What if the boss shows up?" "As I understand it, he's gone into hiding" Johnny replied. "Had it away on his toes. It could be years before he has the front to turn up, if ever. Listen mate, the old Bill are well up for feeling his collar. It's murder they want him for as well as absconding. He'd be insane to show up in the East End, let alone be dumb enough to carry on where he left off. He 'aint bleedin God you know." "Yea spose you're right there Johnny." Bomber then posed a second question. "Where are we gonna have meets and stuff?" Leave that to me Bomber, I've a cousin who runs a dive over near Stepney Green. I'll give 'im a bell and see if he's got a spare room above the place.

I'll get that fired up and then we can get on with some genuine organised crime. Only this time instead of Eddie and his bloody vendettas, brain power's gonna come before violence." Bomber Brown looked on in awe. Johnny the Turk changed the subject. "Anyway, sorry about your flat, you'll 'ave to find yourself somewhere temporary to kip down. It's you and me now running the show with all that goes with it." "How'd you feel like being a crime boss?" Bomber thought about his meetings with Mrs Coleman and shivered. This was a dangerous game he was playing. Bomber ventured another question, "Maybe I could get myself sorted upstairs here to kip down like. You know in one of the girl's rooms?" "As far as I'm concerned Bomber, you can have the whole of the upstairs. Turf out all the brasses, they 'aint bringing in much of an income anyway." "Thanks Johnny, I'll get on with it straight away.

Cor imagine me, living here in the West End, before you know it, I'll start talking fucking proper." "Yea well don't get too comfortable, this place, Steak Bar plus the rooms above, still unofficially belongs to Eddie.

He wrenched it off some Greek bloke for a pittance. There's probably some dodgy paperwork somewhere in the back office with Eddie's name plastered on it. See if you can lay your hands on it sometime or other. We might need to use it as a bargaining chip to buy off Val Coleman." "Christ Johnny, I can see what you mean by using your bonce." As Johnny got up to leave, Bomber asked "How did you get enough dynamite to blow up the entire building?" "Well, it wasn't meant to demolish half the street. A mate of a mate works in a quarry down in Essex somewhere, might be Braintree or something. For a few quid he bunged me a boxful, so I thought in for a penny and all that. He gave me some ideas how to just drop the Oasis. Anyway, it was the gas main that did for the building, the dynamite was just the forerunner."

CHAPTER 22

"That's it then Mr Rolex, we've arrived at our destination safe and sound. What do you think of Bilbao?" Lee said over his shoulder. "Well, it's no great shakes but it's bloody hot for starters." Eddie was not wrong there, being midday, the temperature was up around the eighties. "What you doing now?" he enquired. "Just mooring up, you know, pulling the standing line through the mooring rings. Keeps the boat nice and close in to the jetty." Eddie took a look around him, taking in all the sights and sounds. Fishing vessels of all shapes and sizes were busy unloading, yachts roughly the size of the one that had ferried him across from Jersey to this part of Northern Spain bobbed up and down. Apart from a day in Jersey, this was as far as he had ever been from his home on the Isle-of-Dogs. He felt much like the fish being landed all around him, as in 'out of water'.

"Right then, that's the boat secured, I just need to register with the Spanish officials that we have moored up. They will need to see our passports and need a good reason for visiting their country." "Hey 'old up pal I don't give a flying fuck about all that sort of twaddle and tosh. I don't want to draw any attention to me. If you know what's good for you, you'll do as I say. You go and do what you have to, but don't mention me. I'll nip off when it gets dark and disappear." This was Lee's first inclination of the potential threat of violence. During the somewhat stormy crossing from Jersey, he noticed his passenger becoming more aggravated and moodier as the nautical miles swished by under the hull of his yacht. He became increasingly aware that he could well be smuggling someone on the run, or far worse, a convicted murderer on the run. "Ok, understood. As far as the officials are concerned, I will inform them I have a single male passenger on board, who will not be stepping foot on Spanish soil. That usually does the trick although they will want to see your passport. Eddie reluctantly handed it over. Lee bunged it with his into his back pocket, without glancing inside. Is there anything I can do for you while I am ashore so to speak?" "As it 'appens there is. I want you to find somewhere to send a telegram for me. I've written it down on this here bit of paper."

The address is on the other side. Lee read it out to make sure he understood what had been written adding the word 'stop' in the appropriate places.

'All's well. Made it to S. Let Es know.' "That's right," Eddie nodded. "Let me know how much I owe you but it'll 'ave to be in pounds alright?" Lee stepped onto the wooden jetty and headed for the shoreline. For the first time Eddie was alone on the yacht. He made a bee line for the kitchen area or galley as Lee had called it, because it was here Eddie previously spotted a number of knives, amongst them a vicious looking carving knife. Whilst below deck, he investigated a long timber box that doubled up as a bed base with a mattress on top. Throwing the mattress on the floor, he lifted the hinged lid and found that the box housed various bits and pieces of nautical stuff, ropes, floatation jackets, flares and the like.

It looked long and wide enough to possibly hide a bound and gagged person for a period of time. As the hours passed since Lee had buggered off a plan was hatching in Eddie's head. Having got this far in under a week, he was not about to fuck it up now. His mind wandered back to the slick way he had been lifted, right under old Bill's nose. Ma Val had organised it well, he had to hand it to her. The man hunt back home will now be well underway. If everyone in the know keep their gobs shut then that would make it harder by the day for the filth to work out where the hell he'd disappeared to. The bustling noise of Lee Dean returning to the yacht brought Eddie out of his reverie and back to the present. "So, Mr du Pre'," Lee smiled. "Eh, what?" Eddie replied with the look of someone about to explode. "Well, that's the name on your passport, Jack! What's with all the Mr Rolex stuff then?" A new Name and new identity the Forger said. A new name and new I.D. Jack du Pré he said to himself. So that's what Freddie the Forger meant. "Gimme it back" spat Eddie. He opened the passport up for the first time since Freddie the Forger handed it to him, back in St Aubin.

He glanced at the photo of himself in the passport. Dark brown hair, heavy framed specs then looked up from the passport photo and peered into a circular shaving mirror attached to a shelf containing various bits of shaving stuff, similar enough he thought. Again, he rolled the name Jack du Pré around his mouth. "Seems quite respectful to me" he said to no one in particular. Freddie sure did me proud, guess I shouldn't have given 'im such a bad time even if he is a bleeding queer. "So, who did you sign it off as Lee?" "The name in the passport of course, that the right thing to do" Lee took it back and stuffed it in his pocket. Lee was looking at him with a watermelon smile. Eddie barked "Do me a favour pal, take that sickly grin off your face, or I might just put a permanent smile on it for you. Where you from anyway, Ministry of Mirth or what?" Eddie whipped out the hidden carving knife from under the mattress, and waved it menacingly in front of Lee's face. Lee, however, was not about to let Eddie welch on the deal. As far as he remembered, the deal was to get his passenger du Pré or whoever he really was to Spain in return for the Rolex Submariner. He had done his bit; it was now time for his passenger to do his bit. Lee remembered he had an ace up his sleeve, well actually in his back pocket. He whipped out Eddie's passport yelling "You come near me with that knife and this goes over the side."

Eddie lunged forward, knife in hand aimed at Lee's throat, but Lee was light on his feet, neatly side-stepping the lunge. Put off balance he staggered past Lee. As he fell, he felt a bang on the back of the head. The clout when it came, was a complete surprise. Eddie's knees buckled from the energy of the blow. His vision momentarily gone; Eddie shook his head violently attempting to clear his brain. By the time he could see straight and think straight he felt, rather than saw, the muzzle of a gun being pushed hard against his temple. Lee spoke quietly. "Move and I will kill you." Eddie's eyes glazed over and seemed to be looking over his shoulder. Lee thought he heard what sounded like someone softly singing a kid's nursery rhyme.

Half a pound of tuppeny rice, half a pound of treacle, if he had known Eddie better, he would have been aware of the trance like state he puts himself in before potentially killing someone. Lee pressed on regardless of the unknown danger. "First things first, hand over the Rolex." Eddie had no choice. Slowly unclipping the clasp that held the Rolex in place, he let the watch slip from his wrist into his waiting hand. In an eye blink, the hand holding the watch, shot up flinging the Rolex over the side of the yacht. Lee watched it disappear over the side then swiftly sink to the sea bed. This was Eddie's moment. Lee was momentarily distracted by his ticket to a shiny new yacht disappearing, Eddie was up like lightning and rammed the carving knife deep in Lee's heart. As Lee collapsed, he took aim and pulled the trigger as he fell but there was no bang. He'd left the safety catch on. With both life and strength ebbing away rapidly, this would be his one and only chance of killing du Pré. Eddie, for his part, was glad the gun didn't go bang for two reasons; one, he wasn't dead and two, the bang would have attracted unwanted attention. Pulling the gun from Lee's limp grip, he tucked it into his waistband. A loaded gun on the hip can be a useful persuader, sometimes just shoving it in someone's face was more than enough. He sat on the bed come storage bunker rubbing the back of his head. A lump the size of an egg was the result of the clout he received, but luckily, no other damage. He sat looking down at Lee, knife handle sticking out of his chest and the blade deep in his body up to the hilt. Lee was writhing and gurgling his death throes, legs twitching their last twitches, death cries emanating silently from his mouth.

"Leave it out Pal, can't you die like a man or what?" Eddie smiled. He'd seen it all too often in the past.

For a while, he drummed his fingers, then following twenty minutes of hard labour, Lee's body was put to rest in the bed bunker below the mattress. All the nautical paraphernalia was stuffed on top of his body. Of course, he had to leave his mark on Lee. Eddie wouldn't be Eddie, if he didn't leave his mark. Whenever the body would eventually be discovered, He would be miles away. He could almost see the discoverer looking at Lee's body lying face down with a noughts and crosses symbol neatly carved on his back. Later, under darkness, Eddie left the yacht and made his way to the shore line. He had a fat roll of money, a loaded gun, a passport, and a new identity - what could possibly go wrong?

CHAPTER 23

"Cooee, sorry to bov, it's only Sue and Chris from next door, we've bought some bubbly to welcome you in." Esme thought she was hearing things. The Villa's nearest neighbours would have been at least a quarter of a mile away and downhill at that. The view from Villa Hermosa Vista was uninterrupted straight out to the Med. One needed to crane one's neck looking downwards to catch the merest glimpse of the nearest neighbouring Villa, and only then one would see the red terracotta roof.

It was early evening, however, perhaps her patio lights attracted this pair of nosey busybody moths. Esme looked up and saw a couple maybe in their mid-sixties, standing grinning, there on the patio by the pool. The man was holding up a bottle of Cava in one hand and four flutes in the other. Well, he got that wrong she thought, there's two of them and one of me. Pushing her hair back, she donned her best welcoming smile and opened the sliding door that led on to the patio. "Welcome to Hermosa Vista, I see you've come prepared, how nice of you. Let's go and sit by the pool and have a chat, shall we?" Sue and Chris really wanted to get a nose round the villa, but that would have to wait. "Introductions first," said Sue. "I'm Sue and this is my old man, Chris. Here Chris, get the bottle opened and pour us all a welcome drink." The cork popped; a spume of Cava followed. "Sorry about that love, only I've got Arthurirtus as I call's it in both me thumbs, makes me a bit cack-handed like." Sue doubled up with laughter. Esme reckoned this must be their third or fourth bottle so far tonight.

Sue didn't wait for the intros to continue. Esme though, deciding not to be ignored, shot out a hand and said "And I'm Esme, it's a pleasure to meet you both. I take it you live near here then?" "Oh yes, direct neighbours." Chris jerked an arthritic thumb over his shoulder in the general direction of the sea. He poured two flutes of Cava, one for his missus and one for Esme. "Where's your husband then girly? In town getting some provo's?" Esme looked at him quizzically. "You know, provo's, provisions; eggs, bacon, sausages, beans and stuff like that." "Sorry Chris what makes you think I've got a husband?" "Well, we saw yous two looking around the place and put three and three together didn't we" he said glancing at Sue. She nodded. "Did we come up with five or something then?" Esme explained the chap they saw was the owner's letting agent.

"So" Sue butted in, "you're on your own up here alone?" Not wishing to indulge this couple in her goings on, she switched the subject, inwardly noting, they'd obviously been watching when Javier was showing her around and assumed, wrongly, she and Javier were a couple. She would need to keep these two at arm's length, preferable on the end of a sharp pointy stick. She could hear in her head Eddie saying, "Let's do 'em, dump them in the sea, nosey fuckers." The evening ground on. Esme hearing all about them and they, too busy gobbing off about themselves, to notice they had heard nothing of Esme. As the pair rattled on, Esme slowly tuned out, happy to let them carry on, it gave her a chance to study them both. She could see their mouths moving and heads being thrown back in laughter at some inside or family joke but the voices now seemed a little distant. A bit like being on a bus with two people talking three or four seats away. Couldn't quite get what they were saying above the hum of the engine. Sue was probably a bit of a looker once, Esme concluded. Almost certainly the more graceful of the two. Ageing is not usually kind to women, whereas, men seem to become more distinguished as they get older. With this couple, however, it was the reverse, Chris looked more like extinguished! Sue wore a white blouse together with a lovely vermillion evening sarong which didn't look cheap. Matching necklace and bracelet, denoting care on how one looks, added to the ensemble. Instead of Jesus boots she'd opted for red strappy sandals.

She must have kept well out of the Spanish sun as her skin colour was the same as anyone living north of Edinburgh, white bordering on light blue. Somewhere during the evening Sue mentioned they were in their early sixties. Momentarily Esme's police training kicked in, noting Sue could easily pass for early fifties. Chris, on the other hand, looked like he'd just fallen out of bed and thrown on whatever laid on the floor from the previous night. Dishevelled hair matched a dishevelled dress sense. There was, however, something running a little deeper with Chris. Esme sensed he was the brains, the power behind decisions made, based on well thought out logic and intelligent thinking. If she was to keep her and Eddie's secret from leaking out to the local gendarmerie, this one could be a problem. He might just be too clever for her liking. It was way past midnight so, pretending to stretch and yawn tiredly, her newly acquired neighbours got the message and were soon on their way back to their own villa and their own beds, chatting and laughing on their way, then having a nightcap or two no doubt before falling blissfully asleep. Esme heard Chris curse in the darkness.

"I said to bring a bloody torch you silly mare, I've just stubbed my toe." "Shut your gob, Chris, you should eat more bleedin carrots." Esme however was far from sleepy. This was an unexpected occurrence. She'd only been in residence for a week or so. Nosey busy-body neighbours, however good their intentions, would need to be kept at arm's length at a minimum. The telegram already sent to Val; Eddie's mum, should have arrived by now. At least Val would know where to direct Eddie location wise, if and when he made contact one way or another. Before retiring herself, she decided for the coming day, that a visit to Javier's office in Mojácar town might reveal some useful info about Sue and Chris. She hoped Javier was still enchanted with her. Esme had no qualms about using her femininity in order to extract information. Besides she needed to see if Val had sent a reply back to the local Correos (post office) as being the designated address for Val to send to. It was the same at Val's end. Any telegrams addressed to her, were to be held at *her* local post office.

In the unlikely event the police might be watching Val's house, telegrams being delivered might arouse suspicion and might be intercepted. Esme will be pleased to see one had been put aside for her at the Correos. It will tell her exactly what she wanted to know; Eddie was now in Spain.

CHAPTER 24

Johnny made his way over to Stepney Green. Deep in thought he was trying hard to remember the last time he had seen his cousin Zak, let alone talked to him. It must have been a year or two at least and that was at an uncle's funeral over in Hornchurch. It's been that long he might not recognise him! Having found Sidney Street Johnny was now on the lookout for the dive his cousin ran. Just up ahead was the venue he was aiming for, appropriately named 'Zak's Place.' Johnny needn't have worried about recognising his cousin. As he approached the premises, squeezed in between a betting shop and an old-fashioned barbers, the main entrance door burst open, a body was hurled to the ground, quickly followed by cousin Zak. Yea, that's him thought Johnny. "And don't you bloody well come back" yelled Zak. The grounded guy jumped up and limped off down Sidney Street towards Commercial Road as fast as his good leg would go. Zak was about to dust his hands off, turn around and disappear back inside. But something made him look down the road towards a stranger. Yep, someone was leaning against a high brick wall, looking straight at him. Immediately he challenged the looker on, "You want some 'an all pal?" Johnny nodded, stood up straight, threw back his shoulders and replied, "Only if you think you're good enough." Zak began running towards this new enemy, just as Johnny began running towards Zak, fists raised by both men ready for the fight. Seconds before they met head on, Zak recognised Johnny and skidded to a halt. "Johnny you bastard, you nearly got your flippin head kicked in then. What the fuck you doing over this way?" "Bit of business cuz that's all. How about we go inside and have a sit down." Zak ventured as they walked back.

"I heard you were back in the ring." "Yea, had a few fights, let's get inside and I'll explain." 'Zak's Place' sat close to the site of the infamous gun battle of Stepney back in 1911. Although its close proximity to the siege building and considering how many tourists visited the site, it didn't seem to swell Zak's customer numbers.

Once inside, with the street door closed behind them, the pair were hit with a wall of tobacco smoke, the smell of stale beer, sweaty armpits and some laughter, but only some. A real spit and sawdust hovel with the low earth type hum of blokes mingling and talking; mostly under their breath. A few sat playing poker. As they looked over at Zak and his guest, one player took a peek at the cards held by a guy to his left. His eyebrows shot up and he decided to fold. The dealer ran a nicotine-stained hand through what was left of his hair' threw his cards on the table and declared himself out for the rest of the day. Behind the tiny bar, stood a chap wearing a white apron around his ample middle, a black waistcoat over a blue button-down Ben Sherman shirt. He sported shiny, silver coloured metal arm garters employed to keep his shirt cuffs away from the myriad and constant pools of beer on the bar top. Zak nodded to him at the same time as sticking two fingers up, indicating a couple of beers, then pointing to a table over in the corner by a grimy window. Arm garter man nodded his acknowledgement and got busy. Johnny and Zak sat down just as the bottled beers arrived. "What no glasses Zak?" "No mate, they usually end up in someone's face." "The bloke you tossed out just now, what was all that about then?" "A nuisance he was, getting a bit lippy complaining about this, complaining about that. As I was dragging him out, he said something about coming back with his mates." "Oh, ok, great, more new customers then?" grinned Johnny. "Christ mate you always were a sarky git. Anyway, what's on your mind?" Johnny let the dig pass and got down to the business in hand. An hour or so plus multiple bottles of brown ale later, Johnny left the penny gaff in the knowledge he now had somewhere to base his criminal activities. Next on Johnny's list, was the pressing need to suss out Bomber Brown. During their last meet up, Johnny felt he had perceived a note of divided loyalty. He got the impression that Bomber would run with him only as long as Eddie was away on his toes. One sniff of Eddie back on the manor, and Bomber would be drawn to him like a pin to a magnet. Bomber needs to show some alliance, or he would be useless to the team. Perhaps he could use him as the muscle needed by Zak to keep unwanteds out of his bar.

CHAPTER 25

"Stroll on Javier, how on earth did we end up here?" Javier smiled that smile of men when sated. He'd craved Esme's body since their first meeting and could now chalk her up as yet another conquest. Having used her for his own satisfaction and with absolutely no intention of letting this relationship go any further than sex, he turned over, away from Esme. Sadly, the information she was hoping for regarding Sue and Chris was not forthcoming. Esme was barking right up the wrong oak tree in that department. With Javier beginning to snore gently, she took the opportunity to look around her. Javier's *luuurve* room as he called it was distinctly Spanish. Of course, it would be she thought. Thankfully though, no mirrors attached to the ceiling. She couldn't bear the thought of Javier looking up at her backside whilst she was on top of him, doing her thing. On the far wall there hung a picture gallery of Matadors, the one Bullfighter whose aim is to actually dispatch the bull. Heavily framed pictures of all shapes and sizes. In the centre hung a life size picture of a famous Matador in all his colourful glory. Oddly, a black and white photograph of Javier's head had been cut out and glued on to the Matador's shoulders. Javier's superimposed head was far too small to match the scratched-out head of the Matador, plus he had coloured in his eyes with red ink. Below this macabre sight he'd painted, in crimson the words 'El Diablo' (the devil) with an extended Zorro type slash, underneath the words, as if to underline its importance. On a side wall, two long Espada swords positioned high up on the wall, held in place with a few rusty nails looked down on her. This looked totally incongruous to Esme. From a distance it looked like they had blood on the blade tips. The blood being from the death blow or 'Estocada' to an already suffering bull no doubt. Esme shuddered. Having policed in and around London Town for many a year, she had seen enough weird issues to last her a lifetime. This however was creepy Joe stuff; it fair turned her stomach.

The previous evening when they met for a date, everything seemed gentle and just, well, normal. A shared bottle of red wine or two at the local wine bar, back to his for a nightcap. A goodnight kiss turning into a warm embrace, leading to more frantic kissing. Javier's hands began to explore. The wine, the kissing, the caressing was all too much. Esme let her guard down and allowed Javier to lead her to his bedroom.

Javier stripped off in front of Esme in a matter of seconds. Moonlight shone through a small high up window illuminating his muscular torso and below. Esme almost fainted, Javier exerted his power, lifting Esme onto the double bed and began to undress her. She asked dreamily, "what is that lovely music?"

"You don't recognise Giacomo Puccini; he is one of the greats?" "Well, whoever it is it sounds sad and beautiful at the same time." She had little or no resistance, was like putty in his hands Esme now completely in awe of him. Eddie had the rough touch, but here was this Spanish stud with an, 'oh' so gentle touch. She shooed away thoughts of Eddie from her conscious mind. She was now in heaven, Eddie temporarily forgotten. The music reached a crescendo, just as they did. Exhausted they feel asleep in each other's arms. Daylight came and with it, came Javier's presumably morning after ritual. That of gentle snoring punctuated with the occasional belch, accompanied by some mild flatulence. "Blimey Javier, where's last night's romance disappeared to, you're beginning to sound like a bloody bog monster from the deep. You'll be picking your bloody nose next." Javier slowly rolled back to Esme, grinning like a shark. "Get up Esme, get up, I need coffee. Get up and make me some" he ordered. Esme couldn't quite make her mind up whether to kiss or kill him, her decision was to do neither. Gathering up her discarded clothes from the night before, she headed for the bathroom. Leaving Javier's tiny La casa slamming the front door, she stepped on to the dusty back road that would lead her up to the main part of Mojácar town and perhaps a cabina home. Almost at once, Esme walked straight into a young Senorita who was holding a large bunch of keys tied by a strip of leather to a belt around her trim waist. Esme guessed she would be late twenties or early thirties and very pretty with it. She stood and watched as the Senorita pushed a key into the lock of Javier's front door then let herself in. To Esme, it looked as if she had done this a hundred times or more. From behind the door, she heard a girly voice call out "Ola querida" which she would soon discover meant "hello darling"

CHAPTER 26

"Heard the news Mrs Coleman?" "What's that then Rosie? come in and sit down." Big gas explosion demolished the Oasis a couple of nights ago, so that's me out of a bleedin job in it." Val put her coffee down with a bang missing the saucer entirely. "What all of it?" "Yea, just a pile of smoking bricks now. Weird thing is though, buildings either side are still standing. Bloody strange if you ask me." Val had a major problem taking it all in. The Oasis served as a honey pot for Eddie and she was really looking forward to taking up the reins and control of the income. Plus, it doubled as a meeting place for Eddie and his not so merry men to be able to discuss in a place where the walls actually did have cloth ears to their illegal and dishonest behaviour. Although they would always deny any wrong doings, especially to police. Rosie's job happened to be chief waitress of a staff rota of one, plus senior washer upper in the café area of the Oasis. She knew what went on downstairs in Eddie's office-cum-crime-agenda meeting room. It excited her to be working for a boss who was a known villain, but with him not being around now and her place of work demolished job wise she was buggered. "Mrs Coleman where is Eddie anyway; I've still got some wages owed to me?" "Number one Rosie, I can't explain where he is, cos I don't know myself. All I know is he's away and could be for a while.

I've told you enough now Rosie, so keep your trap shut, I don't want old Bill chasing me up for Eddie's whereabouts any more. Christ, they might as well have set up a substation in my back yard, the bleeders. As regards your wages, I can settle up with you, don't worry you will not go without." Val reached for her purse and bunged Rosie almost double what she was owed. "Aaw thanks Mrs Coleman thanks. I spose it's back to the café over at Millwall docks for me, if they'll have me back." "Don't worry on that count either Rosie, I'll go and have a word in their shell like. My name will carry a lot of clout for a while and I intend to use it as much as I can, as soon as I can. Didn't Bomber live in the flat above Rosie?" "Yea he did, and that's another mystery. Not seen hide nor hair of him. I spose if he survived the gas explosion, the that would make him homeless. He's probably knockin about at the Seamans Mission or found a doss house somewhere. I honestly don't know Mrs Coleman."

Rosie got up to leave, leaning forward as if to hug Val. Not a good move, having just been served up with some devastating news about the Oasis, Val was definitely not in the hugging mood. In fact, she was bordering on white hot rage. This intense feeling was foreign to Val. Up to now she always had full control over her emotions but now they were up to boiling point. Her plans to run things whilst her son was away, had been dealt a severe blow, very nearly a knockout blow. "Gas explosion, my arse" she announced to the door that Rosie had just closed behind her. As Rosie made her way home, she vowed, unless it was a matter of life or death, never again to step inside Val's home at 119 Plenva Street. Rosie knew of the saying 'nest of vipers' and thought that just about summed up the Coleman residence. Not long after Rosie left, Val Coleman rang for a cab. She wanted to see for herself how bad things were over at the Oasis. When the cabbie eventually slowed to a stop at what looked like a bomb site, she could see that Rosie had described it accurately. The Oasis was indeed a pile of rubble. Buildings that would have been abutting either side were shored up with wooden buttresses. Asking the driver to hang around for ten minutes or so, she stepped out onto the pavement, noting that a cordon had been placed around the entire site. Warning signs had been erected. Traffic could pass, only just, unless something big like a double decker bus or lorry needed to pass. Oncoming traffic would be obliged to stop to let them through. Several men from the gas board, shovels and pick-axes in hand stood around. Some smoking, others pouring tea from thermos flasks, none actually doing anything. One or two caught sight of Val and sent wolf whistles in her direction. She stood looking at where the Oasis had been, only days ago. The view reminded her of a well-known smile with a tooth missing. Just then, one of the gas board workers mooched over to Val and leant on his shovel. "Not a pretty sight is it love, unlike yourself." "Val beamed a smile in his direction. "What happened here then?" Mr Shovel moved in closer so as to be within whispering distance. His was a well-worn worldly face and recognisable. However, the recogniser could not quite pin point the person he reminded them of, from deep in their memory banks. He continued "One or two people put it down to a gas leak going up. You know fractured main leaking and all that. We reckon it was a deliberate act. You know blowing the place up which in turn set the gas alight." "Do you now?"

"Yea, the Gas Board aint gonna take the can for this one. Besides neither building either side is touched, got hardly a scratch. I've been to many a gas leak, and nine times out of ten, neighbouring buildings always tend to suffer. In my humble opinion nice lady, I'd say someone who knows a bit about this sort of stuff did it. Or, on the other hand, it might Just have been pure luck. My money is on a professional bloke who knows about explosives and where to plant them for maximum effect." Well, that was jammy thought Val. No need to knock on doors asking questions from any of the neighbours who might have been present at the time. "Anyways, tea breaks over now, so I should get back to standing on my shovel over there instead of 'ere." With a grin and a wink, he made his way over several piles of bricks to where the work was being carried out. The nearest Mr Pick-axe asked "How'd you get on mate, you seein 'er tonight, gonna give 'er one or what?" "Fuck off and mind your bloody language mate." Val, deep in thought, didn't realise the taxi had pulled up outside her house several minutes earlier. In the time it took for the cab to get from the Oasis to 119 Plenva Street on the Isle of Dogs, Val had begun working on her next move.

CHAPTER 27

"How's it going then Errol?" Johnny the Turk, shadowed by Billy and Mel, were paying a visit to the wrecker yard in Creekmouth, not a million miles from Beckton Sewage Treatment Works, just South of Barking neatly tucked away in River Road. Johnny was in Errol's office sitting across the desk from him, Billy and Mel standing either side behind Johnny looking calm but quietly menacing. Before answering, Errol looked from Johnny to the two muscle men, first Billy and then to Mel. He had met all three before when attending the odd sit down at the Oasis. Difficult to be tight lipped with this lot he thought. The Stratford Two knew only too well how to loosen tongues. "Er ok I guess" "You guess?" Johnny smashed his fist down hard on the desk making Errol jump two feet in the air. "You'll need to do better than that my son unless you want me to get these two to ask the same question." Johnny raised a thumb in the direction of the two thugs standing just slightly behind him. "Let's start again. How much in folding are you keeping for Eddie?" Errol shrugged his shoulders. Either he didn't understand the question or chose to ignore it.

Billy and Mel walked around Errol's desk until they were standing either side of him. Johnny gestured with upturned hands and pulled a face that said 'it's up to you pal.' "Be sensible now, or you might get hurt."

The Stratford Two lifted Errol out of his director's chair, lifting him until his feet dangled above the grubby lino covered floor. Errol winced in pain. As the grip tightened under his arms he croaked "I'm holding three grand that's due to Eddie." "Errol, before we let you down, you need to know something.

Are you listening proper now cos I want you to understand what I'm about to tell you?" He nodded furiously. "Forget Eddie, forget the Oasis. Eddie's old news now and the Oasis is no longer. Don't want those names mentioned again, clear?" he yelled. Errol looked aghast, but continued nodding. "Ok, drop 'im down." Errol slumped into his chair. "The money, now." Johnny demanded, not wishing to give Errol a second to rethink things. Errol opened up a desk drawer and fished out a scrap of paper. Johnny jumped up, leant over the desk and snatched it out of his hand. Handing it to Billy, he instructed him to find the safe, use the code on the slip of paper open it up, being careful to take just three big ones. Nothing more, nothing less. "Right pal, now we've got that straight, I'm gonna be instructing Dave to keep nicking cars from up West, bring 'em here for you to do your motor doctoring. What you do with 'em is your business. We just want paying by the car as and when each one is delivered, exactly as before. Billy and Mel will carry on looking after the car-lots and keep up the protection of your yard. All ok so far?" Errol had no choice. He nodded his agreement. "Arnt, I supposed to go through Val Coleman?" Johnny grabbed Errol by the throat, his long fingers wrapping nearly all the way round. "Errol, the name Coleman is old news. You deal with me now. If you go behind my back, I will unleash these two on you and yours. Do I make myself clear? Now that's cleared up, we need a motor." Errol stroked his throat, picked up his phone and rang down to the yard. A moment later heavy footsteps could be heard charging up the outside staircase. Billy and Mel swiftly crossed the office and stood by the door, in case any aggro was looming, hands on weapons. They needn't have worried. Errol's foreman entered the office. "What's in the yard ready to go out?" asked Errol. "We've got a Vauxhall Victor in Silver about to be crated up guv." "Ok, don't crate it. Get it ready to go right now, these gentlemen will be driving it away. Make sure all the correct paperwork is in the glove compartment and the keys in the ignition and fully fuelled up."

"Certainly boss, consider it done." Errol stood and watched them drive out through the heavy gates. He waited until they pulled out on to River Road heading in the direction of the A13. Errol's foreman shot back upstairs again. "What the blazes was all that about then boss?" Errol shook his head. "A change of supplier management, they've got a new boss and I don't care for him one little bit. For the moment, we'll have to bite on the lead ball and see what occurs."

CHAPTER 28

"Bollocks." It was approaching midnight and still very warm. Not a good time for Eddie to be lost wandering around Bilbao. The loaded gun in his waist band gave him a little comfort. Two young Spanish guys had been trailing him for a while as he walked from street to street, not entirely sure of what to do or where to go. He knew he should be getting his head down soon, but these two lads would have to meet their maker first. There was no way he was going to let them knock him out and steal his quite considerable bank roll. Eddie slipped into a convenient darkened doorway and waited until they were within breathing distance. In a moment of pure speed and aggression, he was on them. He flew at them fast intending to hit 'em first and hard. Knocking one to the ground, the other staggering back from a vicious head butt, Eddie yelled out "Stitch that you bastard" at the same time as standing on the throat of the one on the ground, pushing his foot down hard. Next, he pulled out the gun, took his foot off the Spanish guy's throat and held the snout of the barrel hard against his forehead, pulled the hammer back ready to fire. The one with the busted-up face courtesy of Eddie's head butt viewed the scene before him, then scarpered, ran for his life leaving his partner in crime at Eddie's mercy. "Spineless git." Eddie shouted after him. "Now, as far as *you're* concerned pal you need to be taught a lesson." The gun raised above his head and came crashing down on Spanish lad's temple. Once twice, three times. Eddie thought he heard bone cracking. "Must have been 'is skull" he muttered. Spanish boy either passed out or died. Either way, he was out cold. Eddie dragged his unconscious body, not concerned one jot if it was alive or dead, down a nearby alleyway. Ripping off the boy's shirt he used it to clean the blood off his gun barrel. Eddie took several deep breaths, then sat close to the body on some steps for a few minutes to let his head clear and decide what to do next.

The sound of many running footsteps getting louder and nearer by the minute gave him a bit of a clue regarding his next move. He decided he had roughly thirty seconds to have it away before whoever it was would be on him like a pack of hounds cornering a very unlucky fox. An English voice called out. "Up here quick." Eddie looked to where he thought the voice was coming from. The darkness of the alleyway did nothing for his night vision. "Up here, come on quickly, they're just round the corner." Eddie didn't need asking twice, he mounted the stone steps three at a time until he was level with his potential saviour. He found himself on a first-floor open air balcony that served several front doors to his right and a low stone wall to his left running along the length of the building. The second door was slightly ajar letting just the barest minimum of light out into the night-time darkness. "Hurry up mate for Christ's sake." Eddie shouldered the door open, threw himself into the tiny flat kicking the door shut behind him, in a single manoeuvre. The flat's owner instructed Eddie to follow him into the kitchen. As soon as Eddie was in, the owner switched off the light. The flat, like all the others, was now in darkness. Raised voices could be heard in the alleyway, it was all double Dutch to Eddie. His rescuer screwed up his eyes straining to hear what was being said, started nodding sagely. Eddie asked "can you tell what they're saying then?" He put his finger to his lips indicating both should remain shtum, whilst nodding a yes. His eyebrows raised at something that was said from down below. "They're coming up here, keep still and keep very quiet" he whispered. Footsteps could be heard as a group of bodies climbed the stone steps. Eddie and his new found friend, sat on the kitchen floor motionless. Still as stone. Shadows of bodies could be seen outside, door handles rattled. Doors shook on their hinges as they were pushed backwards and forwards, testing their resistance. This continued for ten minutes or so, then all went silent. All one could hear now was the sound of el Grillo's (crickets) chirping. The pair waited another twenty minutes or so before moving a muscle between them. The owner held out his hand "I'm Mitch by the way, and you are?" Eddie hesitated, in the heat of dealing with his two pursuers momentarily forgot his alias, then it came to him. "Jack" he said" Quickly adding "but my middle name is Eddie and that's stuck." "Ok, Eddie it is then," Mitch whispered.

"Stay put for a moment, I'm just going out on the landing to make sure the coast is clear. He stood up slowly and crept to his front door, cautiously opening the door Mitch stuck half his head out. Nothing, just the night sounds. The other half of his head followed, to be joined by his body, slowly silently emerging like a moth from its protective cocoon. He looked left then right and only when he was sure the landing was clear, he peered over the balcony down to the back alley below. No one around, the body, nearly dead, or barely alive gone too. Mitch stood stock still for a couple of minutes, straining to hear something, anything that would tell him that danger still lurked just around the corner. Eddie crept outside and stood alongside him. He was far taller than Eddie, but then again, so were most people. Mitch turned and went back inside the flat, beckoning Eddie to do the same. "I don't think they will be back tonight, let's have a brew and a chat, actually, maybe not. Look mate, it's two in the morning and I'm guessing you've nowhere to go, so why don't we leave the brew and chat until first light, only I'm just thinking if we put the lights on – well I'm sure you know the rest. You can kip on the couch if you like, there's a bottle of whisky on the shelf over there if you fancy a night-cap. I'm going to get some shut eye and suggest you do the same. Oh, and by the way the bog is down the hall first on the left." Mitch turned, shut the door behind him and disappeared to wherever he was bedding down. Left on his own, Eddie's mind raced. This Mitch was a cool customer, so bloody relaxed, almost casual about a complete stranger who'd pistol whipped one local hood and no doubt broken the nose of the other. And yet here am I sitting in his lounge, sipping his whisky, with a loaded gun in my belt. As Eddie's eyes grew more and more accustomed to the dark, he noticed a single photo in a frame stood on a small desk over in the corner of the lounge. He also made a mental note of the tidiness of the paperwork on the desk. Picking up the photo frame, Eddie took it to the window where some ambient light shone in allowing him to study the subject. It was Mitch all right unless he had a twin brother and he is wearing an army dress uniform. Medal ribbons aplenty on his left breast. On his head a sand-coloured beret. Eddie had no knowledge of the army whatsoever but had no doubt he was in safe hands for now.

CHAPTER 29

"Hi there Esme, been out on the razzle then girl?" Esme having indeed been out on the razzle, all night as it happened, was none too happy about the scene that greeted her as she stepped out of the cab. It looked like Chris had camped out on her front door step. Next to where Chris was standing, stood a deck chair that she didn't recognise along with an occasional table with two, what looked like glasses of pink gin and tonic sat on it. Chris looked at Esme and thought he'd better explain. "Thing is sweetheart, while the villa's been empty for a bit, you know before you came along, we've been kind of self-appointed gardeners, you know bit of pruning here, bit of weeding there and that sort of stuff. Thing is we've got kind of used to it once a month or so. Gives us something to be doing." "Cooee Esme over here." Esme looked over to one of the many small flower beds dotted around the grounds at the front of the villa. Sue, bent over double was busy doing some pruning, stood up straight, wiped her brow with the back of her hand, bent down again to finish what she was doing. Jesus thought Esme, those white slacks don't leave much to the imagination. Chris broke in having read her thoughts. "Gives me something to grab hold of when we're, you know, you know, nudge, nudge when we're doing it" he chortled with a sheepish grin.

Sue crossed over to greet Esme with a smacker of a kiss on both cheeks. "I love doing it the Continental way" she grinned. "That was a good night we had, wasn't it?" Not waiting for Esme to answer; "We were thinking of returning the pleasure and having you over at ours." A chill ran down Esme's spine. The words *'having you'* sent a dozen warning signals to her brain. She knew all about the swinging sixties back home in East London. She also knew about bloody swingers too. What with Chris's last comments bordering on sex talk, she had visions of these two greeting her over at their villa, stark bollock naked! She visibly shivered at the thought. "What's up love, you can't be cold it must be about sixty-five, going up to seventy-five a bit later on, according the forecast. Let me give you a hug to warm you up." Esme stepped smartly back; hand held up in front of her. "No, not cold, just a bit tired." *Sod it, that was the weakest thing to have said, I'd better add some more,* "and I think I've got the flu coming on, hope it's not the Spanish type" she laughed weakly. "Oh dear, poor love, well I suggest you go and get some rest and we'll finish up here. Have you got any pills and potions that might help? We've got loads of what we call 'get better' stuff.

We've got Anadin, Phensic or Beechams Powders if you need some," offered Sue. "No, you're ok, I managed to bring some over with me.

But thanks anyway" replied Esme. "Just a question if I may, as I understand it, I have a full maintenance package that came with the villa, but I didn't check if the gardening was part of it." Chris butted in, "That'll be our fault love, we told the people that come and do the gardens they needn't bother as we're quite willing to take it on. They of course agreed cos they don't do anything but still get paid by the villa's agent. I guess in turn the agent bills the owner, funny old world 'aint it." Esme had a fit of phantom sneezes, and bade Mr and Mrs busybody farewell for now. When Eddie gets here, he'll have to take them for a boat ride and come back on his own.

CHAPTER 30

"So, you're Bomber then?" "That's right mate and I take it you're Johnny's cousin Zak?" "Yep, cuz says you're a dab 'and at sorted out unwanteds like. Welcome to Zak's Place mate, make yourself at home, come and meet the staff and some of the regulars." The pair mingled with a few of the customers who were in that night, singling out those that Zak wanted Bomber to meet. Bomber duly shook hands with one or two and nodded at the others. Bomber took Zak to one side. "Got any baseball bats have you mate?" "Sorry Bomber, no. We don't want you killing anyone, simply calm down any agro, and eject whoever is being a nuisance." "Ok Zak, only Johnny told me that a team might be back mob handed like and slapping a baseball bat in the palm of me 'and usually calms mobs down nicely without even throwing a punch." "Let's see how things go, for now, just get used to the place. Have a look around and do please make any suggestions that might be useful for security issues." Bomber asked, "Do you want me to grill any of your workers in case?" "In case of what?" "Well, you know in case." "No Bomber no need, they've all been with me mostly since the day we opened." "Ok, only wanting to do my job proper." "Judging by your boxing background you'll do fine. I need to nip out for an hour or so, see you later. And remember, no one gets killed, clear?" Bomber registered a disappoint look, then beamed a smile. "Got the message boss no messy stuff, no blood spilt."

Bomber had need of the men's room; it was a bit of a journey from his temporary digs above the Steak House over in the West End. Eyes half closed from the stinging sensation given off from a tobacco smoke-fog, he looked around but couldn't see a Gent's sign anywhere. An elderly looking bloke leaning against the tiny bar looked quizzically at him through poached egg eyes. "Here, don't I know you pal?" Bomber turned slowly to face the enquirer and shrugged his shoulders. "I definitely know you; you know, I do." Bomber started to walk away, hoping this geezer didn't connect him to Eddie. "I've got it; seen you in the ring over at Wembley Arena. What was it, er, Bomber ummm, Bomber Brown? That's it yes, the Bow-Bells Bomber. Bit tasty in yer day, still getting the gloves on are ya, what brings you 'ere then?" Bomber moved in closer. "As it 'appens pal, I'm here to keep the peace. Zak's a mate of my boss so, as long as you behave yourself and don't become a nuisance, you're very welcome to sit here and enjoy a drink or two, got it. By the way, what's your name?" "It's Bob-Bob mate on account of I once tried to swim out and round Southend Pier then back again. You see when I swim, me 'ead bobs up-n-down like a bleedin cork, geddit?" Bomber called the barman over. "Where's the gent's mate I'm dying for a Jimmy?" The barman shot a look over to a door in the corner. "Cheers mate." Bomber ambled over, opened it to find himself out in the building's back yard. Tucked away over in the corner stood a lavy. Its door had a foot or so missing top and bottom. Entry was gained via a thumb latch but there was no lock on the inside. "Oh well, better whistle while I piss." Visit over, instead of returning to the bar, Bomber took a quick look around the yard. In one corner there was a pile of old timber, in another a heap of old and rusty metal bars, about three or four foot long. In yet another corner empty beer bottles in brewers' wooden crates, some stacked up six or seven high. The thing that worried him most was yet another door, well more of a gate, leading out on to the street. A tiny padlock held it locked in place, easily kicked in if a mob of blokes was determined to force an entry. What was running through his mind was this. If a gang came through this way mob handed, with minds determined on busting the place up, bent on violent behaviour, this would be their favoured entry. If any would be toe-rags decided to come and fuck the place up a bit, had previously been drinking here at Zak's Place, they would have only needed to have taken a piss in that lav, seen what Bomber saw and come to the same conclusion.

Worse still, they wouldn't need to walk the streets on their way here tooled up. All the weapons needed were lying about in ready-made piles and stacks. "Need to speak to Zak and soon." Bomber said to no one in particular. On his way back to the bar, a big ugly brute of a bloke looking much like a brawny docker type barged passed on his way to the toilet almost knocking Bomber over. Sleeves rolled up exposing a myriad of tattoos, some looking homemade others more professional. Bomber noticed love tattooed on one fist and hate on the other. "Oi, donkey features" Bomber called after him. "What's your game then?" Donkey features spun round to face him. "Wos it got to do with you then matey?" he snarled. Bomber didn't hesitate, he slammed a huge fist to the right side of his face, catching him somewhere between the upper jaw and ear, usually a sure thing, if performed correctly, resulted in a dislocated jaw, more often than not stopping a fight in its tracks. Either Bomber had missed the sweet spot or donkey features jaw was made of steel. Bomber's boxing training kicked in, the initial blow was followed with a powerful uppercut sending donkey features reeling backwards crashing into the pile of old rusty metal bars. Picking himself up, he grabbed one of the bars and began circling Bomber, waving the iron bar in front of him right in Bomber's face. Bomber knew fists alone would be more than useless from here on in. He also knew donkey features would make his move any second; and he did. Iron bar raised above his head he charged. The bar began its arc towards its target, Bomber's game plan was to spring to one side a second before the blow landed. A gun exploded behind him; two shots fired in quick succession. Donkey features slumped to the ground shot through the heart. Metal bar still in his fist, blood and skin stuck to the opposite end to that which he was gripping. Bomber also fell, dizzy, ears ringing, head thumping from the bash, he turned to see who was holding the gun. As he began to lose consciousness, he caught sight of the shooter just prior to his final journey. Which destination was it to be; heaven, hell or hospital?

CHAPTER 31

Eddie heard a mug being placed gently on the coffee table which was just in his line of sight. He smelt the coffee before opening his eyes fully. "Morning mate, or should I say afternoon. It's just after noon, you slept in a bit." Eddie checked his Rolex, but of course it wasn't there, it was in the marina, down in the silt somewhere beneath Lee's yacht. A momentary bout of panic set in as he remembered slaying Lee and dumping his blooded body, noughts and crosses symbol and all, in that long box. Better not let his new and most excellent friend and saviour know about that little bit of activity just yet. He drew himself up to a sitting position, yawned heavily, stretched his arms up towards the ceiling and began to take in unfamiliar surroundings. The flat looked different in the daylight. Warm and comfortable. A place for everything and everything in its place. Centrepiece on the mantle stood a photo of a beautiful young senorita. "Your settee mate is well comfortable." Eddie threw back the blanket, stood up, then checked that his gun, bank roll and passport were still with him, satisfied he sat down again. The block of flats Mitch lived in was situated on the fringe of Bilbao. One block amongst many others, enjoying an elevated position. A reasonable view of the marina and its many yachts could be seen from the lounge window over to his right. Mitch was standing at the window staring at something. "Bit of a fuss going on over at the marina, wouldn't know anything about that would you?" "What do you mean a fuss?" "Can't really tell from up here, it's choc as block with police vehicles plus an ambulance. Police bod's to-ing and froing, you know, been going on since about ten this morning." Eddie got into his coffee. "None of my business Eddie, but what you did to those two bandido's last night was pretty swift and calculated, had any specialized training?" Eddie stood up and moved over to the window. "They were all sauce and no bottle." he muttered. There was indeed a fuss and bother going over at the marina. He shrugged his shoulders, grimaced then shuffled back to the settee. Mitch, referring to the previous night's action said "Don't know if you are familiar with gangs and mobs and that. Thing is, those two you downed last night are part of an organised gang.

They terrorise parts of Bilbao, mostly back streets you know, very few witnesses. They frequently go after travellers or visitors, especially anyone roaming the streets late at night. There is a Mr. Big who controls them, hence as I say they are organised. So, just out of curiosity where were you aiming for?" Eddie mumbled "Train Station I guess." "Well in that case you were well lost. How long had those two been following you?" Eddie changed direction. "Army man then?" he explained himself. "Saw the photo on your desk." "That's correct. Did some time with REME; Royal Electrical and Mechanical Engineers, then after selection got into Special Forces." "Oh yea" replied Eddie with an air of someone totally aware of what Mitch was saying. which he wasn't. "So, how'd you end up here then?" "Love mate, simple as that. I was stationed here for quite some time and fell for a pretty Senorita. I was single, spoke the lingo, so here I am." "Where is she now then?" "She died mat, drivers over here are lunatics, fucking mad men." "Oh, that must have been a blow." "Certainly was. It was three years ago now, but still hurts like fuck. Mia was her name Mia Garcia Martinez. That's her on the mantle above the fireplace. The one true love of my life, snatched away from me two weeks before our Boda; that's wedding to you mate." Eddie wasn't sure what to say next. He somehow knew this Mitch bloke was a gift from God and certainly wasn't going to spoil it by saying something stupid.

He shut his gob and looked at the floor. A few silent moments passed. Eddie then said, "This gang and their boss man, 'ave anything to do with it?" Mitch looked up sharply. "Why do you ask?" "Well last night you saved my skin, so my thinking is, you did it, cos you think they were responsible for your loss and saving me was your way of getting one up on them." "Bingo Eddie got it in one, you cotton on fast don't you." "It's a gift" smiled Eddie. "Ok so why don't you let me pay you back. If you know where this Mr Big hides out, lets me and you go and do 'im and his bunch of bandolero's." "You serious Eddie, only it's an itch I've been wanting to scratch for one hell of a long time." "Right, that's that sorted then. Can we go out for breakfast somewhere and sort out a plan. I'm hungry as a wolf?" Pushing through the busy market square, they found an outside table in the sunshine. A sign above the cafe read El Pirata. Mitch was obviously known here as the waiter greeted him by name, and said in good English, "Usual today, Mitch?" "Thanks Carlos, make it two." Within minutes two plates of fried egg, bacon, sausage and beans appeared. English breakfast Spanish style. It was if they had them sitting by on the hot plate waiting for the two of them to arrive. Eddie looked at Mitch quizzically. "That was bloody fast, were they expecting us?"

"No mate, they get a number of English tourists coming in via the marina from time to time, so they get prepared in advance. Almost all of them, to a man, order the same thing; always an English breakfast." As they tucked in, two steaming mugs of tea arrived together with a couple of rounds of toast, then a jar of Robertsons marmalade found its way to their table. Mitch grinned. "Almost home from home, eh?" Eddie grinned at Carlos who smiled back reciting his favourite saying, "The improbable we do today, miracles take a little longer" followed by a burst of enthusiastic laughter. "Impossible Carlos, impossible." Mitch turned to Eddie, "I must have told him a million times, impossible, not improbable." Eddie wasn't sure there was a difference, but laughed along anyway. "Ok Mitch, how do you want to play it? Barge in tooled up. A steam in job, take on all comers, or do we cut the snake's head off then piss ourselves laughing, while watching all the so-called hard nuts scram in various directions?" "You done this sort of thing before Eddie? You seem very well versed in the art of violence. Actually Eddie, seeing as they did for Mia in a car crash, I favour driving my old land rover straight through the wall of their den, tossing a couple of stun grenades out then beating the fuck out of any survivors left standing, with a tyre wrench." "Christ, so you've got grenades?" "Yep, it's amazing what you can get hold of if you know the right people." "Sounds like a suicide mission to me. Do you really expect us to come out of it alive?" "Sure, all that training with Special Forces has got to pay off sometime or other." "Ok pal, I'm with you." Breakfast over, Mitch enquired "I've heard of people travelling light Eddie, don't get me wrong it's none of my business, it's just that you don't even have a tooth brush! Where were you aiming for when and if you found the train station, would it be the capital, Madrid perhaps?" Eddie's mind was racing, frantically searching his brain for the right thing to say. "That's the one Madrid, yep, that's it, Madrid." "Ok mate, nice one. When we've sorted out our bit of business and providing the Land Rover isn't too busted up, I'll drive you over." "What, to Madrid?" "No mate, I meant to the bloody station. Meanwhile, we can't have you walking about dressed like that, we need to get you some jeans, boots and a zip up jacket so you blend in." "You mean pass muster like?" "That's the ticket Eddie, something like that." This'll be a first thought Eddie. Jeans and desert boots and stuff!

CHAPTER 32

Red Satriani stood outside 119 Plenva Street, Isle-of-Dogs. Hammering on the front door got nil response. A neighbour of Val's, on her way back from the shops called out, "If you're looking for Val darlin, she's out, not back till three she told me. Said to watch out for a caller, so that must be you then." Red Satriani checked his watch, 2.40 pm another twenty minutes to go. "You can come in and wait at my place, it's just two doors along. I'll make you a nice cuppa if you like my lovely." Another much younger voice piped up, "Go on then mista, me muvva makes a nice cuppa, if you comes round, she'll have to get the best cups out, cos you'd be a guest wontcha." A lad of about eleven trailed along behind the shopper carrying two bags, full to the brim. He added, "An I'll get a glass of lemonade see, like I always do when guests come round to see me muvva." Red was a weights freak, he trained almost every day. When he was much younger, his mother told him women much prefer men whose chests stick out further than their stomachs, not so the other way around. Consequently, the weight training paid off handsomely. Once the chest-over-stomach thing had been achieved, he worked on the rest of his body. The result being a young man at six foot in his mid-twenties looking extremely fit and possibly a bit dangerous. This, coupled with a scrubbing brush type haircut, a winning smile and clad in a fine, bespoke Italian suit direct from Saville Row was how he liked to be seen. "Yea ok then, only if itsa no trouble." "That's no trouble at all" the shopper called back. "You just come in and I'll just pop a note in Val's letter box to say you're here with us." Red sat down in the little two up two down. Immediately the young lad opened up a conversation. "Where you from mista cos you aint from round here I know that much?" Red smiled. "No little man I'm not." "You talk funny an all don't cha." "Too many questions little man. Let me ask you one back." "Yea, go on then." "What do your friends call you?" "I'm Robbo aint I." "Course you are Robbo of course you are. Got a nice girlfriend then?"

Robbo blushed a little. "As it 'appens I have." "And does she have a name?" "Now who's asking all the questions mista?" "Sorry Robbo, just curious," "If you must know its Beryl, Beryl White" giving her full name.

"And she's well lush." Red asked, "And how many uncles do you have?" "Quite a few as it 'appens but that's alright cos I gets a lemonade when they visit see. Only trouble is, I don't get to speak to them, I 'ave to go for a walk while they're 'ere. Some leave me a bit of pocket money. Only yesterday I got an 'alf crown 'ere it is wanna see it Mista?" "Now, now Robbo, don't keep asking questions, here we go my love, one lump or two?" A sharp rapping on the front door startled the shopper's guest. He sprang up from his chair accidently knocking over the tea tray and its contents. Her best crockery reserved for guests and visitors only, crashed to the floor, it lay there in bits and pieces. "Bit twitchy aren't you son, it's probably Val" the shopper said, smoothing down his ruffled feathers. Red looked at her as if to say, sorry, in my line of business it's force of habit. He knelt down intending to pick up the pieces. "That's alright don't worry, it can all be replaced. I got a good deal from Manny Isherwood down at Romford market, he's bound to have some more. Seconds they are, but he told me they were brand spanking new he did. Anyhow, he's the most trustworthy Jew boy as I'll ever meet. So, don't make a song and dance about it, I'll clear it all up later." Red pulled out a smart looking leather wallet and dug out a twenty-pound note. "Will that cover it?" he smiled directly in to her eyes which were somewhere near five inches or so from his. "Handsomely my dear, handsomely.

Is there anything else I can offer you?" she asked in a flirtatious manner, smoothing her dress down. Her guest noticed she had applied a layer or two of bright red lipstick, no doubt whilst in the tiny kitchen. "Now young Robbo, be a good lad, finish up your lemonade then go and tell your aunty Val that her visitor will be round hers soon. And then perhaps you would like to go for a little walk."

CHAPTER 33

"Keep still Sir, do please keep still. I'm almost finished, a few more and you are all stitched up." Bomber thought, 'effing *well* stitched up weren't I.' Leytonstone hospital was oddly quiet for a Saturday evening, although it was not quite yet pub chucking out time. Lots of casualties found their way here following all the drunken brawls at closing time. Some with bits of beer glass sticking out of various places. Others with broken this or broken that, all of them well pissed up. "How you feeling Bomber?" Sitting in the little curtained off cubicle sat Bomber, the doctor and Johnny the Turk. "What you doing here anyway Johnny?" "Well, somebody had to run you over here and you know I don't drive, so I got Zak to dig out his old jalopy. He's out in the waiting area. What happened I need to know?" "Didn't Zak tell you?" "He knows less than I do." Johnny replied. "There you are Sir all finished." The night doctor intervened. "Let's see you again in two weeks' time to snip out the stiches." "Yea, cheers doc." Gathering up his medical bits and pieces, he pulled back the curtain and walked swiftly on to his next patient. "Wouldn't want his job for all the cocoa beans in Borneo, would you mate?" "Not on your Nellie Bomber, not a bleedin chance. So, you going to tell me what happened or have I got to beat it out of you?" "That's it, hit a man when he's down" grinned Bomber. A sit down at Zak's, for Johnny to chair, had been hastily put together to take place on Sunday. Timed for late afternoon, the day had been warm and sunny. As a result, Zak's place was filling up fast. Pale ale always was a magnet for serious drinkers following a hot day. Due to the rush, Zak happily lent a hand behind the bar. Those on the attendance list upstairs were, in spite of his recent injury, Bomber, Dave Conti, Billy and Mel the Stratford Two, and a small number of Eddie's ex-army. These lads used to hang out at the Oasis awaiting any orders from their hero. They were on the edge of villainy, always ready for a rumble or two. This would be the first time they had actually sat in on a meet. For now, Errol, although part of the set-up, was to be side-lined from meetings until further notice. The room they were using above Zak's Place was nothing to write to the prime minister about. It was pokey, window less and smelling of damp but would serve a purpose for the moment.

Johnny outlined his plans. His ultimate aim was to take total control as he was convinced that nobody would see Eddie in the country, let alone the East End any time soon or for that matter, any time later. He thought it might be a bit dicey to play all his cards at once as any one of them could fly off the handle. So, for now he would need the blokes sitting around the table to feel comfortable. Especially with him now at the helm, therefore as far as they were concerned Johnny wanted to be seen as merely adopting a caretaking role, well, at least for now. "Right" Johnny said drawing attention to himself. "Until anyone hears or sees any evidence of Eddie coming home to roost, I'm taking up where he left off." Bomber thought, he's bloody well been lying to me. He told me no more murders and to use brain power instead. "Anyone got any problems with that?" Before waiting for any answers, Johnny continued. "The Oasis is no more so, for the time being, this is now our place to meet up. The bloke who owns the dive bar downstairs is Zak. He's a distant relative of mine. Bombers gonna take up the role of chief chucker outer down there, his main aim is to keep the peace. We won't be charging Zak for Bombers duties cos in return; we're getting this meeting room free plus as many beers as we can handle." Just then the door opened. As if on cue, Zak entered the room carrying a crate of ale, six brown and six pale. He nodded to Johnny who nodded back. Zak closed the door silently behind him thinking, 'Christ what have I done, that lot back there in the room look very iffy and they stink of trouble.' He could only hope that a turf war between Johnny's mob and any other gangs in the area, didn't put his beloved bar as the epicentre of any blood-letting and general mayhem. In the short time of allowing Johnny access, he'd already been at pains to organise the body of a brawny young docker type to be dumped in Epping Forest. The blokes he paid to dispose of the body, were instructed to saw the arms off the cadaver from shoulder hight and dump them elsewhere. The tattoos might have given away his identity, **if** he was ever dug up. One of the lads from Eddie's ex-army who went by the name of Monkey Mick piped up aggressively. "So where *is* his nibs then, that's what we wanna know?" His three companions agreed in unison. "Yea" Short Willy added. "And, we wanna know where his bird is you know, that Esme. We 'aint seen niver of them since Eddie was lifted?" Johnny held the wanna be thugs gaze for a moment or two, staring them down, he swore blind they visibly shrank. Johnny smiled that smile he would use after beating an opponent to pulp in the ring. "That's something we all want to know. But before we go any further, show some bleedin respect for your ex-boss Monkey. All you four lads need to know right now is this."

Johnny crashed his two enormous fists on the table. "Just sit in on the meets, keep your noses clean and keep schtum about us. You're here to help make a ton of money. Your time for a bit of extorting cash out of people with the threat of intimidation and violence will soon come round. Got it?" Johnny asked through gritted teeth. "Yea, yea got it boss." Replied Monkey. Short Willy nodded also. For good measure, Johnny added, "and when you're sitting in, just watch what you say, in fact watch what you don't say, right, that's sweet as a nut, so let's move on." Dave Conti had a question. "What's the situation with Eddie's Mum Val Johnny?" Most of the blokes looked from Dave to Johnny who was remarkedly ready for this one. "Look pal, if you want to go and work for her, then you're more than welcome Dave. In fact, if anybody else wants to go and work for Val Coleman, you might as well leave now." He swept a hand around the table, but no one moved a muscle. "Good, that's that sorted then, Billy, Mel, you carry on with keeping the car-lot managers on their toes, plus keep a close eye on Errol's breakers yard in case of any aggravation from the local hoods. Dave, get yourself up West and start nicking quality motors again. Exactly the same routine as before. Drive 'em over to Errol's then bring the payments back here. All went quite for a minute or two as those around the table took in and thought through their individual duties. Monkey Mick was about to put his hand up to speak but remembered just in time, he wasn't at school now. Instead, he stood. "What about us Johnny, what about us?" Again, Johnny was ready for this one too. "Information Monkey, information. I want you four to spread yourselves out and about a bit and gather info. Talk to people in the know. Stay schtum about us and keep your ears to the ground. Pick up anything useful and bring it to me, I need to know whose doin what and to who, understand?" All four nodded. "One more thing before we get into the beers. Bomber, who was it with the shooter that killed that young docker bloke out in the yard? I wanna put a tin lid on it as soon as and by the way are you still dossing down at the Steak House up West?" Bomber looked up and before answering took a deep breath, he knew Johnny would be mightily pissed off. "The shooter was" ……. at that moment, they could all hear a ruckus going on in the overcrowded bar below. Zak called up the stairs, "Bomber, you're needed and fast." Grateful for the timely intervention, Bomber rushed downstairs happy to quell the commotion, and throw anyone out who was being a nuisance. At least *this* ruck would not finish in a shooting, *he hoped.*

Momentarily the room went quiet, all present were more than prepared to nip downstairs and lend Bomber a hand. A roar akin to a raging lion rang out followed by the sound of several people running out of the building. "Bombers earning our keep down there" remarked Johnny. Later that evening, Johnny cornered Bomber and asked him once again. "And the shooter that came to your aid that night was?" Bomber had no choice. Either he held back or told Johnny who he saw. Either way he was dammed. Bomber was not prone to stammer, but on this occasion he did. "Come on Bomber, cough it up. It might be a gold watch." The air was electric. Bomber whispered "It was Val Coleman., In the darkness she thought it was you." Breath bated, Bomber waited for Johnny to explode, but it never came. Johnny simply smiled, turned on his heel and walked out of Zak's bar to an empty Sidney Street.

CHAPTER 34

"You kill people for a living, right?" Red Satriani grinned sheepishly and nodded. "How many people have you killed then?" "Erm, that's not a question I get asked a lot actually." "Alright here's another. Did you get your leg over with her two doors down?" "Sorry Mrs. Coleman, a gentleman never speaks of such things." "Well, you were in there long enough, blimey she's a one she is, knickers always at 'alf mast when blokes are around." Val Coleman and Red Satriani were in Val's sitting-room, he perched on the edge of a fireside chair while she sat back in the other. "Have you heard of my son Eddie?" "I have yes Mrs. Coleman, who hasn't, his reputation for organising large-scale crime, dished out with a healthy dose of violence and mayhem has reached ears way beyond these shores." Val narrowed her eyes. "What do you mean beyond these shores?" "Mrs. Coleman, I am of Italian descent. I've lived in London most of my adult life but still very much in touch with my wider family in Catania, Sicily. "Where's that?" enquired Val? "It is part of Italy, way down to the South. It is somewhere in the region of 500 miles South of Roma. If you look at a map you will see Italy is shaped like a giant boot. Sicily looks like it is being kicked up the arse by the toe of that boot."

"Enough of the geography lesson. We're simple folk us Londoners but we can kick like mules too, especially with a tight rubber band or two snapped around the mule's willy." "Well, I mentioned my wider family because they want to meet with your son to discuss terms and conditions. It seems he has a good thing going with reference to obtaining up-market automobile's, shall we say, for free then shipping them abroad for cash. To have set that up and with your police force not knowing who is doing it, and where the cars are ending up, takes brains and ingenuity. My distant family want to meet Eddie and expand the shipping destinations, to Italy." Val was truly shocked. Shocked to hear this Red Satriani speaking so easily of a big money spinner and that someone as far away as Italy wanted in on Eddie's lucrative caper. "So how did your extended family here of this?" Val enquired. "I have no idea Mrs. Coleman no idea. I can only tell you this. We will not need the usual fee required for me to kill whoever it is you want me to kill. We pride ourselves in a first-class service. There will be no reduction in quality, you will, like all our clients receive the best." Val thought good grief, this one's a cool customer. He talks like he's selling a Hoover or something. "So, let me get this straight. You will do the killing, no charge right?" Her guest nodded smiling sweetly. "In return, you want me to set up a meeting between my son and someone from your extended family?" "That's right Mrs Coleman, that's right. I would add the two are not connected by time." Val was getting vexed, "What do you mean not connected?" "We know your son Eddie is on the run, therefore a meeting might be a little difficult for you to arrange for a while. We are patient people Mrs. Coleman, we are prepared to wait for such an important meeting.

However, I have been told that I can carry out the killing as soon as you would like." Val began to see what was happening. "So, you do the killing then my bit is to arrange a meeting. What if I can't?" "Then Mrs Coleman, you will be in debt to my extended family." "In debt, what do you mean?" "Mrs Coleman. Killing people with no come back on our clients whatsoever is an art. You must have heard in your news from time to time, that so and so has gone missing. No trace, no clues, police baffled. Those that go missing can range from top politicians, nobility down to hardened gangsters. They can be celebrities or hotel porters. What we offer is peace of mind without compromise. All this of course has a cost, now we come to your situation. As I have already said, we will offer our services to you free of charge. In return we all we ask is a meeting with your son. Now, if you cannot comply, we will ask for an in, on your car set up to the value of Thirty percent"

"Thirty percent, you're having a laugh." "Mrs Coleman, you have not been listening, we will increase Eddie's business threefold by opening up the Italian market. From early conversations we have had with members of our extended family which stretch from Genoa to Roma and from Roma to Catania, we could triple what it is currently doing cash wise. Anyway, who is it that you want, how do they say in America, rubbed out?" Val had some thinking to do, how the hell would she explain this to Eddie? Not only was Errol involved but there was his dad in the mix too, and in a big way. Plus, there is car thief extraordinaire, Dave Conti to be put in the know. Could Dave up his game threefold? Probably not. He might be the best car thief around but even he would have limits. On the plus though, the amount of cash it would generate for all concerned would put them in clover for as long as the caper lasted. "Look Mr. Satriani." "Please, call me Red Mrs. Coleman." "Ok, look Red, I've got to speak first with Eddie, which will not be easy. He's travelling across Spain about now." Aha thought Red, the lure of the money is prising open the sealed lips of this lady. He interrupted her flow. "It is just as easy for my extended family to fly to Spain and meet him wherever." Val began to feel a little cornered. "Hold your horse's pal, nothings been agreed yet." "I understand Mrs. Coleman, I understand." From an inside pocket of his immaculately cut and tailored suit jacket, he produced an expensive looking business card and proffered it to Val. She reached out to take it, just as her guest flick it downwards slightly out of her reach. "Ahead of taking this card, should any of our conversation go outside these four walls, all bets are off." The friendly smile suddenly gone, replaced with a mouth closed with corners turned down together with the evil eyes of a manic shark full of menace. Val temporarily went cold, almost shivered. But she was made of strong stuff and would not be faced down. Quickly she snatched card and held his gaze. Red Satriani was the first to blink and within seconds was back to his charming self. Talk about butter wouldn't melt. Val took a peek at the card expecting it to read Contract Killers Inc., or some such stuff. However, nothing so dramatic. At the top in bold letters was his name Red Satriani, in red ink of course. Below that, just two words. Vermin Control. Followed by a London telephone number. Val got up and slipped the expensive looking business card in the top drawer of her sideboard. The same drawer that once held Eddie's hand gun, until Val having discovered it screamed bloody blue murder at Eddie until it disappeared. How ironic she thought, now here am I about to hire a contract killer. She turned to her guest.

"Red, that's not you real name, is it? what kind of a name is that anyway?" she asked. "No Mrs. Coleman, I am called Marco by birth. I go under the name of Red as I have a weakness for gambling, in particular roulette. I love it, have a passion for it, always betting on red." With contempt rather than cynicism, Red asked "Do you by any chance have a weakness Mrs. Coleman?"

CHAPTER 35

The Land Rover with its two occupants flew at speed down a tight alley-way towards its intended target, engine screaming.
 Crashing through the flimsy wall all three came to a halt smack in the middle of the little Spanish bar. A number of flying bricks crazed the windscreen and shattered both headlights. The aged Landy was a tough little bugger, however the designers hadn't designed it to go crashing through brick walls; even flimsy ones. Before the dust had time to settle, Mitch and Eddie had thrown themselves out of the Land Rover and bunged a couple of stun grenades into the room. There were just a few customers in on this quiet Monday evening. This was the known 'hide-out bar' for the gang which terrorised many of the ghetto type areas of Bilbao. The intelligence previously gathered by Mitch had it that most of the gang got together here on Mondays. Mitch looked at Eddie, Eddie shrugged his shoulders. He saw Mitch move his mouth saying "Where the fuck are they?" but heard nothing. Only the ringing in both ears caused by the stun grenades. It was then he remembered he was supposed to plug something in his ears to guard him from the pressure, caused by the blast wave coming from the exploding grenades. To his left, he saw the barman pop up from a crouched position behind the bar and level some sort of antique hunting rifle at Mitch. Hearing or no hearing, quick as a flash Eddie picked up some loose debris from the downed wall, and flung it at the shooter. It caught him on the shoulder just as he pulled the trigger. The shot went downwards and to the right, missing Mitch by inches and catching one of the departing dust covered customers in the calf. Mitch stuck a thumb in the air by way of thanks. The

rifle must have been a single loader as the bar tender was busy shoving in another round. He was about to level the barrel again, this time at Eddie when he was shot in the head dying instantly, with his eyes wide open. As he slumped back down behind the bar, both Mitch and Eddie could see parts of his brain and a great deal of his blood splattered on the bottles of spirits on the second shelf, directly behind him.

Eddie was not uncomfortable with this; he'd had his share of messy killings and of course Mitch was much the same. What was troubling them was the accuracy of the shot. This was no random gun happy shooter, more like an experienced killer. And now he or she was in the same bar. The shooter, whoever it was, for the moment had become their saviour from the barman and his antique firearm but was now their potential nemesis. Framed in the doorway was a big looking bloke holding a revolver. Tall, bulky round the middle with a long pony tail and sneer on his thick lips as wide as the Mersey Tunnel. He was wearing a gun belt loosely slung over his gut, the type used by gunslingers in wild West picture shows. Above this was a multi coloured waistcoat complete with tassels. To Eddie he looked a right fucking idiot, but that six-shooter held him back from falling over laughing. He could see from the revolving barrel there were at least four more shots to come and no doubt another one up the spout ready to kill. Plenty enough to put he and Mitch out of action. The gun he was holding reminded Eddie of his first ever weapon, an American Peacemaker. A gun he'd borrowed off his mate Wossname. The main difference being, Wossnames gun wouldn't go bang, the firing pin had been filed down. He remembered the time he shoved the gun up to Wossnames head right between the eyes. Both knew the gun wasn't capable of firing, indeed it wasn't even loaded. It didn't stop Wossname from crapping in his pants when Eddie thumbed the hammer back, pulled the trigger screaming bang. Mitch held up his hands in mock surrender, "Well, well, well if it aint the head honcho José himself." Eddie kind of heard something being shouted in his direction. A deep voice full of growling menace. He saw the big guy was looking at him waving the six-shooter upwards, possibly motioning for Eddie to do the same with his hands. The big guy moved from the doorway gaining ground into the bar, both Mitch and he held their ground. Streaming in behind José, several bandidos, luckily Eddie thought, unarmed maybe a knife or two, but no visible shooters. One of the bandidos recognised Eddie instantly. This boy had thick sticking plaster plastered over a blooded, bruised nose and busted top lip together with two lovely shiners topping it all off. He jumped up and down rabbiting off to the boss man pointing at Eddie. Something was said between Mitch and the big boss guy.

When the conversation finished, Mitch explained the reason why José shot the barman. "It might have been his uncle, but he wants you alive for his personal pleasure. He's taken umbrage at you killing his son the other night and maiming his young brother." "How do you know his bloody name?" Eddie asked. Mitch called back, "Well known in these parts, a total head case." "By the way, they speak very little English so I will add this little gem. I've brought some *'back-up'* by way of a couple of loaded shotguns in the back of the Land Rover. I need you to cause a distraction while I dig them out, OK?" He winked at Eddie. "Just pretend you're still deaf from the stun grenades." Eddie stumble forward faking deafness. He put his hands behind his ears holding them out like an elephant giving the impression of not hearing a single word. José watched him trip then seemingly fall forwards over parts of the wall that lay scattered about, he laughed loudly. His stomach bouncing up and down in time with the guffaws. Truth is, Eddie was play acting. He'd seen a handy lump of wood laying in amongst the pile of brick rubble. Mitch's dramatic entrance, not only bashed part of the wall down, some of the bar's furniture suffered too. What Eddie was aiming for looked like the leg from of one of the beer tables. Grabbing it, leaping forward he let out a blood curdling scream. "Fuck you pal, this is do or die." The upswing from the heavy table leg caught José on the elbow loosening his grip on the revolver. Instinctively he squeezed the trigger. The gun exploded. In such a small space the noise of the bang was amplified ten-fold. His aim however, due to the table leg doing its job went far wide of its mark. Eddie brought it back down again, cracking the big guy's radial bone neatly in two. Part of which decided to make its way to the surface and out through the skin into fresh air to see what the fuck was going on, sticking upwards at a weird angle all six inches of it.

CHAPTER 36

It was boss man's turn to scream. This time due to complete agony. The gun dropped to the ground, bounced and fired again; the hammer had been cocked ready; the trigger must have been adjusted for an extremely light touch. The bullet bounced harmlessly off the open rear door of the Landy.

Mitch, who was standing behind the open door busying himself with grabbing the loaded shotguns, stuck another thumb up at Eddie shouting "cheers mate." Eddie was now up close and personal with plaster nose. He had no hesitation of head butting him in exactly the same spot, the plaster acting as a perfect target. Sticking plaster nose went down like the proverbial sack of spuds, blood spurting from freshly closed wounds, now opened again. By now the remaining bandidos were beginning to back away. Mitch, having grabbed the two shotguns, ran to the main entrance to cut them off. As he ran, one of the shotguns was thrown to Eddie, he caught it, then with practised speed aimed it at the boss man's head. They were both now armed and very dangerous. "Tell them José is about to lose his face" yelled Eddie. Mitch interpreted. The gang of seven were now at the mercy of two. No one moved. There was a distinct stench of poo in the air a sure sign of someone shitting themselves. 'So, not so hard after all' thought Eddie. "Might be brave enough when its seven against two, but look at you now when things cut up a bit rough." Bullies always melt when put against a wall with a gun rammed into their face. These lads were no exception. Eddie couldn't stop himself, "No so bloody bravo now is yoo gringos" he shouted in an attempt at Spanish. Mitch nearly wet himself laughing partly due to relief and partly because of Eddie's linguistic attempt. Eddie took a few steps closer to the bandidos, the shotgun now inches away from Mr. Busted nose. Just then Eddie went into his killing trance. His eyes glazed over and he began humming his favourite nursery rhyme. Oh, how he relished at being at the working end of a proper gun and not a bleedin pea shooter.

'Half a pound of tuppeny rice, half a pound of treacle, that's the way the money goes pop goes the weasel"

On the word *pop* he dropped the barrel downwards pulling the trigger at the same time. The multiple metallic balls of 'shot' bounced off the terracotta tiled floor straight up towards José and his mob. They howled and hollered as their faces, arms and hands were peppered with tiny little balls of metal. Most of them dropped to their hands and knees others tried to run but were forced back by a smiling, shotgun holding Mitch. José mouthed off something at Mitch who immediately turned the gun around and smashed the wooden stock into his mouth.

Most of the bandidos scarpered through the now unguarded entrance door, left open by Mitch. Eddie let off a second barrel in the same fashion as the first, downwards. The resulting spray of tiny metallic balls peppered a few backsides, mainly belonging to those that were desperately trying not to be the last out of the bar. More screams and hollering. That left just José. "Mitch, why did you hit him in the mouth? When we torture him, we won't be able to hear him beg for mercy." "Oh yes, we will matey oh yes, we will. Especially with what I've got planned for him." "What's that then?" Eddie enquired. Mitch spoke quietly. "When he was gobbing off just now, he told me he would have the last laugh because it was him that did the hit and run on my lovely bride to be, Mia." Instantly Eddie walked over and dealt José a severe blow to his balls. Eddie placed the barrel of his shotgun between the boss man's legs then rammed it as far north as he could. José went white, bent in two and projectile vomited. "That's for Mia you ugly fat gutted bastard." Eddie grabbed him by his pony tail, yanked his head up to meet his then spat in his trembling face. It mixed in nicely with the blood, snot and gore that at one time was his mouth. Mitch picked up the only chair that was still in one piece indicating for the snivelling wreck to sit down and place his arms behind him. From the back of the Land Rover, Mitch produced a length of parachute cord. José was past caring. Blood was pouring out of the open wound to his arm. So, with much discomfort, he obliged.

Mitch tied the cord roughly around the wrists, going for maximum pain for his prisoner. "Right let's get him into the back of the Landy preferably covered by a blanket." "Ok Mitch, what you gonna do with 'im?" "We're going to take him for a little ride." With José hog tied and laying in the back, covered by a blanket, Mitch dared him, "Make a sound and I will gouge your eyes out."

CHAPTER 37

"You were a bit tasty back then mate. Seems to me rough stuff comes second nature to you. And what's with humming a nursery rhyme?" Eddie lied, "Keeps me calm, you know, got to keep one step ahead, keep 'em on the back foot. It comes from me boxing days. Besides I hate bullies, had enough of 'em when I was younger. Anyway, where are we going?" Mitch was driving at speed, the glazed windscreen had long been kicked out, the dust from the side road they were negotiating was beginning to get down their throats. Roughly ten minutes from town, they might as well have been in the Gobi Dessert. Darkness was approaching fast.

The Land Rover's headlights were smashed beyond repair so Mitch was driving on sidelights only. "Come on Mitch, where the bleedin hell are we going, and how much longer?" As he spoke, the Land Rover pulled off into a makeshift lay-by. Eddie jumped out as did Mitch. Eddie looked over the side of the lay-by down into what looked like an abyss. They both heard a low groan, a sort of gurgling from a near dead José under the blanket. "Come over here Eddie, see this?" He pointed to a small mound of stones piled up which held a wooden cross in place standing approximately three feet high. "This is where my Mia was found. Her body lay here for a number of days. When she didn't come home, her parents and me started up a search for her." "What made her come out here then?" My belief is, that bastard lying in the back, ran her down for whatever reason, drove her out here and left her to die. The wild life, possibly Iberian wolves, had their fill of fresh meat. When she was eventually found most of her face and flesh on her arms was gone." "My God Mitch, and you've lived with that all this time, let's go and do the fucker now." "No mate, I'm grateful for what you did back there at their hideout but this is my show now. All I need you to do is help me get him in to the driver's seat." José was coming round and was not too aware of his surroundings as he came to. He shook his head in attempt to clear his vision, then tried to wipe his blooded and clotted mouth with the back of his hand, only to find both his hands were tied to the steering wheel, the steering wheel of the vehicle that conveyed him to this remote spot. In the centre of the wheel a picture of Mia looked up at him, youthful, smiling, so beautiful. He screwed up his eyes tightly, hoping this was a bad nightmare of nightmares. Upon opening them again he saw Mitch by the bonnet holding up a large red metal container with word 'Gasolina' printed on it in big yellow letters. Mitch was all smiles, he'd been visualizing this in his mind for some time and now, it was actually happening. Mitch walked past the open window to the driver's side, leant in then poured a modicum of petrol into the big man's lap. José quivered in fear of his wretched life. He tried shouting out his innocence but couldn't, his mouth was not working properly. They didn't care for it anyway; all Mitch could hear was gibberish. He opened the tail gate and poured the remaining gallon or so over the blanket and side seats. He threw the Gasolina can in for good measure, at the same time he murmured something to José. "If indeed you have a god, you are about to meet him."

Eddie was standing well back, not because he was afraid, far from it, he simply wanted this to be Mitch's show. Ten minutes Mitch waited, ten agonising minutes for both José and Mitch for very different reasons. Finally, Mitch tossed a lit match on to the petrol-soaked blanket that lay in the back of the Landy. Flames roared up; José fought in vain to get free. As he did the parachute cord bit hungrily into his wrists. The pain of his broken arm forgotten as his pony tail caught light, the pain of his broken arm forgotten completely now as he could feel the searing temperature on his back as the fire took hold. He felt his flesh begin to burn and crisp; the air now pungent with black smoke together with the smell of seared meat. A coughing, burning, spewing José fought and fought to get free, he screamed as the pain became too much to bear, he was becoming overwhelmed by the scorching blistering heat. His hair was fully alight, hot melted skin from his scalp now beginning to drip down his face. "Right Eddie, help give us a push mate." Mitch had previously turned the steering wheel to the left so the front wheels were aiming for the cliff edge. He knew the hand-brake was not engaged. Both grunted putting their backs in to it, the Land Rover tipped slightly then began its descent and slowly rolled over the edge. Mitch jogged over to the driver's window so as to politely offer José a cheery wave bye-bye. He yelled at the top of his voice, "ave a nice trip bastard." Gathering speed, it rolled further and further downhill, faster and faster. As they watched they heard more screaming. It seemed the doomed Landy driver had found a new level of screaming volume. Mitch pictured the petrol in José's lap igniting, which would be the likely cause of the increased volume. He smiled, it had long been on his mind that José had had his end away with Mia, therefore in the unlikely event he survived, he wouldn't have the means to repeat his dirty deeds. Just then the Land Rover turned a few cartwheels front first, then hit the ground, roof downward with a sickening crump. As they watched, it burst into flames, thick black smoke added to the already darkening Spanish sky. Mitch mouthed a fond farewell to his beloved Landy then, turning to Eddie asking "How is it you're so good at being so fucking bad?" "Lots of practice Mitch lots." "What about that barman getting his brains shot out" said Mitch in a thoughtful mood. "Yea well at least we saw what he was thinking at the time." Mitch looked puzzled but then nearly kicked himself for taking too long to get Eddie's drift. "Ok, but that thing you did with the shotgun, peppering the bandits faces and arses with shot was a blinder in every sense of the word, wish I'd thought of it." "Did the trick though didn't it?" replied Eddie.

"Don't think they'll be showing their spotty faces around Bilbao for a while. Anyway, what's next, do you want to go down and see if he's dead or something?" "Nah, if he survived that, it'll be a bloody miracle." Eddie asked, "how do we get back to Bilbao then?" "Oh, shit hadn't thought of that, suppose we'd better yomp it back to town." Eddie was confused, 'yomp' didn't register in his brain. If it meant walking, he was not going to be best pleased. "Sorry mate, it's an old army thing, it means a long hike with something heavy strapped to your back. Usually, a bergen or rucksack filled with house bricks. Only on this yomp we won't have the bricks, so should be a cinch matey." Mitch turned and marched off at a goodly pace back along the dusty by-road heading towards Bilbao. Eddie grimaced and silently fell in behind. As Mitch passed the spot marking where Mia was eventually found, he kissed his hand and put it to the cross, gently say "Rest easy now Mia my lovely."

CHAPTER 38

Esme let herself in the Villa Hermosa Vista, threw her overnight bag on the settee then poured herself a long one. She knew Chris and Sue meant no real harm but deep inside she also knew Eddie would see it differently. One thing was for sure, she would ask Javier to get the proper gardeners back on the job and pronto; as they say in Spain. It was a bit weird getting out of the cab and seeing the pair of them doing up the Villa's gardens.

But then again, she thought, the pair were relatively harmless. If it took Eddie a while to get here, that might give her time to keep both of them, especially Chris, at the end of a sharp stick. Downing the green alcoholic drink in one, Esme opened up the patio doors, wandered around the patio area until finally flopping on to one of the luxurious sun loungers. Laying back at full stretch, she allowed her mind to wander back to the night she had just spent with Javier and knew it was a big mistake. If Eddie found out he'd probably go spare, gang-land butcherer that he is. Indeed, it probably wouldn't stop at Javier, once Eddie got a bee in his bonnet, anyone who got in his way would suffer too.

In spite of her craving Javier's company, she was now regretting that last telegram she sent to Val, the one with the address that would lead Eddie to her here, at the Villa Hermosa Vista. The neat alcohol lulled Esme into a false sense of security, climbing out of the sun lounger, she went back inside to pour herself another. Half was swallowed on the spot, the other half transported, rather wobbly back to the sun lounger.

Placing the drink on a convenient side table, Esme threw herself down on the sun lounger once again, before long she was in the land of nod. It seemed like hours had passed when she was woken by someone's lips pressing on hers. Next, she felt hands softly, expertly exploring her body. Gently caressing her, taking care to avoid intimate areas. At first, she thought Chris from the neighbouring villa had crept back and was taking advantage of her. She felt quite sick at the thought. Then she thought no, he wouldn't be so gentle, cautiously opening one eye, it was Javier smiling down at her. He'd pulled the adjoining sun lounger close to hers, making what might be contrived as a double bed in the warm afternoon sun. She opened her other eye. Javier was smiling again, smiling that smile that was supposed to melt knicker elastic at twenty-five yards. Javier was completely naked and what's more, very, very aroused. He whispered in her ear something in Spanish which by all intents and purposes to Esme probably meant brace yourself girl I'm coming in! She felt her underwear going South. Although to be absolutely correct, as her feet were pointing at the afternoon sun, it was therefore more likely to be classed as South, Southwest. Whatever the direction, she had no resistance and was unable to halt their journey. Her white pleated skirt was then pulled gently up around her waist. Again, no resistance from Esme. Javier was now kneeling up and about to climb on to her sun lounger. His mouth crushed down onto hers, his tongue searching every corner of the inside of her mouth. As he made his move to get on top of Esme proper, a vehicle could be heard pulling up at the front of the Villa, a car door slammed then the vehicle drove off at speed. Esme was unable to move or call out. It then dawned on her; the bloody drink was probably drugged. How could she fall asleep for so long, how could she allow Javier to carry on like this? And who the hell was coming from the front of the villa to the back where she lay, under the influence of a drug, administered by Javier.

"Esme, where are you, it's me?" She recognised Eddie's distinctive East End gravelly voice. Esme found her vocal cords at last, "Eddie, Eddie, thank God, come here, get this dirty greasy bastard dago off me." Javier looked heartbroken. 'Dirty greasy bastard dago is she talking about me?' Eddie turned the corner and was able to view the entire scene set out before him. Javier stood up ready for the fight; big mistake. Eddie strode purposefully towards Javier, when close enough he slapped him round the chops twice, really hard slaps. Slapped him like a mother slaps her naughty child. Eddie knew it would remind this greasy looking geezer of his childhood. Javier was shocked alright, right down to his toes, the slaps stung him, stopped him in his tracks. He began to cry like a baby, a baby having been scolded by his beloved mummy. Eddie followed up the slaps with a shoulder charge like a raging Minotaur bundling both Javier and himself into the swimming pool crashing right over the top of poor half-naked Esme. He fell on top of Javier as they entered the water. Eddie surfaced first, grabbing Javier by the hair he pushed him under holding him down until the thrashing arms and legs ceased to thrash. Only then did he release his grip on Javier, whose tanned and swarthy body floated to the surface face down, lily white buttocks uppermost, legs and arms sticking out looking much like a dead frog.

CHAPTER 39

Job done, Eddie waded to the shallow end, pushed dripping wet hair from his eyes and grinned a hello up at Esme. "You okay girl? Looks like we need to dispose of this lad, but before we do, I'm gonna mark him on his back. Might be a bit messy so best to drag 'im out first, don't want to taint the pool with his blood. Much as I like seeing your gorgeous body, there might be nosey parker neighbours bogging in so pull your knickers up. When you've done that, nip and get me a carving knife will yer." Esme was aware of a hand clasping her shoulder, gently shaking her. She shot up into a sitting position to find Sue sitting on the sun lounger next to hers, shaking her awake. "You alright my darlin, we could hear you over at our place, screaming blue murder you were. Havin a bad dream, was you?" "Sorry Sue, yes it was a hell of a bad 'drunken' dream and it was bloody ghastly." " So, who's this Eddie person then, you were shouting out his name a few times amongst other things?"

"What other things Sue?" Esme feared she had unwittingly blurted out stuff about Eddie that she would not like Sue to have heard. "Mostly rude cussing type words that's all dearie.
 Shall I make us a nice cuppa then?" Esme was mightily relieved. "That would be nice Sue and while you're at it, there is a bottle of booze on the work-top, can you pour it down the sink please, it's a bit too strong for me." As Sue got up to busy herself in the kitchen, Esme's hand surreptitiously drifted towards the top of her legs and found what she was feeling for. Knickers intact and not pulled up roughly or back to front as some times can happen. Her white skirt she had bought back

in London was also where it should be. Esme's eyes darted to the pool, fully expecting to see parts of a dismembered Javier floating about in a blood red pool, but thankfully no, all was well there too. Just the afternoon reflection from the sun brightly dancing, like a butterfly on the surface ripples caused by the filtration unit, silently doing its job. "Here we go my lovely, nice cup of Rosy-Lee. Sorry couldn't resist a swig of that stuff you wanted put down the sink, made me quite woozy it has. I've given you extra sugars to help quell the stress of your nightmare. "Now," Sue half breathed in a conspiratorial way, "Tell me all about this Eddie bloke, Hmmmm"

CHAPTER 40

Red Satriani got up to leave. Instructions verbally received from Val on who the target was to be, tucked safely away in his head, no need for incriminating paper work. "Just one or two things Mrs Coleman before I go." Red asked. "You haven't said how." "What do you mean how?" Red was quiet for a moment or two. He needed to remember this was a first for Val Coleman, a once popular clippie to a now fledgling gangland boss. "Do you have a particular way you want him dead? "For example," he continued. "Shot, decapitated, garrotted, drowned, poisoned, thrown off a tall building or simply strangled? The list is without end." Val became fleetingly speechless, then found her voice again. "So, you carry out the kill *and* you offer how, what's the point in that?" "Well, let's say, the target murdered someone you knew and loved by driving a car over them several times and now, you are of course bent on revenge. You might well ask me to arrange for the person you want put in a coffin to suffer the same fate prior to their burial.

"Oh, I get it, well erm, shot then please, in the heart will do. And just before you pull the trigger, tell 'im it's for blowing up the Oasis Bar" Val began to shudder and shiver, *this business* she thought, *is getting more macabre by the minute.* "Lastly, do you need evidence?" "What" she shouted! Red continued "Some customers ask for a body part they might be able to recognise. In cases of infidelity and the target is male, customers occasionally ask for the targets peni." Red didn't get any further; Val cut in. "Stop right there, this is the East End and we are dealing with an ex-fighter cum gang boss. Believe me, I'll know as soon as the deed is done. Now, if I can possibly help it, I don't ever want to see you again. As far as meeting my son is concerned, I'll speak to the people who put me in touch with you and pass on where you can find him-in Spain, nowhere else and definitely not here, got it?" "Certainly Mrs. Coleman, I have got it, I will now bid you adieu." As Val collapsed back down on her fireside chair, Red moved swiftly out of 119 Plenva Street, quietly closing the street door behind him. That was it, no going back, it was only now, the realisation of her actions and what they might lead to came home to roost. Val was sweating profusely, her skin cold and yet somehow clammy. One thing was for sure, a murder was going to take place, she knew how, but had no way of knowing exactly when. 'At least he didn't ask me if I wanted a front row seat.' What now for the rest of Eddies crew? she would need to act fast if she was to gain control again. Red strolled along the street for some fifty yards as if he had every right to be ambling along Plenva Street, head held high and smiling, when a black, previously unseen sports car of Italian descent pulled up alongside him. Engine at idle, exhaust note sounding throaty, guttural even, promising the driver ferocious speed as and when called for. Red stopped briefly, looked up and down the street which for some reason had taken on a quiet spell, then got in. The swarthy looking driver made no attempt to drive off, at least until Red tapped the dashboard, only then the Ferrari drew off at a leisurely pace. Back at number 119 Val was in the middle of a mild panic. Full of trepidation and dread at what she had just unleashed. Up until the point when Red Satriani had offered kill options on how Johnny was to die, it all seemed so correct and above board. A bit like booking a coach trip or something bland and impersonal. However, if you have a snake in the grass or as in this case an enemy in the camp, simply eject them without fuss or bother. Having him shot dead however, did actually now, seem a tad extreme. Perhaps a severe beating, would have sufficed.

She recalled one of the things her son said to her during a visit while he was on remand awaiting his trial. It seemed unimportant at the time; *'Ma, you are the only person I can trust from now on.'* His voice was clear as a bell echoing around inside her head which made her feel somewhat calmer. Although, on the other hand, Johnny the Turk *was* Eddie's number one trusted, but, if Eddie knew he was about to jump in his boots, wouldn't he want him out of the way too? He would very probably do him without thinking, especially as Johnny was shoving me, Eddies mum out in the cold. She must get this news to Eddie and soon, let him know before he heard it from elsewhere. Thank God Bomber was dropping her weekly hints as to what the Turk was getting up to, no bloody honour amongst thieves she pondered. A knock on her front door brought her back to the present, thinking it might be Red Satriani returning, which meant she might now be able to cancel the hit. Or even worse, it might be old Bill, Val was convinced they were still out there, watching her home. She moved swiftly over to the window, drew back the net curtain a few inches. The neighbour who had recently entertained her gun for hire had her face right up close to the window, hands cupped around her eyes straining to peer in. It fair gave Val a shock, angrily, she indicated with her thumb for her neighbour to go and stand at the front door. "Come on get in here, shut the door behind you you're letting a draught in. What is it you want then Mary?" "Well, that's a nice greeting, especially as I looked after your visitor till you got back 'ome." Val shot back with, "there's looking after and then there's *your* kind of looking after. I saw young Robbo going off on a walk around the Island and that usually means one thing and one only. Good shag, was he?" Mary pouted putting on the old innocent look. "Don't know what you mean Val, anyways up, he was fair game plus I was a bit short of doe-ray-me, what with just coming back from the shops and that." Val raised her voice "You mean you charged him?" Mary snorted, then started to giggle; "Well I couldn't be out of pocket could I. I 'ad to give young Robbo half a crown to fuck off out of it, didn't I?

Val joined in the giggling. Before long they were both laughing uncontrollably. "Christ Val," Mary gushed through the laughter, "I'll tell you what, 'e was bloody well 'ung. I said to 'im, listen mate if you're gonna stick that up me you'll split me bleedin cap, honest you will!" By now they were both holding their sides and laughing fit to drop. Mary asked through even more laughter, "What's he do then, for a living like?" "Vermin Control." Val answered.

That was it, the laughing came in major fits and bursts. Mary having done a spoonful or two made a quick dash upstairs to the toilet, shouting as she ran "Christ that twice I've pissed me pants today." Val was in tears, even though she wasn't sure that she should be this jolly at all. Still, no point in being miserable, crabby and complaining all your life, like that daft old cow June a few doors down.

CHAPTER 41

A beautiful crimson dawn streaked over Bilbao; another hot day was on the weather menu with perhaps the odd thunderstorm mixed in. Mitch and Eddie were sat at a table in the gardens of El Pirata awaiting two English breakfasts, busy planning Eddie's next move. Courtesy of Mitch, telegrams had been flowing to and from Val, as a result, Eddie was in possession of an address. An address that would lead him to Esme and safety. All it said was, Villa Hermosa-Vista, Mojácar, Province of Almería. Southern Spain. "That's a bloody long way from here Eddie." Mitch chipped in. "It's all of 600 miles or so." "Well, we'd better get our skates on then hadn't we. Didn't you say we should jump on a train to Madrid or something?" "Yea, might be a few changes on the way, I don't think there is a direct one straight through. Then after that, possibly find yourself a coach to the port of Almería. I should imagine that'll be your best bet. Hang on a mo, what do you mean we?" "Listen Mitch, I'm only thinking of you my friend" Eddie lied. "We've stirred up a hornet's nest here in Bilbao and it's best if you lay low or perhaps disappear for a while. What better than a yomp as you call it, over to Mojácar. By the time you get back here, it'll all be history." "I'm not walking that far." grinned Mitch. "But I s'pose you're right, the mob that José headed up will no doubt surface again, once they've dug the pellets out of their arses and I guess they might well slap some sort of venganza on me." Eddie looked up from his mug of steaming tea quizzically. "It means vengeance in their language mate. Mind you, they will definitely need to relocate; their hideout is now a pile of rubble plus there down a decent barman.

Fuck it let's do it, all exses on you Eddie." "Consider it done

Mitch." Eddie called the waiter over and cleared the bill for their breakfasts plus the substantial slate run up by Mitch over the last month or so. "I'm gonna need some more pesetas' mate where's the nearest bank?" "You'll get the same rate here." Mitch replied waving for the waiter to come and visit their table once again. "And you won't have to show your passport." Eddie peeled off two hundred nicker from his money roll and handed it to the wide-eyed waiter, whilst Mitch explained in Spanish that no, it wasn't a tip, it was a swop for pesetas at the going rate. "Right Mitch I'm in your hands you lead and I'll follow." Mitch scraped his chair back, heading off out into the market place. Eddie grabbed the pesetas from the waiter and duly followed. By midday, Mitch had seen to it that a goodly number of Eddie's Spanish potatoes, as he called them, had been well spent. Jackets jeans and shirts for them both, each item x two, leather holdalls x two, train tickets to Madrid x two road maps, such as they were, x two, then back to El Pirata for lunch x two plus another currency exchange, just in case. "If we're going by train and then coach," Eddie asked, "Why the maps?" "It's ingrained in me from my army days mate.

Map reading before we go, will be invaluable. Besides, maps will be helpful if we need to cover any ground on foot. I may speak the lingo over here but I've never stepped foot out of Bilbao except for a spell up in the mountains of Cordillera Cantabrica for training." "A spell?" "Best part of three months it was. Me and the blokes were on hard routine; most of us came back looking like the original bog monster. Long beards, matted hair and bitten to death by whatever lived up there that wanted something alive and relatively warm to chew on." Eddie tried to imagine such a look on Mitch as he recalled the photo, he saw on the desk back at his flat in Bilbao. In the framed photograph, Mitch looked immaculate in his sand-coloured beret, medal ribbons and nice neat uniform. "I need to shut up shop back at home you know, tell the neighbours I'll be away for a while. Let's base ourselves there for the next twenty-four hours or so and we can sort our shit out. I've got tickets for Wednesdays train, that's two days away, leaving Bilbao at ten in the morning. If I were you Eddie, I'd ditch the shooter, they have roaming guards on trains over here, plus on the odd occasion, military guys use the railway system to get to manoeuvres and such like. They'll be the only ones allowed to have weapons on board. Don't want us to end up in some gloomy drab lacadina miles from anywhere, with no friendly blond hostesses serving hot coffee." Eddie raised his eyebrows. "I take it you mean clink?"

"Yea correct, some of them are right pig holes and well grim. Bring your own bog roll type. A bucket for two and a couple of straw mattresses, if you're lucky. If you're unlucky you might get shoved in a cellar and chained to the wall." "All mod cons then?" Eddie chipped in. "As you say better ditch the shooter, how about I leave it at yours?" Without further ado, they made their way back to Mitch's home.

CHAPTER 42

D.I. Jackson, normally a studied and meticulous Detective Inspector in London's Metropolitan Police Force whooped for joy. In his hand was a communique from Interpol. A communique he thought would never happen. Of course, often he had secretly addressed many a prayer to the almighty asking for it to arrive on his desk one day soon please, and now, here it was. Positive thinking works, he said quietly to himself. Eagerly he read it then read it again, he even asked a passing admin clerk to read it out loud, once again. As he was listening to the clerk, he recalled when he was a teenager the day his father had won a substantial amount on the football pools. Papa ran around the house not believing what was written in front if his eyes, getting each member of the young Jacko's family to confirm that which he simply couldn't take in. Here was Jacko today, doing exactly the same thing, well almost. Finally, and only after sending his heartfelt thanks to God on high, he went back to his office, sat back in his chair and read the communique once again. On this occasion, he took several intakes of oxygen in order to settle his excited mind. The content as far as he was concerned, heralded a direct signpost as to Eddie Coleman's whereabouts. According to Interpol, Spanish police had recently discovered a body of a middle-aged man, hidden on board a yacht moored up in a place called Bilbao. D.I. Jackson called out for a map of Spain. The reason the Interpol communique had found its way to his desk was due to a particularly gruesome twist, in that a pathologist report attached to the document described a noughts and crosses symbol had been carved, post mortem to the upper back of the victim. When Jacko originally posted the details of the wanted man and sent it to Interpol, he'd meticulously detailed all he knew regarding Mr. Edward Coleman and his modus operandi.

Thankfully, someone somewhere within the system picked up on this essential bit of detail, made the connection and this was his reward for the very detailed information he originally submitted. The police at Bilbao, having checked with Customs determined the deceased a Mr. Lee Dean as the yacht owner plus one passenger by the name of Jack du Pré who had recently arrived from England. D.I. Jackson called out to the open office once again, "Somebody please get me the main police station in Bilbao Spain on the blower. And somebody else find me a Spanish speaking interpreter. Jackson was convinced it was Eddie Coleman using a false name. Who else would carve his signature kill symbol on his victim and leave a marker for the police to discover? Bloody fool. Caught up in the excitement, Jackson completely forgot about police procedure when dealing with overseas police matters. His first port of call should have been to take this information up-line to his boss Chief Insp. Ellis. Jackson called out to the open office once again, "Cancel the overseas call and interpreter, just bring me the map." D.I. Jackson sat back in his well-worn green synthetic leather office chair swivelled it round to face the view from the window behind him. His office originally had the desk and chair facing the window, which overlooked the station's car park. He read somewhere that changing it to its present layout as in having his back to the window, meant anyone sitting opposite him would have difficulty seeing the expression on his face, especially on sunny days. Gave him the edge he thought when talking to his subordinates. He looked down at the right arm of his office chair. It was well worn with age. What antique dealers might describe as patination? A good deal of the leather had been picked off by its previous owner, the soft padding material poking through the holes. The seat wasn't much better, in fact Jackson purchased a cushion from the local haberdashery shop, had it made to measure. 'If I do this properly,' he thought, 'it could well mean promotion which in turn could well lead to me occupying a more salubrious office up on the second floor. Just think, capturing Eddie Coleman and a promotion. What a serious double that would be.'

A warm feeling flowed through his veins, 'gosh haven't felt this good since me and the wife last did it.' Briefly he tried to remember when, but could not. " Good God Jacko, he's a complete basket case if you ask me, gets himself safely away then plonks a bloody great clue on your desk, inadvertently or vertently, if that's even a word, but I'm sure you get my drift." D.I. Jackson was once again in the plushest of police offices known to man, belonging to Chief Insp. Ellis.

He even had a beautiful bunch of flowers displayed perfectly in a Cloisonne vase on the corner of his vast shiny desk. While Ellis was sounding off in his usual gruff manner, D.I. Jackson made a mental note that Chief Inspector Ellis also had a green leather swivel chair. Must have been a bulk purchase by procurement. However, *his* did not have the wear and tear or fading signs as that of his own. He was half in mind to ask Inspector Ellis, if he also, had a cushion made to measure. Reading through the communique, Ellis enquired, "Did this come direct from Interpol Jacko and do sit down please, you're making the office look untidy?" D.I. Jackson stood a little while before accepting the order. "No Sir, it arrived by motor cycle courier direct from Scotland Yard." "Did it by golly did it?" Ellis seemed surprised and sat up correctly at the mention of Scotland Yard. He asked Jackson, "And what action have you taken since receiving it?" Nothing Sir, it arrived and I signed for it about an hour ago, all I have done is acquire a map so as to ascertain exactly where Bilbao is. I have brought it to you directly." "Good, good Jacko." Ellis replied, who was beginning to sweat a little. "Did you bring the map with you, old boy?" Jacko hated being addressed as 'old boy.' He might well be a good deal older than his boss but there was no need to rub it in. A young lady entered the office unannounced with a small tray, on it one coffee alongside two chocolate digestives. "Oh, please forgive me Sir, I had no idea you were in a meeting, your colleague must have arrived whilst I was in the kitchen." She placed the tray on the huge desk, out of reach of Jackson, in case he made a lunge for a biscuit. What she failed to realise was, it would be the last thing on his mind. He kept his body very trim and watched what he ate. Chocolate biscuits and sticky type cream buns, for him, are off limits. Ellis waved the young lady away with a cursory lopsided smile, looking at Jackson raising his eyebrows as if to say, 'can't get the staff today old boy.' Jackson watched as Ellis dunked a chocolate digestive swirling it around until it was almost too soft to transport from cup to mouth. He listened as Ellis slurped the soggy biscuit, sucking out the coffee before loading the remainder into his mouth. "So, tell me what do you think you've got here then?" He said talking through a mouthful of chocolate digestive. Ellis, was holding up the paper work. "Well Sir, the most important piece of information is the fact that this Mr Lee Dean, the yacht owner, had a noughts and crosses symbol carved on his upper back post mortem." "Yes, yes I see that, but your suspect goes under the name of du Pré, first name Jack."

Jackson knew Ellis was challenging him, that was his job. "What else can you glean from this Jacko?"

"Well Sir, apart from knowing where Coleman potentially is or was quite recently, absolutely nothing." "Exactly Jacko exactly, please don't tell me you want to fly out there and track him down or some such nonsense. After all it might well turn out to actually *be* someone called Jack du Pré. You would look a right Charlie arresting the wrong man. Besides our budgets for this fiscal year are almost spent." Ellis saw Jacko look from the flowers to the tray with the remaining biscuit, then to the big shiny desk. "What is it that makes you sure it's

Coleman?" "I know this much Sir, over the last three weeks or so since he absconded, I have trawled through police records extensively and cannot find any evidence of a kill symbol, identical to the one Coleman inflicts on his victims." "Hmmm, still not enough, I suggest you contact your opposite number in Bilbao and try to get something more solid. You will need an interpreter, so grab one." "Excellent idea Sir, I will get on with it right away, thank you." D.I Jackson got up to leave. Ellis said, "Before you leave, there's more. I want to be kept bang up to date with any news, good or bad." He then added, "If you need extra man power let me know, and good luck Jacko. Bring me more concrete evidence and I will back you all the way." Jackson turned his back on Ellis, so that he would not see the broad grin on his face. He thought well, that went well, I may not have been awarded a cup of coffee and a biscuit, but I've definitely got the green light to put the finger on that bastard Coleman. And he didn't even ask to see the map. Later that same day, D.I. Jackson organised a twenty-four-hour watch on 119 Plenva Street code name BigWig, Jacko's pet name for Ellis. *Sooner or later, Eddie Coleman is going to come a cropper,* thought Jackson, he very nearly skipped along the corridor and back into his office, he was truly chuffed as a monkey.

CHAPTER 43

Zak's Place was choc-a-bloc, customers wall to wall. A smoke haze hung down from the nicotine'd ceiling almost to the heads of those standing. The seated customers sucked in air that was a little less foggy. Music was doing its best to be heard via the ubiquitous juke box belting out the latest number one 'Pretty Woman.' An over full ash tray sitting on top of the music box was jiggling about to the beat of Mr Orbison and his band, threatening to topple over and spill its contents on already dog-end encrusted floor boards. Since the time Johnny the Turk had started to use upstairs at Zak's as his H.Q. many a young wanabe gangster began to frequent Zak's in the hope of being invited to carry out some bad or immoral deeds. Very likely being intimidation or breaking the odd leg here or there or simply tearing up the local town centre for Johnny, in return for a few quid. For some however, just being in the same building, was equally as exciting as they would be able to tell their mates with whom they were rubbing shoulders with on a nightly basis. A few had 'Fight or go Under' tattooed on both arms and would ensure all could see them. Johnny sat upstairs at the head of an otherwise empty long rectangular table, jotting down some notes. It was time to ramp up the income and he was keen to set things in motion. The meeting this evening was to kick off at around about eight, with all the usual guys attending. Top of Johnny's list read one word- 'Protection.' He'd witnessed easy money coming in whilst working alongside Eddie at the Oasis. They'd installed and old but working safe, which on most days, was stuffed with fivers, tenners and twenty-pound notes, anywhere up to a thousand pounds or two in total. A good percentage came from protecting Errol's car- lots plus any others added in from the good work carried out by Billy and Mel, the Stratford two, who were known as the pain givers. Not a million miles from Zak's Place down in Clark Street a group of Chinese Restaurants had sprung up. *Birds of a Feather,* thought Johnny. The gathering had been christened by the locals, Chop-Chop Square. If they were not already being looked after protection wise by another crew, they soon will be, under Johnny's wing protection wise, quick as you like. And why stop there, thought Johnny, most of 'em had brothers, sisters, mums, dads, aunts and uncles running similar outfits springing up in other parts of London. It's how the Chinese win, they spread faster than a deadly virus. It seemed to Johnny, the Chinese Restaurant angle would be a good one and could bring in a fair wedge.

Next on his list up for discussion would be finding ways to increase the flow of nicked *quality* cars from the West End. This was Dave Conti's and Errol's corner of the business, Dave nickin 'em and Errol doing them up and flogging them abroad. Errol's dad Leroy the Second, was pivotal, he roamed around Europe establishing buyers for the bent motors cash only of course, and they seemed to have pots of it. As soon as deal had been struck between Leroy and a client, a message found its way back to Errol who would instruct Dave to go and nick a specific motor to order. If it was to be a Merc, then that would be the sort to be nicked. Same with a Jag, Roller or even a Porsche, nothing parked up overnight was safe, Dave was up for whatever. As soon as a target car was nicked then delivered to Errol's yard, his blokes went to town on it. When they'd finished, the original owner would not recognise it as theirs. New reg plate, different paint colour and a change of badging. All this coupled with new dummy paperwork that would definitely fool the authorities. Johnny was deep in thought when his cousin Zak stuck his head around the door. "Sorry to disturb cuz, there's a bloke downstairs, wants a quick meet with you, says his name is Mario, something about an Italian

Restaurant that needs looking after. It's well busy down there, I expect you can hear the racket, best you see 'im up here. What time you seeing your boys tonight?" Johnny looked up, took off his worn-out spectacles and raised his voice to be heard above the din coming into the room from the open door. "In about half an hour. Why?" "Well, you've time for a quick chat with 'im then aint cha?" "Yea okay, send 'im up and thanks cuz." Zak nodded closed the door then descended to the smoke-filled noisy bar area. Red Satriani stood motionless in a corner towards the end of the tiny bar. Dressed as he was, he stood out from the crowd of many. Red was always seen in suits of the finest Italian cloth. He had a good dozen or so in his wardrobe to choose from. The one he had on his back this evening, he preferred to call his executioner suit. It was tailored to conceal a hand gun sitting in a smart leather shoulder holster, perfectly. Since his recent meeting with Val and working on the known information she'd handed him back then, Red had been shadowing Johnny for the best part of a week.

The gym Johnny used would not be the best place for an execution, or out in the street, or anywhere there might be a witness or three. Besides, Mrs Coleman's instructions stated that he was to speak a sentence to his intended target prior to pulling the trigger and Red was determined that Johnny would hear it, fully understand it, and why he needed to be terminated. *'It's for blowing up the Oasis bar.'* The sentence had been well rehearsed. Climbing the stairs, Red had no idea who else would be in the room he'd been directed to alongside his intended target or, if any were actually tooled up body-guards. It wasn't a problem though; he'd taken out groups of three or four on a number of occasions, when circumstances dictated. The trick is a fast entry, gun raised and ready, kill or maim all body-guards first, quickly and efficiently, leaving todays target until last. It gave the target a real sense of impending doom. Red's weapon was equipped with a noise suppressor, its primary function being, to reduce noise and muzzle flash, secondary function, not to draw unwanted attention. The shouting, laughing and general hub-bub coming from the large crowd of drinkers in the bar that night, would more than cover any noise Red made on entry and subsequent 'suppressed' gun shots. Red barged in, gun hand outstretched levelled at Johnny, a fast scan of the room told him, this man was on his tod, perfect. "Put your hands on the table, where I can see them." he growled. Johnny complied. Red gloated at this pathetic man, face battered, no doubt from too many lost fights in the ring. Old worn-out spectacles, one lens scratched to buggery. He almost felt sorry for him. Red's usual method was to carry out any extras the client may have previously requested before the kill, then the kill. As far as Red was concerned it was just another day at the office, or in this case someone else's. Killers' instinct warned him; hesitation was nearly always fatal. He recited the sentence and let it sink in. Johnny had not moved a muscle, it looked like he was expecting the intrusion and prepared to die alone. None of the *'no, no, no please don't shoot, please, I have a wife and child'* stuff, all boggle eyed and shaking. Johnny though, didn't flinch as he watched the gun-man begin squeezing the trigger to make his gun go bang. At this range his potential killer would not miss, the gun was held rock steady in Red's hand. Johnny had been on the wrong end of a gun before and was always glad when he saw the gun waving up and down like Tower Bridge. It was a sure sign the holder would probably refrain from shooting. This one however was unwavering, unshaken, secure. He watched as the trigger finger squeezed further into the trigger. "Okay" he told himself, "This is real." He closed his eyes and waited for the inevitable.

CHAPTER 44

As the train pulled out of Bilbao station, Eddie gave Mitch a knowing look. There were indeed a fair number of military guys on the train as Mitch said there might be. Two were actually sitting opposite them. They seemed happy enough, in fatigues or battledress, ready for whatever manoeuvres the top brass had in mind. A couple of senoritas ran alongside the train, as far at the platform end, waving their loved ones' goodbye with pretty little pure white crochet hankies. 'Wonder if they will be so pure tonight' thought Mitch. Having passed the 10-mile marker with the train up to speed, most of the military guys seated up and down the train began to sing. Scattered as they were over several carriages, two in this one four in another and so on, intrigued Eddie. He leaned sideways to Mitch and enquired as to why they were so split up. "Don't they like each other or something?" "Nothing of the sort mate, we're not a million miles from Basque territory and there's always the remote possibility of an attack on trains carrying Spanish military. If a rocket was fired at the train and all the military were stuffed into one carriage and it got a direct hit. See what I mean?" Eddie's eyes widened. Mitch reassured him, "It's just a precaution, that's all, so don't even think about it." Both Mitch and Eddie, Eddie minus his hand gun, were dressed casually in the garb Mitch had chosen at the open market, back in Bilbao. Two Identical leather holdalls perched above them on the luggage rack. Eddie caught the eye of one of the military guys sitting opposite. His assault rifle stood between his knees, butt on the carriage floor, muzzle towards the ceiling. The military guy winked; Eddie simply stared back. It was as if Eddie was looking deep inside him right down to his very soul.

The winker, feeling a little uneasy under the staring gaze from Eddie, absently moved a hand down from the muzzle of his assault rifle towards the middle section, thus making it easier for him to bring his weapon up to arms height and if necessary, point it at Eddie's Head. He clocked the hand movement and was about to jump on the soldier before he could get into a threatening position. Mitch grabbed Eddie's arm in a vice like grip. He spoke very softly in an effort to take the steam out of a possible nasty incident. "Not a good idea Eddie" he whispered, there's roughly thirty of them all told and two of us. At the same time, Mitch smiled at Mr Winker and an uneasy calm temporarily descended.

The two military guys began talking to each other, unaware that Mitch could understand what they were jabbering on about. It seemed they were severely pissed off and would, if pushed further use their rifle butts to cave Eddie's face in. Obviously, Mitch did not translate entirely correctly for Eddie, which was just as well given Eddie's habit of descending into immediate kill or be killed mode. The atmosphere was electric, the military guys seemed to be working themselves up for some pre manoeuvres action, right here on the bloody train! Abruptly the spell was broken. The military guys looked over at the ticket Inspector, half smiled half saluted, then resumed their original relaxed position. Seeing the Inspector, ticket or otherwise, reminded them who and where they were. The military of course didn't need to have to pay for train tickets. So, who were they to bugger up the system by beating a fellow passenger to pulp with army issue assault rifle butts? Each and every one of them on the train had identical papers stating whatever their destination, the papers enabled free passage on the train network. The Ticket Inspector dutifully held out his hand for the appropriate paper work, as he had already done so in other carriages. The two military guys dug them out of their tunic blouses and handed them over. The Inspector scrutinised each one torturously hoping against hope there might be the tiniest mistake which would relieve his ever so boring boredom. There were none. The Inspector then turned to Mitch and Eddie. On this occasion, he didn't look directly at the two customers, he simply grabbed the tickets proffered, stamped them, handed them back and moved on. Excitement over, the train rattled on. Mitch nodded off whilst Eddie remained awake simply fascinated by the Spanish countryside viewed from his position, sat up against the large carriage window. The terrain outside gradually changed as they chugged along. Sometimes merging from lush and fertile greenery to a complete dust bowl then back to green again. It went on and on and then on a bit more, eventually, he too dozed off. The train slowed as it creaked and picked a path over several sets of points, as it negotiated the signalled route offered, to an empty waiting platform, at Burgos station. Burgos being roughly a third of the journey from Bilbao to Madrid would be a fifteen-minute stop. It was here, all the military chaps disembarked, much to the relief of Mitch. "They make me go all twitchy" he said to Eddie. "You know, there are some rocks you don't want to turn over, especially with those blokes.

Half of them want to slit your throat the other half want to fuck you. Look mate, we'll probably be here for a good twenty minutes or so, let's get on the platform and 'ave a bit of a stretch." "Had one of those recently mate when I was on remand at Pentonville" grinned Eddie, adding "don't ask."

CHAPTER 45

"Come on Esme, you're lagging behind again." Chris called out. Esme waved them on, said she wanted to take it all in. Chris and Sue had talked Esme into a day trip to the Southern Spanish City of Almeria.

They wanted Esme to see as much of La Alcazaba the awe-inspiring Moorish fortress that overlooked the city as possible. An entire day could be spent viewing all that was on offer, and there would still be more to see. As usual Chris and Sue were speeding along, it was a structure they had visited many times before and were getting just the tiniest bit wearisome of the whole thing. On the other hand, although this was not Esme's particular bag, the splendour let alone the age of the fortress caught her imagination, making her want to take in all she could. Reluctantly Chris and Sue came to a dead stop, allowing Esme to meander along towards them grinning like a Cheshire cat. "Come on Esme" Sue urged "let's get down to the town centre, there's loads of bars serving Tapas, Almeria's got something of a reputation for gastronomic delights" Esme enquired "Tapas?" "It's small portions of Spanish cuisine" Sue explained. "You can have it hot or cold, more like an appetiser really. Last time we were here, we found somewhere we've christened Tapas Alley. You can stroll, leisurely of course, from one bar to another, I reckon there must be at least ten in a row." "Any of them do burgers and chips?" Esme asked with a sly wink towards them both and said, "Okay let's go, I've had my fill of ancient architecture for today. It is stunning though and to think it's been around for a few years." "Try four hundred or so."

Chris had a thing for numbers and was inwardly pleased to impart this knowledge to Esme. But it seemed to go over the top of her head without so much as a *'How Long!'* much to his chagrin. "Thanks for bringing me here, I really love it, and will want to come back. One other thing though, I need to send a telegram home, so if either of you know of a post office in town, I'd be very grateful if you could point me in the right direction." Sue whispered in Esme's ear; "Would this be going to a certain young man called Eddie?" Esme frowned. Pretending not to hear Sue's comment, she walked on, this time taking the lead hoping she was heading in the right direction. Things turned in her favour due to Esme spying one of the few signposts in Almeria showing English first, Spanish second. It clearly directed her and her friends to Almeria's town centre. As the threesome ambled through the tangle of narrow side streets some with secret doorways to who knows where, heading towards Tapas Alley, Esme's heart began beating a little faster, in fact it missed a couple of beats. There, in a lady's fashion boutique, double glass doors wide open stood Javier with a young and beautiful senorita, draped all over him. Javier looked directly at Esme, his youthful smile, his confident stance, hips thrust forward, everything about him sent a thrill surging through her entire body. The cheeky bugger, she thought, here he is with the same young lady who entered his home on that morning the moment I was leaving, and now giving me that come on let's do it again smile. She remembered that feeling of one lover out, (her) next lover in, (senorita) but had clung to the hope that the young lady on that morning might have been his cleaner or sister perhaps. Certainly not, it would now seem. Had this senorita now hanging all over him, turned up any earlier whilst they were in bed together, what then? A show down, a cat fight? Or a simple shrug of Javier's shoulders, indicating 'I have many lovers my lover, you are just another notch on my bed post.' Esme glanced back towards the shop entrance to see Javier turn his back and disappear further into the little boutique. Thankfully, neither of her companions noticed the mini encounter, they were far too busy arguing whether to turn left or right at the next junction. It was an encounter which, in the space of nano seconds, conveyed multiple mixed messages; sneaking suspicions, green eyed jealousy of that damn senorita, his tenderness whilst in his arms, their insane fondness for one another, all spinning around inside her head.

She had not felt so excited since her first night with Eddie. This, together with the possibility of being found out she had taken Javier as a lover; how would that sit with various people? At some stage no doubt, Eddie would quite naturally in the scheme of things, meet Javier. She couldn't keep them apart for ever. They might even soon be in the same room together chatting about the villa or some such stuff. How would she feel watching them chat away knowing her secret could come tumbling out of Javier's mouth at any moment? How would she feel knowing that both men had bedded her and were now in the same room? Who would she choose if it came to making a choice? She noticed her hands were perspiring, if it was observed by Chris or Sue, she would put it down to the sultry airless weather. Esme had to let it pass, Sue was already asking questions about Eddie, who was he? Was he, her man? What does he look like? When will he be around? Is he great between the sheets? 'Christ' thought Esme what have I gotten myself into? If only I could talk it over with Gwen. *To Esme, her mum had always been Gwen,* she'd have known what to do, she always did. Fancy popping her clogs at fifty-two, that's no bloody age. Chris called out "Here we are Esme, Tapas Alley which one do you fancy then girl?" Before she could answer, Chris who now had hold of her left wrist was guiding her into the first bar. She noticed his hand was sweaty too. The sign above the Tapas Bar door read Bienvenido a Casa Lucio. Esme followed Chris down a badly lit tight little twisty wooden staircase with Sue bringing up the rear. The seating area boasted around twelve tables and the lighting was not much better than that illuminating the staircase. Connie Francis was belting out beso de fuego *Kiss of Fire* as they were ushered by a waiting waiter to a table for three. All other seats were taken bar a few bar stools over at the bar. Sue smiled at Esme and mouthed above the din "time to eat." Esme mouthed back "my shout, don't want you out of pocket."

CHAPTER 46

Red Satriani is the front man of London's East End operation, effectively controlled from the head office in Palermo Sicily, overlooking the Tyrrhenian Sea. The Italian based headquarters enjoyed a beautiful view out to the Med however, due to a broken and unrepaired sewer pipe in the street below it was more like rooms with a phew. The business cover name being 'Exclusive Vermin Control.' His extended family in Sicily were particularly proud of Red's achievements in London. On instructions from highly valued English clients, Red had chalked up somewhere in the region of seventeen executions over the last three years. The format is quite simple. Clean, tidy and no evidence for the Metropolitan Police to discover, then to follow up. Bodies disposed of without fear of being discovered at some later date. Reputation for his organisation regarding quality and class is not up for question and therefore extremely expensive. Targets who needed to die simply became listed as missing. Clients in London plus surrounding suburbs who required person or persons dead with absolutely no come back, benefited from the vast experience of Red Satriani and his extended family. The business and its varying range of product lines was sold to potential clients as the 'White Glove Service,' with gold star quality assured. The huge up-front fee, usually many thousands of pounds was, as in business transactions other than simply killing people, topped up with extras. For example, a client may require a part of the deceased body as *proof of death*. More commonly known as P.O.D. So, add forty percent. The client may request whoever they want liquidated, to die in a particular way. Add another twenty five percent. Or, they may ask the assassin to convey a message, as in 'That's the last time you interfere with my wife' and then be killed. Add on a further ten percent and so on. All part of the 'White Glove' premium service which was not, as it happens, short of interested potential clients. It was a growing business and Red Satriani was constantly on the lookout for consultants to join the company. Consultants were, just that consultants, nothing more, nothing less. Their main task being simply to act as a conduit between new and potential clients and Red himself. He was the only one who carried out the kill, him and him alone, unless Red *wanted* to be known, would remain unknown to the client. The position of consultant attracted very little in the way of perks. No holiday entitlement, no sick pay or any other of the usual employment benefits such as expenses or company car.

Income consisted of cash in hand plus a percentage of any extras sold, all usually paid three months after the confirmed death. Consultancy work within this micro private underworld organisation was a decidedly dicey business. Any whiff of moonlighting, that is, a consultant carrying out a kill then pocketing the entire fee could be fatal, especially if discovered by Red Satriani. When, and if discovered, Red would end the consultant's employment then and there as in instant dismissal. The consultant's body thence to be dumped in a reservoir somewhere up in the North of England – end of employment. This had happened just the once, therefore Red needed to be ultra-careful as to whom he offered these positions to. Meanwhile, Johnny watched as pressure previously applied to the trigger eased forward. *He's not going to shoot*, he reckoned. Quick as a flash Johnny jumped up and rammed his forehead directly against the silencer whilst keeping a steady gaze straight into Red's unblinking eyes. Was this going to be a Mexican stand-off, who would backdown first? If Johnny instigated aggression, might he trigger his own demise? It was worth it, he judged. Time was now very much at a standstill while both men glared at one another, neither intending to be the first to yield. This current situation was somewhat afresh to Johnny's would be assassin. His trigger finger seemed to be acting like a naughty child, it would not obey the command sent from his brain, reluctant to do as his bidding. Here was Johnny's life hanging by a spider's thread and still the bullet was not fired. Red Satriani actually lowered his gun slowly, very slowly, until it was in line with Johnny's heart. He punched the weapon forward, forcing Johnny to fall back into his chair, the stand-off appeared to be temporarily postponed. Red holstered his gun and was just about to open his mouth to speak when Johnny went up the wall. "You bastard, you come in 'ere intending to top me." He then started throwing punches, it wasn't until Red was on the floor battered and blooded that Johnny ceased the attack. Johnny sat on the downed man and felt for his shooter. Red Satriani shrugged Johnny off, stood gingerly, uneasily to a standing position to find his own gun pointing at him, hammer pulled back ready to go bang, Johnny's finger now gently squeezing the trigger. Red held up one hand above his head, the other hand slid unhurriedly behind him, his long bony fingers searching for his back up weapon. Johnny observed the movement, but his face remained deadpan.

Fearing the Italian guy had another weapon tucked in his waistband at the small of his back, Johnny aimed for Red's heart and pulled the trigger, the recoil took Johnny by surprise, the shot just nicking the top of Red's left shoulder. Seconds passed before either man reacted. Zak, having heard what he thought was a gun being fired, raced up the stairs and barged into the room. Red was still standing, face pummelled and bloodied, one hand clasping his shoulder, the other still behind his back. Zak looked at his cousin sitting not too far away from Red, holding a smoking gun. Johnny spoke to Red. "You'll need to get up very early in the morning to get one over on me Pal." He turned to Zak "Check him over mate, I think he's got another shooter tucked away, pat him down just in case eh!"

Zak looked at Johnny again who was waving the gun in Red's direction. "Don't worry cuz, I've already nicked him, so he knows not to be stupid. Zak did as he was asked and began to search Red for anything, anything he might suddenly surprise everybody with. He produced a stiletto flick knife, the handle lovingly crafted from buffalo horn. Zak pushed the little button at the top of the handle and the blade sprang forward ready to cut, slash or simply be buried deep into someone's heart. Zak retracted the blade back into the handle. "You're a dark horse Zak," Johnny chortled. "Where did you get to handle a blade so expertly?" Zak grinned and threw the closed knife on the table at the same time as making for the door. "Leaving already cuz?" "Yea sorry Johnny, there's someone being a bit mouthy downstairs and I was just about to sling him out on the pavement when I heard the shot, anyway looks like you got it all under control." Johnny called out, "when the blokes turn up, get them to stay downstairs for a bit, I want to have a chat with this geezer." "Yep okay" came the reply. The room was quiet again. Johnny indicated his would-be adversary to sit, which he did somewhat uncomfortably. The wound on his shoulder was weeping, more blood was trickling down his face from an open wound above his right eye. Johnny stiffened as Red put his free hand inside his jacket. *Had Zak missed something?* Johnny relaxed as the hand reappeared with a starched white handkerchief which Red folded into a pad then tucked it up inside his jacket sitting it firmly on his flesh wound caused by the shot. His extended family would be most disappointed especially if they knew of his current predicament. Seventeen or so successful kills to date, but this one; a total fuck up, in fact, utterly shambolic. He needed to sort things, needed to salvage something out of this sorry state of affairs. He eyed his stiletto flick-knife there on the table in front of him, it was easily within arms-reach, could he grab it, flick out the blade and plunge it into this man's heart before he got a second shot off.

He didn't think so, Johnny the Turk would not miss this time, no he would be prepared for the guns extra recoil. At this precise moment, Johnny held all the aces. Red decided against the 'leap up and stab him strategy.' Johnny jumped up and walked behind the seated Red, pushed the loaded gun hard into the back of Red Satriani's head just above the neck line and just below the base of his skull, then informed him, "You've been well out of order my son. I'm going to kill you tonight, but not until I find out who the fuck sent you."

CHAPTER 47

Metal wheels screeched, rumbled and complained as the train lurched slowly away from the station. Soon Burgos and the soldiers who disembarked en masse would be far behind them. The last thing Eddie saw, glancing out of the window, was a sign which informed him they were heading in the direction of Madrid. Mitch explained it was a longish journey, so might be best to get their heads down for a bit of a kip. The empty seats opposite gave them room to stretch out. Putting one's feet up on empty seats was frowned upon in general throughout public transport across Spain, so, when in Espanola, do as the Spanish do. However, these two being English adopted the English style and stuck their feet up on the empties, desert boots and all. The train now on a straight through to Madrid meant no more stops and no more passengers to pick up plus, the ticket guy had done his rounds already, so what's the problem with having their feet up? Mitch had been right about the time the train had stopped at Burgos almost exactly to the minute. Eddie was now wishing he had the good sense to have visited the gent's back on the Burgos platform. Mitch was busily rummaging through his holdall and let out a yelp of satisfaction when his searching hand came into contact with a silver object. Eddie thought a rabbit was about to appear, instead it was a hip flask. Smaller than the average flask and no doubt full to the brim with liquor. Mitch took a long swig, offered it to Eddie, suggesting he do the same. "A night cap" he said. "Help us kip down for a few hours or so." Eddie was curious, he wanted to cast and eye over the flask before taking a swig, had a desire to study it, especially the enamel badge slap in the middle. The body of the flask was ever so slightly curved and it felt comfortable as he swopped it from hand to hand. On closer inspection, the badge had a vertical winged dagger with the words 'Who Dares Wins" etched in a scroll through which the dagger passed. He looked at Mitch puzzled.

"It's a trinket from my army days," Mitch offered. "Anyway, drink up, it's a nice drop of twelve-year-old blended Scotch whisky in there, should warm the cockles of your bloody ice-cold heart!" Eddie let it pass, well it was a sort of compliment, wasn't it? Both men knew precisely what Mitch was referring to and they laughed energetically. A couple of swigs each later, Mitch slumped his head forward, chin on his chest and began snoring gently. Eddie decided to keep awake; if it were possible. Mitch might have been a traveller courtesy of the army, however Eddie had not. He wanted to take in all the sights and sounds. He was like a kid with a new toy at Christmas, nestling amongst the Brazil nuts, an orange, some chocolate pennies wrapped in gold foil and whatever else his parents could afford to put in his Christmas stocking. The train had settled to a steady speed, the land it was traversing at this point of the journey was reasonably flat with not much to write home about on the other side of the carriage window. The rhythmic beat of the wheels hitting the track joints was far better for inducing sleep than counting sheep, before long the blended whisky and the trains rhythm moved Eddie's eyelids to droop mode. Gradually he succumbed and was soon in the land of nod too, the rhythm and the whisky gaining the upper hand. However, sometimes sleep was when Eddie's personal devil took over. His unique nightmare took the shape of him needing to be somewhere although he never quite found out whereabouts. He regularly found himself walking alone through the darkened streets of East London, a place he knew well. It started with him hurrying along the East India Dock Road, all well and good he thought, this is home turf, what could go wrong? He would turn left at the next corner and was then immediately lost in totally unfamiliar surroundings. He would turn back; but was unable to find his bearings. Each time he caught the time from a clock high up on a church steeple, another hour had passed. After walking unknown and unfamiliar streets for what seemed like ages, he would find himself back where he originally started. It was now when rain began to fall heavily, oddly though, he remained dry. The rain however turned the road into deep energy sucking mud. As he walked his feet sank lower and lower into the mud. His leg muscles starting to scream with the effort of trying to move. Exhausted and now stationary, unable to go forward unable to go back, ghoulish faces would rise up from the mud and slime, faces he recognised. First it was Wossname, poor Wossname, slashed to death by the razor gang, then one by one the faces of people he had ordered his crew to kill.

The most hideous of them looking directly at him with mocking grins, would be those he had executed himself, and of course left his mark in the shape of a noughts and cross symbol. But this time the symbol had been carved in miniature on each eyeball instead of the victim's upper back. It was against this grim backdrop that Eddie awoke. Slowly he opened his eyes. Dazzling late afternoon sunshine pushed its way through the grimy train window on to his face. His nightmare a distant history once more. Grabbing Mitch's wrist, he positioned his watch in front of his eyes, it was four thirty pm. The pair had been on the train for the best part of six hours, Mitch having slept through most of them, he a little less. Madrid station, where the train now stood, was just about halfway to their desired destination and for them, Madrid was a switch over to yet another train that should take them to the Port of Almeria. From there it will be a hop, skip and a jump preferably by way of a local taxi firm, that would whisk him to Villa Hermosa Vista somewhere close to Mojácar and the waiting arms of Esme. To Eddie's mind, he and Mitch would be parting company once they reached Almeria. There was no way he wanted to introduce Mitch to Esme no way, or anyone else locally for that matter. He certainly didn't want Esme to know of his involvement with the killing of José, his son and that boat owner back in Bilbao. Not only that, but with Mitch hanging around the Villa what if Esme took a shine to him? He'd have to kill him too!" Eddie tried hard to remember that which was agreed when he and Mitch planned this journey over lunch at the El Pirata Cantina in the Market Square Bilbao. His thoughts took him only as far as getting off the train at Port Almeria, nothing onward from there. Not wishing to have a bull and cow with Mitch at this precise moment he decided he'd front him out when they were well on their way to Almeria.

CHAPTER 48

Chief Insp. Ellis slammed the phone down so hard it rocked his oversized desk. He bawled out, "and good bloody day to you too Sir." His secretary on hearing the commotion, popped her head around his office door. She could see her boss was fuming, his face almost purple. "Anything I can help you with Sir?" she asked meekly. "Yes, get Jackson up here today, not tomorrow, today"

"Yes Sir, of course Sir, but it is Friday and it's five thirty, do you not think he may have gone home for the weekend?" "I don't care if he's gone to Timbuctoo, bloody well get traffic to find him and bring him back. All *they* ever seem to do is sit around in their cars nice and cosy, drinking something or other from a thermos, give 'em a proper job to do." "Yes, Sir right away."

Mrs. Meek gently closed the door behind her, at the same time Ellis reached into the bottom left-hand drawer of his desk for something a little stronger than the remnants of the cup of cold tea sat on his desk. He drank directly from the neck of a bottle of Gin. He swallowed a large mouthful and grimaced as the alcohol hit the back of his throat. "Christ, no wonder they call it mothers ruin, bloody awful stuff. I wish that lot out there would buy me something different at Christmas just for once. Gin, gin, gin always damn gin. Just because I stupidly said I enjoy the odd Gin and Tonic now and then. I wouldn't mind, but they never ever buy the tonic to go with it." His face had now coloured down a notch to a slightly lesser shade of purple when Mrs. Meek tapped on the door asking to be let in. Ellis, thinking it was Jackson, shouted "COME" at the top of his voice. His secretary stepped back from his office door, alarmed at the ferocity of the command. Before entering, she straitened her hair, straightened her dress, her composure and straightened her back. "He's on his way Sir, Detective Inspector Jackson was less than a mile from the station, when he was picked up by a mobile unit. They radioed in an E.T.A. of approximately six thirty Sir. Apparently, they have hit *'going home'* traffic." Ellis purpled up again. "God give me strength; I have to get back to the Chief Constable by six tonight. He's buggering off to an opera soon and wants an appraisal as to the whereabouts of that bloody Coleman character before he goes to pre opera drinkies. Tell the mobile unit to turn on the siren or bells or whatever they need to turn on and get back here post haste." Mrs Meek disappeared down to the control room and asked for the message to be passed on. Ellis heard the mobile unit screech into the police car park, narrowly missing Ellis's mode of transport afforded to him courtesy of his rank, a Ford Zodiac Mark 3. Ellis counted down the minutes, how fucking long does it take to get from the car park to my office? More minutes went by. The purple rage was returning, Ellis eyed the Gin bottle sat on his desk commanding him to drink a little more, but instead of downing another mouthful he shoved it out of sight. Jacko might think it was on the desk for a celebration. Two minutes more passed and Ellis was about to blow a number of fuses, when Detective Insp. Jackson knocked loudly and entered. "Sorry for the delay Sir I was taken short and needed the men's room." Ellis stood up and walked over to stand by the door.

He placed his back to the door to prevent anyone from entering, although, he thought his secretary had probably gone from the building by now. Moreover, he stood by the door to prevent Jackson from even thinking about leaving. It had taken Ellis the best part of an hour to get him here and he was not about to let him go, just like that. "Any news on the Coleman case, or should I say chase?" "None whatsoever Sir, I am awaiting information from my opposite number in Bilbao."

Ellis breathed heavily, "Nothing, nothing?"

We've got a crazed psychopathic killer who scribes his fucking logo on his victims with a knife surgical or otherwise, it's positively bone chilling, plus he's on the run from us." Jackson nodded solemnly as if being sentenced to death by a judge wearing a black square of fabric on top of his peruke. Ellis continued his diatribe. "Yes, that's one Jacko, you may well nod in that fashion. The one we let slip through our hands on his way to the Assizes in Oxford basically sticking his two bloody fingers up at us in the process. Apparently under an assumed name he murders an innocent yacht owner and Interpol get jumpy. They keep us appraised of the situ and it falls in your lap. Yes, that would be you, the one man who would give his high teeth to bring Coleman in, and you stand there and say nothing! I've a bloody good mind to swop your duties and put you on zebra crossing patrol. And what the hell were you doing going home at this time of day? The last time we met I made it clear that I would back you to the hilt, and you said you would work tirelessly, not slink off at five. How many times have you done that I wonder? Just bring me something concrete I said, anything, anything, but not nothing. What have you to say for yourself then Jackson?" "Well Sir, I'm not exactly cock-a-hoop about it myself." Jackson looked at Ellis who right now, resembled Jacko's wife at the time she was giving birth to their son, red faced, screaming obscenities, howling at Jacko to keep his smelly thing in his smelly pants in future. "Never again, never again" she wailed, but of course they did.

CHAPTER 49

"If you might be good enough to remove *my* gun from the back of *my* head, I might be in a better position to speak to you, until then I will remain silent." Johnny made no attempt to reply, instead he pushed the gun even harder into Red's skull and thumbed back the hammer. The weapon was now at the ready position, ready to pulverise Red's brain into mincemeat.

With his free hand, he reached over to the flick knife, released the blade and stuck it down into Red's already wounded shoulder. Red groaned loudly, but the pain was not so bad, he'd endured far worse. "You *will* talk you fucker and you *will* tell me who wants me dead. What was it you said a while back? Something about the Oasis being blown up? Johnny pushed the blade in a little further. Something stopped its downward movement, must have hit bone. This time Red yelled, mostly to control the pain, yelling can sometimes make it less severe. They both heard heavy footsteps climbing the stairs up from the bar. Johnny eased the hammer forward, whoever it was coming up stairs he didn't want Red to use the disturbance by jumping up, grabbing the gun and pointing it at him, or the coming visitor. Bomber Brown completely unaware of what was occurring, in his usual blundering way, threw the door open which hit the wall with a resounding bang and stood motionless wondering what the hell he'd stumbled in to. He was supposed to be here for a meet up with Johnny and the boys. "What the fuck's going on 'ere then eh?" he called out. Johnny glared at Bomber. "Stop acting the fucking maggot Bomber, it should be more than clear to you, me and this geezer are discussing the colour scheme for our meeting-room 'aint we?" "Oh, okay well, if you want my opinion, I'd go for magnolia." Bomber Brown was now very confused; he could clearly see the gun Johnny was holding to the back of *this geezer's* neck plus there was a wicked looking blade sticking out from his shoulder. Surely, he wasn't *really* a painter and decorator, was he? Ignoring Bomber's bewilderment, Johnny continued with his quest to get at the truth. "Last time pal," he snarled menacingly, "who sent you, who is it that wants me dead, and how much were they gonna pay you?" Bomber began lurching forward, the penny dropped, this geezer was trouble and he, Bomber, wanted to show Johnny who's side he was on. Red did indeed use the disturbance to make his move, unfortunately for him though, Johnny had anticipated his bid for freedom and crashed the gun down on the top of his skull, sending Red sprawling to the floor. As he fell, he cracked the side of his head hard, on the edge of the huge meeting table which was a very unforgiving table. The sharp crack resonated around the room, both he and Bomber stood looking down at Red, now motionless as blood seeped from the downed man's head towards where they were standing. Bomber kicked him hard twice in the chest, aimed purposely to connect with and break some ribs; no movement from Red "I reckon he's out cold Johnny, didn't half crack his head on his way down like didn't he" Johnny wasn't so sure. He grabbed the blade which had found its way to the floor beside Red and wiped the blood off on his Jacket.

"Jesus Johnny, you 'aint gonna do what Eddie does and carve a sign on his back or something are you?" Johnny didn't answer, instead he knelt down beside Red and placed part of the shiny silver blade directly under his nose and waited, he let a minute pass. The blade showed no sign of misting up. He's fucking brown bread Bomber, dead as a door nail. He was here to kill me, someone called a contract on me for Christ's sake, now I'm gonna have to find out who, by other means. Nip down and get Zak up here mate, I need to ask him a few questions, then stay down at the bar and keep the bloke's downstairs but tell them what's happened." While Bomber disappeared to find Zak, Johnny went through Red Satriani's pockets searching for clues as to who he was and where he came from. Zak appeared, "Bloody 'ell cuz was that absolutely necessary? When I left you, you had a gun pointing at him and his stiletto was on the table. What happened? If he's a goner, that's the second body you've handed to me and you've only been using this room for a week or so. It aint going to do my business any good if I keep having to cart cadavers off to Epping Forest. Who the bloody hell is he anyway?" Red's wallet was in Johnny's hand an extremely smart one it was to; he opened it and drew out a posh looking business card "Say's here his names Red Satriani and runs a company that deals in 'Exclusive Vermin Control' by the looks of it. "Does that mean I'm exclusive Zak? Look, there's a phone number on it." He gave the card to Zak for him to take a look. "I'll go and ring the number now." "No not just yet, he was sent here to kill me and I want to find out who the hell sent him." Zak's eye brows shot up. "Well, he picked on the wrong bloke there then, that's for sure." Johnny's meeting room began to fill with the stench of death. Satriani's blood pool appeared to be ever increasing, before long it would seep in between the cracks in the bare floorboards and start to drip down on to Zak's customers in the bar area below. Zak asked, "Does your lot have to be so bloody brutal?" Johnny looked over at Zak with a sideways glance. "Listen Zak up till now you didn't know too much about me, or what I do. Thing is when your life is based on taking whatever it is you want by force, unfortunately like this geezer here, people get in the way and need to be dealt with. In my world it's kill, or be killed." "Right then, I'll 'ave it away with the mixer, shoot downstairs and grab some bar towels and chuck them 'em up to you. You and Bomber clean up as best you can, the geezer will have to do an overnight up here. There's no way I'm disturbing the peace and quiet downstairs by lugging a dead'n out to the back yard right under the customer's noses."

Johnny asked, "have you got something we can roll 'im up in, you know, an old carpet or something?" "As it 'appens I've got a lock up not far from here with some old tarpaulin lying about. It's well tatty, but it should do the trick." "Thanks Zak, really appreciate that." "That's okay Johnny no worries." He smiled back at his distant cousin and said, "Look, can you stop throwing your weight about and can we have a cadaver moratorium, of say about two years?" "Whatever you say Cuz, just for the record I didn't kill 'im God's my witness, Bomber will back me up. It was the table that did it for him, cracked his head wide open he did, on his way down." Zak did an eyebrow flash and grinned, "what made him hit the deck then I wonder?" Johnny grinned back, "well, just a tiny bit of persuasion on my behalf. I'll hang on to the shooter and knife, I doubt they're traceable, both look like they're imported, probably illegally."

CHAPTER 50

Esme jumped out of her skin at the sound of loud banging, squinting at her bedside clock it informed her it was ten after two in the morning. For a split second she thought it was actually in her head, courtesy of the wine and spirits guzzled earlier before retiring. During the short time she'd moved in, she'd started to do a little decorating. Just a few of the rooms though, the most recent one being the room she was currently sleeping in. Her thoughts as the banging continued turned toward the smell of fresh paint, maybe it was this that was making her head bang so much, that and the alcohol. As the mist and fudginess in her brain began to clear, she realized it was neither, it was most definitely coming from the front door. Courtesy of her police training in the Met, Esme was not one to fear for her life in just this sort of circumstance. She was trained to advance to danger and had learned skills on how to quell dangerous situations. She was however, far, far from the Met without a likewise suitably trained officer around to back her up. The hammering continued and, if anything, it became more rapid almost to a frenzy by the second. Donning her dressing gown and tying the belt tightly, Esme made her way along the hall towards the door, currently rattling on its hinges. She remembered it being a substantially constructed entrance door, definitely not liable to cave in, unless rammed by a raging bull. And of course, this hopefully was no raging bull.

She also remembered the Villa was blessed with garden and porch lighting, controlled by a switch located close to the front door. Esme reached out threw the switch, immediately illuminating the entire front garden, porch area and the whole frontage afforded to the villa. If nothing else, it will give the moths something to home in on and any bats that may be zooming about can home in on the moths. "Lunch is on me" whispered Esme to the swooping swishing brown long eared bats. The hammering stopped, the silence deafening, Esme put an ear to the door hoping to gauge who and how many were on the other side. It couldn't possibly have been Chris or Sue, they would have called out her name by now, or at least identified themselves. Same for Eddie, if it *was* Eddie standing on the other side and couldn't get in, he'd be screaming her name at the top of his voice. That left very few people to come to mind and this disturbed her. Who would want to visit her at almost dawn but not make themselves known to her? Calling the local police was way out of the question, If Eddie found out the bloody filth had had their noses in the villa, he'd go spare. She wished she had a side window which looked out onto the porch area so she could at least see who was on the other side. Esme pressed her ear ever closer to the door, was that heavy breathing she could hear? It sounded like someone had been out running and was now partially out of breath. Next, she heard a thump, a heavy bag or some sort of case being dropped onto the front door step followed by a sigh, a long deep audible breath expressing sadness, then the sound of a body flopping down as if to sit things out until dawn. Curiosity had now got the better of Esme, if there *was* just a single, unknown person on the other side of the door and *if* she opened the door and *was* attacked, (1) she would need a weapon and (2), she would need to figure out an element of surprise. Up until now, whoever was outside, could well be thinking 'Ah well there's no one home.' As it happens Esme had not turned any lights on *inside* the villa, the porch lights now illuminating the front of the villa could well have been triggered by a timing device. Esme reached over to the switch, gently easing it to the off position, the outside returning to darkness. She heard another resounding sigh and not just from the hungry bats. Esme tippy toed back up the hall, this time away from her bedroom, toward the kitchen heading for the patio door. On the way through the kitchen area, she grabbed the bread knife from its personal slot in a neat looking block of wood, ignoring the other five knives, the bread knife being the most menacing. The patio door slid open silently, she was now out of the villa and on the patio.

Night time sounds greeted her, many Grillos were in full song, chirping away hunting for a mate to mate with or food or something to drink, or perhaps all three. Soft bubbling noises came from the pool via the filtration unit gently pushing filtered water up to the surface. Waves could be heard in the distance lapping gently upon the deserted moonlit beach down below. Any other time, Esme would have grabbed a drink sat down on one of the sun loungers and sat quietly listening to the sounds of the night. Knife in hand, Esme's plan was to creep around the side of the villa until she was in a position to see who the hell it might be that she needed to confront. Edging along the side her back close to the wall, she rounded the final corner and for a few moments stood deathly still. Craning her head forward then her eyes, she saw the figure of a man laying full stretch on the front door step, his head propped up by a holdall of some kind as a makeshift pillow. To her complete surprise whoever it was had fallen asleep and was now gently snoring. "Cheeky bugger" she almost shouted. "Frightens the life out of me, gets me out of bed at two fucking thirty, almost bangs the door down then has the bloody front to nod off." Sensing no imminent danger from this stranger, she crossed the final few yards in seconds, knife at the ready to warn him off in case he jumped up and grabbed her. Still no movement, the snoring if anything grew louder, indicating he was slipping into a deep sleep. This allowed Esme the ability to give him the once over. He looked about thirtyish, clean shaven, relatively well dressed in an outdoorsy rugged sort of way. Quite the handsome chap actually again, in an outdoorsy rugged sort of way. She decided against having a poke around his jacket pockets for any clues, instead Esme started to sing, well just hum to begin with, it was a trick she'd learnt from a big burly retiring Sergeant whilst working in the Met. This Sergeant was big enough and ugly enough, given the same set of circumstances that Esme found herself in now, to pick this bloke up and slam him in a police van in a matter of seconds. The trick had helped him over the years to quell many a vagrant or villain alike, so Esme gave it a try. She increased the volume and added just a few words here and there, it was beginning to take the shape of Hey Jude and she hoped this handsome stranger would wake up before she got to the crescendo type ending. At last, her singing brought him from deep to light sleep then to a gentle awakening. His eyes flickered open, Esme switched from Miss Nice Lady to Miss Bastard Lady, it was now she needed to have complete control over this stranger.

"Think of moving pal and you will be well fucking sorry." Esme donned her vicious look at the same time as holding the knife close to his temple. The stranger spoke, softly and directly to her sneering face "you must be Esme then, boy have I got a tale to tell you, my girl."

CHAPTER 51

D.I. Jackson was severely pissed off, Chief Inspector Ellis had torn into him and as far as Jackson was concerned the tirade had been totally unprofessional and completely unnecessary. For more than a fleeting moment, he considered topping himself, then for more than a fleeting moment more, he considered committing murder, in the end he decided to do neither but to talk it over with his Superintendent. Of course, this would be something of a bold move, once the ball was rolling so to speak it would create huge bow waves throughout the entire station. Time had dragged on; it was now passed seven in the evening. Jackson rang his wife Janey to explain he wouldn't be long now, just a bit of paperwork to follow up then he would be home for supper. Janey hoped her minutes silence conveyed her annoyance at needing to put the evening meal on hold yet again. He couldn't have been more right about his paperwork comment. Upon reaching his office he'd spotted a folder which had been placed on his previously cleared desk. Must have appeared he thought, while he was upstairs with the Chief Inspector, getting a right old bollocking. He pulled his shirt cuff back to reveal his watch; it was according to the big hand, creeping towards seven thirty. If he scanned through the folder and it contained something that needed a reaction, he might still be at the station passed eight o'clock so, he wouldn't be home until eight thirty. This would mean his supper could well be in the dog by then, or in the bin or probably both, plus Mrs. Janey Jackson might give him the silent treatment for the rest of the evening! For the first time in his police career, he chose home life over police life. "Fuck it, this can wait till Monday." Without even the tiniest of peeks inside the folder, he put it in a wire tray marked **TBDW** *'to be dealt with'* perched precariously on the windowsill. If he had peeked, he would have found a fair bit of information from his opposite number in Bilbao, exactly the information that would have headed Ellis off at the pass and might have resulted in a more amicable meeting. So, for the second time that Friday evening, Jackson left the building on a second journey home. This time he jumped on a bus, 'let's see if they can fetch me back to the station this time' he thought rather smugly.

CHAPTER 52

"Bloody nigh had his collar felt he did that Jack Du Pré bloke, you know had a tug, nicked by the Spanish Polícia you know the old Bill, it means Eddie, that's his middle name I think, is free." "I know all the jargon matey, I was a police officer once, it's how Eddie and me met." Mitch was talking rapidly, the knife to his temple, the pointy bit beginning to sink into his skin a little deeper causing blood to dribble down his cheek. The whole affair was making him gibber most gibberishly. Mitch had been in many life-or-death situations during his army career; however, this was a calm and confident lady on the handle end of a knife already drawing blood. It was infinitely scarier than facing a bunch of freedom fighters armed with AK-47 assault rifles. "Yea Eddie's free, free as a dicky bird, he's holed up over in that old Moorish City Almeria and wants to keep his head down for a while." At the sound of Eddie's name, Esme eased off the pressure on the stranger's temple by a couple of notches. Was this some kind of trap? Should she be wary? Should she stab him deep in the eye and run back indoors? Mitch sensed what was going through her mind. "Look Esme, before you do anything hasty, what I've just told you is the truth, kosher, all above board, true, cross my heart, how else would I know your name and where you live?" Esme eyed him suspiciously, uncertainty swirled around her mind; there was something in what he said though, could he have known Eddie in some way? Might he be on the level? And who in hell was this du Pré bloke when he was at home anyway? Her choices were, stab him but that would make a mess and if she pushed the blade far enough in his eye socket, he might die and she then would be none the wiser as to who he is. Or should she give him the benefit of the doubt and let him in? Perhaps she could keep him sitting where he sat and start screaming for Chris and Sue. In the end her mind was made up for her, Mitch produced a scruffy bit of lined paper with little torn holes across the top, torn from a wire bound A5 reporter's notebook. He handed it to her waving it back and forth as if it were a white flag of surrender, Esme pulled back the carving knife a little, it was now several inches away from Mitch's face. He visibly relaxed and began standing up. "Not yet matey stay where you are, or this knife will be rammed in your eye." Esme read the words written on the piece of paper.

"Esme, listen to this bloke's story. He's called Mitch and he got me out of a major scrape a few days ago in a place called Bilbao. He's on the level you need to take him in and both keep doggo for a while."

The note was unsigned. "Can I stand up now Esme only I've got a gammy leg courtesy of standing too close to and exploding grenade and if I lay like this for too long on a hard surface like, it brings on the pain chronic like. "Have you read this note?" she asked, "Yea course I did, have a look on the back it's got this address written on it. Apparently, he got your address from his Mum Val via a telegram, said you and Val have been bouncing messages backwards and forwards." The knife fell from Esme's hand to the floor, quite close to where Mitch was still sitting. He didn't make a move to snatch it spring up and hold it to Esme's throat, instead gammy leg or not he kicked it away onto the lawn. "Right then Mitch person, get yourself up, grab your stuff and follow me." After traversing the villa and reaching the open patio door, Esme pointed for him to step inside then followed him into the kitchen area. "I suppose a brew and something to eat is out of the question? only I'm a bit parched and my tummy's a bit tumbley grumbly." Esme put some lights on, slid the patio door shut and threw the lock. Still feeling a tad uneasy she said to herself, '*Esme my girl it's gonna be shit or bust now, we're both locked inside so I really do hope my instincts don't let me down. C'est la vie.'* "Okay sunshine, let's hear the story."

CHAPTER 53

"It goes a bit like this." Mitch started at the beginning, how he had witnessed from his apartment, Eddie being followed up late one night in down-town Bilbao by a couple of ugly looking bandits out to rob him, and how Eddie turned on them and laid them both out. He explained that he hid Eddie from a much larger bunch of Spanish bandidos, out for his blood. He said the two Eddie flattened were part of a fanatical gang headed up by a known blood thirsty killer by the name of José. It was later discovered that it was he, José, that sent his gang to return and search for Eddie mob handed, with blood very much on the menu. They wanted to slice him up good and proper. He explained how he and Eddie managed to evade the mob by lying low in Mitch's apartment until the mob got fed up and fucked off back to their hideout.

The next morning Eddie explained he wanted to get to somewhere down South and meet up with you. We discussed it over breakfast and because José and his bunch of bandits would no doubt be on the lookout for us, we would do the trip from Bilbao to the South together, no need for me to stay put and possibly get topped myself. As soon as we got to Almeria, I was to return to Bilbao hoping that José had forgotten about me and moved onto other things. Mitch broke off for a swig of tea and a bite of a cheese sandwich. He went on, he explained to Eddie that he, Mitch, had a long-standing grievance with José. After explaining the grievance in detail there was no stopping him. Eddie wanted to return the favour and fast, so before leaving Bilbao we murdered José then shot up his gang of bandidos *inside* a cantina, their favoured drinking hole. Unfortunately, the barman got shot too, but that wasn't us, it was José that did for him. Mitch looked at Esme expecting some sort of reaction, but not so much as an eyebrow lift, all this time she had been nodding sagely. He told her about how they travelled across Spain's interior mostly by train with an overnight stay in Madrid. It was in Madrid that Eddie sent a telegram to his mum Val asking her to let you know he was on his way. The next morning a reply was waiting for him in the los Correos confirming your address but didn't say if she'd informed you. "So where does the name Jack du Pré come into it?" asked Esme. Mitch pointed out that at first, he was confused by this too. Apparently, he'd met up with someone in Jersey just off the coast of mainland England, called Freddy the Forger of all things! This guy was an expert in forging passports and new identities, overnight Eddie became Jack de Pré. He'd gone from a red head *his words not mine* to brown and walked around with heavy black framed glasses halfway down his nose, made his eyes look a bit distorted, a dead ringer for the young Michael Caine he reckoned. Eddie told me he was something big back in the East End and was determined to return there as and when the man hunt in England cooled down then take up where he left off. He didn't reveal too much about what he got up to in London, and, as it's none of my business, I didn't like to ask." Esme went about making a third brew for them both and a second sandwich for Mitch. All this information falling out of Mitch's mouth was a great deal to take in especially the going back to London bit. That had really thrown her. Pottering about in the kitchen at five in the morning however tired she was, offered her a little time to let things sink in. "Have you got any idea how he managed to get to Spain" she asked with her back to Mitch.

She asked whilst watching the birth of yet another day, to what some would call a stunning view, a shimmering azure blue Mediterranean Sea. "Well apparently, Eddie hitched a ride on some guy's yacht and paid for the crossing with a dummy Rolex, you know the type you can buy down Pettycoat Lane market in Aldgate, next door to Danny's Café. There's a bloke there who knocks them out for ten bob a throw. Some say, you couldn't tell the difference. Anyway, sorry Esme, I'm digressing, hope it doesn't make you homesick? You know, hearing about your old haunts." "It would have been genuine Mitch, Eddie doesn't frequent Petticoat Lane if he can help it. Just get on with it." Esme hissed. Mitch slurped up the remains of his third cuppa and in doing so acquired a mouthful of tea leaves. It turned out Esme forgot on this occasion to use the tea strainer, Mitch looked over towards Esme, knowing full well the tea leaves would be all over his teeth. He smiled a wide smile and mocked her with the phrase *"That's another fine mess you've gotten me into."* Esme was unimpressed and requested that he carry on. He told her the train from Madrid to Port Almeria had one scheduled stop planned after which it was then full steam ahead for the last short leg of the journey. Most passengers had either left the train at the planned stop, then replaced by others who would no doubt be on going to Almeria. It came as a bit of a surprise then to endure another stop at a tiny, rundown grubby little station just prior to the terminal. It looked more like a shunting yard. Not much about the way things worked in Spain phased Mitch a great deal, manyana *'tomorrow will do'* he called it, but this situation for some reason worried him. A train stopping *off schedule* literally minutes from its terminal destination was a tad worrying especially as their fellow passengers were glancing around a bit, looking non plussed. Eddie on the other hand was becoming very twitchy, he told me he felt something was very wrong. Over the years he'd quietly built up an internal radar and this radar detected old Bill Metropolitan, Jersey, Spanish or otherwise at five hundred yards minimum and right now, his radar was pinging like billy-o. It was then he told me about killing the yacht owner and leaving his blood-soaked body onboard complete with a noughts and crosses symbol carved in his back for Christ's sake. If this was what the police were on the platform for, I would be arrested immediately for harbouring a sadistic and blood thirsty murderer. I stuck my head out of the window and saw what looked like three police detectives and judging by the way they were dressed, looking like a throwback to the German secret police, better known as the Gestapo

All three were wearing long overcoats almost down to their feet, topped off with wide brimmed dark grey trilby style hats, pulled down to one side. All three wore black leather gloves and all three stood questioning the train's only guard who was busily pointing towards the front three carriages. I looked to my left and saw the driver and his mate standing on the platform close to the engine, chatting sharing a fag and laughing, the engine just about ticking over. This train was going nowhere, I popped my head back in and told Eddie that it looked like the three musketeers on the platform way down at the last carriage. Eddie stuck his nose out then sat down smartish like and said, "It's the bleedin pigs and what's more I bet you a pound to a penny the slags 'll be looking for me." Esme went white and slumped down on the settee looking poleaxed, stunned and stupefied. She was now sitting really close to Mitch. Apart from the knife to his head encounter this was the closest he'd ever been to her. Their elbows and thighs were touching. He, could see why Eddie was in love with this bird, lovely green eyes, jet black hair, quite petite, she smelt lovely too and no doubt a right decent shag. Esme's mind was elsewhere, she hadn't noticed the once over from Mitch she was focussed on Eddie, as in what the hell is wrong with the man that she loved and adored. Why can't he leave off all the killing and maiming for heaven's sake? What is it about him and his murderous rampages? I thought he wanted to build a life for us in Spain, but what I hear from Mitch, it seems he wants the opposite. He gets this far and still manages to bring the cops with him. The story Mitch was telling her was a damn sight worse than that stupid dream she had a little while ago when pissed up on Crème de Menthe but sadly Mitch wasn't finished yet, how much worse can it get? "Sorry Mitch, I've got to get some shuteye now or I'll keel over. Stretch out on the settee here if you like, you can finish off the story later?" Mitch was now in full flow and in no mood to stop. Reluctantly though he said, "yea that's fine Esme, it's just that the next bit is the best bit." "Save it Mitch, it'll keep." Esme keeping her dressing gown on, curled herself up in bed and read Eddie's note again and again. Soon she was slipping into a spell casting sleep. The note dropped from her fingers falling gently to the marble tiled floor. As she drifted off, she thought she heard the bedroom door handle click. Far too tired to worry or check if Mitch was trying to gain entry, well if he wants in, I'll not complain, it's what adults do she thought by way of making it in her mind, legit. The bedroom door clicked shut.

CHAPTER 54

"Bands Bomber bands, groups and stuff, rock and roll types. I'm keen to get hold of and manage as many bands as possible, get them bookings and stuff. We get the cash from whoever wants to hire them and we pay the bands peanuts. They'll be happy playing in front of an audience instead of in their bedrooms or garages or where ever they practise. It's all about exposure *and* they'll get plenty of groupies." "How come?" Bomber asked. "Cos we will make sure they do won't we." "What happens if they get famous like?" Johnny frowned, "then we'll get more money won't we, we can get them bookings at bigger clubs, maybe up West and that. "Are you going to tell the others about this scheme?" "No mate, they'll think I've gone bloody soft. Let's keep it between us just for now. When it's right to bring the others in on it, then we will." "Right, so how we gonna find bands and groups then?" "Fuck me Bomber have I got to think of everything around here? Look, this is what we need to do, put an ad in the paper asking for amateur bands looking for a breakthrough to contact us for live bookings. We'll be flooded with 'em, we'll soon find out if they're any good or not, depending on how they get on with live audiences at dance halls and clubs we get them into." Bomber was not impressed, rubbing the recently acquired wound on his head for inspiration, he understood the concept, but lacked the logistical knowledge in order to tie it all together. Johnny grabbed Bomber by the arm, "when we get set up in the music business, I'll offer your services as minder to the bands when they are on stage. We've got a good wedge coming in from the car lots, Billy and Mel are doing a sterling job. Plus, there's more on top coming from the prestige cars being nicked then knocked out by Errol's dad." "That's great Johnny but why are you telling me this?" "If the band thing takes off, I'll double up your wages. Just watch your mouth though, if you go chiming on about it, the others might get pissed off. Just remember, I'm steering the ship now and like I said a while back, if I can help it, I don't want to go about maiming and murdering people. We can always pay some other muggins to do our dirty work when it's necessary." Bomber raised a point. "Don't we 'ave to be licenced in the music business to do this, you know like agents or whatever they call themselves?" Johnny was ahead of Bomber but before coming up with his planned answer he said, "you raise a good point Bomber, good thinking mate."

Bomber swelled up inside, happy in the knowledge he was on the same wavelength for once instead of just being the muscle. Johnny rubbed his chin whilst looking skyward for a couple of minutes. "Got it Bomber, got it. We need to find whoever dishes out these licences, probably some geezer at the council offices and threaten to slice him unless he coughs up the appropriate paper work." "That's a bit harsh Johnny, what about setting up whoever it is with a prosy if it's a bloke or a male escort if it's a bird. Either way, if we set it up properly, we can get some tasty snaps while they're going at it hammer and tong. Then we threaten to send them to the press if they don't cough up the paperwork all stamped correctly like. When they cough up the licence, all well and good but we'll tell them that we'll hang on to the snaps in case they squeal to the filth." "Blackmail, of course Bomber that's genius, where did you dig that up from?" "Dunno mate, must have been that clout on me head with that metal bar, out in Zak's yard." Johnny was seriously impressed and was about to tell Bomber when they were interrupted by a waiter. "Are the steaks to your liking Sirs?" "Double nice as it happens. Bomber, want another?" "Not half boss."

The waiter returned to the kitchen to fulfil the requested order. "Nice 'ere 'aint it Bomber? perhaps we'll come again." Bomber chuckled "I should cocoa Johnny it is our steak bar now after all." "That's right Bomber, as it 'appens, it bloody well is. I was thinking perhaps we could use the upstairs rooms to carry out your grand plan. Do we still have two-way mirrors in some of the rooms? If we do, it will make the photography work so much easier and with greater detail, get some right old juicy shots" "Yea, since I cleared the girls out, I picked the biggest room for me to kip in, it's the only one without a two way, the other three are all still there. "Fantastic mate, we'd better get a plan together." Johnny watched as Bomber scoffed down his second steak that day.

CHAPTER 55

The gentleman presently giving Val the bad news sported an eye cast. His right eye deviated and was sometimes *which he disliked immensely* referred to as cockeye. Actually, it was more of a squint with this chap, which gave the impression he was looking directly at you at the same time as looking somewhere else. Val hadn't noticed the eye deviation during her first visit some weeks ago to see this man, and just for the moment couldn't understand why.

Perhaps because she was wound up about the Oasis being demolished and the fact that she was fast losing her grip on Eddie's so-called empire. It might also have something to do with the fact she'd been here to kick start an assassination programme. The gentleman got up from his desk, turned and from a tray on a shelf upon which stood a single bottle along with two glasses, poured them both a full schooner of Oloroso Sherry. Whilst Mr. Poppy eye was doing this, Val took the opportunity to take in her surroundings, again something she took scant interest during her previous visit. She hadn't noticed on that occasion how small and untidy his office was, to her mind it wasn't really an office, it was more of a broom cupboard minus the brooms. His desk was a mess of paperwork, gloss paint peeling off the window and door frames, sizeable damp patches on the walls visible, gradually turning into smelly green mould. A large cheap glass ashtray sat in the middle of his desk, un-emptied for quite some time by the look of it. The gentleman placed a schooner of Sherry in front of Val, deftly nudging the over flowing ash tray with his elbow out of sight so that it was hidden under loose piles of paperwork. Val as it happens, was partial to a drop of Sherry, and was inclined mostly to drink the pale version and not normally inclined to let this darker liquid pass her lips, but on this occasion, she went for it. Tilting her head back so as to pour it down her throat in one go, her eyes were drawn to a vast brown stain on the ceiling, directly above the desk. She stared at it for a few seconds not noticing the woody taste of the Oloroso as it passed down her throat on its journey to her stomach. The gentleman looked towards where she was staring and shrugged his shoulders. "Nicotine stain" he volunteered as if to lend the stain some sort of credence. Thank God for that thought Val, at first, she thought it looked like an upstairs toilet located directly above them had continually leaked through to the ceiling they both were staring at, Val shuddered. The gentleman returned to his seat, minus his suit jacket which he'd slung over the back of his chair. It was then Val noticed the large sweat patches showing through his short-sleeved shirt under his armpits. They were increasing in size, spreading like a deadly infectious agent. An egg-stained green tie hung loosely around his neck; the top two buttons of his shirt undone. An oversized Windsor knot barely holding it all in place. The gentleman sipped at his Sherry and looked at Val over the rim of his schooner. "Another" he asked salaciously. Val noticed the glint in his good eye. If he's trying to get me sozzled and get his leg over, he's got another bloody thing coming.

Val was well aware her long blonde hair, slim features and feminine ways turned on many a bloke, however very few tried it on after just one Sherry. She stood and turned as if to leave. "Just a minute Mrs. Coleman we have not concluded our business" he leered. Val snapped "If you think I owe you anything then forget it pal, no assassination no money that's what you said." she shouted, making the ancient sash windows rattle. "But Mrs. Coleman there have been extenuating circumstances unforeseen by us. The chappie, a certain Mr. Satriani, we suggested for your contract, has gone missing and has been missing for some time now. This is very strange; he is usually extremely professional." "Don't include me in your *us*, there is no *us*, never has been an *us*, not ever likely to be either. Mr. Satriani came to my house and was given strict instructions on who to kill, how to kill and where to kill. It never happened, so, no introduction fee for you buster." Incorrectly thinking she was short of money, the gentleman ventured. "Well okay Mrs. Coleman I fully understand" he said making it obvious rubbing his crutch area, "perhaps we could find other ways for you to pay." She left out the bit about Red Satriani's extended family in Sicily wanting in on Eddie's car racket, and if they were to be let in, Satriani's fee would be waived. She thought it best to keep shtum about that. "Frankly I didn't trust 'im from the start, far too slimy for my liking and he nearly put my neighbour up the bleedin duff 'an all and now I'm in a cleft stick, thanks to you and his bloody disappearing act." The gentleman began to stumble over his words. Sweating under Val's glare like a saveloy in a chip shop. "I-I-I can find another to assist you and y-you can pay on results, I will even halve my original finder's fee." "Not a chance sunshine, drop dead, twice" she replied, at the same time as throwing a twenty-pound note from her coat pocket on to the floor stating, "Use this to get rid of that stain on your ceiling pal and don't come chasing after me cos if you do, I'll see to it that you'll not walk again never mind work." Val shut the office door with an almighty crash then made her way down three flights of stairs, which descended to street level. She heard the gentleman exit his office and shout down over the banister, "I didn't fancy you anyway you skinny bloody trollop." Val speeded up her descent, high heels clacking away like castanets on the concrete steps. When she reached the stairwell, she pinched her nose to block out the vile stench of urine plus a collection of other stale smelly type smells.

Barging through the wooden double doors which opened outwards, the suburb of Hoxton lay in front of her, in particular Hoxton Square. The gloomy day did nothing to cheer her up, or the drab London neighbourhood and just as a bonus, it started tipping it down. She debated the dilemma in her head, back to the stairwell and a row with mister stinky armpits? Or get a soaking, she chose the latter. Raising her arm, she hailed a passing taxi. The driver smiled and winked as he drove on without stopping. It was only then she saw that he already had a fare. The silly bugger hadn't turned off the illuminated sign which plainly said, *for hire*. She flicked him a v sign, turned up her collar against the commencing downpour and legged it to the nearest tube station. Six minutes of half jogging half running, Val was glad to see Old Street underground station come into view. By now she was wet through, hair sticking to her face, coat shoulders dripping and the shoes, as smart as they were, had no real defence against the large puddles she splashed through. Just as she approached the station, the sun broke up the rain clouds and chased them away. This did nothing to raise Val's spirits. If she'd sheltered in a shop somewhere for five or ten minutes, she could have ambled along happy in the knowledge that she had missed the worst of the cloud burst and not acquired an unnecessary soaking. At the moment the poor cow resembled a wet dish rag. 'Call me dish rag Val' she murmured to no one in particular. Deciding not to get the tube and then stand or sit next to dry commuters, shoppers and day trippers to Camden Town, she opted to find somewhere that would provide her with a hot chocolate, a ladies lav where she could tidy herself up a bit and a place to sit and consider her next move. Her plan to eliminate Johnny the Turk had failed twice, it was time to reconsider her options.

CHAPTER 56

"Good morning, Jacko, how was your weekend? A little dicky bird tells me you have some good news, concerning the imminent arrest of one Eddie Coleman." "Crickey, you're up to date Sir, there's no flies on you." "Only when I'm dead Jacko, only when I'm dead." D.I. Jackson dropped a folder next to his boss's morning coffee and cream bun pointing out, "there is a fair bit of information in the folder Sir that's of interest to us, not necessarily leading to an arrest right away though. I have taken copies of all the documents, you have all the originals" he said, tapping the folder with a forefinger. "So, with your permission I will leave it with you to peruse, while I chase up the relevant stuff and get to work on things at my end. Jackson was in no mood to hang around, he was still fuming and smarting from the dressing down at the end of last week, at the hands of Ellis. Today was Monday and still, Ellis's harsh words were ringing in his head. He spun around, shot through the open office door, nodded to Ellis's secretary and marched swiftly through the open-plan office. Just when he thought he'd reached safety, Ellis called out, "A minute Jackson, a minute if you please." "Cock, nearly made it" he muttered. Jackson re-entered the Chief Inspector's office." "What is it now Sir?" he asked wearily. "Sit down Jacko sit down nothing serious. Look old boy," he said with a face that resembled a Black mamba about to kill its prey. "Just thought I was a bit harsh on Friday." Harsh Jackson thought, who since Friday had been thinking of topping himself or at least grabbing a gun from the station's armoury, charging up the stairs, kicking Ellis's door open and putting as many bullets as possible into his darned head. "Thing is," Ellis continued, "I have had a think about things and the way this case is developing with you leading the investigation, or not as the case may be. I'm sure the contents of this folder will be interesting, however your comments just a moment or two ago, was that an arrest is imminently *not* imminent. Which implies you have concluded there is fuck all of use to us in here", he said stabbing it with his forefinger several times to make the point, "other than what we already know. I'm disappointed, very disappointed Jackson to say the least. My superiors are pressing for some good news. They in turn are just about keeping the home secretary at bay and he keeps threatening to involve the P.M

It is therefore with regret Detective Inspector Jackson that I intend to stand you down from this case, delayed for fourteen days unless we see progress. And by that, I mean an arrest of either Eddie bloody Coleman or his alter ego Jack Du fucking Pré, being imminently bloody well imminent." Jackson clamped his jaws together as some people would do to supress a yawn when in the company of one's superiors. He wasn't suppressing a yawn; it was to save him from bursting out laughing. Imminently imminent, what on earth is he on? Whatever it is I must try some. He stood stock still, upright, shoulders back, waiting to be dismissed. When it came, he followed the same pattern as before, a smile and a nod towards Mrs. Meek Ellis's secretary, scuttled through the open-plan office, ignoring the knowing looks from the various detectives busily typing arrest notes then proceeded to put a finger firmly in each ear so as not to hear a potential second recall. Instead of going back to his office, he went directly to the desk sergeant downstairs and asked him to sign him out for the day. The sergeant looked up and said mockingly, "Going somewhere nice are we Sir?" Jackson murmured and tapped the side of his nose. "Well, I wouldn't be going anywhere nasty, would I? Actually, I was thinking of a trip to Spain, good day Sergeant." Jackson said with a leer.

CHAPTER 57

Esme woke to the sound of something occurring in the kitchen. She didn't recall what, if anything, happened after hearing her door click open the previous night. For the second time this month, her hands felt for her garments. Yes, the nighty was in place and not up around her neck. She spotted her dressing gown sitting neatly folded at the end of her bed. Alarm bells rang, this was something she would never do. Her usual, if she happened to be wearing it, would be to simply throw it to the floor before falling into bed. Further examination by feel reassured her, her panties were very much still in place and by the feel of them, not inside out or back to front. For a milli second, she felt a twinge of disappointment after all Mitch was a bit of a hunk, all six foot three of him. And, what was it about her that Mitch had the audacity to think he could decline a night of lust that only the both of them would love and know of? It was then she noticed her bedroom door was wide open, more alarm bells started to ring, only this time little distant ones. The kettle ceased whistling and was replaced with the sound of cutlery clinking on crockery and liquid being poured into cups.

She noticed her bedroom window blinds had been rotated allowing the sun to dapple onto the marble tiled floor and onto her bedspread. A dressed and refreshed Mitch came in without knocking carrying a tray laden with several rounds of toast and two steaming mugs of coffee. How chivalrous she thought at the same time as thinking 'gosh he scrubs up well' and for the second time felt a twinge of disappointment, 'God he's so dishy'. "Morning Esme, rise and shine, I've got us some breakfast, hope you don't mind me knocking it up in your kitchen? After putting the tray on her lap, he went over to the picture windows and rotated the blind mechanism more fully, allowing the sun to pour in to the room and affording them both a beautiful view, directly out to sea. Mitch ignored the chair in the room, he walked around to the opposite side of the bed to where Esme was propped up, lifted a leg and manoeuvred himself so that he was on top of the bedclothes and sitting shoulder to shoulder with Esme. A fleeting thought passed through her mind, should she throw the tray on the floor, jump all over him and have her wicked way, several times? Gosh it would be oh so easy. Her tongue would search his mouth in a frenzy, while she pulled off his khaki-coloured safari shirt to reveal his manly and hopefully hairy chest. He would respond by gently pulling her nighty over her head then kissing her pert breasts. "You okay Esme, I said, is the toast to your liking?" She came down with a bump. She dared not tell him what she was thinking, there would be ructions if Eddie found out. Being the head case that he is, he'd probably kill Mitch just for fun. Hang on she thought, if she could sort it the other way round, persuade Mitch to murder Eddie, dump his body out in the Med, the pair of them could live happily ever after at the Villa Hermosa Vista. She was so sure that Mitch would agree when she told him of her innermost thoughts and desires. Would he kill for her yes, yes, of course he would? Esme turned to Mitch, their eyes met, their lips inches from each other, "I've something to ask of you." "Fire away Esme." How appropriate she thought, fire away. She began with those three words that most men get very jittery about when they are spoken. "I've been thinking." Someone was knocking on the front door. "Oh shit, who the hell is that?" Esme moaned.

Someone was doing a Mitch only this time in broad daylight however this time the knock-knock--knocking was more of a tap-tap-tapping and much less frenzied. Requesting Mitch to avert his eyes; he could see what's on offer later, Esme grabbed her neatly folded dressing gown, slipped it on over her nighty and pulled the belt tightly, finishing it off with a knot that would hold the Queen Mary to a cleated piling. Turning to Mitch, she said, "Get in the bed, and cover yourself up and if you sniff the sheets, I will know." "Hey Esme, I love it when you talk dirty," he grinned. She made her way along the hall, talk about Déjà vu she thought. As Esme approached the door, she heard Sue on the other side talking to Chris. "She's not responding Chris; shall we take a peek around the back?" Sue's question was answered by bolts being drawn back followed by the door opening a couple of inches. Esme met their worried gazes with a bright cheery smile. "What's up guys, what brings you both to my door? not that it isn't a pleasure to see you." Chris said, "we heard a bit of a commotion last night, followed by you lighting up half of Spain, is everything okay?" "Esme opened the door enough to fit her frame in the opening. Both Chris and Sue tried hard to see past Esme. "Well, aren't you going to let us in lovely?" "Normally I would Sue but I was just about to have a shower when you knocked and I've left the hot water running. You know what it's like around here, once you've used up the hot water, there's no more until the tank on the roof has heated up again. So, I'd better run or it's a cold shower for me. Thanks a million for your concern, I'll pop over to see you a little later on." Front door shut and bolted; Esme's heart skipped a number of beats as she ran back to her bedroom and to Mitch in her bed. "Now, where were we?" No Mitch! She sat on the bed which had been beautifully made military style. How could he do that in a matter of minutes? I was only gone a few and now he's disappeared.

"Oh, fuck or maybe not." Esme was done with shilly shallying about, first there was the unexplained rapid banging on the front door last night, then the *did he didn't he episode,* then breakfast in bed and now he does a runner. She flung on someday clothes and went in search of him. The villa, although grander than most, one didn't need to actually recruit a search party. If he'd buggered off out the back and was making his way back to Almeria to hook up with Eddie, she would need to find him well before he got anywhere near that maniac. It crossed her mind that perhaps Mitch did climb into bed with her last night and perhaps he did have sex without her knowing.

Was that even possible? She knew she had been dog tired, plus the bedroom door did click as if being gently opened, but surely not *that* tired she wouldn't have noticed Mitch laying on top of her. Was he on his way to Almeria to confess to Eddie his undying love for me? Surely, that would be a death sentence and would lead to yet another corpse with a noughts and crosses symbol carved on his back. Her search resulted in a no show, the sofa where he had presumably got some shut eye looked as if it had never ever been sat on let alone slept on. The cushions were neatly displayed, plumped up and ready for the first customer of the day. Right, that's the inside done she thought, next would be a quick tour of the grounds. Tracing what she hoped might be his escape route, she stepped out on to the vast patio and pool area. She emitted a modest gasp, there was Mitch, in the pool in his birthday suit, naked as nature intended. He was performing a gentle back stroke, barely moving across the pool. Mitch heard the gasp, looked up and their eyes met, his hands immediately sought to cover his privates. He rolled over, and none too quickly; Esme could plainly see his bare arse. For a second or two, she was tempted to ask him if he could roll back over again. "Sorry Esme, I was thinking you might be a while with whoever was at the front door." He was now standing in the pool, feet on the bottom, the water just about up to his neck. The rest of him being under water looked like a T.V. out of focus, the gentle waves caused by Mitch waving his hands about under the surface adding to the lack of focus. I heard the bit about the hot water and didn't want to use up your quota, so I dived in here. Hope you don't mind too much?" Esme smiled and shook her head from side to side. "Normally I would say the waters lovely, come on, jump in and join me, but maybe not, eh?" "Why the bloody hell are you naked, those at the door were my neighbours, they were just about to march through to the back here, I can't imagine what they would have made of it, to see you stark bollock naked in my pool, just as well they didn't venture around here. And why are you bloody well naked anyway?" "Esme, when Eddie and me discussed the trip from Bilbao to here, we forgot that we might need a pair of speedos each," he said sarcastically. Esme went back to her bedroom, rummaged around in her undies draw and found what she was looking for. Purchased back in England, a bikini top with two pairs of matching bikini bottoms. She remembered being seduced by the sexy colour description printed on the packaging, 'Burnt Orange.' But didn't look at the size chart until she got to Spain, it was extra-large so no good for her anyway.

Ripping open the cellophane bag, she fished out one of the matching bottoms and retraced her steps to the pool area. Another sharp intake of breath. Mitch, still naked was out of the pool and hitting some press ups on the patio. "For God's sake Mitch have you no modesty?" "Sorry Esme love, didn't have a towel to dry myself and find exercising is always a good stand-by." "Well please stop what you are doing and put this on, I'm going to make us another brew, we need to talk and you need to finish the story." Esme disappeared in to the kitchen. Meanwhile Mitch really struggled to get the burnt orange bikini bottom to fit. His build was tall but trim, a relatively flat tummy meant that the bottom just about fitted, however he had more down there at the front than was intended for such a garment. After much wriggling and moving various things around, his tackle although somewhat uncomfortable was all tuck away. He attempted to sit on one of the sun loungers and catastrophe! As soon as he bent his knees in order to sit down, various bits and pieces of his anatomy popped out both left and right. He jumped up and immediately and set about the 'tucking back in' routine. Then it struck him, he had a brainwave, slipping the bikini bottom down and over his feet, he turned it around and pulled it back up again. This proved successful and unsuccessful at the same time. Wearing it in this fashion, back to front there was more material to cover all his bits, however round the back, the slim width which would normally be at the front, did not sit snugly across his behind. Instead, it fell between his bottom cheeks, which meant he was apt to keep wiggling it about with a forefinger and thumb to alleviate the discomfort. Esme arrived back with the teas; Mitch had positioned himself on one of the sun loungers whereby his back would be facing away from Esme at all times. "Right then Mitch, bring me up to speed with rest of your story but just before you do, when you brought me breakfast in bed earlier, you were fully clothed, so how come you aint got a pile of clothes lying about somewhere near here to put back on again after your swim?" "When you were at the front door, I stripped off and got under the covers as you suggested. Then the smell hit me." "Smell" she called out at the top of her voice. "Not you Esme" Mitch laughed. "Me, I hadn't washed since leaving Bilbao and until I got under your bed clothes I hadn't really noticed. God, I stunk, reeked like a sewer rat, heaven knows what you must have thought. I hid my clothes, all of them under your bed, and while you had the front door opened just a few inches I scooted down the hall towards the kitchen,"

"What naked?" "Yes, as nature intended, I thought a wash was needed." Esme looked perplexed. "Hang on a mo, didn't you arrive here with a leather holdall, the one you were using as a pillow on my doorstep?" "Correct Esme and that's where it must still be."

CHAPTER 58

"He's a spiv an 'alf aint he?" "How can yer tell, then Tel, what's the scooby doo's mate, you know clues an all that? anyway, as it 'appens I don't give a jot what he is, if he's gonna get us some live audience work *and* pay us at the same time, stroll on he could be the King of sodding Siam for all I care," laughed Bobby. "Didn't care too much about our band name though did he Tel, said we should think of something more Rock-n-Roly." "Yea I got that too, thing is we've been known as Bobby Bell and the Bell Ends since we started." "Yea but only our mums know us by that name, that and a couple of mates, I like it, makes people giggle." "Look Tel, I'll tell ya, if that bloke who just signed us wants a Rock-n-Roly band name we'll give 'im a Rock-n-Roly band name won't we Tel, just think about it, paying us *and,* what about all those lovely groupies just gagging for it?" "Yea spose so Bobby, I spose we'd better get a base player and a drummer to join us, won't we?" "No worries with that mate, they're ten a penny, me and you are the heart of the band, you on rhythm guitar and me on lead. That means whoever joins us will have to follow us won't they. What's more we can explain that we've got an agent now, so how bad is that mate." Following their meet with Johnny up above Zak's Place, the two lads were cock-a-hoop. During the meeting, Johnny promised all kind of things that wouldn't happen but only he knew of that. The two young guys sat in awe as Johnny waxed lyrical about fame and fortune, not to mention groping girly groupies, hopefully after one thing and one thing only, and not just autographs. After leaving Zak's Place they walked the streets full of dreams and pots of money. Carrying their instruments in long slim guitar cases and on the lookout for a bus stop, Tel spotted an old boy walking towards them looking all of sixty or older. To Bobby and Tel, he looked ancient and by the grimace on his face he was having a bad day. Tel thought he might try to cheer him up, as they got withing speaking distance Tel said with a wide grin "Good evening, mate." "What's good about it?" came the sneering rebuke. Tel trotted out his usual answer. "Try missing a few matey and you'll soon find out."

"What's going on Johnny, that's the fifth bunch of long-haired teenagers with guitars you've had up here recently." Zak, dropped into a chair next to Johnny, handed over a bottle of beer and holding up his own inviting Johnny to reciprocate. Johnny held his bottle up as Zak clinked them together, took a swig and watched Johnny plonk his bottle on the table without even tasting it. "Look you're gonna need to level with me. Dead body disposal on your behalf is becoming my forte but kids and bands?" Johnny remained quiet. Silently, he wished Zak wouldn't be so nosy and fuck off back to his bar. However, he sat staring at Johnny, his eyes demanding to be in the know. Johnny wished now that he'd interviewed the potential wanabe bands elsewhere, but he hadn't, and he knew now he owed an explanation to his cousin. "Zak, no one's gonna die or get slashed with razors mate, I'm hoping to make you redundant reference your body disposal business. I'm planning, when it's necessary to do my killing anywhere but here." Zak softened his stance and relaxed his shoulders. "Glad to hear that cuz. So, what's with the bands then?" "Okay I'll tell you, so pin your ears back." Johnny smiled and spoke. "Are you sitting comfortably Zak, then I'll begin." Johnny explained about the musical instrument business he and Eddie had gotten into a while back. Some guys from Eddie's team carried out several break-ins to music shops that stocked guitars, drums and so on. Music shops to begin with weren't all that secure so, that part of the operation went well. The warehouse we rented in Basildon started to bulge at the sides with guitars, amps, music equipment and stuff. The idea, according to Bomber was this, lots of groups and bands were mushrooming up so Eddie and me through two guys from Southend, acting as go-betweeners, were gonna flog the stuff to start-up bands at knock down prices. This part of the deal didn't go so well, thing is, Eddie and me went down there to have a little chat. Eddie gave them a right roasting, told them get selling or get cut. The two tossers from Southend, got cold feet didn't they, windy guts Eddie called 'em. Ended up doin a runner, so a week later, we got some of Eddie's boys to clear the warehouse. They took all the guitars and stuff to some woods near a place called Thundersley, don't know how they found that place, one of them must have known a local or something. Had a bloody great bonfire and torched the lot. There wasn't a lot of good trying to track down them two gits that were running the show for us, so we closed down the warehouse, end of operation *Rock-around-the-Clock*. If I ever find them two, I will end their lives on the spot, but to be fair to 'em I'll make sure they get matching headstones."

"Got it cuz, so what's with the bands and groups then?" Zak asked. "I'm gonna manage a few, get them places to play to live audiences, dance halls, weddings, funerals and stuff." "Funerals" shouted Zak, "who wants live bands at a funeral?" Johnny held his poker face for a full thirty seconds. "East Enders mate, you know, when they have a right old knees up after the poor bastards six feet under. All they've got at the moment is a radiogram if they're lucky, and a few scratchy forty fives." "So, why the secrecy?" "Cause Zak, the blokes in my team will think I've gone soft or barmy or both especially after what happened in Essex. So, I want to run it for a bit, see how it goes, build it up then bring them in on it." "Who knows about it right now?" "Just you me and Bomber." "Don't you need a licence or something?" "All in hand Zak, we should get the signed documents in a week or so." "What, all above board and kosher like?" "Too fucking right Cuz, we're getting the compromising photos developed as we speak."

CHAPTER 59

D.I. Jackson sat at his desk, the folder and information within obtained from his contact in Bilbao Spain, in front of him. The weather that day was particularly nasty, howling wind and lashing rain was rushing vertically past his office window. Large black thundery looking clouds congregated directly above the police station. Last time they had a storm of this magnitude bits of the roof got torn off exposing rafters, letting the rain find its way downwards into several buckets plus green metal waste bins strategically placed to catch the drips. Drip-drip drip it was, after a while it started to get people down. Some remedial repairs to the roof had been carried out since then so the hope was, this time, there would be no tiles missing courtesy of the gales tearing at them and therefore hopefully no leaks. Jackson opened the file; studied the information and began to scribble sentences in his police issue note book. Two weeks and I am off the case, unless I can show some forward motion, he thought. Something concrete, substantial, something solid. There is no doubt that Eddie Coleman amongst other things is a slippery bastard. But he will trip himself up sooner or later and I will have him, however time is not on my side and I need to get the ball rolling and fast. Best to concentrate here rather than over in Spain. Let's see what we can dig up from people closest to Coleman.

The following morning D.I. Jackson called a snap briefing, he described the current situation viz Eddie Coleman possibly being in Spain to his team of officers, then described what he wanted to happen. Firstly, Mrs. Coleman was to be brought in to the station for questioning, followed by a Mr. Brown. It was without doubt, out of the two, the one that will resist coming to the station most vigorously would be Mrs. Coleman. However, they would have no problem at all with Mr. Brown. An officer asked Jackson "On what grounds do we bring Mrs Coleman to the station boss?" Jackson answered sarcastically. "Listen, I know a thing or two about a thing or two, her son has committed murder and at present we are not exactly sure how many. He's on the run having been lifted on his way to court in Oxford, and by all accounts he's now on a killing spree, this time in Spain. We know this because at least one of his victims was left on a yacht, somewhere in Northern Spain dead of course, with a noughts and crosses symbol carved on his back. This is precisely his M.O." Another officer spoke, "Well that's not exactly Mrs. Coleman's fault is it Sir?" "Look son, ever since Edward Coleman slid down her birthing canal, everything's her fucking fault." His audience of detectives and constables were stunned. This was not the D.I. Jackson they knew and almost loved. Perhaps if they knew he was working very much to a dead line of just two weeks, they might have understood his ugly attitude, but they didn't, because he didn't tell them. However, Jackson was an officer hitherto to be well respected. He always put his team, his department and his principles first. he was respected for his excellent policing methods, respected for the respect he held for his team. Respected for the fact he brought Coleman to his knees and charged accordingly. It certainly wasn't his fault that Eddie Coleman was lifted on his way to court and is now subsequently on a killing spree over in Spain, whether the slaughtered deserved it or not. His team had become accustomed to Jackson's mannerisms. The straight upright back, the straight upright talking and the straight upright approach to good policing. Jackson continued, "I believe there is a strong link to Mrs. Coleman and the lifting of her son from the prison van in Oxford. I believe there is also a link to Mrs. Coleman regarding the demolition of the Oasis. I have recently been talking to the local gas board which services the area of Limehouse Basin where the Oasis once stood.

Please remember this was the epicentre of Coleman's activities. I firmly believed until recently that the gas board team digging at the site would uncover bodies, but they have not, or haven't yet. Following their exhaustive examination of the site upon which the Oasis stood, they are ninety percent sure, in their view, explosives were involved. The initial explosion fractured the gas main which lay directly under the building leading to an escape of gas, causing a secondary explosion. They have under-taken extensive searches via their own records of gas escapes and of other gas boards in and around the London area. No other site where a gas main had been fractured has the damage been solely confined to just a single building. All cases they looked at revealed damage, not extensive, but damage none the less to adjoining buildings." "What does that tell us Sir? And why the internal paperwork search, are they wishing to wash their hands of it, you know pass the buck, let someone else take the blame?" "Exactly that" replied Jackson. "If they can shift the blame, then they will" quickly followed by "but that's not the point I'm alluding to here. If explosives were involved and it is likely they were, then we need to know all about it. Where the explosives originated from, did they pass from hand to hand. And why the hell did anyone want to blow it up anyway? Was it a rival gang a disgruntled customer or was it an internal feud between two mobsters who work for Coleman? Or perhaps a crime of envy?

Decide amongst you who will develop this angle further, in particular, the source. If we can trace the explosives back to the original supplier, we can then make arrests and squeeze whoever it might be until we get a name or two. Mr. B. Brown more commonly known as Bomber Brown supposedly lived in a flat above the Oasis bar, I would think he might have a thing or two to say about it. Okay everyone, decide who amongst you is going after Mrs Coleman and Mr. Brown, and when you have decided, get the both of them in here for chat, as soon as you can." A voice rang out from the ranks "and if they refuse Sir?" "Explain they are not being arrested, simply helping us with our enquiries. Okay briefing over." Jackson did his trademark exit, back ramrod straight, a quick left right, left right, and was gone.

CHAPTER 60

Mitch was about to finish off the story about how he and Eddie managed to evade the three Spanish musketeers who were searching the train. Esme sat on the sun lounger next to Mitch's, so now they were facing each other, knees almost touching. Momentarily he forgot what he was wearing and, in whose company, he was in. He stood and proceeded to walk and talk, he became so engrossed in the story trying to not leave anything out, not the slightest little bit when he turned around in order to walk along the edge of the pool, his back now facing Esme. Still reciting the story, he became aware that she was having a giggling fit. He was also aware that the burnt orange bikini bottom round the back was disappearing to where it shouldn't be disappearing to. Absentmindedly, he used his forefinger and thumb to hook it out and breathed a sigh of relief. The giggling grew to uncontrollable laughter. Then it dawned on him what it must have looked like. Worse was to come, the action of yanking the bikini downwards to offer him some comfort, displaced some of the bits that were previously tucked in at the front. Esme couldn't take anymore; her sides were aching from all the laughter. She shot inside emerging some two minutes later clutching a jumbo-sized beach towel in one hand, her other covering her eyes pretending not to look, although the gaps in between her fingers were just about wide enough to get an eyeful. "Put this on, you silly bugger, I'll go and make us another brew." Soon they were deep in conversation. Esme was keen to hear the rest of the story. "Okay Mitch, start from where you left off last night." "Right Esme." He explained how the train stopped at a little nondescript station just short of their destination.

Having a train stopped would have to be serious enough for the police to request such a stoppage. He covered the point about the three musketeers looking like the Gestapo with their trilby hats and long coats down to their feet, who were about to search the train before it was allowed to move off again. He described how they watched the threesome all pile into one carriage and no doubt challenge anyone remotely looking English then out again and in to the next one. He said let's do the same and when we meet up in the middle, we'll do 'em. Can't think what he had in mind, but if it *was* Eddie they were looking for, I would be in the shit too.

So, we grabbed our luggage from the racks and hopped carriages in time with the three cop's carriage hopping making our way to the middle carriage of the train.

We were two carriages away before carnage was to begin, when Eddie spotted a bloke snoozing in the corner, head up against the window, with an English newspaper on his lap. Eddie goes, hey mate can I have a peek at that pal? The bloke sort of snuffled and snorted as you do when you wake up from a snooze. This particular carriage was empty apart from us and this bloke. The snoozer stood up and as he did so, the newspaper slid off his lap and onto the floor, various pages fell in different directions. The bloke apologised profusely and got on his hands and knees to gather up the paper. Eddie whispered to me, this bloke is about my size and age, while he's on the deck, go and shove my passport in his jacket that's slung on the seat opposite him and see if his own is there. If it is, lift it. I did as Eddie asked, and when the bloke stood up again and next to Eddie, I thought yes indeed they do look alike somewhat, albeit the snoozer was a little taller. Same height(ish) same age(ish) and same weight(ish). Different barnet colour, but that's easy to alter especially if you're on the trot. Only thing missing was the heavy framed glasses. Eddie had already thought of this, he rolled up what was left of the newspaper and put his specs in it and placed it on the seat next to the bloke. The bloke said in broad English, sorry gents I've had a busy day, then resumed his position up against the window. Before many seconds he was whistling happily through his nose once more and dreaming no doubt of his supper. We waited till the Spanish cops dived into the next but one carriage to us and we dived out while they were not able to see us and back to our original one, then waited for the fun to begin. To me, it was outrageous what Eddie was doing but the alternative didn't bear thinking about. The Spanish cops as far as Eddie was concerned, only had a name, Jack du Pré and a loose description, so his plan should work. If not, it would be a right old workout dealing with the cops. Thankfully the commotion fired up, we could clearly hear the protestations from Mr Snoozer. Apparently, Mr Snoozer had a reasonable grasp of Spanish, but the comment 'you fuckers' was quite distinctly heard in English. The cops no doubt would have asked the bloke to show them his passport him being an alien and all that. Once it was opened and they saw the name Jack du Pré they would have cuffed him, probably given the carriage a quick rub down and found Eddie's horn-rimmed glasses. What more evidence would they need? They'd got their man. The last we saw of him; the poor bastard was being dragged towards the station's only exit and no doubt straight into the squad car to be taken to God knows where. At last, the guard blew his whistle and our train chuff-chuff-chuffed its way out of the station and, as it 'appens, we were a bit chuff-chuff-chuffed ourselves.

"Got to hand it to Eddie though, what he did was a master stroke, built on that bit of luck. I mean, fancy coming across an English bloke about the same size and age, then getting him to be a right patsy. I did ask Eddie, what with the train now well away from the station, if he would have gone at the coppers. Eddie looked at me smiled and muttered." "What do you think pal." "And you know, I do believe he would have." Eddie opened up the bloke's passport and grinned. "Bloody hell" he said, "I'm now fucking Ronald Biggs, he's on the run an all." "Soon as we got to Almeria, we found Eddie some digs and I shot over here in a cab and that's the truth Esme as I live and breathe. Criss cross my heart and hope not to die."

CHAPTER 61

Feeling relaxed and self-assured, Eddie laid back in the huge bath, his body surrounded by a million and one bubbles. He smiled to himself as he recalled when yesterday, the luckless real Ronnie Biggs was unceremoniously dragged off the train to an unknown destination. The moment was made all the better because Mr. Biggs resembled him and what with him holding the passport of Jack de Pré meant he would have a hard time convincing the cops they had arrested the wrong man. So, no supper for him any time soon. Eddie had no regrets for the wrong he'd committed, no remorse what so ever. He looked again at the passport Mitch had lifted for him. The image looking back at him, Eddie thought, was a good enough match. You only needed to close one eye and squint with the other. As far as Eddie was concerned, near enough was good enough. The Parador Eddie checked into the previous night, at first glance looked to be located within a historic building or even a castle perhaps. On second glance it was exactly that, well at the very least within the grounds of a castle with a view to die for on and out over Almeria to the Mediterranean Sea. Talk about luxury, Eddie, as usual had fallen on his feet once again. He sank deeper into the bath until the bubbled surface covered his head. Holding his breath for at least sixty seconds a knock on his suite door brought him to the surface. Eddie yelled through the half open bathroom door. "Yea, who is it and what do you want?" A young lady's voice called out in broken English. "Good morning, Mr. Biggs, sorry to disturb, we are serving breakfast but only for the next forty-five minutes. Would you like me to reserve table for you?"

"Okay, be there in ten." Eddie rummaged through his holdall

and found a fresh set of casuals, white shirt and beige chinos, he towelled himself down and made the hotel's restaurant in twenty. Two other guests were just finishing up leaving the restaurant to Eddie plus three waiters who were gathered by the breakfast buffet area. He called out from where he was sitting "Any of you speak English?" They stopped talking amongst themselves, one of them looked over at Eddie and nodded. He beckoned him over. "Okay pal, have a sit down I need some local info." The waiter looked over at his co-workers shrugged his shoulders and sat down. He'd not been employed that long at this plush hotel and in that short time it was constantly drummed into him *the customer is always right.* "Good morning, Sir, my name is Fabio and how can I be of assistance to you?" "Well for starters you can get one of your mates to get me some strong coffee, and some eggs and bacon I'm famished. Fabio called one of his colleagues over, spoke rapidly and turned back to Eddie. His colleague strode off to fulfil the order. Fabio repeated his request. "How may I be of assistance to you Sir?" Eddie was curious. "How come you're so good at English?" "My mother moved here from London." Eddie's eyes widened. "She taught me, thinking it might help me get on in life. There are not that many prospects in Almeria, a second language is as good as a degree around these parts so she was correct in her assumption. This beautiful Parador, or as you would say, fine and luxurious hotel employed me the instant they knew of my talent for the English language. Good for trade they said. Will draw many more English visitors they said." "Did you say London was where your mum used to live, before she came out here?" "Yes, you are correct." "Whereabouts in London?" Specifically, Sir I do not know it never came up in conversation, I can ask her if it is your wish." "What do you mean you don't know whereabouts in London?" "Well Sir if I was in London and said to you, I am from Almeria I would not expect you to ask where in Almeria." "You've got me there Fabio." Carried between the remaining two waiters, on a large oval silver tray each, Eddie's breakfast arrived. One tray with a plateful of eggs and bacon the other with coffee pot, cream and a few polvorones, delicious looking almond cookies. They laid it all in front of Eddie with practised ease. Fabio spoke quickly to one of them who all but ran to the buffet area. He explained to Eddie. "My Mother likes to have a slice of buttered bread with her eggs so as to dip it into the yolk, I am assuming you would like that too Sir?" "I would Fabio, I would cheer's mate." The buttered bread arrived and Eddie dipped.

"So, what is it you would like to know Sir?" "First off son, call me Eddie." "Oh, but Sir, when you checked in last night, you checked in as Mr. Ronald Biggs." "You're bloody well informed, aren't you?" "It is hotel policy Sir we are all informed of our valued guests' names in case we need to inform them of anything." "Yea well, you got that right, Mr. Biggs is correct but my mates call me Eddie and as you're sitting at my table, you're now a mate." "Thank you, Eddie, that is much appreciated." "Now I come to think of it somebody knocked on my door just now and spoke to me in English too, and she knew my name." "As I said Sir it is policy to know our guests' names. Are you staying with us for long Sir?" Eddie laughed, "Dunno pal depends how good the grub is." "We are sure you will not be disappointed." Eddie slurped some coffee from a bone china cup, which held about a thimble full. When he replaced the cup to its saucer a waiter appeared from nowhere and topped the coffee back up to the brim. "You asked earlier for some local information is it beauty spots, places of archaeological interest, places of worship, what is on your shopping list Sir um sorry, Eddie?" Eddie looked at Fabio and chuckled. "You're a right old bright spark aint ya. Not one to mince your words, eh?" "Sorry that one has me puzzled, if you mean I am straight to the point you must remember I am employed and live here also and obliged to work to the standards upheld by the management, I can lower those standards for you but only when out of earshot of my superiors." Eddie looked around. "Well, if they're here abouts then they must be invisible." Fabio smiled "I think you will understand me when I say," his voice dropped to a whisper "walls have ears." He liked this young man a lot. "You'll go far you will pal." Fabio smiled. He remained at whispering level. "If it is ladies of the night you are wanting, I can help you in that department too. However, it is strictly off the record and as you would say, if I was found out, it would mean the chop for me." Eddie feigned shock first then grinned. "You're okay mate it's nothing of the sort. I've just arrived, want to stay here in Almeria, have a rest up for a bit and get to know the area. Do you know somewhere called Mojácar?" Fabio smiled and replied with a dark husky voice "Aha, Indalo Man country." Fabio was on very familiar ground here, he felt superior now, had the upper hand so to speak. If there was one subject, he was hot on it was the issue of 'Indalo Man', the symbol of a man holding the ends of a rainbow which arched above him, discovered in the caves of 'Los Letresos.'

It was adopted by the inhabitants of Mojácar who turned it into a souvenir item for visitors to purchase and take home. They said the symbol would be a totem of good luck and therefore would not let any bad luck enter the household where it was visible. The fact that 'Los Letresos' caves were some sixty-five miles away in the Sierra de Maria Los Vélez natural park, didn't stop some of the wilier residents of Mojácar profiting by selling images of the Indalo Man, Fabio's mother amongst them. She owned and worked daily in her gift shop in the little town square, which was simply full of Indalo Man items. All for sale to tourists from within Spain or holiday makers from abroad. Fabio as a young lad worked many hours in his mother's shop and would tell anyone who entered the shop, the origin of the prehistoric magical symbol. Some called it the Mojácar Man others the Indalico Man. Whatever, it caught people's imagination especially those that sought-after good luck charms which in turn if the story was spun well, meant the shop's cash register was constantly ringing.

CHAPTER 62

It was Saturday night. Bobby, Tel and their new four-piece band line up had just finished tuning their guitars and about to crash on with their first number. Since the original meeting with Johnny the Turk, the four of them had rehearsed and rehearsed and rehearsed until their fingers got blisters from running them up and down the guitar strings. The new drummer and bassist had come along to join Bobby and Tel from an established group which unfortunately held no real future for them. When they found out Bobby and Tel had an agent cum manager, they joined up pronto. Their opening number was to be a real rock n roller, one that horrified the older generation, 'Move It" by Cliff and the Shadows' The band by now had been re-christened **Robby and the Rocking Rebels.** Johnny approved and was successful in getting them a booking at dance hall in Tottenham. The kids on the dance floor already bopping around, were doing so to rock music being played over the sound system. The Mecca ballroom was like many others spread out across London, a dance floor, some tables and chairs plus a bar at the opposite end to the raised-up platform that doubled as a stage. There was even a glitter ball with spots trained on it to add a bit of class.

Johnny and Bomber stood at the bar waiting for the band to do their thing. The Mecca employed its own security; therefore, Bomber was merely a spectator, just for tonight. Johnny however had persuaded the management to let Bomber join in if a major fracas kicked off, but only if he was needed. New bands always pulled in a good crowd, and there were plenty in this Saturday night. Birds dancing around their hand bags, blokes watching the birds, beers in hand sizing up the talent.

Bobby, guitar strap slung over his shoulder walked up to his mike and whistled to see if was switched on. It responded with some piercing feedback through the mike's amp' so somebody behind him turned the volume down a tad. He tapped it this time, satisfied that all was well he counted out, a-one, two, a one two three four and they were off. First the lead guitar intro, followed by rhythm and bass guitars then the drums cut in. The sound compared to the records being played earlier was deafening. All eyes, ears and attention were levelled at the band. The atmosphere suddenly became electric. Blokes put their beers down, grabbed a bird, any bird, they just had to dance and jive around the dance floor. You simply could not stand still. Before long they could hardly move for couples jiving and jittering everywhere. Johnny who up until now had not heard the band properly, that is to say amplified up to 25 watts via the AC30 Vox amps before tonight, looked at Bomber and yelled above the noise "Fuck me there're noisy but good! I think we may be on to something here." The barman shouted something indecipherable, Johnny turned to look in his direction and stuck a hand behind his ear. The barman pointed in the direction of the main entrance. Johnny looked across to see the manager beckoning him over. Once outside the dance hall and in the foyer, the music was a little less intrusive. It was however loud enough to attract in passing teenagers who were on their way to some other destination, which pleased the manager no end. "What is it then mate?" asked Johnny, he was told by the manager the bingo ladies in the building next door couldn't hear the numbers being called out by the caller-outer due to the bands excessively high volume. On the back of that as they were good, he asked Johnny if he could book the band for the next six Saturdays. Johnny agreed on the spot then sent Bomber back in to tell Bobby the good news about the bookings and to turn the bloody volume down or he would have to do it for them.

By now they were on their second number of the night, being

a great number that kept everybody on their toes, 'Summer Time Blues' which was a nod to the late Eddie Cochran. Bomber strode across the floor barging through dancers unceremoniously, completely unaware of the evil looks from one or two of the blokes he pushed out of his way. Bomber waved at Bobby and drew a finger across his throat, indicating to stop the music. Bobby mouthed fuck off between lines of the song. Bomber thought, 'what was it Johnny ordered him to do? Oh yes, tell the band to turn the volume down or do it for them.' Once again, he drew a finger across his throat. Once again, Bobby, cocky bugger that he was mouthed fuck off. That's it thought Bomber looks like I'll have to shut them up myself. Clambering up onto the raised platform, he was immediately smacked in the face by the guitar belonging to the bass player. He, at the time had his eyes closed and happened to be clowning around swinging his bass guitar wildly about the stage as far as his amp lead would let him. Bomber let out a yell, clambered up to a standing position and nutted the doomed guitarist who fell backward directly into the drum kit. In turn the drummer fell backwards and off the rear of the stage. Being impossible for the remaining two band members to carry on, the music stopped. Bobby looked at Tel and they both looked at Bomber who was busy twiddling knobs on whatever he could twiddle knobs on. However, the knobs he twiddled with, happened to be the volume control knob and instead of twiddling them to minus, he twiddled them to max. In complete frustration, Bobby slashed his hand across all six strings not realizing the amp was set to max. It was too much to bear, the racket was horrendous, some of the bingo ladies next door screamed in horror. The lads on the dance floor didn't need a written invitation. Being a Saturday night, most were filling up with beer and getting stoked up for a bit of GBH. Fists, boots and bodies started flying in all directions. Several blokes attacked Bomber simultaneously, they dragged him on to the dance floor like a hoard of ants would haul a large insect to their nest for the queen's din dins.

Once Bomber was down on the deck a flurry of boots came in thick and fast, Bomber rolled over and curled up in a ball trying to make himself as small as possible, hoping not to get one where it hurts the most. These guys meant business; and were not about to just walk away. The kicking they gave Bomber was real, and could inflict serious damage. A blur from the main entrance was suddenly upon them. Johnny felled two of Bombers attackers with well-aimed punches to the kidney area. Dangerous but effective. The others turned their attention to Bomber's saviour, without hesitation Johnny caught two of them using both fists at once. One attacker received a solid punch to his adams apple from a straight left, the other received a haymaker to his temple from a swinging right hander, both went down on top of the other two. A fifth was about to smash a wooden chair on Johnny's head but it was snatched away from behind him by one of the two doormen who had at last entered the fray. Bomber stood up. He could deal with the pain later. He and Johnny stood back-to-back, both with fists raised ready to take on all comers. One of the doormen stood with them, meaning they now had West, South and East directions covered. To their surprise, there was an instant out pouring of bodies wounded or otherwise through the many fire exits. Even the blokes that Johnny felled managed to limp away. The Mecca ballroom was quickly filled up again with an in pouring of police charging through the main entrance, truncheons raised, equally hoping for a bit of Saturday night action. Bomber and Johnny dropped their collective guards. The barman shouted at the coppers, "It was them two, they started it specially the big guy,

he was mixing it with the band he was." This was a disaster for Johnny, the last thing he needed was a night or two in the cells and up before the beak in the morning. Bomber wasn't too bothered; he'd been there before. Many blokes in the same position weren't able to get a good night's kip in a police cell. Bomber though was famous for his ability to sleep on a washing line. Handcuffed and with a copper either side of them ready to foil any thoughts of escape, they were marched across the now deserted dance floor, picking their way past strewn tables, chairs and broken beer bottles towards the foyer. The manager stood in silence as the two of them were frogmarched to the waiting Black Mariah, waiting to transport the pair to the nearest nick at Bruce Grove.

Bobby and Tel when questioned swore blind they had seen nothing. There was no way they were going to bite the hands of the very people who had shown some faith in them. Besides, they disliked the old Bill as much as anybody and certainly weren't about to give them any pointers as to who did what. Their new band members followed suit. As they made their way out with their musical kit all four glared daggers at the barman who was creeping further and further up the backside of the officer currently questioning him. The Mecca boss thrust two envelopes at Bobby and said "When the dust settles come back and we'll have a chat." Bobby looked in one of them and saw some fivers, asked, "What's in the other one, the one that's got sticky tape all over it?" "That one's for your manager, see to it that he gets it unopened. And by the way, in case you didn't get the message, you're booked here for the next four Saturdays."

CHAPTER 63

"He's bloody well been nabbed Sir, er Coleman that is." Detective Inspector Jackson was overjoyed. One minute he purred like a cat that got the cream, another minute he was jumping around like a dog with two dicks. "And it doesn't end there, a felon known as Johnny the Turk is sitting in a police cell over in Tottenham. "Johnny the who?" Chief inspector Ellis enquired, eyes narrowing, brow furrowing. "Sorry sir, at the moment we do not have his surname, he refuses to give it to the custody sergeant or anyone else for that matter." "Sorry old boy, I don't quite get the connection. What's a turkey got to do with Coleman?" "This Turk chappie Sir was part of Coleman's gang or crew as he called it when they hung out at the Oasis." "When you say Turk, is it that you mean he's from Turkey?" "No sir, for some reason or other it is his gang or nickname. He is refusing to speak and is being most uncooperative. However, there's more, sitting in a cell next door to this Turk is one Mr Brown known in the underworld as Bomber." "Look Jackson as keen as I am when it comes to T.V. quizzes, I certainly don't want them conducted in my sodding office. Will you get to the point and soon?"

Jackson explained, all three were linked to various crimes as yet undetected in and around the East End of London over the past three years. Previously gathered information had shown that Eddie Coleman was the boss man, Johnny the Turk was his number one, and Bomber Brown, not only lived above the bar at the Oasis but at one time owned the entire building. Apparently, he did a dodgy deal and sold the lot to Coleman however, this cannot be confirmed in that the relevant paperwork went up in smoke when the Oasis building was destroyed and, we have no idea as to who the dodgy solicitor might be that dealt with the dodgy sale." "Okay then, let's get back to Coleman for a moment. What do you mean he's been nabbed?" "Sir, the Spanish police arrested him on his way to Almeria which is in Southern Spain, here look, I have brought a map and highlighted where he was heading." "How do they know it's him?" "Fitted the general description Sir, but the clincher is his passport, it's that of Jack Du Pré. This will make you laugh Sir; he is insisting that his name is Ronald Biggs to the Spanish Police, not Jack du Pré." "What not *the*?" "No-no Sir, not him, just an ordinary chap unlucky enough to have the same name." Ellis being Ellis was confused and gob smacked at the same time. "Why on earth would Coleman choose a name connected to a major robbery? It does not make sense at all. Are you sure that the Spanish blokes have got it right? Eddie Coleman could well have paid someone who looked similar to him to pose as Jack Du Pré. He obviously knew the man hunt was on, and it was just his bad luck that this guy really was called Ronald Biggs. If they swapped passports, then Coleman would have to assume that name. There must be quite a number of men floating around the world called Biggs. Have you checked in the telephone directory how many there are just here in London?" Jackson began to lose his bottle, he was so caught up in the excitement of Coleman being nabbed, he hadn't thought things through thoroughly. This is why Ellis was sitting where he was and poor Jacko standing where he was. He needed to take the initiative. "We will send up to date pictures of Coleman on the teleprinter to the police station he is being held at and ask for a more definitive reaction." Ellis scratched his chin.

"Does Coleman have any scars or tattoos that we are aware of?" "Not that we know of Sir, only that he sports a curly mess of bright ginger hair." "Well, there you have it, Jacko." "Not quite Sir, the description we received detailed his hair as being mousey and short." "Well get the Spanish police to do a strip search. If he's gingerish on top and provided he hasn't shaved his pubes, that area will be gingerish down there too.

"Yes Sir, I will get on it right away and as far as the other two reprobates are concerned, I'll get over to Tottenham nick at Bruce Grove and interview them myself." Ellis was about to say remember, this is the last chance saloon for you, but held back. He would hold on for a while before taking Jackson off the case and wait to see what happens next. After all, even though it was something of a good break for Jackson, he didn't exactly engineer any of it himself. "Just before you disappear Jackson, exactly why are the two, other than Coleman, sitting in cells at Tottenham nick?" D.I. Jackson noted the reference to Jackson and not Jacko. "They were arrested for an affray which uniformed were summoned to, on Saturday night at the Mecca ballroom." "Hmmm, bit silly of them to get involved in a fracas in such a public venue, what does the manager have to say about it?" "Bugger all Sir, says he was elsewhere in the building at the time and swore blind he didn't witness anything and has no connection with either of them." "What about members of the staff?" "Same story Sir except for just one of them, the barman. He reckons the two in the cells attacked the band, then attacked everyone else in the building." "Do you believe that Jackson, or is this barman wanting to get noticed? I mean attacking a band then all other members of the paying public attending, sounds like wild accusations to me." "I will not have an opinion Sir either way sir until I have questioned him." "Okay, keep me posted." "Oh, I will Sir, believe me I will." After Jackson had gone, Ellis became convinced that Jackson was holding something back, possibly something big, and big Chief Inspector Ellis did not care for it much at all. He was about to call him back when his phone rang.

CHAPTER 64

A single bolt of lightning lit up the inky black Spanish sky, momentarily turning night into day, blotting out an uninterrupted view of a beautiful starry vista. A mighty clap of thunder followed almost immediately, directly overhead shaking the villa to its meagre foundations. Rain instantly sheeted down, huge rain-droplets cascaded down splattering fine sand dust all around in each and every direction. Sand dust that had sat where it lay undisturbed for weeks on end and was now on the move once more. Not much escaped the wet sand spray. Cars, window sills, fences, shrubs. Tree trunks once painted white, now turned a dull yellowy grey. If the down pour ceased as quickly as it started, the wet sand splatters would remain exactly where they landed until the next rainfall. If, however, the weather god decided to let it rain continually but much lighter for a little longer, the welcome drizzle would wash most of the muck away. It was not to be though, a second lightning bolt heralded full time and the rainstorm stopped as fast as it had begun. Esme counted the seconds until another clap of thunder could be heard. It came after the count of ten. "That's ten miles from here thankfully, hold me Mitch tightly please." She explained her quandary. "As a little girl I hated thunderstorms when they came, I would run into Daddy's bedroom for comfort and he would just laugh and laugh. He even laughed when I cried." Mitch held her tightly, kissing Esme's forehead then slowly placed a leg over her hip, their naked bodies now fully entwined. "Christ Mitch, you always have to go that one bit further. I was looking for comfort and kindness and understanding not another bloody bunk up." "You've got it sweet pea, it's just that you're so irresistible I thought I might take advantage of you in a crisis. And anyway, don't be such a sissy pants, it's only thunder" "Esme sat up and attempted to turn on the bedside lamp. "Oh dear, look" she said, "the electricity is off." "Thought it might be, this aint London you know, it could be down for hours, days even. Those bolts were vicious enough to split an oak never mind the flimsy wooden cable poles they have over here. I think the record as far as Bilbao was concerned, was almost a week.

Yea," he continued, "it was off for so long, it started to affect the local economy." "How come" murmured Esme. "Well, legit companies income went down, thieves, burgliers and robber's income went up." "Burgliers?" "Oh, sorry Esme, I just use that way of saying burglars, I picked it up from me dad." Esme laid back down in the bed snuggling up to Mitch. She loved his muscular torso and enjoyed having his strong arms around her. "Okay" she sighed, "if having your wicked way is the only way I will get some comfort and kindness so be it, off you go then." "Oh no Esme I can't now, you've spoilt it, where's the romance in 'oh go on then' what happened to the chase or taking you by surprise?" Esme was stunned, was he taking the piss or what? Mitch untangled himself, moved further down the bed until his face was level with her navel and blew a massive raspberry on Esme's tummy. He roared with laughter, Esme followed suit and they kept the chuckling and giggling going for a full minute. As they lay there together in bed giggling their last giggles, she turned to Mitch and said, "I'm not frightened anymore thanks to you." Then she professed her undying love for him. He said "ditto baby" Bogart fashion and waited for the inevitable slap to the back of the head. When it didn't come, he pressed his mouth to her ear and whispered, "I love you more." "Do you Mitch, do you really? It's important for me to know." He went to put his leg over Esme's hip once again but decided against it. "Yea I do Esme; you are all I have ever wanted in a woman. Beautiful, intelligent, nice arse, you've got the lot." "You were doing well there Mitch until the last bit, where does that come in?" "I'll tell you, shall I? When you walk away from me your bottom wiggle is the best wiggle I've ever seen, your bum wiggle gives me a twinge in my um my err, my well, you know." He stuttered. "No Mitch. I don't know, I haven't the faintest idea what you are talking about." 'It's a good job its dark, she thought he won't be able to see the smirk on my face.' "Come on, explain a twinge in your what?" Mitch wanted to curl up under the covers and make this embarrassing moment disappear. He was quite happy when chasing insurgents but when it came to women, he was all of a quiver, unless he was blowing raspberries on tummies. Esme pressed for an answer "Come on I'm waiting" She let the silence hang for a few moments more. "Only joking Mitch, I know precisely what you mean."

"Phew, you do? thank the lord for that, I thought I was going to have to tell you that I was referring to my dig-a-ling-ling."

CHAPTER 65

Johnny the Turk sat quietly in the holding cell within Tottenham police station. The cell measured approximately twelve feet by eleven, Johnny paced it out several times. A window let in some light but it was far too high to see out of, besides the glass was the frosted type and probably three inches thick. This window was not designed to be opened. A bench ran along the far wall which doubled up as a bed, opposite the cell door. A folded blanket lay where it was placed previous to Johnny taking up temporary residence. He found it useful as a pillow but totally useless as a blanket, too small and too thin. Behind a low privacy wall sat a stainless-steel lavatory unbreakable of course. Judging by the dents, previous incumbents had done their very best to inflict serious damage to the poor innocent thing, which Johnny found odd. Besides, the cops took away anything worn on the feet so these dents must have been made by fists. Everyone needs a toilet, so why attempt to demolish it? There was of course no seat, of course not, why should there be one? This was Tottenham nick, not the bloody Ritz. The nearest it got to that would be Ritz crackers for afternoon tea, minus the posh bloody waiters. The cell door housed a judas hole for anyone walking past outside to peep in. Somebody at one time, successfully scratched the cell side of the glass centre making viewing from the outside somewhat blurry. Floor to ceiling tiles clad all four walls, Johnny made a conscious effort not to count them. He needed to concentrate on getting out and taking up his duties once again at the head of his crew. So, instead of sitting and moping, he decided to plan some hits on jewellers up in the West End of London. That was much more profitable than counting tiles.

Besides counting tiles was the first sign of madness, followed by talking to yourself and finally looking for hair growing on the palm of your hand. Oh no, a jewellery heist was much more fun to think about and plan. Just lately, Johnny was becoming much of a gemologist. He was able to identify precious stones, which came in handy when sorting through whatever came back from a robbery. A scraping of metal on metal sounded. Johnny looked up to see an eye peeping at him via the peep hole in the cell door. Johnny sat motionless, put his head back on the tiled wall behind him and closed his eyes. More metal sounds, this time a key being inserted in the cell door lock then a clunk as the lock released the door which slowly swung open. A shirt sleeved officer stood in the door frame.

"Outcha come then pal you can go home now, wherever that is." Johnny opened his eyes; this was unexpected. He asked the question why, by using body language, a quizzical look, shoulder shrugging and arms outstretched palms upper-most. The duty officer informed him there are no witness statements therefore no evidence other than hearsay so they were forced to let him go with a warning. Johnny would find out later on that day, word about his incarceration had got back to Mel and Billy, the hated pain givers. They'd set about the tongue wagging barman and politely asked him to retract his statement or end up in the Thames in a sack securely tied up with barbed wire. He did not hesitate, he retracted. The two from Stratford were feared by many. As it happens when they heard of Johnny's eventual release, they re-visited the barman at his flat and made sure he wouldn't be able to grass anyone up again. As they left, the barman's tongue was thrown casually to a neighbour's dog. It sniffed it with suspicion, lifted a back leg, pissed on it and walked away. As Johnny passed through the police station's reception area, he stopped at the main desk. "What happened to Bomber?" The duty sergeant replied, "If you are referring to a Mr. Brown, he was released an hour ago." Johnny shrugged and moved on. Stepping outside the station he heard a shrill whistle then a raised voice calling out, "Over here boss." Across the road and to the left there stood Little Allen, a broad smile on his face, eager to please his new found boss. He was leaning up against a shiny jet-black Jaguar, Bomber already seated in the back. With his two passengers safely in the Jag he asked, "Where to boss?" "Up West Allen, I need to check out some jewellers, want to find one we can hit tonight with the right blokes." Little Allen replied heartily "Okay boss, sounds excellent to me." Bomber remained broodingly quiet. Little Allen fired up the Jag, put it into drive mode and pointed the leaper perched on the front of the bonnet towards London's West End. All three being so caught up in their own thoughts, nobody noticed an unmarked police Ford Zodiac fall in behind them with a driver and one passenger. They were deliberately three cars behind, so as not to arouse suspicion. These officers were highly trained in vehicle tailing and fast pursuit. One to drive, the other to jot down notes, anything that might lead to a bust. The Jag had only gone about seven hundred yards or so. "Change of plan Allen, head for Zak's Place, we need to get a meet organised." "Sorry boss that's a new one on me, not been there before can I have some directions?" "Bomber, tell him how to get there, I'm gonna shut my eyes for a bit."

Johnny pushed himself down in the seat and tried to snooze. Bomber called out, "spin around mate, we need to be facing the other way." Little Allen turned the Jag on a sixpence much to the disgust of traffic coming at them in both directions. He watched in the rear-view mirror with interest as a black Ford Zodiac completed the same manoeuvre and he was immediately alerted. "Think we've got a tail boss." Johnny sat back up. "Have we now, how come?" Little Allen replied, "must have started tailing us from Tottenham nick. When I did a U-turn just now, they did the same. It's old Bill I can smell 'em a mile away." Johnny was silent for a few minutes then said "turn left here and see what happens." Sure enough, the Zodiac followed. "Yep, still with us boss." "Okay, do another U-turn, drive back up to the main road turn left and pull over." Little Allen did as he was asked. As soon as he pulled the Jag over, Johnny shouted everyone out. All three piled out and stood at the back of the car facing the oncoming traffic. "When you see them Allen, start waving and smiling at them." "Okay Johnny, you're the boss." As the Zodiac came into view Little Allen started waving and grinning. Both Johnny and Bomber scowled at the two cops. All three watched the Zodiac until it disappeared. "What now?" Bomber enquired. "We wait," smiled Johnny. "They'll be back." He was right. Several minutes later, the two cops drove by once again, this time on the opposite side of the road going back to where they came from. Johnny asked, "where's this Jag from Allen?" "It's a ringer boss, false plates and stuff, fresh out of Errol's yard. They done a great job on the paintwork, yesterday it was racing green!" "Right let's ditch it here, find a phone box and give Errol a bell. Tell him where the car is and tell him to come and get it, tow it away and crush it. Tell him to churn another one out and get it over to Zak's place. Bomber, you go with him in case Errol needs directions to Zak's." Bomber asked, "and what are you going to do Johnny?" "I'm off to that café over the way and have some breakfast. When you two get back you might want to join me." Johnny then took a table right up against the glass frontage, which gave him full view of the stricken Jag. Stricken because quite soon it was to be crushed to a metal cube, then melted down. He kept a sharp look out for the Zodiac but so far it was a no show. Fifteen minutes later, Little Allen and Bomber trooped in and sat down next to Johnny. He signalled to the chap behind the counter who disappeared into the kitchen area, emerging a few moments later, with three cooked breakfasts on a large brown tray. "All okay with Errol then?" he asked Allen. "Yep, all good and thanks for the breakfast."

Bomber asked, "how we gonna get over to Zak's then?" Johnny grinned. "Well unless you two want to go and nick another motor we'd best black cab it. But let's eat first, before it gets cold."

CHAPTER 66

"Dead on arrival Sir, died in the ambulance. Now then, unless you are a direct relative to the deceased, I cannot tell you anything more. It will be of help however, to know if Mrs. Coleman has any relatives." "How'd you know her name?" asked Bomber." "The neighbour who found her and subsequently called for assistance, passed the information on to the ambulance crew." "Have the police been informed of her death yet?" enquired Bomber. The hospital registrar was becoming a tad concerned. "Not yet Sir but they will have to be informed soon, why do you ask?" "No reason mate, just curious. Anyway, yes, she has a son who is abroad somewhere, don't ask me where cos I don't know. But I can get word to him if that's any help." "Thank you, and may I have his name for the paper work please?" Bomber was stumped. There was no way he was gonna give this bloke Eddie's name or his whereabouts. Besides, if old Bill caught sight of the paper work, which they would, they'd see Eddie's name and start asking bloody questions. Bomber thought about it and came up with a solution on the basis that the police already knew of Eddie's existence, so what was wrong about telling this bloke about him? "Don't know his first name mate," Bomber made one up. "All I know is, we called him the Slasher see, on account of his 'obby." "And what hobby would that be sir?" as he jotted down *Slasher Coleman (son) currently abroad, address unknown.* "Dunno mate, he kept himself to himself, if I knew any more, I'd tell you guv honest." Bomber was slipping into brick wall-mode, self-defence and general hatred of anyone other than his own kind was kicking in. He found he was taking small backward steps whilst registrar man began shuffling forward in an effort to keep pace with him. "That's all I can say to you mate, so don't ask me any more questions. " Bomber rose to his full height and gave the registrar a menacing look. The registrar, however, was not one to be intimidated. "Just a few questions sir about yourself, I am going to need your name, address and contact number. Since Mrs Coleman's arrival, you are the first and only person to come forward with positive information." "Information?" Bomber's voice rose up a number of decibels.

"Information, that makes me sound like an informer, I'll 'ave you know, I'm no bloody grass not now, not never so stick that in your pipe and smoke it!" The registrar knew when he was beaten and backed off. The hospital had had their fair share of belligerent patients and visitors of late. All hospital staff had recently undergone an 'In house' training course on how to deflate potential threats or aggressive hot spots and how to cool them down. Here then, was a brewing hot spot to deflate and cool down right in front of him. He loved his job at the hospital, it paid well and kept food on the table for his wife and five kids. But no job is worth a couple of black eyes and a broken nose. Admittedly if he received any rough stuff, he would be able to walk straight in to the emergency centre and queue jump for medical attention. He applied the cooling down techniques learned at the one-day course. First off, no direct eye contact, second off, half turn away and begin to smile. Unbeknown to him, Bomber was about to disappear anyway. When he did disappear, registrar man congratulated himself on dealing with the potential confrontation and promised to speak to the course director to tell him how well it all worked. Before leaving Bomber gently asked one final question, a question that should really be answered by a qualified doctor. "How'd she snuff it then?" The registrar, still totally flushed with the success of cooling this guy down, overstepped the mark and told Bomber the following. "Mrs. Coleman died of a cerebral haemorrhage or cerebral bleed." "Hang on, you said she died in the ambulance, how come and where is she now?" "I'm afraid that's all I can tell you Sir. If you want more information you need to go to reception and request to see the duty doctor." "Yea okay but I still wanna know which ward she's in." "Not in a ward Sir, she is in the hospital morgue." Bomber was aware of brain bleeds. Being a pro boxer for many years the subject had come up a number of times. It's something you have to push to the back of the mind,

it can happen to anyone, especially when you're pummelling your opponent in the ring for several rounds. 'Poor Mrs Coleman, Val' he thought. He hated having sole responsibility of letting Eddie know his mum was dead. His first port of call would have to be a return visit to 119 Plenva Street on the Isle of Dogs, get some more info from the neighbour and have a rifle through Mrs Coleman's sideboard. He needed to find the postal address in Spain, so as to let Eddie know. Earlier that same day, Bomber called in to 119 Plenva Street for his weekly update with Val. When he arrived, the front door was wide open with no sign of Mrs. Coleman. Bomber stood in the doorway and called out. "Anyone home?"

A voice was heard from an open window next door. "She's been taken to hospital; she'd just come out of 'er house to go shopping I think and fell. Straight down onto her path, never made it to the gate poor cow. Didn't deserve that, I can tell yer." "Bang! 'orrible it was. She just lay there moaning 'er face all twisted up in pain like. Just goes to show, you don't know when or how. The lord above can take you anytime you know." She quickly made a sign of the cross at the mention of the lord's name, possibly for the first time in her life. Bomber leapt over the low dividing garden fence to get a better look at the neighbour. "So where is she now, is she indoors?" "No son, somebody must 'ave rung for an ambulance, it wasn't me, cos we're not on the blower see." "So, where the fuck is she? Is she dead or what?" Gawd no she gave a little wave as she was stretchered into the ambulance. Anyway, keep your 'air on mate, I'm only trying to 'elp. They took 'er to Whipps Cross over in Leytonstone." Bomber jumped back to Val's side of the fence, pulled the front door shut and called out to the next-door neighbour, "don't let anyone in." He began jogging towards the housing estate nearby where he hoped to grab a taxi. One or two usually loitered around the shopping area hoping to pick up little old ladies laden with their weekly shop then drive them home via Limehouse. Well, it was only an extra two miles, but it should beef up the meter a bit!

CHAPTER 67

Following his visit to Whipps Cross and subsequent discovery of Val Coleman's demise, Bomber made his weary way back to Val's home on the Island. It was a good seven miles therefore a long walk was ahead. He was in a bad mood and felt the walk would help him clear his mind. The fact that a direct bus route from Whipps Cross to the Island didn't exist, helped him decide on using Shanks's pony as a means of transport. When he finally arrived, it was getting dark. Street lights were popping on and lights in people's windows doing the same, at least for those who could afford it, those that couldn't sparked up their Tilley or Aladdin mantle lamps.

119 Plenva Street remained in darkness, seemingly out of respect for the deceased Mrs. Coleman. The sight brought a lump to Bomber's throat. He thought she was a strong woman who would be around till the cows come home. Always a ready sparkling smile, brain sharp as a pin. He began to wonder if he should track down her ex, Micky but then again why should he? That bastard would be all over the house like a shot claiming this and claiming that like a bloody vulture picking over the bones, no, he should be the last to know. Out of respect for Mrs. Coleman Bomber would take care of that. As he entered the house the next-door neighbour scuttled in behind him asking "how is she not too bad, I hope?" Bomber shook his head. "Not good as it happens. She's asked me to keep an eye on this place, so I might be staying here for a week or so." On his way to Val's home from the hospital Bomber worked out a bit of a plan.

If he told the neighbour Val was dead, the news would spread like a bush fire. Indeed, the bush fire could well reach the ears of undesirable people that might use the info for their own gains. He felt it was important that her son Eddie should be the first to know. This little old lady, no doubt was a good friend to Val. It was like that in the East End, people looked after each other, borrowed stuff from each other, shared secrets with each other and would offer up their home if husbands got violent. She will know about Val soon enough, just not right now. He thanked the neighbour for keeping an eye out and slowly hustled her outside, pointing her in the direction of her own home, she got the message. On her way up the path, she offered help in any way she could, again Bomber thanked her and shooed her out of his sight. Gently closing the front door on the world, he made his way into the little front room, sat down and fell asleep. When eventually he awoke it was daylight. He'd been out around twelve hours solid. Bomber sat up, back aching from sitting in a fireside chair all night, cramp in both legs. 'I must have needed that he thought'. Within an hour Bomber located all the paperwork regarding telegram contact with her son Eddie. A biscuit tin hidden up the chimney on a small shelf held all the messages received from Eddie; plus, the address he was aiming for in Spain. He congratulated himself on finding it before anyone else, especially old Bill. From what he understood from the bloke at Whipps Cross, the filth was to be advised about Val and no doubt would be round soon for a rummage. "Over my dead body." He said to no one in particular.

Just then Bomber jumped out of his skin as a loud knocking commenced at the front door. He looked in the mirror at his refection saying "bloody 'ell that was quick" and stuffed the biscuit tin back in its original hiding place. The knocking intensified. Bomber yelled "All right all right I'm on my way, where's the bloody fire?" Bomber threw the door open, fully expecting to see the place surrounded by armed police, pockets stuffed with search warrants. "Oi pal wot you doin 'ere then eh?" the young voice came from below Bomber's eyeline. He dropped his gaze downward. A young boy stood on the doormat looking up at him hands on hips, legs slightly apart. Bomber ventured "You're not the old Bill then" and laughed. "No, I aint, I'm Robbo from a couple of doors down and this is my auntie Val's house, so unless you wanna bunch of fives and a punch up the throat, I'll ask once again wot you doing 'ere?" Bomber explained the situation asking him to keep it to himself at least for a day or so. He purposely avoided telling him anything about the hospital or the reason she was there, only to explain, that it was her express wish that he should stay at her house for a while to keep things ticking over. Robbo quietly thought things over. "Listen up dumbo, you'd better not nick nuffink. Coz If you do, I've got some well tasty mates that'll sort you out see 'an you'll come a right cropper." Bomber smiled. He saw that Robbo was serious, so he replied. "Cross my heart and hope to die, I'll be on my best behaviour." This lad's genuine concern for his auntie plus his fierce loyalty in the face of a giant of a man, touched Bomber, this was beyond fear and if Val was still alive and he was able to tell her about the confrontation, she would probably scold Robbo but secretly she would no doubt swell up with pride. Robbo wagged a knowing finger and marched off back home. Bomber ceased to be visible to any nosey parkers bogging in from the row of terraced houses over on the other side of the street as he gently closed the front door. Back in the tiny living room his hand felt for the biscuit tin and retrieved it from its hiding place. He stuck it on the sideboard, in full view of the street window. It was time to conjure up some tea and sarnies. Rifling through Val's larder he found half a loaf, some cheese and a carving knife.

As he cut off two thick bread slices, he remembered this was the same knife, the one he'd wrestled off Eddie when he was about to shoot off and murder Lenny the Scrotes's gang who'd done for Wossname. Bomber slapped on some butter, cut off two large chunks of cheddar and pressed the slices together to form a doorstep sandwich. Before devouring his home-made snack, he popped the kettle on as he thought he might be needing something in liquid form to wash it all down. Balancing the doorstep sarnie and a mug of tea on a small tray, Bomber made his way from the kitchen back to the living room readying his tummy for some grub. A shadow passing the living room window put him immediately on high alert. Another shadow, then another passed the window. Bomber eyed the biscuit tin sitting on the sideboard in plain sight. Before ducking out of view he grabbed the tin and disappeared back to the kitchen to await the inevitable banging on the door. It didn't come. Bomber decided on an aggressive exit. Steaming out the front door, fists raised he was taken aback somewhat. Stood in front of him was a startled and worried looking chap with two teenage boys. One carrying a bucket of water and sponge the other a ladder. "What's going on 'ere then?" Boomed Bomber. The eldest of the three stuttered. "Were here to clean the windows mate, we come round once a month we do, don't we lads." Both lads nodded in tandem. "Okay if we get on then?" Bomber eyed them suspiciously, perhaps they could be old Bill in disguise. "You mate, can fuck of now cos the jobs cancelled.

If you don't, I'll knock you from 'ere to next Wednesday. The trio decided it was time to go.

CHAPTER 68

For the fifth time that wet and dreary London morning Dave Conti walked the length of Hatton Garden cursing the rain and cursing his lack of courage. Nicking cars was a cinch he was a professional and enjoyed relieving the filthy rich West End bastards of their shiny motors. Each time he passed the premises where the safety deposit box was held, he halted briefly then moved on again. "Tell me again why we're 'ere then Dave." Dave stared at his lookout lad. "You got a slow-moving brain or something, no wonder people call you Slug." "Alright Dave mate, no need to get all pissy." Dave had explained more than once about the safety deposit box stashed in the building they'd passed now five times, full of jewellery courtesy of a raid some time ago from a jeweller's shop on the same street.

What he didn't tell his young companion was, the tom foolery had been deposited by himself and Mrs. Coleman and he, Dave, had memorised the box number and its location within this world-famous diamond centre known to most villains as sparkler street. To Dave's mind the proceeds in the box belonged not to Mrs Coleman but to him and Eddie, who'd arranged the original raid.

The very idea of nicking the already nicked and deposited jewellery from his absent boss was extremely audacious. If it went wrong and Eddie found out, he would be on the run for the rest of his life. However, the lure of the diamonds and the possible wealth they would give him was a tough one to resist. Dave was running a large tab possibly in the hundreds, to a number of gambling clubs across the West End of London and could only stretch it out so far. The jewellery in the deposit box would be the key to his freedom from debt and perhaps he could open a bloody club of his own and start fleecing clients himself. "So why don't we go straight in, grab the stuff and 'ave it away?" Dave smiled. This lad was the best 'look out' he'd ever recruited, he could sense the police well before they appeared. He would carefully work out in advance what bobbies were on what beat, daytime or night beats, within a square mile of the car park Dave was working. This of course was most useful, but it was his sixth sense that made it possible for Dave to carry out his quality car nicking before the old Bill ever got near them. This was the main reason he had asked Slug to go with him to Hatton Garden, Dave's big idea was to collect the diamonds, lift a roller using Slug as lookout and drive off in conspicuous style. Something he could not have known about just now, was that Mrs Coleman is lying in a morgue and as soon as Eddie found out he'd be back in the East End like a shot facing a definite arrest or not. At the forefront of Dave's mind, strictly speaking, he should have told his new boss Johnny the Turk of his whereabouts and intentions. "Sod telling him." He said out loud, "He's not sharing the spoils, I need it to clear my debts or 'ave my hands cut off." Slug didn't bother asking what Dave was mumbling on about he was far too busy clocking a uniform strolling towards them with a knowing look on his face. Slug cleared his throat, loudly. Dave got the message, as he had done a hundred times before. "Let's go grab a cup of tea somewhere Slug, I need to think things through." "Okay Dave, as long as you're paying." He grinned. The copper watched as the two of them passed him on the pavement. He'd noticed them walking up and down and was about to ask them if they needed directions. Good job he didn't, the pair would have instantly broken into a run.

Dave's background bounced between the three points of his particular life style triangle. Prison, fighting and leggy blonds. None of these attributes required too much of a thinking man's brain. Working out the odds at horse racing was the nearest he got to methodical deliberation. He was however a perfect candidate as a gang member and was well liked within his circle of violent criminal associates. Growing up as he did in the rough house of East End London, fighting was almost second nature. Belt someone in the mouth first, discuss why later. He was known to have a strong dislike of nonsense and would take none from no one. He was not frightened of anybody, perhaps only Eddie Coleman just a bit, mainly because Eddie was an unhinged psycho who had lost touch with reality. His contempt and scorn for the law or anyone in a position of officialdom earned him respect amongst his peer group, be they jail birds or gang members alike. It also turned on the blondes no end. Being over six-foot-tall with jet black, swept back hair, plus being a snazzy dresser made him a magnet for the birds, made them go dizzy. Especially when he turned up in a smart motor and flashed the cash about a bit. Since Eddie's disappearing act, his daily routine of nicking quality motors and driving them to Errol's, was peppered with frequent visits to either betting shops by day and gambling clubs by night. In other words, he was slowly going off the rails. It was principally this that led him to Hatton Garden and the possibility of scoring big money and being able to pay off his gambling debts, which were mounting up fast. Some had percentages added by the week, others by the day. The one he feared most was for a monkey. It had been sold by the gambling club he owed, to a recovery agent business that went by the name of the Bazanov brothers, a particularly nasty pair of Russian individuals, known for their brutal debt recovery methods. To date they had achieved a one hundred percent success rate. With Eddie at the helm, the Bazanov's might have given Dave a wide berth. However, Eddie is now on the trot, a fact known to the Bazanov family and many others. Dave didn't fancy going up against them so he was keeping a low profile until he had enough cash to pay off the £500.00 debt, before it grew any more. Having sweet Fanny Adams to his name as in potless, didn't sit well with Dave neither did being cornered by the Bazanov brothers. He stood outside the building where the deposit box contents had been deposited by Mrs. Coleman and himself then pressed the intercom button. A voice immediately said, "Good morning, Sir, how may I help you?" He peered through the thickened glass door backed up with a thick metal grill and saw a young lady sitting behind a desk holding a phone to her ear.

The female voice repeated the question. "How may I help you Sir?" He leaned forward to the intercom and announced. "I need to check the contents of my deposit box" adding "please" by way of common courtesy. Slug had been detailed to scout round for a suitable motor to nick, either a roller or something approaching that level of class and style. Dave must have said the magic words. A buzzer sounded and the heavily fortified door unlocked itself electronically. Dave pushed it open gently then let himself in to what presumably was the front office, somewhere for the staff to meet and greet their rich customers. Tasteful furniture, flowers in vases, portraits of previous chairmen greeted him in advance of the young lady. She came out from behind her desk and made her way towards him right hand out ready to shake Dave's. Mini greetings over, coffee or tea offered and declined, he was invited to sign the visitors' book that sat on a smoked glass coffee table just in front of a stunning racing green three-seater Chesterfield sofa. Coming as he did from a poor family and brung up in Whitechapel, he had no idea of the cost of the three-seater, he just knew he wanted one because to him it looked the bee's knees. He turned back to the young lady and gave her a wink and grin. Turn on the old charm he thought, I might get lucky here! Faint heart never one a fair maiden! He gave her the once over, lovely blonde hair, his favourite, tight fitting dress, black stockings, his favourite again, with a winning smile. He noticed the absence of a wedding or engagement ring. and said, "how's a lovely girl like you not been taken up yet?" "How do work that one out then?" she enquired. Dave held up his left hand pointing to his ring finger. He leant towards her and said in a low voice "When I've done here how about you and me going out tonight?" He signed the visitors' book with an indecipherable squiggle and before being asked, he put a piece of paper on the young lady's desk upon which he had previously written the box number. She picked up a different phone and spoke quietly into it. Dave was sweating like a racehorse, if he kept it together and played his card right, he might be able to pull the whole thing off and pull her and all. The thought of Eddie tracking him down and cutting him up was now farthest from his mind. Diamonds and this lovely young blonde bird, as far as he was concerned, put Eddie straight on the back burner. The young lady beamed at him saying "Someone will be here in a moment Sir to accompany you down stairs to where we are holding your deposit box."

CHAPTER 69

Zak's Place was busy. People from all walks of life crammed themselves into the tiny bar area with more waiting outside on the street. One customer trying to squeeze his way to the bar said to another flippantly, "Strewth I swear if I jumped up in the air I would bloody well stay there!" He continued, "this place used to be much quieter when it was just us thieves, robbers, muggers and swindlers. I've got the right hump with that Zak. It's all 'is bloody fault. Getting greedy for profits no doubt. I'm going to have to straighten him out. Only thing is, I've got to get passed that body guard of his, that Bomber bloke." Johnny the Turk appeared from his upstairs den, as if by magic, a hush descended. Zak's customers shuffled left and right respectfully leaving a clear pathway to the bar. The people in at Zak's today were mostly thrill seekers. Ordinary people who got a kick out of rubbing shoulders with villains. The sort of people that would run a mile if faced with proper aggro. Word was out and about, psycho Eddie Coleman was on the run and this establishment now served as the nerve centre for Eddie's crew, currently headed up by Johnny, the man of the moment. To some he was a local hero, others actually wanted his autograph, not that they ever got one. As Johnny sauntered on over to the bar, a crate of brown ale appeared on the beer wet bar top. Johnny grabbed the crate then made his way back to the door that led upstairs, somebody quietly mentioned, "looks like there's a pow wow on tonight, maybe we'll get to see some more villains." A Kodak flashed straight into Johnny's eyes. The person who clicked the go button on his Kodak found himself on the ground knocked spark out by Johnny rather sharpish like. "Who the fuck are you?" He bellowed. The Kodak fell to the ground with him. Johnny put the crate down and stamped heavily on the camera. It was no match for Johnny's size ten cherry red hob nail bovver boots. The force of the boot-stamp broke the Kodak into a number of jagged plastic pieces. Johnny picked up the largest piece rammed it into the photographer's mouth and stamped on that too. The photographer come reporter guy, now minus a camera, screamed in agony as the sharp corners cut into his mouth, gums and throat. Then the bleeding started. He tried to close his mouth to staunch the flow but was unable to as the broken plastic courtesy of Johnny's stamping, lodged between the roof of his mouth and his lower jaw. Johnny continued casually on his way to the upstairs meeting room without so much as a backward glance.

Show over, the gap made for Johnny closed in again. In the rush to get more beer the guy on the floor was all but forgotten. He was kicked accidentally, trodden on accidentally, had some beer spilt on him accidentally. Somebody even gobbed on him, accidentally. During all the accidental accidents the poor chap spotted the film canister which had come loose from the busted Kodak, it was but a few feet away. Bruised and battered he got up on all fours, made a grab for the roll of film them crawled his way through a crowd of legs to a corner of the room leaving a trail of blood behind him. Happy in the knowledge he would heal in time, at least he hadn't been shot. The blood quickly soaked up in to layers of sawdust primarily scattered around to soak up beer spills and the odd bit of blood and shit of course. He was happy despite his injuries to his face and pride, in that the roll of film from the Kodak was clutched firmly in his left hand. With a bit of luck, the film might have not been exposed to light and with a bit more luck perhaps that last shot of the gangland boss would develop perfectly well, then his newspaper editor boss of 'The London Scoop' for once, might be pleased with his efforts. With his right hand he felt around in his mouth, taking hold of the main bit of plastic he bravely but gently sawed it left and right until if fell out. As it did, he let out an agonising scream. The nearest punter looked down at him saying, "You still here mate? If I were you, I'd fuck off out of it, before Johnny comes back down?" He did just that and thought he would head back to Fleet Street where the newspaper he worked for was based, by way of a hospital to get his mouth sorted. The thought of a good story which might even make page two with his name on it, accompanied by a candid snap of a notorious gangland boss muted the pain in his mouth somewhat. In fact, he thought he'd got off quite lightly. At least he'd not been tortured or killed. On his way to Mile End hospital, it crossed his mind that he should try and sell the story and snap-shot to the highest bidder. Might even get him a nomination for a Pulitzer Prize. That will definitely be worth a hob nail boot in his north and south! Good old Joseph Pulitzer, a great legacy gifted to the world for excellence in journalism. Face, teeth and mouth patched up, the photographer-come-reporter got back to his bedsit in Stepney, pulled the curtains, covered them with blackout sheets and dug the roll of film out from his pocket. Next, he half-filled an enamel tray with developing agent and added some sodium carbonate. He placed the roll of film into a changing bag so as to remove the film from its cannister. Light bulbs in the bedsit were switched from standard 60 watts to red and the process began. After the final rinse he now had a roll of perfect negatives.

Within a few hours the final negative from the film roll, the one with a mug shot of Johnny, had developed well. It was pegged up on a string line to dry. He now had a negative from which he could produce many a copy and one fully developed black and white. A snarling startled photo of the crew's king pin. What a story this would make, he thought. The following day found him at his tiny desk at the offices of his newspaper in Fleet Street, banging out a story on his typewriter to compliment the mug shot. Sub titled, Exclusive to 'The Scoop.'

Eddie Coleman got a mention as did his mum. It was made all the better due to E.C. being on the run from the Metropolitan Police, reportedly charging around under the Spanish sun, according to the reporters' informants, on a killing spree. He'd have to submit the story to his editor for approval then wait to see if the story would be appropriate and fit for purpose. Not every paper wanted the hassle of dealing with gangland goings on, there could be deadly repercussions and had been in the past, like them blowing up newspaper's offices. Plus, stories of this nature were often shown to the police first. The police frowned upon gangland information going out in print, especially if the information might jeopardise any current investigations. It was all very well keeping the old Bill on side with the press by giving large donations to the annual policeman's ball but a slip up would soon do away with any goodwill, and all those ridiculously high donations would then be wasted. On the other hand, a major increase in circulation might out-weigh any repercussions, after all that is every editor's goal. In fact, for most it was their only goal. Increased circulation equalled shareholders' wealth. Everyone's a winner. The eighth attempt at the story line looked just right, definitely having the edge over the previous seven endeavours. It was a winner and he thought his editor, when he saw it, would probably get it in Friday's edition, which was always for some reason, the best day for sales. All that was needed now was a suitable header, something to grab the reader's attention. After a cup of lukewarm coffee and a piece of stale cake he let out a joyous, "*eureka!* I have it. Tingling with a front-page stop press moment, a moment of the kind he rarely experienced, he set to work on the reader grabbing headline to accompany Johnny's mug shot. Jogging over to the type setting area he happily grabbed some sheets of dry transfer lettering in Helvetica bold and set to work. Before starting the process, he needed a burnisher so as to transfer the lettering to an A4 premium smooth sheet of paper.

As luck would have it, The Scoops graphic designer left one on his desk over in the corner. No sign of him, must have popped out for a Jimmy. Great, now to proceed. Another ten minutes passed and it was ready. He held it up, scrutinised the text for any spelling errors and, more importantly, all apostrophes were where they should be. 'Dare I he thought?' He read the headline out-loud. Yes, most definitely he should, The London Scoop has a long and proud record of complete impartiality, as in equal treatment of all rivals or disputants. Well, at least that's what it says in the dictionary. And who in the squeaky-clean press business would vary from that mantra? The Headline read...

East End Gang Boss Wears Women's Underwear!

The photo of Johnny's startled face was clipped just below. The text under the photo read 'Full story on page Two.' The full story set for page two would reveal nothing about the undies, by then the paper had been purchased, the circulation upped considerably, shareholders wealth increased and a happy editor. The organised crime boss in question would not be named, not for now at least, not that the story's author knew of it anyway. He attached page two's ready typed story via a paper clip, tucked the completed effort in a buff folder, marked it 'Hot Stuff' and placed it on the editor's desk. He'd done his bit, now it was up to the powers that be, hopefully to spot the opportunity for greater circulation.

CHAPTER 70

Dave Conti followed his escort to a level one floor below the reception area. He found himself standing on the fringe of a room with private booths on one side and a wall banked with hundreds of deposit boxes opposite. Before entering the room, he needed to pass through a floor to ceiling metal vault door, flanked either side with vertical floor to ceiling metal bars. It reminded him a bit of gaining access to the canteen when he was inside doin a bit of bird. His escort unlocked the vault door and let Dave go through. Once he was in, his escort locked the door and stood outside turning his back to face the other way. Without moving his head, he scanned his eyes over the wall chocked full of locked deposit box doors. To his relief and delight he saw one particular door with a key inserted ready and waiting for him. The key turned with a satisfying clunk. Dave pulled out the metal container from within, took the key with him and settled himself down inside the first booth.

Slamming the metal container on a table for the use of, he unlocked it using the same key and slowly lifted the lid. Before peering inside, he plonked down on the softly furnished chair provided and took a couple of gulps of air to steady his jangled nerves. He didn't need a spine donor, he had plenty of backbone when it was needed. However, his stock in trade was nicking up-market motors not nicking from his now ex-boss, psychotic or not. He was keenly aware the diamonds and gems herein would be separated from any gold or silver they were previously attached to. After all, it was him all those weeks ago that ferried the stolen stuff over to that bent geezer in Romford, who was a specialist in that department with no questions asked. Mr Romford was to keep all the gold and silver as payment. All the loose gems and diamonds given back and deposited here in a box, in a vault not more than three doors away from where the original diamond break-in took place. Eddie, who masterminded the diamond heist, worked on the basis that Hatton Garden would be the last place anyone would look for the proceeds of a robbery which took place in Hatton Garden itself. And he was right, here they were sitting right in front of Dave. From an inside jacket pocket, Dave pulled out a leather bag about five inches by seven with leather laces that would pull the top tightly together. Pulling the box lid fully off, he leaned forward and peered in. There sitting, awaiting an owner to give them a good home sat three white cloth bags, all with similar drawstrings to Dave's leather one. On the table sat a large deep blue mat, the type a jeweller would use when showing a customer an expensive necklace. He carefully opened the first of the white bags and shook the contents out onto the blue mat. He gasped as the sparklers poured out. These were all crystal clear. He knew this meant they were the most valuable, having no inclusions or blemishes. Suppressing a whoop of excitement, he scooped them up and poured them back in the bag. The second bag revealed a great many larger gem stones, in a myriad of colours. Reds, greens, blues, Topaz yellows and so on. Dave quickly worked out the three bags had been pre-sorted no doubt in terms of value. He tackled the third, pouring its contents onto the waiting mat. It was all pearls. He didn't know a cultured pearl from a freshwater and certainly didn't know about the tooth test. To him they could possibly all be fake and therefore almost worthless. Best to bag them up and put them straight back in the box.

In the end he decided to take all of the diamonds and only half of the gems. At this point, he was unsure in his mind, if Eddie knew exactly what was in the deposit box, probably not. If he didn't, then so much the better. He thought he'd best get over to Romford pronto and speak to the geezer who separated this lot from their original mountings. Get him to keep his bleeding mouth shut or he would shut it for him, permanently. The escort called out, "All okay Sir, anything I can help you with?" "Nah mate, almost finished here ta. Be out in a mo." He closed the box, locked it then placed the two bags sitting on the blue felt mat into his leather pouch. He thought about penning an I.O.U. then signing it Micky Mouse and leaving the note inside the box, but bottled it as that would be a major piss take. Back upstairs he waited for his escort to go back to where he came from. When he did, Dave said to blondie "Okay babe, I think I'll take you up on that offer of a coffee now." He sat himself down on the large sofa and stuck his long legs out in front of him and patted the area next to him. "Yes of course, do please make yourself comfortable, I will be right there with you sir." Blondie disappeared into another room. Whilst she was rummaging around in the kitchenette, he cultivated an image of her coming over, throwing herself on the sofa muttering in his shell-like 'take me, take me here and now, you great big sexy hunk'. In my dreams he thought in my dreams pal. This *was* bloody weird though thought Dave, I've got a ton of hooky gear on me recently nicked from a jewellers three doors down, probably fence in the high thousands. I'm sitting on a pretty lush sofa which back home would be called a settee, and about to be served coffee and cake by a nice bit of stuff. What more could I ask? He was about to say, 'I suppose a shag is out of the question, is it?' But thought no, it might spoil the moment. A tray bearing a delicate bone-china cup filled almost to the brim with black coffee arrived, together with custard cream biscuits, a sugar bowl, a tiny silver teaspoon and a cream jug. It was placed carefully on the smoked glass coffee table in front of the sofa. "Would you like me to be mum sir?" asked the young lady. Dave winked and smiled a lewd smile. "No way blondie no way, not me mum I'd much rather you be me bird like. What's your name anyway?" After a few seconds delay, she replied "I'm Sally, Sally Pantz" adding quickly "and before you say anything, I've heard them all." Dave just about kept a straight face and said, "Don't ever get married to a bloke with a last name of Down, cos if you went for a double barrelled jobby, well I'll leave you to work that one out."

A hand vigorously waving from outside the heavily secured street door caught his eye. Slug motioned that Dave should get the hell out and fast. A dally with Sally would have to wait. As he kissed her goodbye on the cheek a piece of carefully folded paper was placed in his jacket pocket. Dave looked at Sally who was smiling a come get me smile. 'Eh up' he thought, I've cracked it with this cracker right enough. I've only gone and got her phone number!

CHAPTER 71

"Fabio mate, call us a cabola can you or whatever it is you call a taxi over here." Eddie was standing in the Hotel's vast reception area. All stone and shiny white marble as far as he could work out. "Certainly Mr. Biggs er sorry, Eddie. I will telephone for one immediately. Where are you going, the driver will want to know the destination?" "Mojácar if you must know and can you ask the cost? I don't want the driver to rip me off with some ludicrous excess charges." "Please be assured Eddie, the cabina company we use is as honest and trustworthy as we are here in this fine hotel and upholds all we stand for in client care." "Oh, and can I change up some English coinage in to Spanish money?" "Yes of course you can. Someone at the hotel reception desk will help you. A question Eddie if I may, what time do you want the cabina to pick you up, and will you be checking out?" "As it happens yes pal at about eleven. I know it's only ten, but I want to have a quick walk around. I need to buy something nice for a lady I know, any suggestions?" Fabio furrowed his brow deep in thought. "Yes, yes, I know exactly the place. They specialize in beautiful traditional Spanish musical boxes to keep jewellery in, which when opened play the classic music. Your lady friend will love one. If you like, as I am on a break right now, I can accompany you to the correct outlet' will that be, okay? It is but five minutes' walk away." "Sure thing pal, so what are we waiting for, let's go, as long as you aint leading me up the garden path." "Just let me book the cabola and I will be right with you." Twenty minutes later, gift purchased and beautifully wrapped, Eddie and Fabio were sat at an expresso bar, located on the pavement outside a large cantina. It was busy with people passing by in front and behind them. "Thanks for that mate, my lady is gonna love it.

Look Fabio." Eddie lowered his voice. "Something tells me you might be useful. I pay bloody good wages for good people to look after my interests, probably treble what they pay you back at the hotel." "But Eddie." Fabio intervened. "I live and eat there for free." "Well get yourself some rented digs." "Sorry, explain 'digs' please." "Somewhere to live and get yer 'ead down. Somewhere I can shack up if I need to. I'll pay your rent and keep. It's just that if things go tits up over in Mojácar, I might need a bolthole." "Eddie, my English although fluent, you speak words I do not fully understand." "Such as Fabio?" "Well, there's shack up, digs, 'ead down, tits up, keep and finally bolthole." Eddie laughed, then went through all the necessary translations, three times for each one just to be on the safe side. Fabio took notes. "Okay, I will try to keep up and many thanks for the explanations." A second, this time un-ordered expresso's found their way through the throng of passers-by and put in front of them. "Eddie, I have a good idea, I think. How about this, I go part time at the hotel and still organise somewhere for you, as you say, a bolthole. That way I will continue to be fed by the Hotel but go home to the digs each night. It will save you the 'keep' and will provide you with a place to stay if things go 'tits up', day or night." Fabio smiled long and contently having mastered some East End lingo. "No need to think too hard about that one Fabio, just get cracking." Eddie pulled out a few 1000 peseta notes he'd obtained from the hotel exchange clerk and thrust them at Fabio. Fabio nodded sagely, stuffed the money into his back pocket and stuck out a hand for Eddie to shake. Eddie looked at Fabio's hand aghast and half shouted "Put that bloody disgusting thing away I don't know where it's been!" Instead, he gave Fabio a great big East End hug and the deal by dint of the hug was sealed. "Get it sorted son. I'll be back at the hotel in a couple of days or so then you can show me where the bolthole is. Just make bloody sure it's got two toilets and two bedrooms." "Yes Sir." Fabio mock saluted. "Look, it's getting close to eleven Eddie; shall we make it back to the hotel. I have seen to it that your belongings are washed, ironed and packed. Your holdall will be in a luggage holding room next to the reception desk ready for when you check out." Eddie gasped in horror. "What will have happened with my guns?" Fabio stiffened, "Guns, what guns? Are you being serious?" Eddie held his stare, this was face to face, eyeball to eyeball stuff. Eddie roared with laughter and mock punched Fabio in the chin, "fucking got you there mate you should have seen your boat race."

Fabio moved in closer, bearing his clenched teeth like a rabid dog he growled "Do that again and I will tear you limb from limb you English piece of shit." It was Eddie's turn to be taken aback. Not that he was afraid of Fabio, far from it. It was just very unexpected. Now it was Fabio's turn to howl with laughter, he almost bent double. Eddie said, "Fair do's mate you had me worried just then, cos I was about to kill you with my bare hands. Yea, I was worried that if I did you in, old Bill would cart me off to clink before you could say Jack Robinson." "English Eddie, English." cried Fabio. As the cab drove off from the hotel, Eddie looked back to see Fabio smiling and waving just as he would with any client who checked out and given him a small tip. He waved a bit more heartily to this departing customer, due to the tip bordering on ten thousand pesetas. Shortly before Eddie left, Fabio informed him, "If there is anything you want to know about anyone in Mojácar, I will be happy to oblige."

CHAPTER 72

"Do you know where you're going pal? Only when we got to that junction back there the sign for Mojácar pointed right but you turned left and now other signs are saying 'Malaga 200 kilometres' so what's your bloody game then pal?" "Oh, so sorry sir, there are no filling stations on the road to Mojácar and we need to fill up, there is a filling station a little way along this road we should just about make it." Eddie leaned forward and peered over the driver's shoulder. He saw the fuel gauge registering full. Eddie sat back and rummaged through his holdall which was sitting by his side. Luckily the people back at the hotel had missed an inside pocket in which sat a wicked looking Bowie knife. One that he'd purchased on his overnight stay in Madrid. Whipping it out, he brought it up to the back of the driver's head, pointy bit forwards. Eddie was about to ram it in and sever this guy's spinal cord but remembered they were travelling at around fifty miles an hour and he would be powerless to control the car from the back seat. Eddie waved the knife at the driver's reflection in the rear-view mirror and snarled, "Pull up or this goes in you" and placed the knife point to the back of the driver's neck once more. He got the message and brought the taxi to a sudden stop. Eddie leaned forward, making damn sure the knife stayed where it would do major damage and pulled open the glove compartment to the right of the driver.

To his surprise, inside was a police issue pistol in a leather holster together with a black plastic pouch which had a police badge attached. Eddie grabbed both items, sat back in his seat murmuring "well, well, well." So, you're a bloody copper, eh? Not a very good one though cos now you're up shit creek without a paddle." The officer laughed nervously, "Not heard that one before, If I get out of this mess alive, I will tell it to my sons." Eddie had the loaded pistol in one hand with the safety catch off ready to go bang and a Bowie knife in the other which was beginning to cut into the flesh at the back of the officer's neck. Eddie's curiosity was working overtime. "Right, shit for brains, time to talk and no bloody porkies." The officer had no idea what porkies meant and he was not going to ask. He was not about to talk anyway, he stayed quiet. Silent ears were listening in on the cabs two-way radio. Eddie needed an angle to get him to cough up. "How old are your sons' pal, only I ask cos it may be difficult for them to grow up without a dad?" This was the trigger. His back seat passenger, seemed to be indicating potential loss of his life. "Look sir, just calm down, we had a phone call from your hotel, strangers get noticed fast in Almeria and we had someone tell us you where you were staying. We know about the murder of a gang boss in Bilbao and a yacht owner in the same town. We thought we had you on the train but the man we arrested believing it was you, was able to prove his innocence." "Hold up pal what do you mean a phone call?" "A waiter who works at your hotel got in touch." "Right pal, I've heard enough, turn this car around and head for Mojácar, don't look back at me and don't drive like a maniac, either way I'll blow your bleedin 'ead off and laugh at the same time" The officer responded. His hands were clammy, sweat dripped from his forehead into his eyes, dark sweat patches appeared under his armpits, legs started to tremble. His mind went back to earlier this morning when he and his police colleagues sat around in the meeting room as the boss outlined todays intended capture of the correct Jack du Pré, currently going by the name of a train robber.

A request was put forward for one of the officers, posing as a taxi driver, to go and pick up their quarry at the Hotel and he immediately stuck his hand up. He was a natural for the job as he spoke good English. Could be a promotion is this he thought. However, he had sorely underestimated one ruthless Eddie Coleman. The remainder of his colleagues were to man the road blocks a mile or two along the road to Malaga not far from where Eddie forced the taxi to stop. Little did he imagine the situation would come to this. He hoped his colleagues who were manning the road block would second guess what was occurring by now and come look for him.

Surely the waiter snitch at the hotel would have rung the station and informed them of Eddie's departure time and the station will have then radioed the message on to the guys at the road block. The road to Mojácar was not exactly treacherous but there were some nasty bends and in some places with equally nasty drops down to rocks below. If his passenger suggested they should out-run anyone chasing them, he was not entirely sure of his overall safety. However, his brothers-in-arms hopefully would radio ahead to the station at Mojácar who could use a couple of their cars to form a make shift road block somewhere about half way between Almeria and Mojácar and then, this bandit would be like a rat in trap, no way forward, no way back. Eddie's mind was racing too. Why did that bloody Fabio squeal on him? If it *was* him, he would have his guts for garters. 'I wouldn't mind' he thought 'but I bunged him all that fucking money the sodding little toe rag.' He pushed the gun hard onto the driver's neck and barked. "Give us the name of that grassing bloody waiter, or this goes off now. He looked at Eddie in the rear-view mirror. His eyes seemed to be glazing over, this could be it thought the driver. He didn't sign up for this, so he blabbed. "His name is Pedro, Pedro Garcia, he's the son of one of the hotel owners. Nobody likes him, he is for ever being *how you say*, the big I am." Eddie spat. "He's going on my kill list, you tell 'im next time you see 'im. I'm gonna fuck 'im up good and proper. And what's more with your bleedin gun. The police driver doubted he would be likely to see anyone again soon. Mojácar, being just about 50 kilometres away Eddie needed to think, and think fast. He put the Bowie knife back in his holdall and rather swiftly brought the pistol up to the side of the officer's head again and growled "Take the next left." He knew the police would now be aware of his destination. He remembered Fabio asking him for an address to let the taxi driver know.

"Tell me, did you know the address we were going to then?" "No sir, we didn't think that was important because I was to simply drive you straight to a road block where you would have been arrested." This little tid-bit meant Villa Hermosa Vista was still a safe house. Christ, what a balls-up, so near too. If Mitch is still with Esme, he will have to wait up a bit as best he can. Have to hope they're getting on alright. Eddie reminded the driver "Next left." "Sir that is the road to Nijar, very famous for beautiful pottery." "Look mate I don't need a guided tour just take the left. "Yes sir, taking a left to Nijar.

Eddie suddenly twigged what was going on. He barked "Pull over here and get out." Eddie jumped out too. "You've been using your two-way fucking radio to let someone know where we're going. Get down on your bloody knees." The officer did as he was told.

His own police issue gun was pressed hard into the back of his head. Was this an execution? "Your boys are gonna miss you, start saying your prayers pal right now." Eddie heard the officer mumbling Dios té salve, Maria Llena de gracia. Eddie lowered his voice seeing as how he was in the presence of the almighty. "That's it matey you tell your God you're on your way up to see him, hope you've been a good little boy lately." The officer jumped out of his skin at this remark. He suddenly remembered that recent fling he'd had with his wife's sister. He was going downstairs if he was going anywhere, with no time to confess his sins to a priest. Instead of pulling the trigger Eddie side swiped the officer's head knocking him to the ground. Blood from the head wound splattered onto the sandy dusty surface on the road side. A tractor chugged into view and passed them, the driver looking concerned slowing down as if to investigate. Eddie aimed the pistol at the cab driver's head at the same time as holding up the shiny metal police badge. That was message enough, he took off at a speed the tractor hitherto, had not been successful in reaching. Eddie turned back to the copper who was now standing, albeit a bit shakily, and stabbed the gun muzzle hard into his guts. "Right, get back on the radio and relay on this message to whoever's listening in. The driver sat back in the cab, reached over to the two-way radio and turned up the squelch knob adding to the normal channel noise. "Tell them, *in English,* you've changed direction once again and now heading back towards Almeria." He did as he was told, the channel noise making it harder for the listeners to hear clearly. "Step out again." As he did Eddie reached in and felt behind the two-way radio. He found what he was looking for, the connecting wires. Yanking hard on them the radio went dead. "That'll keep your mates busy for a while. Get back in and drive." "Where to sir?" "I'm not falling for that one pal, just go straight and don't bleeding well repeat what I said, got it? In fact, you can keep yer trap shut from now on otherwise it's bang-bang." The driver, glad to be alive for the moment, nodded vigorously. Eddie needed time to think. The Hotel was a no-go area, the villa at the mo, was a no-go area, just in case. He would deal with that spineless rat Pedro in the fullness of time, but right now a hideout of some sort would be top of his shopping list.

CHAPTER 73

Mitch stood gawping out through the bedroom window, as usual stark naked. Esme roused herself, sat up in bed and pulled the bedsheet up to cover her top half. "Heavens Mitch, I know we're not overlooked by anyone, but Chris and Sue have a habit of trapesing into the garden when they pop over to see me, and there's you naked as nature intended!" "Sorry love" he muttered as he donned her dressing gown. Esme had a little giggle. "You look a right goof in that, what with your long hairy legs sticking out, it's a good job it's not any shorter else the end of your thingy would be on show. What am I going to put on then?" He threw her his shirt saying "Button it up though don't want you looking too sexy, might have to drag you back to bed again." Esme smiled wryly. "If it's all the same to you, I'm going for a swim." Beach or pool?" Mitch enquired. "Beach, I think, it's early and will be deserted not that it ever gets that busy. If you come and join me after I've had a swim, we can walk round Goats Head point to where it's really deserted, I call it Robinson Caruso Bay and we can get an all over tan without being disturbed. What do you think?" "Sounds interesting, I'll be down in twenty minutes or so." Mitch watched as Esme slid back the patio door, stuffed a couple of towels in her beach bag and tootled off. She was still clad in Mitch's shirt which amused him no end. "Where's your cossi then girl?" he called out. Esme reached into her beach bag and held up a tiny black bikini set. "So, what you got on under my shirt then?" Esme slowly undid the shirt buttons and revealed her nakedness to Mitch. "Christ" cried Mitch, "Talk about the pot calling the kettle black. What if Chris and whatsername see you like that?" "They won't Mitch." Quickly buttoning up again, she produced a black five-inch-wide clasp belt from inside her bag and fastened it around her waist offering her the perfect hour glass figure. Mitch could feel the sap rising fast. "Is that a magic bag or what? You got anything else of interest in there?" Esme reached in the bag once more and pulled out the flimsiest pair of silk briefs and waved them around her head. "If you behave yourself, you can let me chase you along the water's edge with just these on." "What, me or you?" "You of course you daft dollop, a gals got to have some fun now and then you know. Only one thing I ask, well two actually. You have to shout out chase me chase me." "And the other thing?" Mitch enquired. "You have to let me catch you of course.

The rest I will leave to your imagination. See you soonest dearie bye-bye." His gaze followed her as she disappeared through a security gate at the bottom of the grounds that led to a sandy path that would take her all the way to the beach below. He knew now that this would be the last time, he would set eyes on her.

CHAPTER 74

The road to Nijar was risky and unstable to say the least, very narrow and not a great deal of tarmac to write home about. At places, especially sharp bends, it would be oh so easy to meet a lorry coming the other way, put a tyre over the edge by a few inches and they might tumble over the side, then down an almost sheer drop to whatever lay below. Eddie had the beginnings of a plan. He remembered the *Indalo Man* story Fabio spouted on about, especially the bit about his mum who used to live in London and now the owner a shop in Mojácar. Thing is, what to do with this bloke and when he's been dealt with, how to get to Mojácar. "Pull over here you, and get out. They both stood on the road edge that looked down on a ravine, Eddie smiling, driver frowning. "I'm gonna spare your life, that's bloody generous of me, isn't it?" The driver remained silent. "Isn't it?" Eddie screamed. The driver nodded furiously once more. "Go on then fuck off, start walking back to Almeria. The driver stood motionless, not sure whether to turn his back or not. This madman was certified, mentally unstable, a true psicópata! He turned and ran, ran for his life. He heard Eddie laughing, also the gun shot. The next thing that came to him was a sensation of floating up to the sky, whereas in reality his now dead and lifeless body was tumbling down the mountainside, limbs being torn from him by the uncaring razor-sharp rocks as he fell. Eddie watched him tumble until he couldn't see him anymore. I guess the local night life will be having a bit of a feast tonight, he thought. Mooching back to the cab he separated the cab sign from the roof, this being the only outward indication of the car being a taxi and flung it in the same direction of the driver. Next was the two-way radio and mike. They were ripped out and sent the same way. The car now looked like any other dosser's private motor.

He walked slowly around to the front, fumbled for the bonnet catch, lifted the bonnet until a ratchet system clicked into place, stood back and scratched at his head. Twenty minutes passed before somebody pulled up. Plenty had sailed by in that time, some waving a hello sign, others staring straight ahead. None of the passing traffic had a clue as to the horrific goings on that had occurred here just recently. And why would they, it looked like an innocent motorist had been unfortunate enough to break down in a precarious spot. A voice behind Eddie said something in Spanish. He spun around and with a broad smile, arms outstretched palms uppermost and said, "Me no speaka elspaniola." "That's okay, I speak a little of your tongue. What is wrong with car?" Eddie shrugged his shoulders, arms still outstretched palms still uppermost. He briefly studied his new found friend. Well dressed, might be a professional, about fortyish, and driving alone. He pointed at what he assumed was Eddie's car saying "I am medico, doctor. Not good with engines, I can take you Almeria." Eddie was not sure if this was a statement or a question. He smiled some more and nodded in agreement. At least he could find a proper cab company and get himself to the villa and Esme under his own steam, right under the copper's noses. "Cushty mate, that's very good of you." "It is okay, I visiting a cirugia there to see some sick people and then to my home in Malaga. That's proper handy thought Eddie, by the time this doc has finished at his surgery that road block the driver told me about, will be long gone. As far as the Spanish plod are concerned, my trail will have gone well and truly freezing cold, slipped through their net, yet again. If they took the road to Nijar, all they will find is an abandoned car. With a bit of luck, by the time they get there it will have been nicked. Wouldn't take long for anyone nosing around to see the keys in the ignition. Christ, I can hear them now, sod taking the battery out, might as well nick the whole bloody car.

Few words were spoken between Eddie and the Doc during the journey. The Doc was inwardly willing his passenger to begin a conversation, his grasp of English although good, could always do with a little improvement. However, it was not to be, his passenger remained stony silent. As they hit the outskirts of Almeria, Eddie casually said "Just here will do Doc, look there's a garage over there, maybe they can send out a truck and get my car, I'll shoot in and see if they can help. The Doc obliged by pulling up on the forecourt, waited till Eddie jumped out, reached over to the rear seat, grabbed Eddie's holdall and handed it to him through the open passenger door. Eddie dug out some Spanish currency and offered the paper money to the Doc.

He smiled, held up a hand and shook his head from side to side all in one motion. "Okay Doc, I got the signals but still want to say thanks for getting me out of the shit." "Qué?" "No worries, mate see you around, be lucky." The Doc smiled, shrugged his shoulders then pulled out into the flow of traffic, promising himself he would try this new English phraseology when saying adiós to his patients. What was it he said? *"See you around, be lucky,* yes that was it." Eddie waited until the Doc's car was well out of sight before walking towards the main area of Almeria, hoping to meet with a cab company on the way. Passing a smallish street market, he purchased a flat cap from one stall and a denim jacket from another. No point in walking around with a bloody great arrow pointing in my direction. Donning both items, his next stop was to find a cabbie company. As he walked on, suburbia became the beginnings of the town's outskirts. Houses either side of the road became shops. This was not a main drag by any means, which is why what happened next, surprised Eddie somewhat. Two fully loaded cop cars, blue lights on, came screaming up the road in the direction Eddie had just come from. He took more than a passing interest in a shop window full of pots and pans. He watched the reflection of the two mobiles disappear up the road and out of sight. Was this due to someone finding the body or perhaps just an uncanny coincidence? Which-ever, it posed a problem for Eddie in that he was more likely to be nabbed now by the cops than ever before. In a foreign country, can't or won't speak the lingo, out on the streets in full view. Alone, no back up and just killed a cop. No, this was a bad time. He looked down at his holdall. Someone at the hotel, someone now top of his kill list, might well have told the police that he was carrying a brown leather holdall. As far as Eddie was concerned being as it is a luxury item afforded to the few, it might stick out like a spare prick at a wedding. Up ahead was a tiny street that led off the main road which took him down a dusty side road, with dwellings either side. Taking the Bowie knife out and slipping it through the front of his belt, he buttoned up his newly acquired Levi jacket and drifted down an alleyway between two dwellings, looking for a suitable dumping ground. A few dogs growled and barked announcing his presence. One of the dog's owners appeared through a plastic multicoloured striped curtain and walked to towards Eddie, who tightened his grip on the knife. This guy, obviously a local, smiled a warm greeting. Eddie had never seen a smile with so many teeth missing. One upper and one lower, offset. He wondered how this bloke, who looked about ninety but in all probability was no doubt nearer sixty actually chewed his food?

He was about to show this chap the holdall and begin negotiations, when he remembered the police gun and the badge. Why the fuck didn't I chuck them over the side as well he thought. Rummaging inside the holdall his hand came into contact with the badge. Eddie held it up right in the face of this grime ridden old boy, who cowered down immediately. Even his dog whimpered. Eddie marvelled at this show of fear and respect of the police. Fuck me he thought, it's the other way around back home. He indicated that the old chap should spin round. As he did so, Eddie fished out the gun and stuck it in a handy inside jacket pocket. He thought he might frogmarch this bloke back indoors and do 'im when a pretty senorita appeared through the same multicoloured curtain, hands on hips and a half-smoked fag hanging from the corner of her mouth. "Don't tell me," Eddie laughed "You've got to be fag ash Lil." It didn't occur to Eddie that anyone living or possibly just about surviving in this hovel would understand him, such was his arrogance. He was in for a shock. "Not Lil thank you but close" she smiled "I'm Luciana and this is my father. Why are you arresting him?"

CHAPTER 75

Mitch dived back into the villa heading for the main bedroom, on the way he grabbed a piece of paper and a pencil. Stuffing his belongings into his leather holdall would not take long. As he did so, he concentrated on what he would write in the note to Esme. Using the house phone, he dialled for an operator. Having lived in Bilbao for what seemed forever, his grasp of the local lingo was fair to middling. No problem there, he asked the operator to put him through to a taxi firm and put the receiver back down. He waited a full five minutes before the phone rang. "Ola" he said into the mouthpiece. A voice at the other end having been tipped off by the operator said "Good day, sir, where would you like to go to?" "Mitch was momentarily taken aback, but quickly recovered his composure. "Almería Por favor." "Yes of course sir and when would you like us to collect you?" "Straight away." Mitch gave the guy his address, slammed the phone down and continued to shove his scant amount of clothes into the holdall. His mind flew back to a little earlier and he played back the bit about Esme waving her briefs in the air. He all but cancelled his plans to fuck off, run down to the beach and take up where he left off. He knew though Eddie was not far away and might even be on his way to the villa. Mitch did not want to be around and face him off, especially regarding his love for the gorgeous Esme.

Fifteen minutes passed by the time the cab finally arrived. Mitch stood and read through the note he was leaving for Esme.

"Darling Esme, from the moment I first saw you, I fell, crazy barmy in love with you. I would give anything to have you by

my side from now to all eternity. However, you belong to another and that is something I must respect. I am going back to Bilbao, if you ever visit, please look me up and we can remember together all the lovely encounters we had. You are an extraordinarily, sexy, intelligent woman my lovely and you have a nice arse too. (Sorry, couldn't help myself, trust me to spoil it) ...... I will miss you Esme but you will be in my thoughts every minute of every day.

Love n kisses, your Mitch."

This he left on her pillow just as the Mojácar based taxi arrived. With a huge sigh Mitch closed the front door, strolled down the neat flower bordered path towards the waiting taxi with not so much as a backward glance. As the driver fired up the engine, selected first and pulled away, Mitch turned his head briefly in the hope of a final glance at Esme. He needn't have bothered; she was enjoying the thrill of bathing naked in the warm Mediterranean waters. "Estas bien?" asked the driver. "Am I okay?" answered Mitch. "Yea I'm good mate. It was just as well Mitch had some knowledge of the language. This was going to be fun he thought. He asked the driver if they could take a detour on the way, by way of El Paso where some of the filming took place for a spaghetti western, he wanted to have a walk around the disused film set, the one he had heard so much about when living up in Northern Spain. His driver obliged with a nod so Mitch settled himself down, took a swig from his flask, closed his eyes and hoped Esme would understand.

CHAPTER 76

"What's the bleedin panic Slug? I was doing alright in there. Got blondie's phone number and everything, why the panic stations?" Dave asked as he absently patted his jacket pocket to make sure the sparklers were still there. He was the type to check his passport a million times, whilst on his way to catch a flight. "There's a well tasty Daimler just around the corner in Kirby Street boss. This suited up geezer jumped out and disappeared, didn't even bovver to lock it, had a smart looking briefcase an all, might be full of diamonds."

"What, the Daimler or the case?" Dave enquired. "I dunno do I? By the looks of 'im, might even be both." "Anyways, don't need them, got my own now, must be worth a right fucking bundle thousand probably. Come on you little toe rag, let the dog see the rabbit then. Fifteen minutes later Dave was at the wheel of the Daimler, heading not to Creekmouth, that could wait, but over to Romford instead to sort out the bent jeweller. On the way he dropped Slug off having bunged him a couple of score for his troubles. That will keep him happy for a while, he wrongly thought. Everything was running smoothly as he weaved the Daimler through the thick London traffic. Passing the Barbican tube station and on towards Shoreditch, Dave ticked off the major gains of the day so far. His order of importance being as follows, blondie's number, almost new Daimler and of course the sparklers. He took a hand-off the wheel and patted the diamonds in his jacket pocket. All in all, he thought, it's been a blinder of a morning. The icing on top will be getting Mr. Romford to keep shtum regarding the number of stones, and what numbers of 'em went into the safe deposit box. That bit should be a cinch, he had his gun with him and was not afraid to use it as long as it was the knees, or below. Poor fuckers got to make a living, even if he is doing dodgy business. The Daimler was the best of the best, top of the top most, they didn't come any better. Hardly any miles on the clock, the leather interior smelled new and delicious. 'Bet that suited geezer Slug spotted will be well brassed off when he can't find his new wheels.' Dave could see him now, going back to where he'd parked up at a suitable spot, only for it to have been replaced by another motorist who was glad of a space opening up in such a prime position. 'Well, fuck 'im, it's mine now. I shall see to it that Errol's mob get to do a full respray and turn over the paperwork accordingly. Then when I'm good and ready, I'll bell blondie and blow a fortune on her, just as soon as I can fence this ice. Once more, he took his hand from the wheel and patted the diamonds and glanced at his cocky smiling face in the rear-view mirror. At that precise moment, out of nowhere, a cyclist shot out in front of the Daimler. His speed being much about thirty, meant the cyclist had no chance, her head hit the windscreen with such force it cracked instantly, in a thousand directions. This, mixed with blood from her head smashing against the screen, restricted Dave's view to almost nil. For a few moments he was driving blind. He heard screams and people shouting from the busy pavement and knew instinctively he was in the kack. Bent gear in his pocket, driving a stolen motor, potentially killing a cyclist.

His instinct was to ram his foot down and get away and out of sight as fast as he could. Still driving blind and with a dead woman on the bonnet the Daimler sped up then hit or rather went under, the back of a stationary flat-bed lorry, lifting the lorries rear wheels a couple of inches off the tarmac. There was nothing to stop the momentum of the Daimler. The bed of the lorry, being at a height for the car's bonnet to go straight under; until the windscreen and top portion of the car met with the rear of the flat-bed. The woman's body was crushed between the two as the lorry's bed sliced off the top part of the Daimler, decapitating Dave into the bargain. A grisly scene of various body parts, blood and gore awaited the ambulance and fire service crews along with the police that were soon to appear. Bystanders were busy throwing up, some fainted, others screamed. Nobody rushed to help as it was all too clear there were no survivors.

CHAPTER 77

Eddie stopped in his tracks. "You speak good English girl, how come?" Luciana replied, "My boyfriend is English and I spent a year or two in England at his parents' house." A tiny smile developed on her lips at the thought of her time there. Instant running water, lights went on at a throw of a switch, a fridge to keep the milk cool. No such luxuries here though. Eddie didn't want any boyfriends around; he'd already sussed this place as drum to hang about in until things old Bill wise, calmed down. "Is your lover about to pop out and join us too then?" "Oh no, he is travelling on business, in America just now." The smile faded to a pout at the thought of no cuddles again tonight. Although this stranger looked a bit interesting, she thought. Waving the badge about had no effect on Luciana, she was made of sterner stuff. "You're not police, are you?" "What makes you think that?" "It doesn't add up, no uniform, obviously English, shall I go on?" "Never mind about all that malarky, just the both of you get indoors, now." Eddie was getting a bit pissed off. Apart from being tired, he was hot, bothered, dusty, thirsty, hungry and in need of a sit down. He may be a raving lunatic on a killing spree, but even raving lunatics need the basics occasionally. The old boy, Luciana and the mangey old dog did as they were told and trooped through the plastic multi-coloured curtain and into the front room. It took a few moments for Eddie's eyes to adjust.

He'd gone from dazzling Spanish sunshine to near total darkness. As his vision gradually came into focus, he could make out a few chairs, a table and a double bed over by the only window, which had sacking for curtains. These were drawn tightly.

Only a slither of daylight peeped through due to them not entirely meeting in the middle. To the left, a shelf stacked full of the world's collection of little brass nick-nacks. Eddie looked at Luciana who explained, "My mother once said she liked little brass ornaments, so my father bought her one for every birthday and Christmas since then." The bed seemed to have all the blankets curled up in a heap near to the bedhead. Eddie moved closer; it looked like the heap was moving. Luciana snapped, "Don't go any closer, that is my mother who is gravely ill. This is why we keep it dark and quiet in here." The old boy did a crucifixion sign on his chest and began to weep. "What's wrong with her?" "We don't know," "you don't know?" "No, we don't." "How long has she been like this?" "A long time." "What about seeing a doctor?" "She is bedridden and we cannot afford a house visit." House, thought Eddie, more like a bloody cave. "Do you know where the local surgery is?" Luciana looked at him suspiciously. "I know of one nearby, why?" "Right, you and me will get there by cab, come on you can speak the lingo for me." The pair of them entered the cirugia, brushed past the receptionist and all the customers politely awaiting their turn and straight into the consulting room. Eddie knew he was taking a chance; this might have been an entirely different surgery to the one mentioned by the doc he met earlier. As it happens the gamble paid off, here was the same doc who drove him to the outskirts of Almeria, administering to someone's ailments. He paused at what he was doing, as if he was entirely used to such interruptions, then spoke quietly to his patient and finished off with '*see you around, be lucky*' in a genuine sounding East End dialect. "Tell 'im a distant relative of mine is half-dead and needs his attentionano. Tell 'im there's a cabola outside and he needs to come now." Eddie fished out a goodly wad of notes and threw them down on the doc's desk. Luciana obliged; the doc got the message; he'd joined up all the dots. Grabbing his medical bag, he filled it with all kinds of potions and pills and they were off. On his way through reception, he barked something at the nurse who was standing open mouthed, Luciana interpreted for Eddie, explaining that he said he would be back within the hour. Whilst the doc was doing his thing with the old boy's wife, Eddie and Luciana sat in the kitchen sipping cups of tea which washed down some bread smeared with home-made marmalade.

"Nice, very nice," Eddie remarked, as he did that thing people do, biting off a chunk then holding the remainder in his fingers nodding, looking at it, and waving it in the air. "Nice." He said once again. "And so, it should be." Luciana replied, "We are lucky enough to have a few orange trees in our little garden. Sometimes my sick mother will help with the squashing of the oranges by standing on them in an old tin bath. She says it cleans her feet better than washing." Luciana watched Eddie's face contort with horror. He was about to say, you tellin me that stinking old mess in there stomped all over this jam in her bloody bare plates of meat? Before he could speak, Luciana was squealing with laughter, shaking her head from side to side, Eddie got the message and relaxed. Even so, he decided he would not eat any more, just in case. "I think the doctor is finishing up" whispered Luciana. "How do you know?" asked Eddie, "He just said *see you around, be lucky*. Did you teach him that?" she asked. "I don't reckon so, might be something he picked up in Malaga." Doc appeared, wiping his hands on a paper towel. He spoke rapidly and at length directly to Luciana. Eddie noticed a grave look on his face. He must have told the old boy the bad news already, as sobbing could be heard coming from the other room. He turned to Eddie and watched him closely as Luciana interpreted. "He says, he is very glad you brought my mother's illness to his attention. She is very ill and that it is not terminal but it might have been, if you had not intervened. When he arrives back at his surgery, he will organise an ambulance to come and pick my mother up and take her to the hospital in Malaga, where she will receive the best possible care. He will attend to it personally. He also said if you need a doctor any time soon, you are to give him a call, she handed Eddie the Doctors business card. The doc smiled warmly at Eddie, shook his hand vigorously and said, "Thank you," in good English. Shortly after he went Eddie asked, "What's up with your old man, what's all the sobbing about?" "He and my mother have not been apart for more than thirty years or so." "Oh, I get that but surely, he wants her to improve, you know get better?" "Yes of course but now he is thinking who's going to wash and feed him and occasionally wipe his bottom." Eddie looked aghast. "She did all that while being bloody ill, he ought to be ashamed of himself, is he any good at anything?" Eddie spat in disgust. "Well, he must have done something good once in a while, because my mum had me!" "By the way, what's his name?" enquired Eddie "We call him el héroe, it means hero in English'" replied Luciana. "Anyway, what's wrong with your ma?" "Acute appendicitis which needs emergency surgery before it sets off peritonitis, because then, it is life threatening.

Please wait here while I go and console my father." Luciana threw her arms around Eddie, gave him a long hug, nuzzled into his neck and thanked him profusely. Tears were running down her face, some for the relief and some for having a real man in the house who got things done for once.

He could hear Luciana gently talking to her father however, it was in their native tongue and the whole conversation went whooshing over his head. "I've explained to my father that I will be going to the hospital with my mother." She called, from where she sat by her mothers' bed. Hearing no answer, a quick visit to the kitchen revealed no Eddie. On a shelf by the back door a pile of Spanish money in high denomination sat, with a note on top. It read, 'For your ma's op.' Luciana flew to the kitchen door, flung it open and ran on out into the back garden. She just caught sight of Eddie rounding a corner and he was gone. She stood there silently sending him her heartfelt thanks and wishing for him to return one day. She said with loving thoughts "I will pray for you."

CHAPTER 78

The sun was getting low as Eddie sat back and watched the scenery of Spain's forgotten province passing by. He was roughly halfway to Mojácar when it occurred to him that he'd managed to kill someone today, and helped to save the life of another. A long, long time ago his Ma read him part of a story from a book called Gulliver's Travels. He wondered if anyone would write about him and his current excursion. Nah probably not, probably not interesting enough. *Eddie's Travel's* didn't have the same ring about it, so why bother. Daylight was dropping fast as were Eddie's eyelids. The sun sinking in the West behind them resembled an enormous orangey glowing satsuma, waiting for someone to reach up and give it a squeeze. It reminded Eddie of when as a boy he used to help out at the local market back home on the fruit and veg barrow, the owner of which would tell Eddie how to keep the lady customers from squeezing the produce, testing for ripeness. If any customers come near to squashing the fruit in their fingers, he was to shout out "Okay darling, don't squeeze me till I'm yours." It worked a treat, most of the time! Soon darkness would be on them. He hoped the cab driver was conversant with this particular road as he had yet to see evidence of any lamp posts. Traffic was almost nil in either direction. It tended to come in blocks of five or ten vehicles at a time.

Overtaking at certain places would have been almost suicidal, hence all the tailgating. It was close to dusk, the dipping sun almost vanishing bar a small thumbnail shaped red slither, when his driver shouted in broken English, "hey look, it's my hermano!" Eddie would find out later he meant his brother. He opened his eyes to see a fellow taxi to the one he was sat in coming from the general direction of Mojácar.

The driver's brother and he were excitedly flashing their headlights on and off at each other. Both slowed down to a snail's pace, wound down their drivers' windows and exchanged greetings before speeding up again. It was at that exact moment Eddie locked eyes with Mitch who was sitting in the back of the other cab. Before Eddie could gather his thoughts, he was gone. He turned around to look out of the back window and saw Mitch was doing the same. He saw him offer a military style salute. Eddie simply put a thumbs up in the direction of Mitch. He said nothing to the driver, didn't want to distract him from the dodgy looking road ahead, which was now illuminated by the taxi's headlights, but only just. Well, well thought Eddie. What are the chances of that happening? Me from the Isle-of-Dogs, Mitch from Bilbao, both murderers of one nasty bit of work in his home town, passing on a remote bloody coast road, somewhere South of Madrid. Stick that in your book about *Eddie's Travels* Mr Publisher. If anything was untoward, or if Eddie was driving into a trap, he felt sure Mitch would have got his driver to turn around and stop us. He speaks the lingo and it would have been easy for him to sort it. So, maybe everything is under control. Eddie felt sure Mitch would have contacted Esme and no doubt told her the story about their time together, possibly leaving out the killing of that Spanish gang leader slag in Bilbao. He rather fancied telling her about that one himself. "Two of a kind me and him." He said out loud. His driver looked at him in the rear-view mirror, shrugged his shoulders and laughed. Eddie shot a look at the clock on the taxi's dashboard and reckoned he would be in Mojácar at about seven-ish. Shops would be reopening about then following the late afternoon siesta. His aim now was to seek out that shop and introduce himself to Fabio's mum. Shouldn't be all that hard if all she sells is Indalo Man stuff.

CHAPTER 79

Val Coleman's funeral was a quietish affair. A goodly amount of her workmates turned up, all the ladies had their barnet's done up in a bun, and temporarily gone blonde as a nod to Val's favoured hairdo. No sign of Eddie though, he wasn't even aware his Mum was dead. Nobody had the guts to tell him and, until Bomber released all the telegrams, he'd found at Plevna Street, nobody knew how to, except possibly Rosie. However, no one had seen hide-nor-hair of her for ages. If Eddie knew about things, he would have moved heaven and earth to be here. He would have taken care of every little detail, right down to the smallest of smallest.

As it turned out the bus depot, and all who worked there stumped up most of the cost. Val was well liked at the depot and would be sadly missed. The burial took place on a wet, wretched old day at the cemetery off Hermit Road, Canning Town. The 'knees-up' to be held later that same day at the 'Bag-O-Nails' pub back on the Island. Bomber informed Eddie's most trusted men of Val's sad demise a week or two ago. He, Johnny and some of the others sorted out the when and where stuff. They also put a couple of hundred sov's behind the bar at the knees-up venue in case anyone wanted to get majorly pissed up. Eddie's men, to a man, stayed silent while the rest of the congregation sang along to Amazing Grace; singing was not for them. They wondered silently how their missing boss would react when the news finally reached him. Val's body had been identified by one of her sisters at the hospital who took the whole episode badly. Although not terribly close, there was always that sisterly blood bond, even if it was just the occasional one-page letter in the post. Considering she lived on the Island you'd have thought they would have lived in each other's pockets. But both Val and her sister led busy lives however, Val working on the buses, day and night, her sister looking after a number of foster kids which was her thing. They never met up other than on special occasions, and of course this was one of them.

Irish Jimmy, poor sod, stood at the back of the congregation; heart-broken, heart cleaved in two. He was the only male present with tears in his eyes. Val had been the love of his life for an all too brief a period. Now she was gone, so the least he could do was to pay his last respects. Before the service ended, he slipped out of the little chapel and laid a huge bunch of roses next to Val's intended burial site. On the card he wrote, 'To wake again in heaven.' Then without looking back, he made his way back to his crummy little flat in Poplar wondering how the hell he was going to move on.

First off, he opened a fresh bottle of whisky and would see it off that night, if it didn't see him off first. The do at the Nails went well, a good number of Eddie's mob or crew crammed themselves in to the function room set aside for Val's wake. The talk amongst the lower ranks was, what happens now? Most if not all, were unaware of Eddie's whereabouts and most if not all, were not going to pose that question to those who worked directly with Eddie. As it happens Eddie Coleman is now on the run from the old Bill, and the less those motherless bastards knew, the better. Thing is however, the motherless bastards did know better. They knew he was in Spain; they knew he was aiming for Almeria and they now knew he was moving about with a passport in his sky rocket in the name of Ronald Biggs.

They also knew he was a slimy slippery bastard and, as Ellis called him the gingery turd, had slipped through net put in place by the Met and was now slipping through the Spanish equivalent. They also knew but had yet to gain solid evidence, that Mr E. Coleman had committed at least three atrocious, vicious and vile murders in this foreign country, at least that was the body count to date. They felt sure there would be more. When most of the 'knees up' revellers drifted away Johnny asked Bomber and a few others including Errol, if anyone had seen Dave Conti. No's all round. "Should have showed up," remarked Bomber, "Least he could have done," said Errol. "Well, he'll have a thing or two to say when I catch up with him" growled Johnny. "I'll pin 'im to the wall and pluck his bleedin eyes out. He'd better have a bloody good excuse for not turning up." Nobody gave a thought to the fact he was well and truly brown bread.

CHAPTER 80

The Scoops headline: -

'Violent East End Gang Boss Wears Ladies Underwear'

caused a mini sensation in the underworld, and for that matter, the overworld too. Sales of London's daily "The Scoop" hit an all-time high, trebling its usual daily sales quota. The editor in chief decided to stick the story, plus the picture of Johnny the Turk, bottom right of the front page, instead of at the top as a header head-line, which would have been in large and bold red print. A very subtle move on his behalf.

A second, then a third edition found its way to newspaper shops and street vendors right across London in order to satisfy the hungry retail demand. Other newspapers on sale were shunned by the buying public in desperation to get their hands on a copy of The Scoop. For the first time in newspaper printing history, competing newspaper houses sent their own photographers to camp outside the offices of The Scoop so as to get as many shots as possible of the brave reporter who had the audacity, almost suicidal nerve, to put such a story together. The trick worked beautifully for The Scoop, grab the readers' attention, get them to part with their hard-earned money, then it's too late, once they saw there was nothing substantial to back up the attention-grabbing headline.

If anyone was to read the follow-on piece printed on page two in very small type, they would find no names named regarding the gangland boss pictured, that was because the paper didn't have one. There was no mention of the style of undies he wore and when or why, because they didn't know about this little tid-bit either. However, the original reporter was going to have his day, that's for sure. It certainly made up for getting his mouth and camera busted, that day over at Zak's Place. The rest of Fleet Street were livid. Livid that a tiny paper such as The Scoop, could hit all the big boys in the goolies. The entire might of Fleet Street was kicked very much into a cocked hat by a minnow for once. A few, in retaliation and hopefully to pick up some lost sales, ran follow up stories the very next morning. Early editions plus second editions hit the newsagents in the hope of rebuilding customer confidence and lost profits. There was no telling at this point how many loyal customers, loyal for many years, proved to be un-loyal in an eye blink. Such was the throat cutting logic of the press. Most of the competing papers now had a name *the reporters*, plus various pictures of him, courtesy of all the photographers elbowing each other, jostling one another for the best shot. One of the stories that went to print asked,

'How long before (*name and picture)* **feels heat from ganglands wrath?'**

This approach was of course very dangerous and could lead to The Scoop's reporter being hunted down and possibly murdered by whoever fancied getting his name about a bit, in the hard man's who's who. Those that ran such stories didn't give a shit, this was a sales revenue war. Money, reputations and loyal customers are at stake.

Bite back stories were particularly frowned upon by the Met, who voiced their concerns to all who mattered within Fleet Street and the wider publication houses within the London area. And as usual, all of the competing newspaper houses completely ignored the wise words from the Met. The original reporter having seen the outcome of his report in his paper thought, in hind-sight, it was a crazy stunt that's blown up out of all proportion and he now wished he'd ditched the idea. However, the need to put himself in a good place with his boss at the time, blinded him to any follow-on consequences. Too late now though, the rat was definitely out of the bag. 'I might well become a posthumous receiver of the Pulitzer Prize' he said to himself, 'no good to me if I'm brown bread and pushing up daisies in Epping Forest minus my limbs, fuck it.

Best go and see the editor and hope the paper can put me up in a safe house somewhere.' "In time son people will forget all about it and the story will be yesterday's news, you know history, fucking fish and chip paper." The reporter stared at his editor. He couldn't believe that sentence had just dropped out of his mouth. "But what about my well-being?" he asked. "Look son, the past only exists if you let it." The reporter almost cried. "I need the paper to look out for me. Sales have double or trebled for that matter, plus we might well have increased our circulation by at least twenty five percent!" The irritated editor asked "What is it that you want?" He had a paper to edit and this idiot was getting in his way. "Is it a raise you want or what, come on hurry it up, I've work to do?" The reporter was dumb-founded. For a few moments he was unable to think, let alone speak. "Okay" he said, "how about I put myself about a bit now that I am becoming well known in Fleet Street and get a job with another newspaper?" Mr irritated hissed "Do you expect *they* will up your income then?" "They might, when I tell them how shabbily you've treated me. Goodbye, stick that up your nose and in tomorrow's news." He turned and walked out of the Editor's office. As he skipped down the stone steps to the street, he could be heard whistling the tune "My Way." A favourite song he'd listened to many times.

CHAPTER 81

Major success regarding high volume circulation and high-volume sales, in addition to many new readers, encouraged The Scoop to capitalise on the favourable outcome by printing a follow up feature. This time they decided to turn the readers' attention towards the reporter.

'Ace reporter seeks adulation elsewhere on Fleet Street'

The article ran on page one yet again, and yet again the buying public, eager for more dirt on the subject, drove sales skyward for The Scoop the second day running.

The full story on the inside pages, on this occasion was written by the editor himself, and contrived to ensure none of his competitors on Fleet Street would touch the reporter with a ninety-foot-long barge-pole with a snooker cue tied to the end of it.

If Mr Reporter went cap in hand with a sob story, it wouldn't wash at all now. The whole episode didn't go down too well with Eddie's crew either. Zak, Johnny's cousin, happened to be the first to bring it to Johnny's attention. "What's all this about then?" "All what cuz?" "Shit Johnny, don't you read the papers?" "No Zak they're full of crap, lies and sensationalism, I only get a paper so I can check out whose running and who's not, on the gee-gees." Zak showed him the front page of The Scoop. Johnny the Turk read the story slowly and the follow up text inside on page two. "Hmmm, good likeness." He murmured. Zak expected him to burst out of the premises promising hell, mayhem and the odd murder starting with torching the offices of The Scoop. He certainly wasn't expecting the complete opposite. Johnny murmured,

"How the fucking hell do they know I wear knickers? How did they find out? When I get changed at the gym, I'm really careful when I'm slipping them on. I always make doubly sure no one's around. So how the fuck then, eh?" Zak almost fell over. He never did know too much about this distant cousin of his, now he knew even less. "Bloody hell Johnny, don't tell me you're bleedin bent mate, you know, one of them." Johnny looked at Zak aghast. "What the 'ell do you mean one of them?" "You know backs to the wall at midnight and all that." It slowly dawned on Johnny what Zak was driving at. "Listen Zak, before the boys arrive for tonight's meeting, why don't you pop downstairs and grab us some beers. And that's beers with a B not a Q" he laughed.

A few brown ales later, Johnny explained. "Have you heard about footballers who have pre-match rituals, you know put the left sock on first? Or comb the side parting in their hair to the opposite side of their head just before a big match? There are tons of rituals like that,

it's supposed to obtain a lending hand from lady luck. Some have been doing it for years and years. With me, it all started when I was eleven and had my first bout in the ring. Me mum packed me sister's knickers in me kit bag instead of me underpants. I had to have something on under me boxing shorts otherwise I might develop a rash or something, what with all the rubbing away down there on the inside of me shorts. No silks in those days, boxing shorts might just as well be made of rough bleeding serge. Anyway, I was pissing myself that I might get knocked out and stretchered off and the St. John ambulance chaps would discover my secret. So, I fought this bloke like a bloody deranged tiger and knocked 'im cold in the third and final round. Fuck me, I've won I thought and there you have it. It is now my ritual.

I never enter the ring now without a pair of knickers on, under my shorts of course. Admittedly they're not my sister's anymore and they are a bit skimpier and silkier now. Thing is,

I hate going into Marks and Sparks for replacements. I always say to the girl, they're not for me. Always get a giggle though." Zak thought for a moment or two letting the story sink in. "Doesn't explain how that newspaper knows about it though does it?" Johnny looked up from writing his meeting notes. "No, it doesn't cuz. Must have been a lucky guess, I guess. I do remember a geezer taking a snap shot of me downstairs in your bar recently. I seem to remember grabbing his camera, shoving it down his throat, knocking him to the ground then stamping on his face." "Did you now, I don't recall that, I must have been out the back 'avin a piss." "All I know Zak is it was bloody crowded, so I didn't see what happened to him. Frankly I don't fucking-well care, I thought he was out stone cold. Tell you what Zak, have an ask around some of your regulars, see if anyone can shed some light on it." "Yea okay Johnny, consider it done. Meanwhile, what you gonna say to the blokes?" "Nothing cuz, it's none of their business, if anyone's got the balls to bring it up, thanks to you mate, I'll be ready." "If that's your line of thinking Johnny, you'd better sit right down and write yourself a sick note." "Yea well, like I just said, thanks to you I'll be more than ready."

He threw Zak a steely glare then looked down to read his meeting notes. Zak took the hint and made himself scarce.

CHAPTER 82

The first police officer on the scene to Dave Conti's unfortunate road traffic collision had long since decided an officer's life was not for him. Ten years down the road from the training academy at Hendon was more than enough. His problem being he was trapped in a circle of longish hours, lowish take home pay, three hungry kids and a wife whose favourite shopping haunt happened to be in the West End. For a while now this particular officer had been looking for a way out. He did the pools regular as clockwork, but that's where his gambling started and stopped. The chances of coming up trumps stood firmly against him in that department. Prayer was his latest hope, divine intervention would appear if he put his trust in the Almighty, something the vicar told him when he last policed his local village fete. Fat chance of that he thought. Today, however, somebody up there in the clouds above London was looking down upon him and about to give him his long-awaited break. A ton of rubber neckers gathered around the ugly and gruesome event.

The lorry driver whose goods vehicle sat with a car stuck four feet along under its rear end was sitting on the kerb with his head in his hands. The officer pulled him to his feet, shook him roughly to bring him round. "Is this your lorry mate?" "Yes, it is and my boss is going to go bleedin spare, look at the bloody state of it." "Just for the minute sir sod your boss, I need to summon help, I want you to keep people from getting too close. There's a Police box across the road. You get on with marshalling the public while I get some people to help me here." The officer took a closer look at the carnage and saw that the car driver's head was missing and the cyclist's limp and very dead body was cruelly sandwiched between what was left of the car's bonnet and the underside of the lorry bed. As he ran for help, he turned and called out, "Especially the bodies, keep the public away from the bodies." The driver gave the officer a nod. Fifteen minutes later emergency service vehicles began turning up. First was a single ambulance, followed by two fire engines, hopefully one with metal cutting facilities onboard, a tow truck and three police vehicles. Barriers were hastily set up roughly one hundred yards in either direction of the crash site in order to close the road from passing traffic. Being as it happened in central London at peak traffic time which in this part of London, is all day long, traffic havoc ensued and would ensue for many hours to come.

During the interim period between the first officer to arrive on scene and the emergency vehicles arriving, he requested the lorry driver to sit in his cab, turn off the engine and to await further instructions. On no account was he to move his lorry, not an inch. The driver grudgingly did as he was told. The officer he thought, would not be aware that his boss back at the depot in Bedford was a complete and utter bastard face. In fact, his work mates, behind his back all called him Barry bastard face. He knew he was totally innocent. All he did was to stop at a pedestrian crossing and thump! he was hit from behind. Would his boss Barry have pity on him? Fuck no. So, he did as the officer asked, sat in his cab, switched off the engine and visualised the notice of 'employment termination' that would no doubt be in his next and last 'ever' little buff coloured pay packet. Meanwhile, just prior to the emergency teams arriving, the officer felt for a pulse on the young lady cyclist. He doubted he would find one seeing as how she was tragically crushed. No, no pulse. Next, he checked on the headless car driver. Not for a pulse' but perhaps something that might help to identify the unlucky bugger.

Gingerly, not wishing to disturb any evidence, he slowly reached into Dave's inside jacket pocket in the hope of a wallet or some other form of identification. His fingers felt something damp, warm and leathery? Aha he thought is this the unfortunate man's wallet? The sound of bells heralding the advancing service vehicles could be heard, no doubt encountering heavy traffic on their way. It didn't exactly feel like a wallet however, he proceeded to lift it from Dave's pocket until it was fully out and he could see what it was. "Ello-ello-ello, what is it that we have here then?" he said out loud. With one hand holding the pouch, he put his other hand in and examined the contents by pulling open the draw strings. His eyes bulged. They stuck out like they do in a cartoon, on very, very long stalks. He peered into the pouch and saw his new future life flash before him. New house, new car, new wife and no more, well, no more everything. He had heard of some of his colleagues emptying the wallets of poor unsuspecting murder victims. This lot of tom however, is very big bangers in anyone's book. Must be upwards of twenty-five big ones. What the hell is this bloke was doing with them, is anyone's guess. A skilful and deft slight of the hand saw the leather pouch find its way into the officer's tunic. It was far too good an opportunity to miss. A further rapid search of other jacket pockets yielded up just one item. A neatly written telephone number on a piece of headed paper, followed by two large kisses.

He had just enough time to pocket this too before the area was deluged with swarms of emergency personnel. Had he delved a little further he would have encountered a hand gun tucked into this headless man's waist band.

CHAPTER 83

Eddie's taxi rolled into the little town of Mojácar bang on seven. Night had just been handed the batten from day and was weaving its starry skied magic together with a lovely warm breeze of salty sea air. Mojácar by day resembled a pretty chocolate box vista, a plethora of whitewashed Moorish dwellings. By night it was a gentle, seemingly innocent place to walk leisurely through the narrow streets lit up by colourful shop lights selling colourful items displayed outside for all to see and hopefully purchase. Lanterns with lit candles shone on restaurant tables, Spanish guitarists effortlessly strummed their instruments for the small number of early evening eaters drifting to the tabernas.

Mojácar by night gave off a mixture of soft music, sizzling cooking aromas, popping wine corks, in all, it added up to a lovely sultry laid-back feeling.

Mojácar is one of those rare places to meander hither and thither, or perhaps just sit quaffing or sipping a glass of Rioja whilst people watching, watching as they pass by in search of somewhere to do the same. Sometime a little later, no doubt, the singlies would be out and about hoping to get lucky.

All this went straight over the top of Eddie's head, he needed to find a certain shop before he could take in the night air and all that a Mojácar evening under the stars, could offer. A waiter appeared from the nearest taberna to where Eddie stood. "Please come in and sit-down sir. We have the finest Spanish cuisine in Mojácar." It was this guy's job to put bums on seats. Anyone within ten yards of the taberna he worked for was a legitimate target, Eddie ignored him. The waiter grabbed

Eddie's arm in an attempt to steer him toward a table already set. Eddie fiercely yanked his arm away and told the waiter to cut it out or get hurt. Instead of apologising and backing off as requested, the waiter continued to ply his trade and only stopped when Eddie landed him one in his midriff. The waiter bent double, completely winded by the blow. The next one came crashing down to the side of his head very nearly ripping his right ear off. Nearby early diners started to back away, even more so when other staff from the taberna came toward Eddie with menacing scowls, one with a large meat cleaver to hand.

Eddie fished around in his holdall, grabbing the gun, he inched the police revolver above the central zip, just to let these potential attackers see he was armed and very dangerous. They retreated rather smartish, which gave Eddie the opportunity to slowly back away keeping his eyes on these guys as he left. As soon as he was at least fifty or so yards away, he turned and went in search of the 'Indalo Man' shop and Fabio's mum. "Good evening, may I help you?" Eddie looked up to see a pretty woman, as of this moment age undiscernible, shortish but stylish auburn hair, slim build and smiling. "Are you Fabio's mum?" Straight in, no messing, he didn't have time for sodding around. "Oh." she said. "I wondered if you had called in to buy something that might remind you of your visit to Mojácar, before you leave?" Eddie looked bewildered. She looked down at his smart leather holdall. "Cabin luggage I assume?" she laughed. "I get it," he smiled back having temporarily run out of words. "As it happens, I've just this minute got here, anyway are you Fabio's mum then, or what?" "Might be, who is asking?" "Look, I met him at the hotel he works at in Almeria, in fact I stayed there and we kind of hooked up. He said, when I get here, I could find you in your gift shop and you might be able to help me." On hearing this, she relaxed. "Hi I'm Anna and yes, I am Fabio's mum, how is he, I haven't seen him in ages?" Eddie replied "Bright little spark; a right live wire he is, me and him got on well." "And you are?"

she queried "Well, my passport says Ronald Biggs but everyone calls me Eddie." "Well then Eddie, with a name like that you must either be loaded from that daring train robbery or on the run." "Neither Anna, just unfortunate enough to have the same name as the bloke you're referring to." "Okay. So, what brings you to Mojácar at seven thirty in the evening, are you on holiday?" "Yea, sort of, although I might stay on for a while. Someone I know has sorted out a villa somewhere nearby and I might bunk in there for six months or so." "Where's the rest of your luggage then?" Anna enquired. "In the boot of the cab that got me here, silly sods buggered off back to Almeria with it" Eddie lied. "Not to worry though, I can sort that out in the morning, it's no problem; no biggy honest. I'd love a cuppa and a bacon sandwich or something, if you don't mind?" "I can do better than that" Anna replied. "Look, it's been quiet for a while, let me shut up shop and you can buy me a meal. There's a nice cosy little restaurant just around the corner, I'm sure they could come up with something a little better than a bacon sarnie. Perhaps then you can fill in the gaps for me."

Eddie hoped it was not the same one he'd had the bust up with earlier. The one she took him to was indeed quiet, almost semi-private. Anna and Eddie were ushered to a tucked away table out on the rear veranda. From their table one could look up and see a million and one stars, the milky way was out to play for all to see, at the same time they could hear the waves meeting the beach some way below them. Eddie liked this spot, not too many prying eyes, quiet and peaceful, it was just perfect for him. Anna wished that Eddie would say something like 'Hey, what a romantic little place,' but of course romance couldn't be further from his mind just now. "Fabio tells me you lived in London once, where abouts was that then?" Before she could answer a group of five or six people were ushered to a nearby table. A real noisy and rowdy group, scraping their chairs out and bum hopping them back in again. They were beginning to get on Eddie's tits. He had no idea where they came from, definitely not English. To Eddie they sounded about as clear as a giggling gaggle of girls from bonny Glasgie, bent on getting pissed on a good night out. Across their own table Anna fascinated, watched a change come over Eddie. He was clearly niggled and unhappy with the racket the rowdies were kicking up, and clearly about to do something both he and Anna might come to regret.

She watched as his eyes glazed over and his hands became fists, he was humming a far-off tune, sounding like a nursery rhyme. She put her hand gently on his arm, at the same time as putting a finger to her lips in that very recognisable signal, calm down, keep quiet and I will deal with it. Eddie of course was more than capable of shutting this mob up but was curious to see how she would go about it. He smiled, filled his lungs with warm sea air and slowed his heart rate down. Unseen by the rowdies, Anna signalled to the waiter who was quickly by her side leaning over to hear whatever it was she was whispering. Two minutes later the guy returned with another plus his boss. The boss was all suited up, and by the look of him, didn't suffer boisterous fools easily. Whatever the three of them said to the rowdies, it had the right effect, they upped and left rather rapidly. As the two blokes and five girls filed out, peace descended once again. Eddie was more than impressed. His way of dealing with the problem would have been ugly and bloody, possibly leaving at least one dead and most of the others out cold. As the chosen evening meals came to their table Eddie ventured. "What the 'ell happened there then?"

Anna grinned and said "I'll tell you my secrets if you tell me yours." Eddie wasn't fazed but thought, caution, there's more to this bird than meets the eye, I'd better watch my step. I know I could've run rings round those noisy bastards, one of em had a face you like to punch hard twice, but her way means we can enjoy our evening undisturbed. From that moment on they had the entire veranda to themselves. "So," Eddie asked again, "Fabio tells me you lived in London, weren't in the Met or something were you, you know, old Bill and that?" Anna winked and moved the conversation on to other subjects. As she rabbited on about stuff intermingled with her life story, Eddie tuned out.

He could hear her voice and saw her lips moving, but didn't register the actual words. This was quite honestly the first time he had, to properly draw breath since escaping from that prison van back in Oxford. The night time magic of Mojácar took care of that. Made him feel right mellow for a change. The company he was presently keeping added to his relaxed state. Somehow, after witnessing the chucking out of the rowdies, he felt somewhat protected, just like he did at home in Plenva Street, where his lovely Mum Val was always in charge. The whole escape shebang in Oxford was down to her. She had it planned down to a 't' she did. Didn't drop a single clanger or anything. He realized he hadn't spoken to her since being on remand and vowed he would make contact as soon as he could, if only to let her know his journey was almost over. He would tell her he was safe and nearly in the arms of his precious Esme. The occasional nod and smile kept Anna yattering on. Next, his mind drifted to Johnny. How was he coping with running the show back in the East End? Before Eddie did a runner, he'd amassed a powerful and talented crew, as he preferred to call them. Some capable of pure violence to be dished out whenever necessary. Others very proficient in jewellery raids plus a large number ready and happy to wrench protection money from local businesses. He thought about the original money spinner he'd set up himself, using Dave Conti to nick tasty motors from up West and sell them on the car lots, yea that was a winner if ever there was one. He made a mental note to up Dave's wages and give him a bit more support. Meanwhile, he thought he'd better catch up with the present day and tune back into Anna. "You haven't heard a word I said, have you?" Eddie smiled weakly. "Thing is,

I've had a bit of a journey getting here. Oxford to Weymouth, Weymouth to Jersey, Jersey to Bilbao by yacht, Bilbao to Madrid, Madrid to Almeria then on to here. I've kind of lost track of dates and times plus, all of a sudden; I think it's because I'm finally here, I'm bloody dog tired.

"And Eddie, you haven't touched your meal." Eddie stuck a mouthful of tortilla and chewed on the delicious Spanish style omelette. "Amazing, very tasty." Anna asked, "When was your last proper meal, Eddie?" He stared up at the sky, then it came to him. "Orange jam on a slice of dodgy bread." "Oh, substantial stuff then," Anna laughed. He was beginning to like being in her company. Especially the way she threw her head back each time she laughed. "Look, I take it you've nowhere to sleep tonight?" "Yep, spot on, I was hoping they might do bed and breakfast here perhaps?" "No, sorry, it's a restaurant, not a hotel." "Oh well, I'll have a traipse around and see if I can find some digs then."

"You'll be lucky, there's only two hotels in Mojácar, one in the town overlooking the square and the other down on the beach front. Both will be chock full of holiday makers. No, I have a spare room back at my place but no funny business, okay?" Anna laughed that head thrown back laugh again and said, "Mind you, by the looks of you just now, I don't think you'd have it in you. Come on, finish your omelette and we can go." Eddie shoved another mouthful in his face, threw some money on the table and they were gone, off into the night.

CHAPTER 84

Billy stared up at the nicotine'd ceiling as he thought about fronting Bomber out about Johnny and his bleedin knickers. "What do you reckon then Bomber?" "I dunno what to say mate," he replied, "who would have imagined him, the big boss man wearing ladies' knickers he must be as daft as a brush, and what with it splashed all over the papers an 'all." Billy chipped in with "To be fair though Bomber, it was only one paper, and it's a tiddler compared to all the others, it only goes out in London." "Yea I know mate but still, London is where we do our business, you know, beating people up, robbing, stealing, putting the frighteners on people and then demanding protection money. It's our back yard init?" "Good point mate and yea you're right, but what I'm really worried about is what our so-called customers are gonna think of *us* you know, like you and me for instance." Bomber went white. "Christ I never thought of it that way round" Bomber had arranged to meet up with Billy so they could chew things over.

He'd always held the belief that Billy would take the helm instead of Johnny the Turk if Eddie was to drop out or got himself killed or something. Billy got up, sauntered over to the bar and ordered two more beers. The Ship in Hackney had a good number of drinkers in this particular evening. It was not well known as a gangsters' favoured boozer; therefore, it came as a bit of a surprise for Billy to see a couple of bad lads he knew of, who usually hung about with the brother's firm, especially surprised as he didn't clock them coming in. The one closest to Billy turned to him, sneered and said laughingly "Johnny got you wearing kinky stuff an' all has he?" Billy went berserk. The unfortunate sneerer had a mouthful of ganky green teeth from a life time of eating raw Brussel sprouts. Not for much longer though, Billy grabbed a beer bottle from a nearby table and rammed it neck first into sneerer's mouth, then punched the bit of the bottle sticking out as hard as he could, plunging it painfully into the back of this guy's throat. Sneerer's companion leapt to his assist his mate but Bomber was quicker. The two were now on the deck. One gagging on a beer bottle and spewing bile out of the corners of his mouth, the other out stone cold from a single blow to the temple courtesy of Bomber. Billy pulled out his hand gun from the back of his belt, aimed it at the sneerer who by now was actually more than out of it. He couldn't see clearly due to blood seeping into his eyes from within, and totally unable to speak other than the odd gurgle. It would take a skilled surgeon, plus a capable medical team, to remove the bottle now.

Billy lowered his gun, the blokes on the floor couldn't see it anyway, instead, he knelt beside his bottled-up victim and whispered in his ear, "the next one's going up yer jacksie pal. Done you a favour though, no more stinking green Hampstead Heath eh?"

Up until now most of the punters had been happy to watch, however, at the sight of a shooter, many began to melt away. The Landlord who'd been watching the goings on from behind the bar, arms folded, upon seeing the gun being waved about turned to dial for the cops. Bomber saw the move and shouted out a warning. "Do that mate, Eddie Coleman and his crew will be in to bust this place up good and proper." The name Eddie Coleman still held some sway in the East End, even if he was on the run, not that everyone was in the know. The Landlord was aware of nails in the eyes and so forth, so the telephone receiver went back in its cradle well before the 999 call was answered. The pair left their two beers on the bar and calmly walked out. As they sauntered along Mare Street the topic of conversation got around to Dave Conti. He seemed to be missing which was not that unusual, except this time it was for a couple of weeks or more.

Plus, he didn't attend Val Coleman's funeral which they thought was entirely disrespectful. Other things bothered them too, this business about Johnny and his bloody knickers. The whole issue could undermine everything that Eddie had grafted for and possibly make his entire crew targets for piss-taking which would never do. The mystery surrounding the disappearance of dangerous Dave Conti could wait. They decided that little problem might resolve itself as and when he eventually turned up. The main issue now was to reclaim some respect. If what had just happened in the Ship was anything to go by, they would need something big and decisive to happen and they would need to sort it soonest or possibly see the crew dissolving, a laughing stock. Losing their hard men reputation would lead to disaster. As they walked past the Blind Beggar pub, Billy glanced sideways at Bomber as he drew a finger across his throat, Bomber nodded in agreement. Topping Johnny would be a very audacious move, especially with Eddie incommunicado. If it was going to be done, it would have to be done without his blessing. They were confident though Eddie would agree.

CHAPTER 85

Eddie awoke in yet another strange place and yawned heavily. Gone three o'clock, it was dark and for a moment he had no recollection of where he was, or how he even got there. Something stirred near his feet, holding his breath he could just about hear low volume snoring. Piecing together the last few hours or so he rapidly concluded it was Anna snoozing at the foot of his bed. She must be laying across the bottom, probably put him to bed then curled up just wanting to be near him, to protect him. His eyes grew accustomed to the darkness, he lifted his head to gain sight of exactly what or who was lying there. By slowly spreading his arms outright he worked out the bed was a double but, at the same time, couldn't work out why she wasn't lying beside him. Lifting his head up a little higher he saw what looked like an arm gently waving. He screwed up his eyes tightly then reopened them, clearing the mist. That was no arm, it was a bloody tail, a large dog's tail at that. He shoved his feet downward inside the bed hoping the mutt would jump down, bugger off and find somewhere else to sleep. Instead, it jumped up, still on the bed and barked his flipping head off. The noise was eardrum splitting, bearing its fangs didn't help much either. The light clicked on illuminating the room, in the doorway stood Anna, tying up the belt of her swish looking blue silk Kimono. She threw her arms around her pet in order to calm him down, thankfully it had the right effect.

Eddie breathed a sigh of relief, he'd not much savvy when it came to dogs. As far as he was concerned, dogs this big usually came on a long lead with an ugly looking copper on the other end shouting stand fucking still or he'll bite yer bollocks off. "Sorry Eddie." Anna apologised and introduced Vinny. "Eddie, this is Vinny, Vinny this is Eddie. So sorry Eddie, he's my best friend and the reason I sleep well at night. It completely slipped my mind; Vinny occasionally beds down in here. I must have left the door ajar when we finally turned in." "Don't remember seeing him earlier." Eddie grumbled. "That's because he quite often sleeps outside, he probably jumped up on your bed not realizing you were here." "So, what do we do now?" asked Eddie. Anna pouted and replied in a sensual tone "I can't chuck Vinny out, he's just a dog and wouldn't understand." I guess you had better come into my room, the beds big enough for the both of us and like I said earlier though, no funny business. Eddie grabbed his chinos and followed Anna down the hall in his under-pants. Anna's bedroom startled him. It was in complete contrast to the one he had just left; this room was more of a boudoir.

A six-foot high five-foot-wide velveteen headboard in purple dominated the room. Rounded off at the top corners, it resembled a purple-coloured half-moon, rising up to the heavens. Heavy curtains of a similar colour draped from ceiling to floor fully covered the windows. A chaise longue type sofa sat at the foot of the bed, and judging by the amount of dog hairs covering part of the cushioning, this was a bed for Vinny too. Lucky lad thought Eddie, one of three snoozing spots for him. An antique dressing table sat against the far wall, littered with different brands of make-up, potions, creams and smellies all reflected to double the amount due to the oval mirror in the centre of the table. But the thing that got Eddie's attention the most, there must have been upwards of thirty candles placed in candle burners, all lit and giving off aromas, filling the air to almost choking level. It put him in mind of a major whore house back home and was just about to say something when he felt Anna's arms curl around his waist from behind and hug him. "I think I know what you're thinking Eddie, but you couldn't be thinking of things any further from the truth, so don't think them. I'm not on the game, never have been, never will be. Don't need to, I do okay for male company when-ever I want and what's more, that happens to be right now. Eddie realized she must have lit all these candles very recently, so all of this was contrived to get him into bed with her.

"The blue Kimono with gold dragons printed on either side fell to the floor, leaving Anne naked apart from a gorgeous smile and a pair of the briefest of briefs. "Your turn Eddie."

CHAPTER 86

Johnny stood stock still at the head of the table in the meeting room above Zak's bar, waiting for people to get themselves seated. It was a sullen bad-tempered crew who assembled for tonight's get-together of villains, hoodlum's thieves, pickpockets and gangsters. The mood downstairs in the bar, for a change, was boisterous and jovial. The sound of much laughter and cheer seeped up the stairs into the ears of the guys sitting around the table. Some inwardly thought the laughter was directed at them, clearly thinking downstairs was taking the piss out of those upstairs due to that knicker wearing Johnny thing, recently exposed in the papers. Billy and Bomber being the only two gang members so far who had been exposed to any direct piss taking and that affront was dealt with accordingly. Neither opened up to Johnny about it or put forward the possibility of retaliation from the sneerer and his gang related member.

They were not obliged to discuss that, or any other subject, with someone about to be deposed or in this case dethroned and possibly replaced by the young Billy Maggs. Johnny brought the meeting to order. "First of," he barked. "Anyone know the whereabouts of Dave Conti?" No one spoke, lots of eyes remained staring at the table rather than directly at Johnny. Johnny slammed his fist down hard on the table in front of him hoping to wake them up. "Look you lot, you will fucking speak, if not you can fuck off and ply your poxy trade elsewhere." Nobody moved a muscle, no one wanted to be the first to front Johnny out regarding the story in the London Scoop. He had, of course, yet to explain himself just as he recently did to his cousin Zak. Seeing as how the sit down was going, he didn't have the slightest inclination to do so. Instead, he thought mentioning Eddie's name might get their undivided attention. "To remind you lot, Eddie Coleman left me in charge. He's off somewhere keeping his 'ead down and out of sight of old Bill. You all need to know; he'll be back soon and will be mightily pissed off with you." Johnny instantly regretted saying what he'd just said. Using Eddie's name to gain the upper ground actually undermined him even further. These guys were not totally daft.

The mood swung from ambivalence to one of a wolf pack turning on its injured leader. The first to react was Bomber. Who, up until this moment had been a faithful follower of Eddie, without hesitation, would kill for him. He did this because Eddie had one outstanding quality that Johnny didn't and would never in a million years possess. And that quality was respect, Eddie knew the meaning of respect. He'd craved it from a very early age. Having now gained such a high level within his crew and the local community, and knew how good it felt, and he was keen to dish it out. If necessary, by the bucket load especially to his most trusted blokes. However, Johnny was bereft of such a refined quality, sometimes much needed when in a position of leadership. Johnny fought for any respect by using his fists in the ring, and occasionally his teeth, as in biting off an opponent's ear. All that is well and good in a boxing bout, but no bloody good with Eddie's crew or any other collection of misfits. If he wasn't careful, he could end up a sad and lonely bloke wondering how he'd dropped so far. One minute the top boy in a well-established and feared notorious gang, the next walking the streets of London, constantly looking over his shoulder. Bomber stood and glowered at Johnny the Turk. "You know nothing about Eddie and even less about respect for him, and for that matter, respect for us." he scowled. Johnny went on the offensive, it was his first instinct to get the first punch in, then the second and third, before whoever he was hitting knew what the hell was going on.

As Johnny stood, so did Billy and Mel, one either side of him. They grabbed an arm each and roughly forced them up behind Johnny's back, almost breaking them into the bargain. He let out a blood curdling roar as they lifted him off the floorboards by pushing his arms up his back a little further. All went quiet downstairs. Any moment they would hear Zak racing up the stairs, Billy asked Bomber to bar anyone from entry. Bomber obliged. As he did so, he turned to Johnny. "We can't live with the story in the papers about you wearing women's underwear, kinky bloody git you are. It's making you and all of us," he swept a shovel like hand around the table, "a bloody laughing stock." Johnny opened his mouth to explain and was halted when Billy stuffed a handkerchief in his mouth. "Shut up and listen," he instructed. Johnny had little choice. Bomber continued "Listen to this." He relayed the incident that recently took place in the Ship. Gave a blow-by-blow account of the event including the fact that the two blokes he and Billy dropped, worked for the firm run by the brothers. "And that's not gonna be the last of it.

Far from it." "If they twig what's going on, this place could become a blood bath." Johnny scanned his eyes around the table at the hard looks at him and could see the impact the tale from Bomber had on them. There might just as well be an old geezer with a flowing white beard holding up a banner announcing 'The end is Nigh'. The door leading to the stairs opened with such force, Bomber who was standing guard, felt the full force and was flung forward. Zak entered the room before Bomber could throw his weight against Zak and force him out of the room. No need to have worried, a couple of the other blokes grabbed Zak by the hair and literally threw him downstairs head first. "Fuck you, you bastards," he shouted as he fell "I'm going to call the cops." Hearing his voice, the language and ferocity in his tone, indicated no serious damage from falling down the stairs. "Must have been a bit pissed." Billy smiled, still holding an arm up Johnny's back. "Happened to me once on New Year's Eve, got well pissed at this nightclub then fell down a full flight of iron steps. Top to bottom in no time." Some bloke asked me if I was alright, I thought he said wanna fight, so I obliged him and knocked him into the new year."

Nods of appreciation all around. For the moment, Billy assumed a very temporary (I'm in charge) role. He said, "let's put this to the vote. All those in favour of me taking the reins." Hands up all round, some of the junior lads stuck both hands in the air. "Right so that's unanimous." He turned to Johnny and warned him, anymore rough stuff and he would follow Zak and be thrown downstairs and told to sling his hook.

Billy and Mel slowly ungripped Johnny's arm and let them fall by his side. They both stood beside him in case he was not a man of his word. Johnny slumped into his chair. Billy thought it was a bit off to ask him to vacate the chairman's chair, that will come to Billy in good time. "Okay, thanks everyone, somebody needs to drop down and see if Zak rang the filth, somehow, I don't believe he's got the bottle, but just in case, who is up for that?" Monkey Micky stood, indicating he was up for it. "Okay Micky, go and sort it out mate. Once that's done get back here on the double cos were going to have another voting session." Other blokes sitting round the table started to feel good. Taking votes was new to them, they enjoyed the notion of being part of decision making, which pleased them no end. It was no longer a dictatorship with a power crazed dick at the helm.

Micky came back sharpish as was requested swinging his head from side to side, indicating no phone call. Billy enquired, "What's he up to then Micky?" "He's nursing a broken wrist boss. The one call he made was for an ambulance, but just in case he tries to bell old Bill, I've ripped out the phone line. One or two of Zak's customers complained because they won't be able ring for a taxi ride home. I told them to shut it or get hurt." "Right Micky thanks for that, you did well." Micky felt his chest expand with pride. A good job well done he said to himself. Billy addressed the blokes. "I want to ask you all for a show of hands for these next three issues. Number one, a second in command. Number two, does Johnny stay and number three does he go? Here we go then; I propose that Mel is second in command. All those that agree hold up a hand or get shot. "Only joking." Laughed Billy. It was unanimous, Mel was now Billy's right-hand man. "Thanks lads, Appreciate that." He winked at Mel who gave him a nod of appreciation. "Secondly, does Johnny stay?" Nobody voted they all ducked. "Right thanks last one, does Johnny go?" All hands shot in the air. He turned to Johnny. "Well, you saw what happened, so why are still here?" Johnny spat back, "You haven't heard the last of this, and you can be certain you will not have this place for meets again," Billy replied, "I was counting on that, coz it won't be long before this place gets a visit from the firm especially now since me and Bomber stuck it to a couple of their followers. Mind you, if I can get word to the brothers themselves that two of his men were disrespecting us blokes while working for Eddie Coleman, they might even shake my hand and top those two sneering bastards. There's still honour amongst thieves you know. The other thing is, that job we did over at Hainault you know, snuffing out the mob that operated from there might have done the brother's army some good.

Haven't heard any rumours yet, but I do know when the Hainault gang broke up, some of the blokes upped sticks and joined the firm, probably taking some tasty deals with them. Mel here is a distant cousin of the brothers, so I guess if I was to ask him nicely, he might get a message to them about the goings on at the Ship over in Hackney." Billy looked around for approval and he got it. He turned to Johnny. "If you're in a two and eight and stuck for some where to get your head down, until you get something sorted, you can stay in one of the bedrooms up West above the Steak bar in Wardour Street. Tell them Billy sent you, Little Allen will drive you over there. He knows the story so he can intro you to Mac the manager. You alright with that Allen?" He stuck both thumbs up. "Stick it up your arse Billy fucking Maggs.

I don't want handouts or sympathy of any kind from you, or anyone else in this room." "Fair do's mate," said Billy. "Bomber! escort him off the premises would you please?" Bomber jumped up, "consider it done boss, consider it done." Bomber led Johnny the Turk downstairs, through the bar where Zak sat open mouthed as he watched his cousin being frog marched out. He heard muffled shouting and a scuffle out in the street and that was it, Johnny was history. Upstairs, Billy had a private word with Mel encouraging him to get word to the brothers about The Turk getting his arse kicked, and that new management was in now place. Billy looked up at the remaining blokes around the table. "Well, that went well everyone, thanks for backing me. Since Zak and Johnny are related, I would think this will be our last meet here. I suggest we let today's dust settle and keep a look out for a new place. Micky, you and your two mates have a dig around and find out what you can about Dave Conti. If he's done a runner, we'll need another specialist in car nicking business, any ideas?"

CHAPTER 87

"Well, that was a fun filled night if ever there was one." Anna remarked. "You sleeping in my bedroom snoring your head off and me sleeping in your bed with Vinny for company, also snoring his head off." Eddie shoved another marmalade smothered piece of toast in his mouth, washing it down with a slurp of steaming black coffee and nodded. "Lovely table manners Mr. Biggs, you know how to turn a girl's head don't you?" Eddie continued, munch slurp belch, munch slurp. He sat giving Anna the once over while she talked and boy, could she talk.

Both were wearing to the floor dressing gowns, both of which belonged to Anna.

He was aware he was naked beneath the gown, and could not or didn't want to remember where his Y fronts had disappeared to. The sexy blue Kimono Anna wore last night was replaced by a frumpy but comfortable thick green woolly gown, he had the same, but in royal blue. He wondered how many other blokes had worn this gown on the morning after at breakfast with Anna, just as he was now. He hoped she washed it thoroughly after every episode. Out on the veranda at the little restaurant last night, her face was youthful and aglow with the candle lights placed between them on their table. This morning, minus the war paint, of which he remembered seeing copious amounts on her dressing table, she looked so much older.

That worried him slightly, he was in his mid-twenties and by the looks of Anna just now, she could easily pass for early forties. "Eddie, you kind of know my story now. I'm a single woman living in here in Spain, cock mad with a son; Fabio. One gift shop to my name and that's about it." What Eddie really wanted to know however, was a bit more about the time she lived in London and how she ended up here. He decided to drill down a little further but only when the time was right. "Come on then," Anna jabbed a finger in his arm, "What's your story then, and no holding back, I'm all ears?" His eyes settled on her ample cleavage attempting to burst out of her gown but declined from offering up, 'well from here darling, it looks like you're all tits, not ears.' He decided to tell her the truth, the whole truth and nothing but the truth, on the basis that if you tell someone the truth, they rarely believe it. "I'm a psychotic, unhinged. fucking cop killing madman," he said grinning like a shark. "I kill people sometimes for money, sometimes for vengeance and sometimes when I'm simply bored. And that goes anyone who gets in the way of the business I run. Anna threw her head back and laughed uncontrollably, she held her sides shouting "stop it my ribs are killing me." Eddie jumped straight in and with a menacing growl bellowed "right, where's me fucking knife, I'll soon sort your ribs out." Anna shrieked with laughter again. "Eddie, that was brilliant no doubt you're going to tell me next; you've killed more people than smallpox! You've been watching too many films you have." Taking a big intake of air to quell the itch to laugh some more, she asked, "And what business is it that you run?" "I'm top dog of a powerful gang in the East End. That's me, a right evil cockney bastard, I'm like a misguided missile. My crews got a fearsome reputation for doling out beatings, murders and general mayhem. Must be twenty-five to thirty blokes under my control, more joining by the day." He remained silent, letting this information sink in. "You know Eddie, it's a great story but I don't believe a single word of it. What you've left out though is this, what are you doing in Mojácar?" "Believe it or not Anna, I stuck a pin in a map of Spain, and here I am. I told you earlier, someone I know came out here a few weeks ago and moved into a villa not too far away from here, I think." "What do you mean *think*?" "Well, I'm not entirely sure exactly where this villa is, all I know is it might be near." Anna's interest was getting the better of her. She enquired, "Do you know the name of the villa?" Eddie dug out of his holdall a bit of paper on which was scrawled 'Villa Hermosa Vista.' She screwed up her eyes trying hard to read what was written. "Christ, spidery writing or what, is that yours?"

"Here let me." Eddie held out his hand and retrieved the scrappy piece of paper and read out the villa's name. "Anna shook her head. "Can't say I've heard of that one. Tell you what though, I know a guy in town who runs a sort of villas for hire or sale outfit. When we've finished up here let's take a walk into town and I'll introduce him to you his name is Javier. We had a thing going once, his dad's a bit of alright too." Eddie looked down at the blue dressing gown he was wearing, he felt queasy and shuddered.

CHAPTER 88

A warm sunny Spanish morning greeted them as they made their way from Anna's two bed cabaña towards the town. At ten o'clock most of the locals were up and about busying themselves. Road sweepers sweeping up last night's litter. Shuttered shops became un-shuttered as shop workers lifted the heavy shutters ready to pack them around the back. Market stalls already laden with fruit and veg full to the brim with colourful fruit and veg displays, most of it looking too good to disturb, such was the art of the street stall holders. It would be a while before any one on holiday was to be seen in the town's little centre, they were either still at breakfast or heading down to the beach in order to beat the Germans to the sun loungers. Fat chance of that, Jerries get themselves sorted by seven. They passed the restaurant that received the wrong end of Eddie the previous night. He mentioned the kerfuffle to Anna. She grinned, raised her eyebrows and said, "You never give up do you? If what you just told me is true, the whole town including me would have heard about it."

They walked on in silence through some very narrow streets turning left, turning right then left again. It was clear Anna knew her way around. Almost everyone they met greeted her like an old friend.

"Hola Anna cómo estás?" Anna always replied in English. "I'm fine today thank you and you?" "Here it is, these are the people who rent out or sell villas. It's all they do; and they're registered with the correct authorities. If they don't know where the Hermosa Vista is, then it doesn't exist. Eddie stopped in his tracks; this was something he'd not contemplated. Could it be

Esme had tricked him into coming all this way for nothing. A tingle of a warning bell rung inside his head last night, when Anna said she'd not heard of it. Fuck me, if this turns out to be a bloody goose chase, I'll…… Before he could finish his internal sentence, Anna pushed the door open and they were in.

Eddie clocked a young man standing with his back to them studying some map or other. He said over his shoulder without looking back "Un momento" Anna looked at Eddie and put a finger to her lips, he assumed it was for him to keep quiet. She moved quickly over to the young man still with his back to them, clasping her hands over his eyes at the same time as pressing her thighs into his bottom, "guess who?" Javier spun around, on recognising Anna, he exclaimed, "Anna, Anna my lovely Anna, what a wonderful surprise." He looked over her shoulder and spotted Eddie. "Oh, I see you have brought your body guard. He's not the one that caused a problema at the La Tasca cantina last night, is he?" Anna looked aghast. "Why, what happened there?" Javier told the tale exactly as Eddie had told her on the way. Looking directly at Eddie, all he had said to her earlier this morning came flooding back. Javier continued, "It is okay if it was your friend here, he did the owner at La Tasca a favour indeed. Eddie spoke. "Oh yea and what would that be pal?" "The waiter was how you say, a big pain in the arse. He is bully and nobody will stand up to him. He is a wife beater too, so next time you see him, warn him if he carries on beating his wife, you will hit him again." Eddie couldn't understand why some of his workmates came to his rescue, so he asked Javier to explain. Javier brushed aside the question saying "please be seated, both of you I must make a quick phone call then you will have my full attention." While Javier gabbled on at very nearly shouting volume down the phone, Eddie's attention was drawn to the myriad of framed photos exhibiting differing sizes of villas plastered all over the walls, ranging from tiny to enormous.

There must have been about fifty of them, many with pools,

others with security fences, electric gates complete with hard-wired intercom systems. Javier looked up from his phone conversation. He instructed whoever was on the other end to stop yabbering for a second, and for Eddie's sake, swept a hand over the photos and said, "take your pick, they are all ready for moving in, most are fully furnished too." He returned to the phone and gabbled on again. Eddie lent over to Anna. "How comes he speaks reasonable English?" Anna explained, "He studied for a while in London, his papa who currently owns this business paid for him to do three or four years at a top college, Imperial, I think." She continued "According to Javier he had the best time ever and boasts of having three children by various partners while he was there." Eddie grimaced, "sounds like a right bleedin' charmer."

While Javier continued with his call, Anna whispered, "if that was you at La Tasca last night you'd better sit tight, this guy can be of help to you in locating the villa you seek. I can see you've taken a dislike to him but let's not have any rough stuff, at least not right now. Eddie took the hint and breathed heavily for a moment or two. Javier finished his call, stitched on a happy face and formerly greeted Anna and Eddie. "Welcome to our establishment, would you like some coffee or perhaps some English tea? We have Earl Grey; it is well known to have blood pressure lowering effects." He said whilst looking directly at Eddie. If Javier was attempting to get Eddie's goat up, he was succeeding. Anna spoke first indicating two coffees would be just fine. "My assistant will not be in until midday today, so I will have to leave you for a moment and make the refreshments for you both." He disappeared from view. Eddie leaned into Anna. "Is he a piss taker, what's all that about blood pressure?" "It's alright Eddie, it's just the way he comes across, I know he seems a bit cocky and I agree there was no need for the blood pressure thing. If you want to do him over, which I have no doubt you can and probably will, just do it after we've gained the whereabouts of the villa and preferably when I'm not around. Just don't actually kill him please." Eddie grinned. "You sound just like my Mum. She'd definitely approve of you girl. When she pops over to Spain like, I'll get her to call into your shop. You two should get on like a house on fire. By the way, what's that music he's got on?" "He's a great lover of Puccini, it's operatic stuff mainly, why?" "Basically, it's getting on me tits." Javier entered the showroom carrying two coffees. Placing them on a nearby occasional table, he turned to Anna and Eddie saying, "now, how can I be of help to you?" Eddie jumped up, looked him straight in the eye for a few seconds and snapped,

"where's the pisser mate I need to splash me boots?" Javier pointed a finger in the direction of the toilets, bringing to Eddie's attention he was to use the one with a male symbol on the door. That was it. Eddie went from ice cold to boiling hot. There are crazy nutters, then there's Eddie. Within a matter of seconds Javier found himself on the floor, out cold from a vicious right hook to his tanned and very weak chin. To Eddie's surprise Anna didn't scream. In fact, she didn't do anything not even budge an inch. Just sat there, fiddling with one of the fasteners on her denim dungarees. Eddie spoke first.

"He was well out of order he was, had it coming from the moment we walked in. If there's anything I detest more than bullies, it's cocky bastards like 'im." He kicked Javier who moaned a little. "Well at least he 'aint dead, yet"

Eddie sat down again and sipped his coffee. "Shows you what contempt he had for us," he said looking down at his saucer, "shouldn't there be a biscuit or two thrown in?" Eddie lazily placed his cup back on the saucer then sauntered over to a trio of three drawer wooden filing cabinets. He rummaged through, flinging out anything unconnected to the Villa Hermosa Vista. File after file hit the floor, each one scattering its precious contents. Some landed on the prostrate Javier which made Eddie grin. That which he was searching for surrendered itself halfway through the third cabinet. "Eddie,"

Anna dragged a sentence out from her bemused mind. "If you'd gone through those files alphabetically you would have come across the one you were looking for sooner." "Bit late for advice now girl, besides it gives 'im a bit of tidying up to do, when he comes round. Sitting down again, Eddie read through the details within the file. From what he could make out, it looked to be situated on the very road the taxi driver used to get to Mojácar, the previous evening. "Bloody 'ell Anna, I passed it on my way here." Anna said astonishingly. "What, as we walked here this morning?" "No, not today, yesterday. Must have driven by it, shit, that close and I missed it." "What does it say for an address then?" she asked. "It doesn't, it just gives directions, it says from here take the main road for Almeria, drive for seven miles/11 kilometres then, on your left you will see a sign saying 'To the Beach.' Hmmmm a talking sign. Turn left here and the Villa Hermosa Vista will be the first on the left. A key can be found under an Aloe Vera plant, in a pot by the pool at the back of the Villa. What's an Aloe Vera plant when it's at home then?" " Ummm a bit like a green cactus but with long pointy type stems sprouting up from its base. Actually, when you break the leaves, the milky white gel it produces is good for minor burns and ailments." "Thank you nurse Anna, leave out the gardening advice if you don't mind." Javier stirred. "He's coming round Eddie." "Yea well he 'aint gonna up jump too quick is he, take him a while to come to, that's if his jaw 'aint broken." Eddie noticed a written note attached to the villa's file. If he had not turned the file over' he would have missed it. On inspection it was just a few lines written in Spanish. "What's all this about Anna, can you read the lingo?" "Of course, give it here, I'll translate for you. He handed it over and watched Anna's face as she read the note. Instead of relaying the contents on to Eddie, she walked over to Javier's desks and pulled open a few drawers. Anna found what she was looking for. She was looking for something with Javier's hand writing on it.

She compared the two and let out a long audible sigh, it was definitely his hand writing on the note. Anna sank into her chair and sighed again. How on earth was she going to tell Eddie exactly what was on the note. It was dynamite, actually no. It was more like a nuclear site with a ruptured reactor. Anna could almost hear all the rods hissing and about to explode. "Is the person you know at the villa called Esme?" Anna asked nervously. Eddie smelt a rat. He was short on guessing games and long on violence. "Yea why?" "It's just that her name is mentioned in the note." "Well, that makes sense, she's the one I asked to find us a drum, didn't I?" "A drum Eddie?" "Yea, somewhere we could rent for a bit, lay low for a while an' all that." Anna was beginning to shake a little and her voice was moving up the frequency scale.

"So, what's it say, come on girl spit it out?" Eddie was moving up the impatient scale himself and was now staring hard at Anna. Javier gasped for air as he finally came round. Sitting upright he looked about him at all the scattered paperwork whilst rubbing his sore but unbroken chin. Eddie, sensing something was afoot regarding Anna's reluctance to read out what was on the note, grabbed Javier lifting him up with one pull and threw him into his wheeled office chair, it rolled halfway across the sales room before crashing into the far wall. Javier's head was thrown back and with a sickening thud hit the wall behind him. Blood seeped down the wall towards the shiny marble floor, exiting from the nasty gash at the back of his head. Eddie grabbed the hand written note from Anna's trembling hand and stuck it under Javier's nose. Eddie put two fingers up Javier's nostril and yanked skyward. The scream was probably heard all over Mojácar, not just from the pain in his face but the upward movement banged his head once again against the wall behind him. For good measure Eddie pulled Javier, with fingers still up his nose, away from the wall by three or four feet. He put his left foot on the chair seat between Javier's legs and kicked it forward, once again banging his head against the wall inflicting more damage to the wound. "Read it you bloody gutless Spanish git." Javier opened his eyes to see the note and the words he had written in haste a short while ago. He looked up at Eddie as the last vestiges of anger welled up inside him. This was his turn to hurt this man. "Esme was a bloody good fuck" he cried. "Satisfied now, English freak, every time you make love to Esme, you will know I've been there too." Eddie had to think about this. Here he was at the mercy of a madman and yet he could still think clearly. Javier screamed, "get out, get out of my premises.

I'm going to call the police. Eddie backhanded Javier across the face so hard it hurt his hand. Blood poured from Javier's nose down onto his cream silk shirt. Before any phone calls could be made, Eddie threw the expensive looking telephone onto the marble floor and stamped on it hard rendering it unusable, and for good measure, ripped out the connecting wires. He looked over at Anna. "You got a car?" he barked like a sergeant major on heat "Yes" she replied weakly, "why?" "Go and get it and when you get back, hit the horn twice leave it running then bugger off and whatever you do, don't come in here." Anna got up to go. "You do something stupid Anna and I'll find you and cut you up and that goes for your dopey son and all." He turned to Javier. "Stand up pal, take your shirt off and turn round." Eddie's plan was to carry out his ritual and carve out a noughts and crosses game on Javier's back, only this time while he is still very much alive. Eddie moved to the entrance door as Anna left and locked it. There happened to be a door roller blind which he pulled down tightly. The two side windows were plastered with pictures of villas 'for sale' or rent. It would be difficult for anyone to see anything that was going on inside. Just in case though, Eddie switched off all the lights placing the main office in semi darkness. "Now then my friend, let the ritual begin." Javier heard Eddie singing gently, and because he was facing away from him, what he couldn't see was his eyes glazing over with his head tilted to one side.

Javier screamed at the blooded wall. "Get on with it freak, you can't hurt me anymore, I've won, I've beaten you checkmate, mate." He started giggling uncontrollably at his own brand of humour. It was obvious he was not aware of what was coming. Eddie dug the blade out of his holdall.

Knocked Javier to the floor, stood on his outstretched arms and began carving. To cover the screams that would no doubt come, Eddie turned the stereo up to full volume before cutting his way into Javier's back. The music dramatically matched the macabre scene.

"This is no bleedin opera matey, shouted Eddie above the din, as his hand pushed the wicked knife blade on into Javier's flesh.

CHAPTER 89

Eddie exited the building, leaving Javier for dead. He'd laid a bloody great marker down for the police a virtual signpost. As far as he was concerned, he'd not heard of anyone else carving kids' games on the backs of their victims. So, this was his signature, and it wouldn't take long for the authorities to put two and two together. They may be daft but they were not bloody stupid. Therefore, time was of the essence. Anna pulled up in her battered old mini which served her well these last three years and was about to blast the horn twice. Eddie came from nowhere, yanked the passenger door open, threw his holdall in the back, jumped in and ordered Anna to get going. She rammed the mini into gear spinning the front wheels creating a screeching noise together with the smell of burning rubber. "Not so bloody fast, don't want to attract the wrong sort of attention for Christ's sake." "I thought I was supposed to leave the car and bugger off." Anna shouted above the racket." "Change of plan Anna, change of plan. I can't drive, totally forgot, so you'll have to drive me to the villa. I've got the instructions here, it says, take the Almeria Road out of Mojácar and drive for about seven miles and look out for a speaking sign saying 'To the Beach'." He chortled at the thought. "What have you done to Javier?" she begged. "He's history the dirty little bugger, just drive and let me think. "I can't do this Eddie, it's okay for you, but for me personally, I've too much to lose." "And I haven't? Don't be thinking just of yourself Anna. Too late anyway, your dabs are all over that place now, especially what with you going through his desk and that. The old Bill will conclude that you helped me top the greasy bastard." "You've topped him?" She yelled. "Yea sort of," he answered.

"So, that puts us both on the run, a bit like Bonny and Clyde. When I was banged up on remand, I read all about them you know, it was the only book I was interested in. Bloody shame they were shot to death in a police ambush. It happened way back in 1934 in a place called Louisiana." "Eddie, stop it, you're frightening me, I don't want to be shot in an ambush!" "No worries, I've got the villa file with me intacto. I dunno how long it will take for matey boy's body to be found, or for that matter for you to be identified from your finger prints. And as I've got this file, where are the plod going to look for Javier's killers? They won't have a scooby bloody doo." "How do you mean *killers* Eddie, I had nothing to do with it." "Try telling that to the judge darlin.

As they motored along the road to Almeria a police car passed them in the opposite direction. Anna shuddered then burst into tears at the thought of ending up in a stinking Spanish correction facility for women only. "Come on Anna toughen up will yer, the only two people who know what happened to Javier is us, you and me and that's it. The stronger you are, the more I will admire you. Look, if you've never been in trouble with the police over here, then they won't be able to tie you in with what's just gone on." Anna explained, "well I did get into trouble with the police back in London and they took my finger prints, so, I am on record over there." "In that case, you'd better stick with me. When the heats off, you can drive over to Almeria, meet up with your son and fuck off somewhere remote for a while. It's me they'll be after not you. Anyway, you're innocent until proven guilty." Anna asked, "where is Javier's body, in his office for all to see?" "Here we are, take left here Anna." "Well, answer my question Eddie, or this is as far as I go." "Fine by me love, piss off and find your boy over in Almeria, then shoot off somewhere remote and keep both your heads down. Six months should do it, just let me get my holdall." Anna screamed at the top of her voice, "you bloody bastard, you've dragged me into your sodding seedy murderous underworld, go to hell." Eddie walked away from Anna and the Mini towards the villa; it was sure to be here somewhere. If he'd bothered to look back, he would have seen Anna's head bent forward resting on the steering wheel sobbing her heart out poor cow. He would also have seen her come to her senses as she spun the car around in anger and shot off in the direction of Mojácar.

CHAPTER 90

Monkey Micky and his mates had been busy as requested by Billy, busy gathering snippets of info here and bits of gossip there. Billy was busy setting up a temporary meeting place for the crews meets. It happened to be in a hall at the back of a run-down disused office block close to Mile End tube station. Nothing luxurious but it would do for now. Ironically, very nearly next door to a working police station. As Billy would say when meetings took place, 'tea leaves in here, thieves next door.' Always got a laugh.

The single-story hall was once used as a meeting room come training centre for those that worked in the office block, but those people were long gone now, and Billy believed the whole lot was due for demolition soon anyway.

On offer was some furniture sat about the place, chairs and tables, that sort of stuff but with no power supply, the crews' sit downs would need to take place during daylight hours always a bit dangerous being so close to the old Bill shop. A distant uncle of Billy's used to be employed as a cleaner in the office block and held on to the keys to the hall when he was made redundant. He'd passed them to Billy only yesterday for safe keeping and wished him luck with his new found employment as a business consultant. Billy didn't pass on to his distant uncle the terms and conditions of his firm. "So, this is the new nerve centre?" asked Mel with a twinkle in his eyes and mischievous grin. "Sure is" replied Billy "until it's pulled down that is." "Stone the crows Billy it's close to the old Bill though 'aint it?" Mel asked. "They're only just up the frog a short way." "Yea, you're right Mel but I can't see them coming round here too often unless it's to bring a bird for a bit of how's your father behind the giant dustbins, and if they do, we'll take some photos and blackmail the bastards." "Nice one Billy, ever the businessman, always looking out for the main chance." Billy asked, "has everyone been told about the meet, only we've got to get things moving before The Turk has a go at starting up on his own and using our contacts." Mel replied, "I doubt that will ever happen, what with 'im being exposed as wearing girly bloomers." "Girly bloomers, where'd you get that from mate?" "It's me mum Billy, old fashioned as the bloody ark she is, well old school." Bomber entered the hall and opened up with. "Bloody 'ell Billy, bit close to the filth 'aint it?" Billy looked at Mel, they both fell about laughing, "It'll be okay Bomber, just as long as you don't knock em up for a cup of milk when we're having a brew." Bomber got the drift and laughed too. When the laughter died down Billy announced, "Look, before the rest of the team turn up, I've got some news about Dave, Dave Conti." The other two looked up sharply. "Micky and his mates have been putting their ears to the ground and come up with the following. And, I might add, it fits with his sudden disappearance. Micky knows a little turd called Slug. He's been doin' a look out job for Dave up West when he's nicking motors. He went with Dave to get some hookey gear up in Hatton Garden he told me. Apparently, Dave laid his brass bands on a pile of jewellery from a safe deposit box, then the both of 'em had it away in a nicked Daimler." Bomber asked "so why did this Slug thing spill the beans to Micky?"

"Well, the tom-foolery according to Slug, was worth thousands, that's what Dave told 'im and yet, he only bunged Slug a couple of twenties or something for marking the Daimler, the tight fucker. Slug was steaming mad about it and told young Micky so.

The other thing is, Slug hasn't seen Dave for a few weeks now, and that ties in with 'im missing at Mrs. Coleman's funeral. Errol aint seen him about neither." "If he's had it away with the gems and that," Mel cut in, "he could be halfway up the country and 'avin it large by now." "That's right mate, tell you what then, go and jump in next door and report him to the old Bill." All three laughed. "Actually, that's not such a bad idea."

Billy said thoughtfully, "I don't mean stroll in there or anything, what we could do with, is a tame cop, one that's happy to be on the take you know bunged a ton once in a while. There's bound to be a copper's story behind the jewellery and Dave thing. Probably knocked off stuff" guessed Billy, "then stashed away in a safe deposit box in a vault in Hatton Garden. We could do with tracking that Dave down and grabbing what's left. We need to put the word out to anyone who might have exchanged the diamonds for cash, you know, fenced it for half its bloody worth. Tell them the stuff belongs to Eddie and Dave nicked it, that should get the desired result. Even if we don't know where he is right now, whoever fenced it for him might be able to shine a bit of light on it and point us in the right direction. When all the lads are here, we'll get them to circulate the story and see what turns up. Secondly, let's see if we can find someone in the Met we can lean on for the odd bit of info. But for now, we'd better get back on some money making blags again and sharpish like, coz the cash is getting low. I think a bank job is on the cards. There's one just past the old Bill shop, I dropped in there this morning. Couldn't see any security or cameras or nothing. Let's raid the soddin' place, let's do it right under coppers uniformed noses." "There's big money to be had and what's more it's all in notes, none of that shifting stuff through greedy bloody fences." "Which one do yer mean then Billy?" Bomber asked. "Snatch West mate. We'll get Monkey Mick and his mates to clock it for a week or so and get some idea when cash is delivered and suchlike. Case it round the back to see if there is an easy entry point or two. If it's done well and word gets out, villains from other gangs will want to join us, if only to get their snouts in the trough." Later that same day the meet up chaired by Billy Maggs proceeded.

Two recent crew members, high up in the scheme of things were absent. Johnny the Turk and Dave Conti. Bent Johnny as they now called 'im, kicked out and Dave Conti missing, presumed completely minted.

And bloody good riddance to both of them, to which all agreed. The rest got their orders and a further get together was shoved in the diary. Billy and Mel held back after the blokes disappeared. "It's all about survival now Mel my son," Billy mused, "we need to rebuild the crew back up again in readiness for when Eddie gets back."

CHAPTER 91

Villa Hermosa Vista, as promised by the information in Javier's manila file, would be the first on the left from where Eddie was standing. In fact, it was the only one on the left and it was a big one too. He looked past the villa and saw others grouped on the right-hand side, but not close by any means. What he could see, through the foliage of some almond trees, was the odd flat roof with big silver-coloured barrels like water butts on their side, one to each flat roof. Instead of entering the villa he took a little stroll down the path that led to the beach below. He covered a hundred yards or so when the path narrowed and the beach, a fair way below, came into view. He noticed it was empty which he thought a bit strange. Whenever he'd hit the seaside back home it was always crawling with people, kids and dogs. He saw a single swimmer, a small speck in the sea from where he stood, not too far out and could have sworn whoever it was, raised an arm out of the water and waved in his direction. Instinctively he turned around, expecting to see someone behind him waving back. He turned back to the swimmer, but the swimmer was gone, perhaps he thought, the swimmer was swimming under the water. He decided to head back up to the villa in search of Esme. He tapped several times on the front door. Odd he thought, she's not about. He banged and rattled the villa's front door several times to no avail. Checking the file to remind him of where the key to the front door was hidden, he trotted to the pool area at the back of the villa. Luckily, only one Aloe Vera plant sat in a pot close to the pool, all the others were safely tucked away in flower beds. He kicked the plant over, grabbed the key and made his way back to the front door and let himself in. The entrance hall was cool and shady, offering some respite to the sun's midday heat outside. Eddie called out, "Esme, where are you, anyone home?" It would seem the place was empty. He walked through the villa towards the kitchen. As he passed an open bedroom door, he spotted a piece of paper that looked like it had some handwriting on it sitting on a pillow. Thinking it might be a note from Esme, perhaps something about gone shopping be back soon, that sort of thing.

He snatched it up, sat on the bed and began reading it. The opening line read *'My darling Eddie.'* Down on the beach Esme was getting a little concerned. She was sure it was Eddie she saw, here at long-last, standing on the sandy path watching her swim.

She waved but for some reason he didn't wave back. She gave it another fifteen minutes before decided something must be up. Esme gathered up the beach towel, donned her bikini top and sarong, grabbed her beach bag and headed for the villa. It's not easy going during the heat of the day, uphill on a windy sandy lane, saps the energy from you soon as you like. Out of breath and sweating profusely she pushed open the front door, already ajar calling out "Eddie, Eddie, where are you?" He appeared in the bedroom doorway scowling, looking like thunder, in his hand a paper note. Not the one she had left for him, in case he turned up, but the one left for her by Mitch the previous day. The first line read *'My darling Esme.'* "You should be more fucking careful girl." He growled. "What do you mean Eddie, I left it for you in case you turned up while I'd gone for a swim." Eddie produced the note she was on about in a crumpled and torn state. "Not this bleedin' one, this one, *this one*" he yelled holding up the note Mitch had left. Eddie started to move towards her menacingly, she screamed at the top of her voice, dashing out of the villa, she was now running for her life. She knew all about Eddie and his psychotic sadistic ways and wasn't about to let him carry them out on her. Eddie slammed the door after her yelling out "come back here an' I will cut you into tiny pieces." Esme continued running, she may have been mildly exhausted due to the trek up from the beach, but having a murderous dog on her tail was enough to lend her the pace of an Olympic sprinter. She ran in the direction of the beach, heaven knows why, perhaps the thought of drowning herself would be miles better than having Eddie torture her and eventually kill her. Chris happened to be pruning some bushes in his garden when he saw Esme flash past, dressed only in her black bikini and sarong. He called out "Hi Esme in a rush for a dip in the briny then, are you?" She stopped in her tracks, however considering the speed she was going, and together with soft fine sand underfoot, it took her quite some time to come to a halt. Totally out of breath and scared shitless, she fell to the ground completely wrecked. It took Chris a few moments to gather what on earth was going on. Sticking his head over the low fence, he could just make out Esme lying face down, arms and legs akimbo like a star fish, on the sandy path sobbing and quivering in fright.

By the time he'd legged it over the fence and got to her, she was kneeling up and talking softly to herself. All he could hear through her sobbing was, "why, oh why didn't I destroy that note from Mitch, why oh bloody why?" Chris was bemused, he hadn't heard the name of *Mitch* in relation to Esme.

His wife Sue, mentioned the name Eddie more than once. Apparently, Esme referred to an Eddie in a dream when she was asleep one afternoon on a sun lounger by her pool. Sue tackled her about it but Esme had remained tight lipped. Chris knelt down beside Esme and was about to put a comforting arm around her shoulder, when a voice rang out with "and what the hell is going on here?" Chris looked up to see Sue striding towards them, hands on hips and looking decidedly dodgy. "It's not what it looks like my darling wifey," although it was secretly what he had been dreaming of since first setting eyes on Esme. "It's exactly what it looks like," Sue exclaimed.

"My God, put her down you bloody sexed crazed animal, she's at least half your age and besides you could have waited till I had gone into Mojácar or something. Chris shouted back, "oh you silly old mare, don't you think I would have chosen a better spot than here, right outside our villa on a public footpath; besides I'd get all sand in my willie, can't you see she's upset?" Sue was not to be appeased by Chris's attempt at smutty humour, "I would be upset too if that's your only chat up line you stupid milksop, sand in your willie indeed." A serious ruck between Sue and Chris ensued, Chris protesting his innocence and Sue who didn't care one jot for his innocence, but was determined to find him guilty of the wrong offence.

"I knew you fancied that slut from the moment you clapped eyes on her." "No, no Sue, you've got it all wrong my little daffodil." Sue ignored the assumed pleasantry. "If you were twenty years younger, you'd still be ten years too old, you dirty old git. Get away from her now." Chris reluctantly stood up and moved away from Esme. "And what have you got to say for yourself, you, you hussy, you husband stealer?" "Esme, stung by the unnecessary name calling as in slut, hussy and husband stealer of which she was none, brushing sand from her elbows, knees and hair, proceeded to explain her predicament. The atmosphere around the three of them changed dramatically, it became alive, fizzing with electricity. "A crazed killer on the loose," Sue screamed, "a killer in the villa! right this very minute? You'd better not be making this up Esme by way of covering up your dilly dallying with my Chris." "Oh, so I'm *your* bloody Chris now, am I? Just a minute ago you were accusing me of having it off with her," he said pointing at Esme. "Shut up Chris. the girls said in unison."

"Sue look, as God is my witness what I'm telling you is true. I saw Eddie from down on the beach and came racing up to greet him and he turned on me. He is a vicious murderer who kills people that cross him or get in his way." "So, what made him turn on you?" Sue enquired.

Esme faltered at this point. If she mentioned the situation regarding Mitch and the note, Sue would rebrand her as a slut and a hussy and blame her for attempting to lure Chris into her web of wicked ways. "Look," she said, "I can't make something up, you need to know the truth." Esme held her breath for a few moments and was about to reveal all when a single shot rang out from the direction of Hermosa Vista. All three stood stock still for a moment or two glancing at each other for answers, but none came. Sue said "for Christ's sake let's get indoors and lock ourselves in and fast, don't know about you two, but I'm bloody well scared. Perhaps we should call the police." "No, no please don't" shouted Esme, "not until we find out if it *was* actually a gun shot, I mean, perhaps it was a car backfiring up on the main road." A figure loomed into sight. All three froze assuming it was Eddie coming down the path in search of Esme. As the figure neared them, it became clear that it belonged to a much older man, definitely of Spanish descent and armed with a gun. Chris dived into the hedge opposite leaving Sue and Esme on their own. They watched stupefied, rooted to the spot as he came nearer and nearer. He was now no more than twenty or so yards from them. Raising the gun in their direction he spoke loudly and in good English. "Believe me," he called out as he closed on them, "I would like to kill you too *Essssmeeee*." He dragged the name out. They watched mesmerised as he threw the gun down in the sand burying it by kicking a heap of sand on top. "My son Javier is dead; he was brutally tortured and left to die. Before he died, he confessed all to me, yes, all about your affair with him *Essssmeeee*. Oh yes he told me in fine detail, where and how you had a night of sex together, that's how I know your name *Essssmeeee*." Sue shot a knowing look at Esme which conveyed 'so you are a bloody slut then.' Javier's dad continued. "You have but a few minutes left to see that monster alive in Hermosa Vista, I have left him near to death just as he left my poor son Javier. I bid you adiós," He bent down slowly, picked up the sand covered gun, dusting it off he called lovingly out to Javier,

"I'm coming son," pressed the gun to the side of his head and without hesitation he smilingly pulled the trigger and blew his brains out. Sue having never witnessed such a strikingly suicidal performance, threw up violently, the resulting spew gaining some distance.

Esme, made of stronger stuff, leapt over the twitching body of Javier's father and started running towards the villa, the deep sandy path seeming to slow her progress like in a bad dream.

She called out at the top of her lungs, "hang on in there Eddie, don't you bloody well leave me." She counted down the distance, only a few more yards. "Eddie, Eddie" she screamed, "I'm nearly there, please, please don't die." The front door sat wide open as Esme ran into the hall and she wasn't expecting to see what she saw. Chris, on the hall floor cradling Eddie! He looked up saying "he's barley alive, he keeps passing out." Esme howled "call for an ambulance, shit, shit, shit look at all the blood, where is he hurt?" "He whispered to me," said Chris "to look for a doctor's card and call him, then he passed out again." "Did you find it?" Esme cried out. "Yes, it's here, go phone him Esme, Eddie can't have long." Esme rushed to the phone and with shaking fingers dialled the number on the card. While they waited for the Doctor to arrive, Chris explained *when he heard the shot, he bolted up to the villa entering Esme's through the security gate at the bottom of her garden, so he must have missed the killer who was on his way down the path towards you and Sue.*

I found Eddie in here on the deck with a great big hole in his shoulder with loads of blood spurting out all over the place. I would guess the bullet missed anything serious but it probably shattered his shoulder. I've plugged the hole with a flannel from the bathroom to stop the blood flow, but I've no idea how to do anything else." Chris was shaking, shock was about to set in. "Bloody hell Chris what a mess, the man who did this to Eddie, did for himself right outside your villa. Blew his brains out he did, shouting out *'I'm coming Javier'* Sue saw it all poor cow. She is in a bad way, you'd better go and see to her and do something with the body if you can, I'll wait with Eddie till the Doctor gets here. We have to hope he gets here in time to save him; he's lost so much blood poor thing." Esme sat down next to Eddie and whispered; "this was not the home coming I had planned for you, my darling." She cuddled up to him and swore blind his body temperate was lowering.

GLOSSARY

Agro = Aggravation.

Andy Pandy = Puppet.

Brown Bread = Dead.

Bell = Call on the phone.

Bundle = Fight.

Boat Race = Face.

Brass Band = Hand.

Bees Knees = Good quality.

Blower = Telephone.

Bobbies = Police.

Brasses = Prostitutes.

Barnet Fair = Hair.

Bookies = Betting Shop.

Bird Lime = Time (in prison).

Bull and Cow = Row/Argument.

Case the Joint = Observation.

Clippie = Bus Conductress.

Cotton on = To understand.

Cozzers = Police.

Come a cropper = Suffer a defeat.

Circs = Circumstances.

Caper = An illegal act.

Clink = Prison.

Collar felt = Arrested.

Drum = House/Home.

Deep sea diver = Fiver (five pounds).

Digs = Rented Accommodation.

Duff = Pregnant.

Frog and toad = Road.

Filth = Police.

GBH = Grievous bodily harm.

Gaff = Slang for building.

Hampstead Heath = Teeth.

Hammered = Drunk.

Ingrate = Ungrateful.

Jacksie = Arse.

Jack Jones = Alone.

Jimmy riddle = Piss/Urinate.

Jam Jar = Car.

Knees up = Party.

Lippy = Showing little respect.

Lacadina = Spanish prison.

Loaf of bread = Head.

Lump hammer = 10lb Hammer.

Mothers ruin = Gin.

Meat wagon = Prison Van.

North and south = Mouth.

Nicker = Money (10 nicker = ten pounds etc).

Pork Pies = Lies.

Plates of meat = Feet.

Potless = Poor.

Popping one's clogs = To die.

Pen and ink = Stink.

Persuaders = Hammers.

Plod = Police.

Reddies = Money.

Sky rocket = Pocket.

Shank's pony = Walk.

Shtum = Tight lipped.

Snouts = Police informers.

Shell like = Ear.

Snuff it = Die.

Sov's = Sovereigns (Coin of the realm).

Slate = Money owing.

Shebang = The whole lot.

Tooled up = Armed/ carrying weapons.

Toe rag = Low life.

Topped = Murdered.

Two and eight = State.

Printed in Great Britain
by Amazon